PRAISE FOR SIMON

"Simon Wood's *The One That Got Away* turns the serial-killer convention upside down in a genuinely suspenseful novel."
—Charlaine Harris, author of *The Day Shift*

"Wood is a master at ratcheting up the suspense—he starts strong on page one and doesn't let up until the final sentence. Wood is at the top of his game."
—Allison Brennan, *New York Times* bestselling author of *Notorious*

"Wrenchingly intense—the talented Simon Wood goes psychologically dark and deeply disturbing. For those who like their thrillers twisty, shocking, and relentless."
—Hank Phillippi Ryan, Agatha, Anthony, Macavity, and Mary Higgins Clark award–winning author of *Truth Be Told*

"This author is a master at taking a simple situation and making it suspenseful."
—*Midwest Book Review*

"The tension is unbearable, and it gets worse as the pages fly by."
—*I Love a Mystery*

SAVING
GRACE

SAVING GRACE

A Fleetwood and Sheils Thriller

SIMON WOOD

THOMAS & MERCER

Text copyright © 2018 by Simon Wood

Published by Thomas & Mercer, Seattle

www.apub.com

Amazon, the Amazon logo, and Thomas & Mercer are trademarks of Amazon.com, Inc., or its affiliates.

ISBN-13: 9781542046442
ISBN-10: 1542046440

Cover design by Damon Freeman

Printed in the United States of America

SAVING GRACE

CHAPTER ONE

Wandering through Fisherman's Wharf, Gavin Connors watched the tourists and sightseers flocking from one attraction to another with their kids in tow. They demonstrated everything he found wrong with parenting. Kids ran wild while parents did their own thing. Smartphones and tablets replaced conversation. All these attractions, and no one took the time to engage their kids. Tourist traps like this were just an excuse to have someone else play babysitter. Essentially, the parents had their hands off the wheel and let someone else drive for them. If they were willing to do that, then he was more than happy to take over the driving.

If these people endured the kind of loss he'd endured over the last decade, then maybe they wouldn't be so careless. It would only take one example to change things. Today was that day. One family was about to learn a lesson for a whole generation.

He wandered up and down the Embarcadero and Jefferson Street in search of his example. He felt like a lion in search of his prey. As a predator, he looked for the weakest of the herd. He searched for a straggler, the lost, the ignored, and the foolhardy. Any of these archetypes would do. Because, like a predator, he was going to take his prey in broad daylight and in plain sight.

Although he was a predator, he didn't look like one. The *California* print T-shirt over cargo shorts with a 49ers baseball cap and sunglasses provided the perfect tourist disguise. He threw in a couple of deceptions to hide his true appearance. The T-shirt was two sizes too big in order to hide his athletic physique, and he bolstered his out-of-shape appearance by wearing a swimming flotation belt to give the appearance of a paunch. He'd grown a neatly kept beard and added a little gray, which made him look closer to late forties than his midthirties. His disguise didn't have to be perfect, just good enough to throw off eyewitness accounts.

He latched on to a family of out-of-towners with two boys. He put the oldest at eight and the youngest at six. None of them focused on one another. Their gaze was on the stores and attractions. The parents led the charge. They debated whether to eat or visit Ripley's Believe It or Not. They never once turned around to check on their boys. The boys lagged behind, their attention grabbed by every tacky tourist shop offering trinkets with *San Francisco* or *Alcatraz* printed on them. The younger of the boys was at eye level with every cheap, mass-produced toy. Connors watched the kid's hunger grow for some toy-related gratification. He fell behind his slightly worldlier brother. Connors liked this little straggler. He'd spent a long time thinking about the age of a kid to abduct and decided younger kids were better than older. The younger ones wouldn't question an adult, and their fears would keep them compliant. But he couldn't go too young, as toddlers were too labor intensive. Older kids were just too unpredictable. A kid between four and seven seemed the right age.

He maintained his distance, twenty to fifty feet back. He slipped his hands into his jacket pockets, and his right hand found the chloroformed handkerchief he'd prepped. He'd be swift and decisive. The kid and the people around him wouldn't know what hit them.

The kid stopped at a store with an open storefront. He picked up a toy cable car.

This was Connors's moment. He moved in. He maneuvered the handkerchief into his palm so that he could bring it out of his pocket in a single, seamless move. He closed in on the boy.

Just as he got within striking distance, the kid's brother turned around. His gaze went straight to Connors. A flicker of confusion crossed his face. He recognized *something* was off, but it was clear by his expression that he didn't know what. Fear kicked in, and he doubled back to his little brother. Connors aborted the abduction and let the boys go. Snatching two in public like this wasn't an option. Big brother grabbed his little brother's hand and hauled him in the direction of their clueless parents.

Losing his fish like this didn't upset him. He admired the brother for his simple and prompt action. It was a good sign that the survival instinct was alive and well.

He peeled off and bought an ice cream from a store. By the time he'd rejoined the flow of people, his little family of out-of-towners was gone.

He spent the next forty minutes stalking prey without finding anything suitable. Things looked promising as he approached the aquarium at Pier 39. There was a nice concentration of people. The higher the density, the easier it was to pull off a snatch and grab.

He estimated that at least two hundred people milled around in bulky lines, waiting to buy tickets for the aquarium and other attractions. Here, he saw his opportunity. Families were separated. One person waited in line while everyone else wandered off to do something else. Some looked out at the water. Others took in the street performers. Others window-shopped. With everyone separated, it would be easy to pick off an ignored child.

A large family—he judged from their accents they were British—drew his eye. He guessed there were eight to ten of them spread out across the sidewalk. It was a multigenerational affair with parents, kids, and possibly uncles and aunts. A couple of guys stood in line at the brightly painted, can't-miss-it information center and box office. They called across to a pair of women with a waifish preteen girl. Four or five kids between six and twelve, lost in a game of their own devising, ran around between people's feet.

"Matthew! Matthew!" one of the women yelled. She was heavyset with overly bleached blonde hair. Despite the chill in the air and the cloudy day, she sported a sunburn across her face and shoulders.

A boy of around twelve stopped running.

"Where's Grace? I told you to keep an eye on your sister."

"I am. She's over there," he said.

Connors looked over in the vague direction of where the boy pointed. It took him a moment to spot the lone figure of a young girl, maybe five or six years old, looking at a sign for the aquarium, a stuffed rabbit dangling from one hand. She was the perfect candidate in every way.

"Make sure you look after her. That's your job for today."

"Yes, Mum. I know."

"Just see that you do."

Matthew shook his head and rejoined the game with the other kids, at the expense of any and all concern for Grace.

Connors wandered over to the girl, who was now watching a street performer juggle bowling pins. She was part of a semicircle of a dozen or so people. No one asked the kid whom she was with. Everyone seemingly assumed that she was with someone. That someone would be Connors.

He dropped to his knees in front of her. "Hey, Grace, there you are. What have we said about wandering off, kiddo?"

The girl looked at him blankly.

His attention drew only a couple of glances from the onlookers. He made sure his 49ers baseball cap shielded his features from view.

"Look at your face. You've got schmutz all over it."

He deftly brought out the handkerchief from his pocket and pressed it to the girl's face. The chloroform worked in seconds. Just as her eyes rolled back, he scooped her up into his arms. The girl's head fell against his shoulder, the rabbit falling from her grasp.

He picked up the toy rabbit. "Okay, Gracie, let's find Mommy before we both end up in hot water."

He walked off with the kid slack in his arms. Barely anyone registered his departure. It was such a self-absorbed world.

Now that he had his child, he moved swiftly and with purpose. He put a moving wall of people between Grace and her family. He brought out a beanie hat and placed it on the kid's head, then swapped his 49ers cap for a Yankees cap. These were subtle changes but enough to confuse identification in most cases. He crossed the street and headed back to his minivan parked in the Trader Joe's lot.

An elderly woman grinned at him as he strode toward her.

"Someone looks tuckered out," she quipped.

"Yeah, it's an early day. She's paying the price for keeping us up all night, so it's back to the hotel."

"Overexcitement will do that to a kid. Have a good vacation."

He agreed and kept on walking.

When he got back to the minivan, he loaded Grace into the kid's booster seat that he'd installed. He removed the beanie, placed some brightly colored sunglasses on her, and covered her with a blanket. Grace was no longer Grace but some other kid, if someone cared to look.

He used the cover of the blanket to inject Grace with a sedative. He couldn't risk her having a meltdown when she awoke.

With the girl secured and sedated, he climbed into the driver's seat and gunned the engine. He brought out his cell and dialed the one and only number programmed into the burner.

"Yes," Connors's employer answered.

"I've got you a kid. Now what?"

5

CHAPTER TWO

At the sight of Nelson Marsters ambling toward her with his wad of papers pressed to his chest, Lehny Corbin reminded herself that as receptionist, she was the *San Francisco Independent*'s first line of defense. She was the first person the public encountered either by phone or in person. Their attitude and need determined how she handled their requests. She screened people as she deemed appropriate. She liked to think her valiant services were appreciated even if they weren't reflected in her paycheck. If management ever needed evidence of her efforts, they only had to come to reception right this minute to witness her doing battle with Nelson Marsters.

She wondered if Nelson owned any other clothes than the ones he seemed to always wear when he came—a food-stained white shirt tucked into a pair of brown pants too big in the waist and short in the leg. If it weren't for the fanny pack cinched around his waist, she was sure those pants would be around his ankles. At least that scuzzy raincoat would prevent him from mooning anyone if his pants did fall.

He represented the half a dozen or so eccentrics, if she was being kind, who came to the newspaper to share their conspiracies and manifestos. As much as these guys were difficult, at least they were polite, unlike the ultraconservatives who spilled bile down the phone at her because the *Independent* was a weapon of the liberal left, or the rabid liberals who accused the *Independent* of selling out their liberal principles in the name of staying in business. She figured since the paper was pissing off both extremes of the political spectrum, then it had to be doing something right. While the oddballs were a drain on her time and her patience, they were altruistic. Their dogma was for the betterment of everyone and not just themselves.

Mike, Lehny's security backup, rose from his seat, but she waved him away.

"No, it's okay. I've got this," she said before calling, "Mr. Marsters, nice to see you again. What can I do for you?"

"Hi. Hello. How are you? I need to speak to Mr. George Moran. I need to discuss the issue of drones. San Francisco is the first city in the United States to authorize the use of drones."

"Yes, I believe it's to help with law enforcement."

He cocked his head to one side and looked at her like she was a naive child. Oddly, it was the same look most people gave him after five minutes of listening to him, although she doubted he would recognize that.

"Really, Ms. Corbin? You really believe that?"

"Call me Lehny."

"I prefer not to, Ms. Corbin. Etiquette dictates that we should keep our association on a formal and professional level, seeing as the information I am bringing to the *Independent* could end up as part of a congressional investigation . . . not that it will make any difference. Congressional investigations are nothing more than a smokescreen for government control."

Lehny caught an eye roll from Mike.

"Right. So, drones, you say."

This ignited a ten-minute diatribe on the misuse of drones for monitoring people's movements, recording their phone calls, listening in while they talked on the sidewalk, and their use of dispersants.

He'd at least cleared the San Francisco Police Department of these civil-liberty crimes. He claimed the whole scheme was driven by several branches of the federal government, namely, the FCC, CDC, NSA, and the FBI, just to name a few. San Francisco had been singled out because it was one of those cities that closely mirrored the cross-section of American society as a whole. The brief was simple—succeed in San Francisco, succeed across the United States. He backed up his claims with reams of handwritten notes, maps, pictures, and manufacturers' specifications.

Lehny found letting people like Marsters rant took the steam out of them before passing them over to someone else. She found it was hard to maintain the heat of a tirade in a second telling, although the weirdos never seemed to lose their appetite for telling their claims again and again. It just toned down the crazy.

Other visitors in the lobby watched Marsters with amusement. Some did little to hide their smirks. Someone actually recorded the diatribe on his cell phone. She nodded at Mike to stop the recording.

While some derived enjoyment from Marsters's craziness, she only pitied him. Over the three years or so he'd been coming in with conspiracy claims, she'd gotten to know him. He'd been a high school teacher once. Something had happened. There'd been a nervous breakdown. He'd lost his family, contact with the world, and reality. No one was ever going to listen to him, but someone should, so she would for the betterment of mankind. She didn't know if this was the wrong thing to do in therapy terms, but it seemed the right thing to do for her.

She picked up her phone. "I'll call Mr. Moran and see if he's at his desk."

She punched in the editor in chief's number.

"George Moran."

"His line is ringing, Mr. Marsters."

"Crap. Is he here again?"

"Still ringing, Mr. Marsters."

"I don't have time for him today, Lehny."

Lehny smiled painfully. "It's just clicked through to voice mail."

"Thanks, Lehny. You're a star," Moran said. "My gratitude will be shown in the form of Peet's."

She could do with a nice caramel macchiato. She set the phone down. "Sorry about that, Mr. Marsters."

Marsters frowned. "Where is he?"

"A meeting, or he could be out. He might be the editor in chief, but he still likes to be a reporter and pound the streets for a story." It was a lie, but it was one that Lehny found worked on Marsters.

Marsters nodded. "I know. It's why I trust him with a story like this."

"Would you like to make an appointment?"

He shook his head violently. "No appointments. No records. It's the only way to be safe."

Lehny nodded skyward. "Because of them."

Marsters nodded. "Yes. Just tell him I'll be by later."

"I will."

Poor guy, she thought as he scurried out the door.

Her switchboard lit up with a new call. She was still watching Nelson Marsters when she picked up the receiver.

"*San Francisco Independent*, how may I help you?"

"Scott Fleetwood, please."

The caller's voice stunned her into silence. Or was it callers? Each word in the request was spoken by a different voice—a man's, then a woman's, then a young girl. Each voice came out stilted and robotic. It had to be scrambled or a recording.

"Scott Fleetwood, please," the caller repeated. This time the words sounded as if a boy and two different women took turns speaking.

Two weirdos in a row, Lehny thought. This was a record for her. Maybe she should buy a lottery ticket.

"I'm sorry. Scott Fleetwood doesn't work here anymore."

"Get him," the caller demanded, the words broken into a male voice and a female voice.

"I can't. I'm sorry. He's not an employee. Can someone else help you?"

Lehny found herself stumbling over her words. The weirdos usually didn't scare her, but this one did. She didn't know if it was the random voices speaking one word at a time, but she detected menace in the deception. She wasn't holding up this call anymore. They didn't pay her enough for this. She was handing this one off to the first person to pick up.

"Just Fleetwood," a boy's, then a girl's, voice said.

"I'll direct your call to Mr. Fleetwood's editor. He can help you better than I can."

"No," a girl said.

Lehny listened to static.

"I want to discuss the ransom," a string of voices took turns in saying.

A shiver worked its way through Lehny. "What ransom?"

"The ransom for Grace."

Lehny went cold. "Who's Grace?"

"Grace is a girl that I abducted two hours ago. I want Scott Fleetwood to deliver the ransom. I will speak only to Scott Fleetwood. Get me Scott Fleetwood, or I will kill her."

The litany of different voices, men and women, old and young, scraped away at her soul. She wanted to hang up on the son of a bitch, but that little girl needed her. Keeping this asshole satisfied would keep this girl alive.

"I have to find Mr. Fleetwood. You'll have to call back."

"You find him. I will call back tomorrow. The same time. Understand?"

Lehny closed her eyes to block out the fear, but the image of a man in the dark standing over Grace's trussed-up body filled her mind. He was wearing a ski mask. He opened his mouth, stretching the fabric tight, and the different voices leaked from the mask's opening.

"I understand."

"Good," a girl's voice seemingly mocked her. "Don't you want to know my name?"

She didn't, but it would be important to the police. "Yes."

"The Shepherd."

CHAPTER THREE

George Moran told Lehny to get to his office with the added proviso, "Not a word to anyone," the second she'd called him. Minutes later, he had her in Editorial's boardroom with the *Independent*'s publisher, James Cardone, and the head of legal, Valerie Richards, to relay what had just happened. Even Richard Thorpe, the business consultant, had been drafted into the meeting. George could feel everybody's eyes on them from the bullpen. They knew something was up but didn't know what, which was a tough thing for a bunch of reporters to stomach.

"And that was everything he said?" George asked when Lehny was finished.

She nodded.

George felt for her. Normally sharp and full of joy, she was the perfect first point of contact for the *Independent*. Right now, she looked deflated and lifeless. It might have just been a call, but she, like everyone at the paper, had suffered through the fallout of a previous child abduction. The perpetrator, who had called himself the Piper, had connected himself to the paper twice over the last decade and not without a price. He prayed they weren't about to go through that again.

"Okay, Lehny. Thanks. I think that's it for now. I would say take the rest of the day off, but I'm sure the police will want to get a statement from you."

She nodded again.

George held the conference door open for her as she left, then turned around to face the *Independent*'s brain trust.

George didn't particularly like Thorpe being there. Thorpe had been brought in to thrust the *Independent* into the twenty-first century. Print media was losing its relevance and its advertising revenue because of it. In a world where people got their news as soon as someone put it up on a social-media account, print media was always going to lose. Events that happened today wouldn't get reported until tomorrow. It was the nature of the beast, and the beast was dying. George had to give Thorpe credit for some of his changes. Thorpe had turned around several papers across the country and had been recognized for doubling the viewership of one of the smaller cable-news networks. His plan was to use the *Independent*'s website as a running news feed and use the print edition to run a deeper analysis of the issues with more pictures.

"Thoughts? Suggestions?" George said, returning to his seat.

Thorpe held up his tablet. "The news has already broken that a six-year-old girl on vacation from the UK with her family was kidnapped at Pier 39."

"Any mention of Scott Fleetwood?" James said.

"Nope."

"We call the SFPD right now," Valerie said. "We want nothing to do with this. This paper can't afford to get burned by the court of public opinion again."

The response from the paper's legal counsel didn't surprise George. History was repeating itself. For a decade, the infamous Bay Area kidnapper, the Piper, had kidnapped children of the rich and extorted them for money. Nearly nine years ago, he had committed his eighth for-profit kidnapping—Nicholas Rooker, the young son of San Francisco property mogul Charles Rooker. Someone claiming to be the Piper had contacted the *Independent*, and Scott Fleetwood, then a reporter for the paper, had taken the call. Scott had publicized the Piper's exploits. Unfortunately, that contact had been a hoax perpetrated by the Piper's biggest fan, Mike Redfern. The FBI had followed Redfern's leads instead of the real Piper's directions. When the clock had run out on the true Piper's demands for the first and last time, he had taken the life of Nicholas Rooker. Redfern had gone to jail, Scott and the newspaper had taken the heat for buying into the hoax, and no one had heard from the Piper for eight years.

Then, six months ago, Charles Rooker had kidnapped both of Scott's children while posing as the Piper. Rooker had masterminded these events to punish Scott and Redfern for the death of his son while drawing out the real Piper. It had worked but had resulted in four deaths, including Rooker's, although Scott's children, thankfully, had been rescued. Still, the paper had taken heavy hits on its reputation both times, and Valerie had been forced to navigate through the legal minefield of both debacles.

"I think that goes without saying," James said. "We're calling the police. The question is, what position does this newspaper take?"

"We have no position to take," Valerie said. "Stand back and get out of the way."

"We can't stand by," George said. "This guy has tied us to him. He's calling back here in twenty-four hours to speak to Scott Fleetwood. The cops will be all over this place when the call comes in tomorrow, and they'll be seeking our cooperation."

Valerie shook her head and rapped at her legal pad with her pen. "He may have tied us to him, but he's made a pretty messy knot. Scott Fleetwood doesn't work for us anymore."

"He doesn't have to," James said. "We just need his cooperation. The police will ask for it, but I think we should ask, too. I can't see him turning a request down with a child's life at stake. George, will you make the approach?"

George wasn't so sure. Scott had pretty much turned his back on the world since Rooker had abducted his children. He'd heard the kids had struggled with adjusting to normal life since their rescue. When your family was in trouble, you looked out for your own.

"George, will you do it?"

George nodded.

"We're assuming something here," James said. "How do we even know if this call is legit? Just because someone calls in saying they have a girl, we can't just assume it's true. Redfern burned us nine years ago with the exact same line, and we bought it hook, line, and sinker. I don't think this paper could weather another hoax, so we need to do our due diligence."

"Our due diligence is that we bring in the police. It's up to them to determine whether the guy is for real or not. We'll assist where needed," Valerie said. "Christ, why did this asshole have to pick this newspaper?"

George echoed Valerie's sentiment. He just wanted to report on the day's events, not be part of them.

"I think everyone is looking at this in the wrong way," Thorpe said. "This situation shouldn't be viewed as an adversity but as an opportunity—and a golden one at that."

"I don't want to contradict you, but you weren't here during the Piper debacles. I was. It was a train wreck both times. This newspaper got scammed," Valerie said. "We can't get dragged into something that could blow up in our faces again."

Thorpe smiled a somewhat condescending smile, but Valerie seemed to miss it. "I'm not saying we do anything reckless or cross the line between the news service and private crime fighters. What I am saying is, a situation has landed on this newspaper's doorstep and at the most opportune time. You should be thanking your lucky stars instead of cursing your bad luck."

"That's a pretty callous thing to say, considering a child's life is at stake," George said.

Thorpe held up his hands. "Yes, you're right. That was a poor choice of words on my part. My bad."

"My bad," Valerie parroted. "I thought we brought you in for your foresight and good judgment."

Thorpe let the insult bounce off him. "You brought me in to change the fortunes of this newspaper, and I am telling you that if you handle this correctly, this will make the *Independent* a household name across the country, let alone the Bay Area."

He paused for effect. The man was grandstanding. George wasn't about to bite, but James did.

"What are you saying?"

"I'm saying we've got a great narrative going on here. A kidnapper has selected this newspaper as his voice to the family and the public. Not only that, he's chosen the one reporter who knows kidnappers more than any reporter should know them to broker the ransom and release of this little girl. This story will go national. Hell, it'll go international, because the girl is a foreign tourist. Every news organization will have to turn its gaze on us and come to us for every tidbit. We're on the front line of this story, whether we like it or not. We will become the center of the news cycle for the duration of this piece. How we deal with it is down to us. We can turn our backs on it and let the police do their thing while we act as spectators, or we can be embedded with the police and Scott Fleetwood. I guarantee this story will propel the *Independent* into the stratosphere, bringing advertisers in its wake."

Silence followed. George couldn't deny Thorpe made some valid points, but he was playing to a gun-shy audience. Thorpe's bravado could backfire without any consequences for him. He was a consultant. He got to walk away. No one at the *Independent* had that luxury. They'd all take the heat if this went wrong. Still, despite George's reservations, he did see an angle here if handled correctly.

"Decision time, people," Thorpe said. "Are we going to sit on the sidelines, or put some skin in the game?"

CHAPTER FOUR

It was midafternoon, and Scott had been staring at the page on his computer screen for the last couple of hours. How much had he gotten done? Two hundred . . . three hundred words? The book should have been easy to write, but it had turned into a chore. Worse, it had become an ugly obligation.

After Charles Rooker had kidnapped his sons, the book offers had flooded in. He'd accepted a six-figure deal to write his account. It was enough to leave his job at the *Independent*. He couldn't be a journalist anymore. His mistakes had cost people their lives.

He'd expected the book to pour out of him. It was his opportunity to document all the errors that had ended up costing the lives of six people. He'd thought that telling his story would be his way of exorcising the demons and healing wounds and every other cliché for closure, but it hadn't worked out that way. Reliving every moment, from receiving the two calls that first Sammy, then Peter had been snatched to finding his kids, had been excruciating. Men had died in front of him. His children had been held captive. He and Jane had been forced to live their worst nightmares day after day as the carrot dangled in front of them. There was a story to tell, but he was coming to the realization he wasn't the one to tell it. He was too close to it.

His cell phone rang.

"Scott Fleetwood."

"Mr. Fleetwood, this is Tracy Devore from the Assisi Academy. There's been an incident at the school involving Sammy, and I need you to come in."

Scott's heart rate quickened. Anything involving his boys had this effect on him. Their ordeal was still with them, and they were struggling with adjusting. They'd been through four months of therapy and had returned to school only two months ago.

"What's happened?"

"Sammy struck another student."

He cursed under his breath. "Why?"

"I think we should discuss that when you arrive."

He grabbed his keys and ran out to the car. While he drove, he called Jane. He got her voice mail. He filled her in and told her he was handling it and not to worry.

He and Jane had taken the boys out of their original school and put them in a new one. The boys couldn't go back to the school where Sammy had been snatched. The memory of it was just too raw.

He pulled up in front of the school half an hour before classes ended for the day and found parking easily. He didn't have to ask for directions to the principal's office. Parent-teacher meetings had pretty much become a weekly occurrence.

Despite Sammy being the only one in trouble, both Sammy and Peter were huddled together outside the principal's office. They'd taken their twin status to a new level. They never left each other's sides in a crisis now. He saw so much of Jane in them. It wasn't just their black hair and olive skin but their quiet reserve during situations like this. It was something he wished he possessed.

The secretary sitting at her desk across from his boys picked up her phone.

"You two okay?"

They nodded.

"Good. It's going to be all right."

"Ms. Devore will see you, Mr. Fleetwood," the secretary said.

He let himself into Devore's office. She was a small woman in her early fifties, and he towered over her with his tall, lanky frame. She stood to shake his hand, taking in his appearance. His jeans were stained, he'd worn this T-shirt for two days, and he couldn't remember the last time he'd shaved. It certainly wasn't a red-carpet moment.

She retook her seat and indicated for him to sit. "I won't beat around the bush, Mr. Fleetwood. During afternoon recess, Sammy lashed out at a group of children, striking one and knocking him down. It would have been a lot worse if a passing teacher hadn't broken it up."

Impulse control had been an issue with Sammy since his abduction. He didn't think or reason; he reacted. The therapist had given Scott and Jane the tools to help Sammy work through this problem, but it was slow going. They'd learned one thing over the months. Impulse behavior tracked back to one thing—a flash point. It took a pressure point applied in just the wrong place at the wrong time to set Sammy off. If Scott could get to the root of it on this occasion, it would go a long way to averting another.

"What were the circumstances leading up to the incident?"

"I'm not sure that's relevant."

"It's very relevant."

Devore sighed. "As far as I can ascertain, the children were playing, and Sammy was shut inside a supply closet."

"Was the closet lit?"

"No. I don't believe so."

Scott didn't have to read too hard between the lines. The kids weren't playing. It was a cruel prank. He smacked his fist down on the principal's desk. "This was bullying. Don't try to sugarcoat it."

"Mr. Fleetwood—"

"You know my son's history, and you let a bunch of kids shut him in a closet? That child was kept in a mine shaft. He can't sleep without the fucking lights on."

"That doesn't excuse his behavior."

"Or yours, Ms. Devore. I entrust my children's safety and well-being to you, and you let something like this happen? This is totally unacceptable. What disciplinary actions are being taken against those children?"

"None of those children hit anyone. And frankly, Mr. Fleetwood, I find your reaction wholly unacceptable."

Scott stood. "My son will apologize to the child in question and to his parents, because that's how I raise my children. However, I expect the children in question and their parents to apologize to my son. Got that?"

Devore floundered for an answer.

"We're done."

In the handful of steps it took to open the office door, he recovered himself. He couldn't let his boys see him seething. He let himself out, closing the door carefully.

Sammy and Peter hopped off their chairs. They looked frightened. He dropped to one knee and placed a hand on each of their shoulders.

"It's okay. We need to talk, but it's okay. Got your things?"

They nodded.

"All right then. We're going home."

Devore's secretary glowered at him when he left the principal's office. The dressing-down he'd just given her boss must have penetrated the walls. He ignored the venomous look and walked his kids into the hall.

The bell rang, and kids spilled from classrooms into the corridors. He saw his sons stiffen at the sudden onslaught of children making for the exits. He dropped a hand on their shoulders and pulled them close to his side. Just as he neared the main entrance, Jane crested the stairs, pushing against the flow of kids heading out.

"What happened?"

"We're changing schools. That's what happened."

• • •

Scott and Jane drove the boys out to Golden Gate Park to let them talk through the incident. They'd learned over the past months that just giving the boys the chance to talk without criticism or interruption helped them get over the event faster. Scott and Jane took turns reinforcing the fact that the man who'd taken them would never do it again. They were safe. They had nothing to fear, but the consequences of today couldn't be ignored, and Scott had to play the bad guy. He explained that as much as he understood why Sammy had lashed out, the second he had, he'd lost the fight. There were alternatives to fighting. Naturally, Sammy kvetched, but Jane backed Scott up. The kids seemed to get the message, but Scott knew there would be more trips to the principal's office. On the way home, they got ice cream, and he put a smile on their faces with a couple of risqué jokes for nine-year-olds. It was good that Jane was driving her own car home.

As the Fleetwood family convoy slowed to pull into their driveway, they saw three cars lining the street in front of the house. His old boss, George Moran, FBI agents Tom Sheils and Lucy Guerra, and a man he didn't recognize were standing on their stoop.

"What the hell?" he murmured to himself.

"Hey, it's Uncle George with Agent Tom and Agent Lucy," Peter said.

Sheils had worked all eight Piper kidnappings as well as Sammy and Peter's abduction. There wasn't a lot of love lost between the FBI agent and himself. For many years, Sheils had held Scott responsible for botching the Piper's last kidnapping, which had resulted in the death of Charles Rooker's young son, Nicholas. Scott held himself responsible, too. Guerra had been part of Sheils's team.

"Who's that other man?" Sammy asked.

"I don't know," Scott said.

"Why are they here?" Sammy's voice caught on his own words.

Scott didn't know. It couldn't have anything to do with Rooker or the Piper. That was over.

He didn't like the nervous tone in Sammy's voice. The kid had had a rough day, and the last thing he needed was another trigger. It would set him back weeks. Scott drove the car straight inside the garage.

"Up to your room, guys."

"Can't I see Uncle George?" Peter asked.

"You will. I just need to speak to his friends first."

The boys charged up the steps to the kitchen and disappeared into the house.

Jane stopped her car behind his on the driveway, frowning. He simply shook his head. She got out, and together they walked over to greet their welcoming party. It was cramped on the small stoop, putting them all face-to-face.

"What are you doing here?" Scott asked.

"We need to talk," Sheils said.

"And I have a phone. You call me. We meet someplace. You don't turn up at my door unannounced. You know the rule when it comes to the boys—no unexpected visits, and no strangers." Scott made a point of eyeballing the man he didn't know.

"I know. I'm sorry, Scott . . . Jane," George said. "Really I am, but we didn't have much choice."

"It's important," the mystery man added.

"Who are you—FBI?"

He smiled. "Good God, no. I'm a consultant with the *Independent*. My name is Richard Thorpe, but you can call me Richard for short."

"Is that supposed to be funny?"

Jane placed a hand on his arm. "Scott."

"Scott, we do need to talk," Sheils said. "We're working against the clock."

Scott didn't like the use of the word *we*. It implied he was now part of their problem. "Okay, come inside."

Jane pulled out her keys and opened the door. "I'll talk to the boys."

Everyone followed her inside.

Scott put an arm across the doorway, blocking Thorpe's path. "Wait here."

Thorpe raised an eyebrow at the arm in front of him. "Feels a little personal."

"It's not," Scott said. "I'm sure you're aware of my family's situation. We have rules when it comes to strangers. George should have explained it. We have a procedure. You have to be introduced."

Thorpe raised his hands in surrender. "I understand. My apologies for the intrusion."

Scott closed the door on him.

Jane called out to the boys. When they called back, she asked them to come down.

Scott showed everyone into the living room and asked them to sit. Scott leaned against the fireplace. He didn't want to be sitting for whatever they had to say. He blamed it on his fight-or-flight sense.

The boys bounced down the stairs. Jane waited at the bottom for them, then walked them into the living room.

It astounded Scott how quickly they bounced back from a setback. A couple of hours ago, Sammy had been traumatized and throwing punches. Now his boys were excited. He wouldn't call them resilient. They were still just a trigger warning away from a meltdown. It would pass. They just needed time and stability. Something like a run-in with the FBI did nothing to help.

"Hey, boys, you know everybody here," Scott said.

The boys said hi to everyone. George got a hug, as did Agent Guerra. The boys were developing an eye for the ladies, despite their age.

"Got any questions?"

This was a technique both Scott and Jane had developed. Unexpected visitors, even good friends, explained why they'd come and answered any questions the boys had. Scott hoped this would instill some confidence because they had control of the situation.

"Why are you here?" Sammy asked.

"Is it anything to do with us?" Peter asked. An edginess had crept into his question that Scott didn't like.

"No," Sheils said assuredly. "We're working on a new case, and we need your dad's help."

"I've got a friend outside," George said. "I'd like to bring him in, but only if it's okay with you two."

The boys looked at each other. They were looking for a weakness. If one of them flinched, the other would back him up. Scott loved that his boys had each other's backs.

"He can come in," Peter said.

"Thanks," George said. "His name is Richard Thorpe. He works with me."

George went to the door and let Thorpe in. Thorpe was tall and rail thin, which his $5,000 suit failed to hide. His suit wasn't the only expensive thing about him. He was high-rolling it from his shoes to the Rolex hanging off his wrist.

"Hi, boys. I'm Richard." He raised a hand. "Sorry to turn up unannounced. I need your dad. Is that okay?"

"Is it important?" Sammy asked.

"Sure is. Your dad is the only person in the world that can help."

The boys beamed with pride.

"So if everything's cool with you two, back up to your room so your dad can talk," Jane said.

The boys shouted bye and clambered back up the stairs with Jane following behind.

"A couple of great kids," Thorpe said, sitting down next to George.

Scott wasn't in the mood for any ass kissing, so he cut to the chase. "So what's happened? You wouldn't be here unless something's gone wrong."

"It has," Sheils said. "A child, six years old, was kidnapped earlier today. She was here on vacation with a British family."

A sudden pressure swelled inside Scott's chest. The suffocating sensation always hit him now at the mention of a child abduction. A nasty cocktail of personal experience and empathy usually fueled the reaction, but not this time. Fear was at the center of it now. Fear of what had brought everyone to his door and what this kidnapping had to do with him. Suddenly, he realized everyone was waiting for him to respond.

"That's terrible, but what it's got to do with me?"

"The kidnapper identified himself as the Shepherd," Sheils added. "Does that name mean anything to you?"

"No, should it?"

"He called the paper," George said. "He says he'll talk only to you."

Scott shoved himself away from the fireplace. "No, no, no, I can't do this again. I can't put my family through this. I can't put them at risk again."

Sheils stood. "I know what we're asking isn't ideal."

"Ideal? You've got that right."

"This kid is just six years old," George said.

"Don't lay that shit on me."

"I just want you to be aware of the facts."

Scott saw through that bullshit. It was emotional blackmail.

"You don't want to be part of this, I get that," Sheils said. "I can probably make this work without you, but if you talking to him gets me the traction I need to get this girl back to her parents, then I'm going to push for it."

Scott understood this. He didn't need it explained to him. It was because he understood that he gave the answer he did.

"I can't. I'm sorry."

George shook his head. Sheils showed no reaction. It was probably the answer he'd been expecting. Only Lucy Guerra looked disappointed in him.

"Can I have a moment with my husband?" Jane asked.

She was standing at the bottom of the stairs. Scott didn't know how long she'd been there.

"Sure," Sheils said.

"Agent Guerra, do you mind visiting the boys? They were asking about you."

The FBI agent smiled. "Of course not. And call me Lucy."

Scott followed his wife into the kitchen. He closed the door on them.

"How much did you hear?"

"Enough." She leaned against the countertop. "Why don't you want to help?"

"You know why. I put this family through this twice. I can't do it for a third time. Don't tell me you want me to."

Tears welled in her eyes, making them sparkle. They escaped when she shook her head. He crossed the kitchen to embrace her, but she put out her hands, stopping him before he could get close.

"There's a family out there who is missing their child. That's something you and I both know about."

"That's why I said no."

She raised her hand. "Let me say this first. If it weren't for the people in the next room, we wouldn't have our boys back. If it wasn't for you, we wouldn't have our boys back. That is something I give thanks for every day."

"I do, too."

"That's why I know if something happens to this child without your help, you'll never forgive yourself. I'll never forgive myself."

Jane had said everything he'd already thought and tried to ignore. He wrapped his wife up in a hug. Half a head taller than her, he lifted her onto her tiptoes. She squeezed him tight and dug her chin into his shoulder. Her tears dampened his shirt.

"You want me to do this?" he asked. He needed her blessing because once this got going, it was going to be hard on everyone.

"No, I don't," she said. "But you don't have a choice. You have to help them."

"God, I love you so much," he said. "But what about us? This family? I can't put us at risk again."

"Tom won't let anything happen to us."

He prayed that was true. His kids were fragile. The whole family was. If his boys broke, he knew he and Jane would shatter along with them. But as Jane had said, he didn't have a choice.

"I'll do my best to keep us safe."

"I know you will." She patted him on the shoulder. "Let's get back out there."

When he and Jane returned to the living room, Sheils was in conversation with George and Thorpe.

"I'm in, but I have a couple of questions and a condition."

"Name them," Sheils said.

"I get why the FBI is here, but what's the *Independent* have to do with it? You took the call and passed it on to the Feds. You're out of it now."

Thorpe shook his head. "Not in this case. We have exclusive rights to this story."

"Exclusive rights?"

"Yes. Whether anyone likes it or not, this newspaper is the voice of this story, and it needs to be that way to ensure this child's safe return. To that end, the family doesn't speak to any other media outlets. We speak for them."

"And the family is on board with this?"

"They're looking for guidance and support," George said. "Also they don't want every media source badgering them 24-7. They just want to focus on getting their daughter back. We can be their buffer."

In exchange for their exclusive story, Scott thought.

"We are giving the FBI full access to the *Independent*. Access to our sources, phone lines, you name it," Thorpe said. "In return, the FBI shares any developments with us first."

"You're kidding me, right?" Scott said to Sheils.

The FBI agent said nothing. That said a lot about how he felt about giving a newspaper access to his investigation.

"Scott," Thorpe said, "a kidnapper comes from nowhere and will deal only with the reporter who broke the Piper case. We need you. Hell, this girl needs you. Whether you like it or not, you're the *it* guy."

He didn't agree.

Thorpe reached inside and pulled out an envelope. "To that end, I have an offer for you. We'd like you to come to the *Independent* on a contract basis, just for the duration of the case. We'd need some copy from you, and we'd want you to be available for interviews. I have a generous contract all drawn up." He held out the bulging envelope. "I just need a signature."

Scott made no attempt to take the contract.

"This is for your protection as well as ours. If anything goes wrong, you'll be legally protected against the fallout."

Fallout. Scott knew all about that. He didn't like that everyone was already thinking in negative terms. It was as if they'd already written this kid off as dead.

"This would also be good for your career."

Scott looked to everyone in the room. George couldn't make eye contact, and Sheils remained stoic. "Is this guy for fucking real?"

No one answered.

"Do you think I care about bylines and fame? There's a kid's life on the line, you asshole. Get out of my house."

Thorpe showed no sign of embarrassment or shame, but he looked to Jane for some backup and got none. She squeezed Scott's arm to tell him she was backing him to the hilt.

George rose, taking the contract from Thorpe. "I think I'd better handle this."

Thorpe nodded. "Okay. Good idea. Thanks. I have a few calls to make, anyway."

When Thorpe had let himself out of the house, George pointed to the seat next to him and Scott sat down.

"Who is that guy?"

"He's a print-media rainmaker, and management is hoping he can make it rain. I don't have to tell you what a pounding newspapers are taking—circulation is down, ad sales are in the toilet. He's been brought in to change that. Naturally, he sees this story as a boon for us, and to be honest, I have to agree. I don't want to make a big deal of it, but the *Independent* is barely hanging on, so I hope you'll sign the contract, Scott. Everything about this story is intertwined with the newspaper, the FBI, and you. The FBI has granted us limited access to the investigation, and we just need your sign-off. Having you on board as a consultant will simplify things."

Scott took the contract. "I'll get this back to you tomorrow."

"Thanks."

"Can we move this along?" Sheils said. "I know I have to indulge the *Independent*, but I don't have to indulge it that much. I have this girl's family waiting to speak to you."

"What's the girl's name?" Jane asked.

"Grace Pagett."

Scott etched the name into his brain. Grace was now the most important girl in the world.

"You said you had a condition," Sheils said.

"Just one."

"Name it," Sheils said.

"I'm putting myself in the firing line again. I don't know what's going to happen and where it's going to take me. So promise me that you'll keep my family safe."

"You got it."

Sheils answered without rancor. It was a solid promise. Considering the history between them, it surprised Scott but also reassured him.

"What happens now?"

"We meet Grace's family."

CHAPTER FIVE

Scott said goodbye to his boys and Jane and followed Sheils out the door. He'd cleaned himself up before leaving. It had taken him fifteen minutes to shower, shave, and change into fresh clothes. He hadn't done much with his hair. He never could. Regardless of what he did, it remained an untidy brown mop.

Lucy Guerra got behind the wheel of the Crown Victoria. Sheils held one of the rear doors open for Scott and slid in next to him. Guerra hit the gas, and the car lurched forward.

Scott cast a look back at George and Thorpe, standing on the street. "I don't think Thorpe liked you cutting him out of this meeting with the family. You screwed up a photo op he had in mind."

"He'll live," Sheils said. "My orders are to work with him, not involve him."

"I'm surprised you're giving the paper any access."

"It's a case of quid pro quo. The Shepherd has targeted the *Independent* and you. My point of contact starts there, so I need their cooperation. The agreement is simple. All FBI press releases are given to them only. You get to write stories for them about your involvement in the case, but let me be crystal clear: you don't reveal a single detail without my approval. I don't want anything getting out that'll jeopardize this investigation. Got that?"

"Absolutely. I'm here for the girl, not the headline."

"I'll hold you to that."

Their relationship had mellowed during the hunt to track down his sons' kidnapper. Scott couldn't have imagined having such a candid conversation a year ago. Mistrust had turned to respect to the extent that they'd had dinner together a few times after the crisis had passed. Scott hadn't seen the man in recent months. Sammy and Peter's rehabilitation into normal life and his book deadline had gotten in the way. Scott wasn't sure if Sheils viewed him as entirely trustworthy. Yet another kidnapper seeking his help probably didn't do a lot in the faith department.

Scott turned back around. He knew Sheils had hit mandatory FBI retirement age. He looked good for his age, except for the additional twenty pounds he carried around his waist and the receding hairline. "I expected you to be retired by now."

"I will be soon, but leaving the FBI isn't like leaving an ordinary job. It has to be planned."

"And this has thrown a wrench in the works," Guerra said.

"Meaning what?" Scott said.

"I'm supposed to be closing out cases, not taking on new ones."

"But you got it because of our past association."

"Correct."

It was just another reason for his relationship with Sheils to remain on a rocky footing. Rather than pick at an old wound, Scott turned the conversation to the current kidnapping.

"What can you tell me?" he asked.

"Very little at this point. The girl is on vacation from the UK with her family. She was snatched on the Embarcadero while her parents were buying tickets for the aquarium at approximately ten thirty this morning. The kidnapper made contact with the *Independent* a little after one p.m. asking for you. He's named himself the Shepherd. He's calling back tomorrow at the same time to talk to you. That's it."

Memories of the Piper contacting him flashed through his mind. That case had also started with a call, and a child had died because of it. His children were kidnapped because of it.

"Is this connected to the Piper? Is the Shepherd some partner of the Piper we never knew about?"

"I don't think so."

"I'm looking for a little more than that. I need to know what I'm walking into."

Sheils raised a hand. "We don't have enough information to say one way or another. We haven't even made contact with this person, and we don't know what his demands are yet. I think we'll learn a hell of a lot once you've talked to him tomorrow."

"It might be a bit late by then if he plans on snatching my family while we're playing his damn fool games."

"I'm aware of that. Your family's security is just as important as getting Grace back. I have people watching your house now."

Sheils was saying all the right things, but it was doing nothing to loosen the knot in his chest. "I just don't get why he wants to speak to me. What have I got to do with this?"

"That's what I wanted to ask you."

"You must have some theories."

"Too many at this point until he makes his demands, but if it makes you feel any better, I don't think this is connected to the Piper."

That answer was a double-edged sword of its own. It was a relief to think the ghost of the Piper wouldn't be coming to haunt him again, but that meant the Shepherd was something new. Of all the people in the world, why had the Shepherd chosen him? The dark unknown of that question almost made him wish that Grace's kidnapping *was* connected to the Piper. At least then he'd have some idea of why the Shepherd was dragging him into this.

It didn't take long for Guerra to scythe her way through the city to the federal building, where the FBI was housed. She parked in the underground parking lot, and the three of them took the elevator. Sheils pressed the button to the thirteenth floor.

The thirteenth floor. Scott wished for a more positive omen.

When the elevator doors opened, Sheils said, "Let everybody know we're back. I'll get Scott checked in."

Sheils signed him in and gave him a visitor's badge. He took Scott through a door for official personnel only, then pressed a hand to his chest. Scott had four inches over the FBI agent, but he carried the bulk to stop Scott in his tracks. "I'm going to ask you this just once more. Do you know who the Shepherd is, or have you had any prior encounter with him?"

Any goodwill Scott thought he'd had with Sheils disappeared with that question. Sheils didn't believe him. After all they'd endured six months ago, Sheils still didn't trust him. He understood, though. An eight-year grudge was not going away in a hurry. Sheils viewed him as a problem and not a solution. That had been the FBI agent's opinion during Nicholas Rooker's kidnapping, and rightfully so, because Scott had inserted himself into the hoax, diverting the investigation. Sheils's contempt had turned into a grudge once the Piper had taken Nicholas's life. In his opinion, Scott's interference and headline-grabbing stories had gotten Nicholas killed. And Sheils was right, but Scott's deep guilt—and then Charles Rooker himself—had made Scott pay for those mistakes of ego and carelessness. He didn't expect Sheils's forgiveness, but he'd thought he'd at least earned the FBI agent's empathy. It looked as if he hadn't.

"I'd tell you if I did."

"Would you? Prior history isn't on your side."

They really weren't friends, Scott decided. "After what I went through last time, and what I'm still going through, how can you even ask me that?"

"I wouldn't be doing my job if I didn't ask. Nothing is off the table or out of bounds at this point."

"I'm not chasing something here. You came to me, remember?"

"So this Shepherd hasn't reached out to you in any way?"

"The call to the *Independent* is it."

"Okay, good."

Sheils put out his hand, and Scott took it. The FBI agent's grip was fierce.

"Just don't keep anything from me, okay?"

"I won't."

"Good. Now let's give this family some hope."

• • •

Sheils opened the door to a conference room, and Scott walked in. Ten faces looked his way—five adults and five kids. The kids ranged in age from five to twelve. They were arranged around the room in a tableau that conflicted with their surroundings. They sported the tourist uniform of T-shirts and shorts with either soccer teams or San Francisco sights clashing with the banal surroundings of a windowless conference room.

"This is Scott Fleetwood," Sheils said.

No one said hello or offered a greeting. They were a family decimated by fear, which was something he understood all too well. He resented the Shepherd for dragging him into this, but in some ways, he ought to be thanking the kidnapper. He was one of the few people who could help this family get through this nightmare.

Sheils introduced everyone. Grace's father, Brian Pagett, was a beefy guy with a shaved head. He leaned against a wall with his arms draped over the shoulders of his daughter Tabitha. His wife, Emily, sat at the conference table holding the hands of her two boys, Matthew and Patrick. Matthew, despite being the oldest child in the room, was sobbing. With them was Pagett's younger brother, Phil. He and his wife, Karen, sat at one end of the table, holding hands, while their two daughters sat in the corner on the floor. Keith Draper, a small, untidy-looking man in his forties, introduced himself as a family friend traveling with the Pagetts.

Agents Shawn Brannon and Terry Dunham had been babysitting the Pagetts before his arrival. Both agents had been part of Sheils's team during Sammy and Peter's abduction. They said their hellos before leaving.

"Why's he want to talk to you?" Brian Pagett asked, although the question bordered on an accusation.

"I don't know."

"It must be something, or he wouldn't be asking for you." Brian Pagett's face turned red.

"Brian, don't, please," Emily said.

Scott took a seat at the conference table. He positioned himself opposite Emily. He hoped the move would bring Pagett to the table, too.

"Six months ago, my children were kidnapped. It was high profile. There was a lot of press coverage. I'm guessing that's the reason why."

"Were your children released?" Emily asked.

"Yes."

"Could this be the same kidnapper?" Draper asked.

"The people involved in my kidnapping were all captured." Scott avoided saying they were all dead. That was a detail they didn't need to know.

"What are your children's names?" Emily asked.

"Sammy and Peter. They're twins. They've just turned nine."

"Why were they taken?" she asked. "It doesn't just happen. There's always a reason."

It was an insightful question and one that burned Scott. There was a big difference between these people and himself. He'd brought the kidnapping upon himself. These people hadn't.

"I was a reporter with one of the newspapers here. I incited the kidnappers."

"See, this is what I don't get," Emily said. "We don't know anybody. We haven't done anything to anybody."

"That's why we don't believe Grace's kidnapping and the kidnapping of Scott's children are connected," Sheils said.

"I swear to Christ if you caused my Grace's kidnapping, I'll put you in a hole," Pagett barked.

Pagett's nieces jumped up from the floor and clung to their parents.

"For God's sake, be sensible," Emily said. "You're not helping."

Draper jumped up from his seat and put himself in front of Pagett. "Mate, mate, it's okay. Everyone is a good guy in this room. We're getting Gracie back. Sit down."

Pagett did as his friend told him and fell into a seat next to his wife, pulling his daughter onto his lap. Draper dropped into the empty seat next to Pagett.

"I know you're scared. I get it. I truly do," Scott said to Pagett. "I'm the only person in this room who's been through what you're going through now. Agents Sheils, Guerra, and the people here at the FBI rescued my children, and they're going to do the same for Grace. They'll bring her home safe and sound and lock up the son of a bitch who did this."

"It's my fault," Matthew said without raising his head.

Scott stretched a hand across the table at the boy. "Please don't say that. Never blame yourself for what other people do. My son Sammy blamed himself when his brother was taken."

"Your boys were taken separately?" Pagett asked.

Scott saw the gears turning in Pagett's head—more than one child was at risk. "Yes, but there were mitigating circumstances for that."

"While I don't believe there are any similarities between your situation and Scott's, you will receive around-the-clock protection to ensure no one is at risk," Sheils said.

Scott decided to steer the conversation away from imagined fears and to the practicalities of what he had to do. He pulled out his cell phone and opened up the notepad app.

"Could you tell me a few things about Grace? It'll help me when I talk to this person tomorrow." He refused to call him the Shepherd to rob him of the power he held.

"She's sweet. Silly. Like any other six-year-old."

"She loves Derek," Matthew said.

"Who's Derek?"

"It's her toy bunny rabbit," Emily said. "Won't go anywhere without it."

"Don't ask me where she got the name," Pagett said, palming a tear away. "She could have called it Cottontail, Flopsy, Bunny, or something, but she went with Derek. That's Gracie."

"She had it on her when the Shepherd took her," Matthew said.

Emily stroked her heartbroken son's head.

"Do you have a picture of her?"

Emily brought out her phone and handed it to Scott. He flipped through the photos she'd taken and got her permission to text a head-shot of Grace to his phone. He wanted a picture of the girl for himself more than anything else. He never wanted to lose sight of who and what were at stake.

Scott spent the next half an hour asking the Pagetts for biographical information about Grace. He asked about her likes and dislikes and little-known information, all of which were good nuggets he could use to obtain proof of life. He asked whether she had any favorite foods or if she required any medication.

"This is really good for us," Sheils said. "Anything forces the Shepherd to make a special or unique purchase is great in tracing their location or identifying him."

"She takes something for hay fever. Just over-the-counter stuff. Nothing prescribed," Emily said.

"But she does have her quirks when it comes to treats," Pagett said.

"The quirkier the better," Sheils said. "Anything that would be tough to find here in the States. It'll be easier for us to trace any unusual sales."

"Jaffa Cakes," Pagett said.

"Jaffa Cakes?" Sheils said.

"It's a biscuit with a layer of orange covered in chocolate," Emily said.

"You mean *biscuit* as in *cookie*," Sheils said.

"Yes," Pagett said. "She'll eat them by the box if we don't stop her."

Things wound down after that. There wasn't much anyone could do other than wait for tomorrow's call. Scott thanked the two families for their time and told them to call him anytime. He went around the room shaking hands with the Pagett family. Emily took his hands in hers.

"Thank you for helping us."

"People helped me when I was in your place. This is the only way I can repay that debt."

"You'll bring her home to us, won't you, Scott?"

"I will."

Sheils's expression hardened. Scott knew Sheils would read him the riot act for saying this. Law enforcement never promised safe returns or happy endings because so much could go wrong. But he didn't care. He wasn't a cop. Sheils had told him to give these people hope, and that was what he was doing. They needed to believe Grace was coming back to them, and so did he. He needed to save this girl. He was already responsible for one dead child. He couldn't live with a second.

CHAPTER SIX

Connors looked in on Grace. Finally, she was asleep on the cot. That was thanks only to a mix of sedatives and exhaustion. He'd done his best to make the room as comfortable as possible by having a bunch of plush toys and games available and decorating it with various posters from the latest animated movies. Not surprisingly, she hadn't shown interest in any of that. At the end of the day, the room was what it was—a cell where she was being held captive. She'd come around, though. Everyone did. No one could maintain that level of panic long-term.

The girl turned in her sleep, murmured something he couldn't make out, and pulled her toy bunny rabbit to her. The grubby thing was the only thing that gave her any solace. Whatever worked.

"Hang in there, kid. This shouldn't take long."

He backed out of the room, which was actually a six-foot-by-six-foot wooden cell he'd put together and bolted to the concrete floor of what remained of a TNT factory. He'd rigged it with lighting, an air vent, and a potty. He was keeping a six-year-old in a cell. How the hell had it come to this—kidnapping kids?

He'd set up camp at the former World War II explosives factory set into the Marin Headlands. Long decommissioned, the buildings weren't much more than husks. This building wasn't too bad. The window had been smashed, and anything wooden had long since rotted away, but the concrete ceiling provided cover. The other buildings hadn't survived as well. Most resembled ancient ruins, just a couple of walls or only the foundation in some cases. He'd chosen this place because it was isolated, and he didn't need reservations to use it. Despite being parkland, it was accessible only by water or a very determined hiker. It was pretty much perfect.

He closed and locked the door before returning to his center of operations, which consisted of a bunk, a picnic table with all his equipment, and a chair. Grace had more in the way of creature comforts than he did. He didn't need them when he was working. If he was being honest, he didn't need them when he wasn't.

He dropped into his chair and eyed the video link monitoring Grace in her room. This would be a learning experience for her parents . . . or so he hoped.

He reached into his hunting-vest pocket and pulled out a creased and dog-eared Polaroid picture. The photograph was in pretty shoddy condition from years of carrying it with him across three different continents. It wouldn't last much longer, but he couldn't bear the idea of losing it. Aamir had loved his Polaroid camera so much. The boy had carried it around his neck all the time. One of the rare times he'd broken from this habit was when he'd given it to Connors to snap this shot of him. The boy had stood with a soccer ball in flight high above his head and a grin that could light a night's sky. And those steel-gray eyes—how did they sparkle so bright? Behind him, a barren Afghan landscape stretched into the horizon. Out of shot, snipers hid, waiting to slay him and his family. Yet the kid could smile like that. He always managed to have a joke on hand and believed in a better future where hate and death wouldn't exist. That boy could have changed the world—and should have—if Connors hadn't screwed up his mission.

It had been a simple one—keep his charges safe. He palmed away a tear and placed the photo on the desk.

He picked up one of the cell phones on the table. It was his phone, untraceable and unregistered. He punched in the number he knew by heart.

He listened to the ringtone drone on and on. Karima always took a long time to answer. She'd be deciding whether to take his call. She would take it, though, because of the simple fact that if she didn't, he'd call back again.

"Hello, Gavin."

He loved the sound of her voice and the way its cadence didn't fall in line with a natural English speaker's. It was almost musical and certainly hypnotic to him.

"How are you?"

Her sigh traveled down the line. His calls weren't intended to hurt her, but they did. He was an ugly reminder of all she had lost. Still, it was his duty to make amends for his failure.

"You shouldn't be calling, Gavin."

"Why? Have you been compromised? Your new identity should be safe."

The WITSEC program she was in was good. It had taken him months of investigation to break their witness protection protocols and find her location. Very few people could accomplish this, but if he could, so could someone else.

"Do you need an evac? I can be there tomorrow to get you out and get you into a safe house."

"No, Gavin. I'm safe. It's you. You know you shouldn't be calling."

He ran a finger across Aamir's photo. "I was assigned to protect you. I won't stop."

"But you . . ." She didn't finish the sentence.

But he what—failed? Yes, he had. They all had.

"But your mission is over. I'm not your problem anymore."

"You were never a problem."

"I know." She sighed again. "What can I do for you?"

She was shutting him out, pushing him out to the sidelines and squeezing him out of her life. Didn't she understand what he was trying to do for her?

"I just wanted to let you know that I will be FedExing you some cash."

"Please don't. I've told you before to stop."

"Don't think of it as charity. One thing I know about my government. They'll do the absolute minimum to honor their obligation. You need to have other means to ensure your own safety."

"Gavin, I'm not your responsibility."

She was. She always would be.

"I don't need your money. I don't want your money. I've told you before."

"I'm still sending it."

She laughed. It might have sounded exasperated, but it brought a smile to his face. He liked her smile. Was she running her hand through that long black hair? It was a nervous tell. Whenever she smiled, she combed her hair over her right ear. He didn't think she was aware of how beautiful she was.

"Gavin, I wish I could fix you."

So did he, but no one could. He deserved to stay broken.

"Good night, Gavin. Don't call again," she said and hung up.

"Sorry," he said and powered the phone off.

He checked his watch. It was time to check in with his client, who'd dubbed himself Elvis for anonymity. He didn't know the man's identity, and they'd never met—his policy, not Elvis's. The client didn't know his real identity, either. Connors created a fresh identity for every client. That way if anyone sold him out, he'd know the rat's identity right away. Elvis knew him as John.

45

He picked up the cell phone marked *Elvis* and walked over to one of the many busted-out windows. He stared out over the bay, listening to the phone ring. Elvis had unnerved him this time around. This was the fourth assignment he'd given Connors in the past five years. Previous jobs had included stealing information or planting damning evidence, but nothing that involved abduction. When he'd said he wanted a child snatched at random, Connors had almost turned it down. The only reason he'd taken the job was because he knew he'd keep the kid safe. There were people in his line of work who wouldn't.

"How's it going, John?"

"Fine. The girl is quiet. I don't foresee any problems with her. I placed the call with the *Independent*. Everything is going according to your timetable."

"Good. What about the law-enforcement angle?"

He'd been monitoring police chatter since he'd grabbed Grace. "Nonexistent. It was a clean abduction. The *Independent* wasn't expecting the call. The police have nothing to chase down or any reason to check out this location."

"Where is that?"

Elvis used a voice changer to disguise his voice. It wasn't as sophisticated as the one Connors had used to call the *Independent*, but it got the job done. He couldn't distinguish whether Elvis was young or old or even if he was a man or not. His client kept his colloquialisms middle of the road to hide regional origins. But the voice changer couldn't hide everything. He was certain that Elvis wasn't military or law enforcement. From their prior conversations, the man had shown he knew little about protocols and procedures. Also, if Elvis had a military or police background, he could pull these jobs off himself. That begged the question—what was he? He was a blank sheet. Connors would do some digging after this kidnapping was over. It was in his interest to have something on his client should anything go sideways.

"You don't need to know my location."

Elvis laughed. "I like your caution."

"It's what keeps me safe . . . and you."

He laughed again. "So you're all set for tomorrow's call with Fleetwood."

"Yes."

"Remember to play up your demands. Make a big show of everything. I'll check in with you after the call."

"We do have one problem."

"We do? What's that?"

"My payment. I haven't received it."

The only thing Connors had received was a $5,000 advance payment. He was supposed to have received an additional $25,000. Elvis had been straight with him until now. He hoped the situation wasn't changing.

"Don't worry about that. It's just a small change in payment terms, but in your favor. The ransom is yours. I don't want it."

The windfall should have pleased Connors. Instead, it unnerved him. They'd agreed to a plan, and they should stick to it. Sudden changes were always a bad sign.

"You don't want your cut?"

"Nope."

"What's in it for you?"

"Plenty. I have a nice side hustle that will pay out just as well."

"Which is?"

"Oh, that would be telling. Talk to you tomorrow."

CHAPTER SEVEN

As the FBI agent drove away, Scott let himself breathe a little easier. Grace Pagett's kidnapping hadn't left his thoughts, but there was distance now. Home was his safe harbor. Nothing was allowed to destroy that.

He let himself in, and Jane came in from the living room to greet him. She wrapped him up in her small arms. There was so much strength in them. He let himself melt into her.

"How'd it go?"

"About as shitty as you'd expect."

"Those poor people."

The image of Grace he had on his phone popped into his head. Her family got to share their fears and sorrow in a hotel room. He had Jane and their boys to keep him warm tonight. God knew what Grace had. He just prayed the Shepherd was treating her well and keeping her safe.

"Where are Peter and Sammy?" He'd hoped they'd be waiting for him when he walked in the door.

"Up in their room. I let them stay up. They didn't want to go to bed until they knew you were home."

He hadn't realized it was that late. George still wanted two thousand words from him tonight for their front-page feature article. George could wait.

"I'll go see them."

"We've got a problem, though. The boys know all about the Shepherd, the kidnapping, and you."

He'd wanted to insulate them from this. He imagined all the progress they'd made getting over the trauma of their own kidnapping and rebuilding their confidence going up in smoke. "Goddamn it. How?"

"A cocktail of screwups. Lucy Guerra told them a girl had been abducted, and the Internet filled in the rest."

"Shit." He reached for his cell. "I'll have Sheils ream her out, and if he doesn't, I will."

Jane raised her hands. "It's okay. We can make this work. This has the potential to be a learning experience."

"A learning experience? You can't be serious. This has the potential to set them back months, if not years."

"It won't if we handle this right. I spoke to Dr. Nichols. She thinks involving them in the process is constructive. We make them stakeholders in this situation. Give them some control over their destiny."

They'd been working with Dr. Vivian Nichols since Sammy and Peter's rescue. They engaged in family therapy, and the boys also met with her one-on-one. She had come highly recommended by several support groups specializing in childhood trauma. Scott thought she was an insightful therapist but felt she was off base on this occasion.

"I don't know. Shielding them from all this makes more sense."

"We can't cocoon them. It's too late for that. They already know some of what's going on. All we can do now is answer their questions and support them when they need it."

He still wasn't sold on it, but he'd give it a try. But he reserved veto power to use at the first signs of trouble. Jane must have read his concerned expression because she stood on tiptoes to hug him. The strength in her embrace blunted the horrors of this shitty-shitty day.

"I'm going to chew out Agent Guerra when I see her next," he said into his wife's ear.

"I'll do it. I don't want you to damage your relationship with the FBI."

What relationship? he thought.

Climbing the stairs, Jane said, "I've been thinking about the Pagetts. They came here on vacation. They don't know anyone, and they're scared. It might be nice if we all get together. They can talk to us about what to expect and to the boys about their experiences, if that's what they need. It might give them some comfort and also let the boys feel like they're helping. It's just a thought. Feel free to say no."

"It's a good idea. It's up to the boys, though."

"Sure thing."

In their room, his boys welcomed him with hugs and questions. They wanted to know all about the kidnapping, the kidnapper, Grace, and her family. They weren't being sensationalistic little boys in their questioning. It was more of a need to know that this had nothing to do with the man who'd abducted them. He showed them the photo of Grace on his phone.

"She's little," Peter said, handing the phone back. "Why does this man want to talk to you?"

"I don't know. I think he knows I've talked to men like him before. I can help things go smoothly to reunite Grace with her family."

"If he knows about you, does he know about us?" Sammy asked.

Sammy's hands were balled into tight fists around his comforter. Scott shared a glance with Jane. She'd seen it, too. He had to handle this moment carefully. If he didn't relieve his son's tension, there'd be night terrors. They were contagious in this household. If Sammy had them, they'd spread to Peter.

When it came to handling the boy's fears, Scott found himself on awkward ground. The truth provided no comfort. Lies provided a nice salve for a sore spot but risked exposure—and worse, mistrust. His boys could never lose their faith in him or Jane. He always erred on the side of truth but supported it with the unshakeable fact he and Jane were their protectors.

"Yes, I'm sure he does, but he only wants my assistance."

"What if he comes here?" Peter said.

Damn, he thought. Fear had made its parasitic jump to his other son. He had to work fast to stop it from fully infecting them.

"He won't. I won't allow it."

"You allowed it when the Piper took us."

That was the truth that destroyed every solid argument Scott could ever make. Yes, he'd let a kidnapper take his children as easily as picking fruit from a tree. Promises and assurances lacked credibility against those facts. That simple fact cleaved him in two.

"That's a little unfair," Jane said.

"It's not," Scott said. "I was unprepared."

"*We* were unprepared," Jane corrected.

"It's different now. We have a security system. We have rules and procedures to keep you safe. I won't let anything happen to you. Your mom won't, either. And Agent Tom and Lucy, who were here today, have sworn to protect you. This man won't harm you. I guarantee it."

Sammy's tight grasp on his comforter lessened but not all the way. Scott had a little more to do.

"I've got a big favor to ask you two," Scott said.

They perked up in their beds.

"The Pagett family is on vacation from England. They're all alone and scared because they don't know what's going on. We've been where they are now. Your mom and I thought it might be nice if we all did something together to let them know they have friends in this country. Would you like to do that?"

He got a pair of excited yeses.

"You guys are awesome. Now, it's time for bed."

By the time he and Jane left the room, the boys were giggling. No white-knuckled fists. He might have just pulled it off, although he might be in for a different kind of restless night. The boys were hyped up planning their get-together with the Pagetts.

Jane leaned into him as they descended the stairs. Scott followed her into the kitchen. She pulled a previously opened bottle of wine from the refrigerator and grabbed a couple of glasses from a cupboard.

"Not for me," he said.

"I thought you might need something after the day this family's had."

"George wants a piece from me."

She poured herself a more than generous glass. She picked it up, stared at the contents, frowned at it, then put it back down on the countertop.

"Do you really think they believe we let them be kidnapped?"

That remark was going to eat at her. He knew it would eat away at him.

"I don't think they meant it like that. It was more of a statement of fact than trying to place blame. It's a kick in the balls, but they aren't wrong."

"Christ, some days being a parent isn't worth the salary."

He smiled despite the situation.

"Do you think this Shepherd will come for us?"

That was the Fleetwood family's $64 million question. "I don't know."

"Jesus."

He held up his hands. "I don't think so. I don't see a reason for him to. I'm a publicity stunt. Not a target."

"It's the Piper all over again."

"It's not." He truly believed that. "If you're worried, take off with the boys. Go somewhere. Don't tell me where."

"I'm not having another one of these bastards run me out of my home."

"He won't. We just have to be vigilant. I'm going to keep this guy as far away from this family as possible, and your job is not to let those boys out of your sight. You cool with that?"

She nodded. "Come be with me. Lie to me, and tell me everything is wonderful."

He wanted nothing more. "I have to do this thing for George."

She frowned. "I've lost you to this, haven't I?"

"The second I agreed to help."

"How long do you think it will last?"

"Two days. Maybe three."

"Okay. Go. Do what has to be done. Just don't do anything crazy."

He crossed the kitchen, pulled her tight against him, and kissed her. She ground her body against him. He liked the heat building between them, but there wasn't time. Like she said, he didn't have a choice. He pulled away from her. She groaned. He picked up the wineglass and handed it to her.

"This'll have to tide you over," he said and left her in the kitchen.

"It's a poor substitute."

He was glad to hear it.

He went up to his office. Excited voices spilled from the boys' bedroom. He rapped on the door and told them to get to sleep.

His office could have made for a separate bedroom for either Sammy or Peter, but it was significantly smaller than the one they shared. Whoever got it would have complained. Luckily, the boys preferred a shared room, meaning he could have his office guilt free.

He closed the door and sat down at his PC. He'd barely written anything for the book worth reading in the last three months. Now he was supposed to write two thousand words for George tonight. Why the hell had he ever agreed to this?

He stared at the screen. What to write? He just needed a jumping-off point. The only thing that sprang to mind was why. Why had the Shepherd grabbed a random child? Why a foreigner at that? He had to have known it complicated things. And why pick him to be his envoy? None of it made sense, but Scott got the feeling that to the Shepherd, it all made perfect sense.

"What's your game, Shepherd?" he said to himself.

He didn't intend to play into the Shepherd's hands by throwing theories at the readers. That would only serve to embolden the kidnapper. *Hey, readers, there's a new big bad wolf out there, and he's called the Shepherd, and I think this is what he wants.* He didn't see any point in feeding this asshole's ego. If the Shepherd had a mission, he'd have to spell it out for himself. Scott wasn't about to do the heavy lifting for him.

The way forward was to stick to the facts and report what had happened. It might seem like a cop-out, but it wasn't. He'd be damned if he'd turn this son of a bitch into another boogeyman like the Piper.

He started typing. He started at the beginning. His beginning, where the Shepherd had tethered himself to him. The words came hard, but he slogged away at it. Then something broke, and he found his rhythm. He outlined his thoughts, quickly adding depth and texture to them. After a couple of hours, he was more than half done. In three, he had something for George to review.

How come he hadn't been able to do that with his own book? He hadn't put out this kind of material since he'd started that project. It took him a while to come up with the answer. He was angry at the Shepherd. He was ashamed when it came to the Piper. Writing about his entanglement with the Piper was writing about his mistakes and the failures that ultimately put him in a compromised position. A position that put his children's lives at risk. Admitting that burned him up with guilt.

Maybe that was where he was going wrong. Guilt wasn't the way to go. Yes, he'd made mistakes, but there hadn't been any malice behind them. A monster had decided to take his mistakes and twist them into a campaign of terror. That wasn't something to be guilty about. That was something to be angry about.

Jane knocked at the door and let herself in. "How's it going?"

"Good. I want to play with something for another hour. Cool?"

She smiled and let herself out.

He put away the assignment for George and pulled up his manuscript. "Time to get angry with you."

CHAPTER EIGHT

Sleep came hard for Scott. He kept playing the past, present, and future over in his head. He was in this again, tied to another kidnapper. If he'd thought he could cut the tether that now bound him to the Shepherd, he was wrong. Whatever this guy asked, he would have to do. Grace's life depended on it. He would do whatever it took, but he had to keep it separate from his family. He could be dragged into this. They couldn't. He just hoped he could control that.

At some point, he drifted off but awoke to the inevitable media circus outside his door at 6:00 a.m. He called both George and Sheils with one simple demand—deal with it.

He and Jane peered at the crowd on the sidewalk and spilling onto the pavement. News vans filled every available parking spot.

"I guess we won't be going anywhere soon," he said.

"We knew this was coming," she said. "I already called in a personal day with work. We aren't going to be popular with the neighbors, that's for sure."

"It should be only for today."

She eyed him with a wry smile.

"And maybe tomorrow."

Within half an hour, Thorpe arrived. He didn't knock, for which Scott was grateful. He simply took care of the media by acting as a spokesperson. Despite him asking the media to leave, they didn't. They still clung to the hope they'd get a sound bite from Scott.

At seven thirty, Sheils arrived. Jane let him in.

"You still up for this?" he asked.

"Yes," Scott said.

"Let's get you ready."

Scott hugged his boys and Jane before leaving.

"Get this girl back to her family," she said.

He couldn't bring himself to do anything except nod.

Sheils carved a hole through the news crews to where Guerra was sitting at the wheel of her car. Sheils held open a door, and Scott clambered inside without answering a question.

"A touch of déjà vu," Guerra said as they pulled away.

"Let's hope not," Sheils said before turning to Scott. "We're ready to take the Shepherd's call at any time. AT&T is looped in. A trap and trace is in place. Any call to the *Independent* will be caught by our people."

"When's he supposed to call?"

"If he's true to his word, at one-oh-three p.m. That will give us plenty of time to get you prepped."

No media greeted them at the FBI office. Sheils put Scott with a hostage negotiator in a small room and sat in on the meeting. For two hours, the negotiator coached Scott on various techniques that would build a rapport with the Shepherd, instill empathy for Grace, drag out the call, draw information from the kidnapper, and bargain down his demands. It was easier to absorb these techniques this time around, when his kids' lives weren't on the line. The negotiator excused himself and Scott thanked him, although his head pounded from the information dump.

"Got all that?" Sheils asked.

They were all great strategies and made a lot of sense, but Scott knew from bitter experience this worked only if the kidnapper allowed it. The kidnapper held all the cards. If the Shepherd was anything like the Piper, he'd dictate the pace. And if he was really smart, he wouldn't even give Scott an opening. He'd state his terms and hang up. The only avenue Scott could follow was to stay flexible and work any opening this scumbag gave him.

"Yeah. Got any Tylenol?"

"I'll get you something on the way to the *Independent*."

"I thought you'd divert the call here."

"Ideally, we would, but this guy is expecting you at the newspaper. I don't know if he'll have someone watching the place. At this point, I know the name *the Shepherd* alludes to being one person, but it could be a team for all we know. If he wants you taking the call from the *Independent*, then so be it. I'll have people monitoring the streets."

"But he must know the Feds are involved."

"It's all about giving him the illusion that he's in control and that we're three steps behind."

Isn't he, though? Scott wondered.

Sheils dug in his jacket pocket and slid a smartphone over. Scott picked it up. A strip of masking tape was stuck to the back with a number written on it.

"What's this?"

"Should the Shepherd want you to contact him, do it on one of our phones and not yours. Keep it on you at all times. We can use the GPS to track you."

Scott had the feeling Sheils wouldn't be tracking him if it weren't for their past. He'd kept the FBI in the dark when his kids had been kidnapped. It wasn't by choice but out of necessity. Sheils knew and understood that, but it still meant Scott was an unreliable element in their investigation. He wished he could say he wouldn't color outside the lines, but he would to save Grace. As a sign of good faith, he powered up the phone and pocketed it. Let them track him.

"You know I don't want to be part of this. I want to help, but the second you don't need me, I expect to be kicked to the curb."

"If you want to make it easy on yourself, the second he calls, hand him off to our negotiator. That way, you'll be done with it."

Scott knew it wouldn't be that easy. The Shepherd had called him in for a reason, and now that he had him, he would keep him to the bitter end.

"Let's get you over to the *Independent*. They want you for a press conference."

Scott found himself in the back of Guerra's car with Sheils at his side.

"We're on our way," Sheils said into his phone. "Okay, will do."

He put his phone away.

"Lucy, they want us to come through the back. Looks like Scott's got a fan club outside."

"Shit," Scott murmured.

The short distance from the federal building to the *Independent* on the south side of Mission Street meant that Guerra was soon sweeping by the front of the building. News crews, probably the same ones who'd parked themselves outside Scott's home, were now here. None of this could be good for Grace. Too much publicity possessed the power to screw up events. If the media failed to live up to the Shepherd's expectations, he'd take it out on Grace.

Guerra ducked down a couple of streets to get to the *Independent*'s staff parking lot and the rear entrance to the newspaper's offices. Sheils had been on his phone to George before they'd pulled up, so George already had the door open when they jumped from the car.

George led them through the building Scott had called home for more than a decade. They passed through the bullpen. Old colleagues acknowledged him with a smile or a handshake. His encounters with the Piper had quashed any feelings of nostalgia. This was a place he'd never expected to return to.

He spotted Brian and Emily Pagett in the conference room with Thorpe. The parents looked wiped out. Dark rings encircled their eyes, and Emily's hair was uncombed. He willed them to hang in there. A lot of road still needed to be covered. He raised a hand in greeting, and Emily waved back. Thorpe turned and gave a thumbs-up.

"It's getting crazy out there. People want a piece of this story, but Thorpe isn't sharing," George said as he led them to his office. "A lot of friendships are being burned today in the name of exclusivity."

Before anyone could sit down, Thorpe let himself into George's office without knocking.

"You're here. Great."

Thorpe shook Scott's and Sheils's hands.

"I have a press conference scheduled at eleven. That way we'll hit the lunchtime news here."

"You have the Pagetts here, too," Scott said.

"Yeah, I was hoping to have all the family, but they didn't want to be part of it. Sometimes you just don't get what you want. Shame."

Scott couldn't tell if Thorpe was just tone deaf or a complete jerk. He gave the consultant the benefit of the doubt and put his callousness down to overexuberance. He'd been brought in to get circulation up, and the Shepherd had just handed a solution to him—and no doubt his bonus.

"I'm going to have Brian, Emily, and you answer questions after I make a brief statement. Don't say too much."

"I can't. I don't know anything."

"Perfect. We don't want to give the family silver away."

"You might want to remember that we have a kidnapped child out there somewhere and a family losing their minds," Sheils said.

"You're right. I'm sorry. I get carried away sometimes trying to stay objective. I focus on the story and put the feelings to one side. That's the only way to say sane."

"Sure," Sheils said.

"Shall we do this thing?" Thorpe asked.

The press conference was in the lobby of the *Independent*, which would have seemed low-rent if it weren't for the eighty-year-old marble floors and the art deco architecture. A temporary dais had been constructed with a backdrop that read *San Francisco Independent* with the web address below. The Pagetts took their seats at the center of the long table. Scott and Sheils sat to their left with Scott sitting next to Emily. Thorpe sat on the right of Pagett. George stood off to one side with his arms folded across his chest, rocking back and forth on his toes.

"Thank you to everyone for coming. I'm Richard Thorpe of the *San Francisco Independent*. I'd like to make a short statement about the events that occurred yesterday with the kidnapping of Grace Pagett. I'm joined here by Grace's parents, Brian and Emily Pagett; reporter for the *Independent* Scott Fleetwood; and Special Agent Tom Sheils of the Federal Bureau of Investigation. I should point out that both Scott and Agent Sheils were instrumental in the capture of the kidnapper known as the Piper."

Scott shifted at the mention of his so-called claim to fame. He glanced over at Sheils for his reaction. The FBI agent remained stoic, but Scott guessed the agent liked the shout-out as little as he did.

"I ask that everyone hold their questions for the end."

Scott thought it was interesting how Thorpe gave the impression that he worked for the *Independent* and hadn't mentioned he was just a consultant.

Thorpe picked up a prepared statement. "Yesterday at approximately ten thirty a.m., Grace Pagett was abducted from her family on the Embarcadero near the ticket center for Alcatraz Island. Grace is six years old and is British. Her family is here in California on vacation. They were in the Bay Area before carrying on to LA to visit Disneyland."

Emily Pagett let out a moan, and her husband slipped an arm around her shoulders and pulled her to him.

Thorpe didn't let Emily's outburst slow him down. "At one-oh-three p.m., this newspaper received a call from a person claiming to be the kidnapper. He called himself the Shepherd and claimed he was holding Grace. He demanded to speak to *Independent* reporter Scott Fleetwood. Scott has agreed to speak to the kidnapper to help with Grace's safe return."

A wave of questions from the media hit them.

Thorpe raised his hand. "Mr. and Mrs. Pagett would like to say something to their daughter and the kidnapper."

Pagett took his wife's hand in his and held it tight. "Gracie, I can't imagine how scared you are, but you just have to know your mum and I are doing everything to get you back. To the Shepherd, I don't know why you took our daughter, but I will do whatever you need for Gracie's safe return. I just ask that you keep her safe. You have the world's most precious cargo."

Scott guessed he wasn't the only one being coached on how to speak to kidnappers. Pagett talked about Grace in casual terms. At no point did he make any threats or aggressive overtures. Scott could hear the restraint in Pagett's voice. The man was playing nice because he had to for the safety of his daughter. Scott noticed that Pagett's free hand was balled so tight, every joint shone white. That man was keeping his wrath in check, and the Shepherd should hope to never see it.

"Gracie, your brothers and sister can't wait for you to come home. That's all I wanted to say."

"Mrs. Pagett, do you have anything to add?" Thorpe asked.

"Just please don't hurt my baby," she managed before breaking down.

Pagett pulled his wife to him and rocked her back and forth. He whispered to her again and again that it would be okay.

Scott could only sympathize. He'd been where the Pagetts were now. Platitudes wouldn't help. They were trapped in a private hell that would release them only when their child was safely back in their arms.

Pagett looked up. Scott met his glance, trying to telegraph his sympathies.

Thorpe gave Emily a moment to gather herself before continuing. "I'd like to open this up for questions."

Thorpe pointed to a local affiliate reporter.

"John Teehan, Channel Six. Question for Scott."

Scott knew he'd be the first one quizzed. He was the story's hook. Outside of the Shepherd, he was the It Guy.

"Why you? Why did the Shepherd call you out?"

"I don't know."

"Have you had prior contact with the kidnapper?"

"No. None."

"Do you think Grace's abduction is related to the Piper's kidnapping of your sons?"

"There's nothing to suggest that," Scott answered. "Naturally, that will be a question for the man holding Grace against her will." He was in no mood to boost the asshole's ego by using his self-proclaimed nickname.

"So what's in it for you?"

Scott fought the urge to tell this jerk to go screw himself, but they were on national as well as local TV. That was the point, though. Teehan was obviously posturing in the hope of being recognized.

"Nothing is in it for me. I'm just here to support the Pagett family and want the person who took Grace to know that I am here to cooperate and help facilitate her safe return."

"So this has nothing to do with the book you have coming out about your experiences with the Piper?"

"That's enough," Sheils barked. "Mr. Fleetwood has volunteered to assist this family and the FBI. That should be applauded, not derided."

Teehan withered under Sheils's glare.

Scott hadn't expected the FBI agent to jump to his defense. The man was full of surprises.

"I think we'll move on to someone else with a respectful question," Thorpe said.

Sheils's reprimand set the tone for the rest of the press conference. The questions were all the obvious ones—who, what, where, why, and how. Sheils shot down anything that pertained to actual details about the case. Everything came to an end after fifteen minutes, although it seemed far longer than that to Scott.

Thorpe ushered them from the dais and away from further questions lobbed in their general direction. He got them out of the lobby and into the hallway, where Scott could breathe again.

"That Teehan jerk a friend of yours?" Sheils said.

Scott shook his head. "Don't know him. Just someone trying to make their bones on camera."

"Congratulations, everyone. Nicely handled," Thorpe said. "Hopefully, the Shepherd now knows we've met his first demand. We have Scott."

There was only one thing left to do—wait for the call.

CHAPTER NINE

Scott was staring at an image of Grace Pagett on his phone when the Shepherd called. She was at an age where her natural pudginess hid her true features. Her long blonde hair looked like a breeze had been blowing through it. Right now, she was the world's most precious girl, and he was going to do everything to bring her home. *You're safe with me*, he thought and pocketed his phone.

Everything was set up to take the call in the editorial department's conference room on the second floor. The attendance had been restricted to Scott, Sheils, Lucy Guerra, the Pagetts, and the negotiator. Despite everything taking place at the *Independent*, no *Independent* staff was allowed in the room. Even Thorpe wasn't allowed to sit in on the meeting. He paced the bullpen with his phone as the clock ticked down to zero hour.

Now the conference-room phone was ringing. Thorpe stopped and stood outside the glass-walled room along with everyone else in the office.

Nothing like having an audience, Scott thought.

Sheils was on his phone, talking to his tech guys back at the office. "They're ready whenever you are, Scott."

"Just try to draw this guy out," the negotiator said.

Emily Pagett held on to her husband. Both of them looked petrified.

"This is the first step to bring Grace home," Scott said and picked up the phone. "Scott Fleetwood."

"Do you have a cell phone?"

The question came out as a series of disconcerting, digitized voices, each word switching from male to female, from child to adult. It gave Scott the chills.

"Yes."

"Give me the number," another series of voices demanded.

Scott pulled out the cell Sheils had given him. He turned it over and read the number aloud.

The line went dead.

"Shit," Scott said.

"What happened?" Sheils asked.

"He hung up."

"He's switching to our cell," Sheils said into his phone.

"Jesus, please," Emily Pagett said.

"Don't worry," the negotiator said. "It's all part of the negotiation."

A moment later, the phone rang. Scott looked to Sheils for the go-ahead. The FBI agent nodded, and Scott answered the phone.

"Scott, are you alone?"

Again, the Shepherd's question was a series of voices. Scott couldn't tell how he was masking his voice. The flow of each word was stilted, like it was being read by a text-to-voice app but obviously far more sophisticated. Scott thought it was a smart move on the Shepherd's part. Whatever he was using, it nixed any chance of a voice print. It was another sign that the Shepherd was going to be no pushover. He was smart and professional. That made him dangerous. One mistake from Sheils and his team, and Grace's life was no doubt on the line.

"No, I'm not alone. I'm here with Grace's parents. They'd love to talk to their daughter."

A simple no would have sufficed, but he was using a couple of the techniques the negotiator had given him. First, stretch his answers out to keep the guy on the line, and second, humanize Grace. He was supposed to remind the kidnapper that she was a girl with a family.

"No."

He looked over at Emily Pagett, who had her hands out for the phone. He frowned and shook his head.

"Just a few words. That's all I ask. It will make all the difference to them and Grace."

The Shepherd shot down Scott's plea with a new question. "Is the FBI with you?"

"Yes." Scott didn't see any point in lying. No doubt the kidnapper had seen the press conference. He would have seen Sheils, and if he hadn't, the *Independent* had gone public with the story. Either way, he had to know the cops were involved.

"Why did you involve them?"

"I didn't. You kidnapped Grace. You had to know the police were going to be called. These people are tourists. They don't know anyone here. You called the *Independent*, telling them you had Grace. What did you think would happen?"

It was easier to take a strong tone with the Shepherd than it had been with the man who'd taken his children because he wasn't in a state of panic. He was fearful for Grace—he held her life in his hands—but it wasn't a father's terror. That made him far better equipped emotionally this time around.

"Just tell the FBI to stay out of my way, and nothing will happen to Grace."

"I think they're aware of that."

"Good."

"How's Grace?"

"She's fine."

"Good, good, good. I've got some information that will make things more comfortable for her."

"You're not here to talk. You're here to listen," came the litany of unconnected voices.

That was true, but the FBI needed information. He had to keep this call going and not let the kidnapper just state his demands and hang up. Any nugget of information could prove crucial.

"You've taken this child, but what do you know about her? Do you know her medical and dietary needs? Do you know what makes her happy? You called me in for my assistance, and that's what I'm trying to do. I just want to make sure Grace is well looked after, and I'm sure you do, too."

The response to this question would be telling. If he knew anything about Grace, it meant he'd targeted the Pagetts. If he didn't, it proved Grace was a random abduction and the Shepherd was an opportunist.

"What does she need?"

The Shepherd was an opportunist, then.

"She has bad hay fever, so she'll need Benadryl. She also likes Jaffa Cakes, which are a type of English cookies. I don't know where you can find them, but they're her favorite thing. I'm sure she's scared, and they might help take the sting out of this situation."

"I don't intend to harm Grace. She will be treated very well."

"Glad to hear it. Could Grace speak to her parents? Just for a second."

"No." Again, a short reply to a big request. "I will send you proof of life."

Proof of life. Law enforcement had coined this term, and Scott detested it. It was a sanitized phrase that reduced a human to a faceless, shapeless organism to take the emotional pressure off the cops and the kidnapper. They kept their sanity while the victim's family lost theirs.

"When?"

"Soon."

"Why not now? She has to be right there. It would only take a second."

"I say when—not you."

"Why are you doing this?"

"I'm teaching parents to love their kids."

"That's it?"

"Isn't it enough?"

Frankly, it wasn't. Scott expected a manifesto. If the Shepherd was on a crusade, where was the speech? Where was the rhetoric? Maybe the Shepherd was a minimalist who didn't drone on. Scott didn't buy it. Maybe there was no crusade, and he was just in it for the money.

"Why'd you take Grace?"

"Absentee parenting. The Pagetts weren't paying her the proper attention."

"That's a little harsh, don't you think?"

"No. If they'd been diligent, I would never have been able to take her."

The Shepherd obviously didn't have kids of his own. A kid could disappear out from under you if you took your eyes off them for a second. Scott found the remark telling. *Is a lost kid at the heart of this? Did the Shepherd lose his own kid in the past?* That would explain why parenting and kids were a flash point for this guy. That was good. It was an angle he and Sheils could exploit. But if the Shepherd had a flash point, Scott also didn't want to do anything that would blow up in his face.

"What do I call you—the Shepherd?"

"Yes."

"Why that name?"

An answer was slow in coming. It was a good thirty seconds before the kidnapper said, "I watch over the flock. Sometimes I have to make an example of the sheep who are careless."

Questions whirled through Scott's mind. That answer had taken time in coming. Did that mean he'd just made it up, or he'd lied to hide the true reason? Second, when he talked about making examples of the sheep, did that mean he'd done this before? Finally, did this mean the kidnapper saw himself as some sort of crusader who had taken it upon himself to hand out justice as *he* saw fit? That element disturbed Scott the most. Potentially, it made him unpredictable.

"Who are the sheep, Shepherd?"

"Enough. I know what you're doing. You're dragging this call out. No more."

"Sorry. That wasn't my intention. I'm just trying to understand what's going on."

"Don't lie to me, Scott. I don't want to hurt Grace, but I will. Have no fear of that. Now, do you want to keep screwing around, or do you want to hear my demands?"

The negotiator passed a note over to Scott with the message: *Don't push it.*

Scott nodded his understanding.

"Sorry. Go ahead."

"I want two hundred thousand dollars in hundred-dollar-bill denominations only. I want the bills in four packs wrapped and sealed in plastic."

"These people don't have that kind of money. They're tourists on vacation. Be reasonable."

"This isn't up for negotiation. Two hundred thousand as I've requested. How you come up with it isn't my problem."

"Then it's going to take time."

"No. Have the money ready by one p.m. tomorrow. I expect you to be at the *Independent* at this time with the money. You'll also need a vehicle and this phone. I will call with instructions."

Listening to all those digitized, emotionless voices spew out the Shepherd's demands made Scott's skin crawl. "Do you know what you're asking?"

"Yes. It's more than feasible. I expect it to be done as I requested. I don't think I have to tell you what will happen if you fail."

The Shepherd kept saying *you*. Scott didn't like it. This wasn't his problem to solve. It was the Pagetts' and the FBI's. He was supposed to be the go-between, the conduit, not in charge here. Except he was, the second that son of a bitch had invoked his name. He was never going to be on the sidelines.

"I'll be ready," he said.

"Good. I won't tolerate any excuses."

"I have a question."

"What?"

"Why me? I don't know you. I don't know Grace and her family. So why me?"

There was a pause before the answer came.

"Not many people in this world understand what it's like to be wrong, but you do. You have one child's death to your name. I'm sure you don't want to make it two. Talk to you tomorrow."

CHAPTER TEN

"Two hundred thousand?" Brian Pagett bellowed. "Where in God's name are we supposed to come up with that?"

The glass walls in the boardroom shook from his protests. Scott knew to let the man have his moment of fury. The Shepherd, like all kidnappers, robbed loved ones of their strength and made them feel impotent by rushing them and taking away their power. An exorbitant amount of money that no normal person could lay their hands on only served to pour salt in the wound.

Emily grabbed her husband's wrist. "We can sell the house."

"Sell the house? He wants his money tomorrow. To-mor-row. There's just no way."

Emily's grasp on Pagett's hand fell away, and she sobbed.

"You people must have a contingency for this, right?" Pagett aimed the question at Sheils. "You must put up the money for these things."

"It doesn't work that way, I'm sorry to say."

Pagett tore across the room and loomed over Sheils. To the FBI agent's credit, he didn't flinch. Not to say he wouldn't take Pagett to the floor if he crossed a line.

"You're sorry to say? My kid's life is on the line, and you're sorry to say? Enlighten me. How does this work?"

"We will assist with arranging the money and delivery of the ransom, but you have to put up the funds."

"You have got to be shitting me."

Sheils's lack of response said that he wasn't.

"You've been through this," Pagett said, turning his attention to Scott. "Is this true?"

Scott nodded.

"How did you come up with your ransom?"

That was a complicated story for another time. It was best to simplify. "One of the previous kidnap victim's family donated it."

"Nice to have other victims to help out. Just my bad luck to have a guy on his debut." Pagett zeroed in on Sheils again. "My daughter was snatched in your country. You're telling me you have no obligation to pay the ransom?"

"No, we don't."

"It's not like you're going to lose the money. You're going to get it back when you catch him." The sarcasm was impossible to ignore.

"Brian, please," Emily said.

Pagett whirled on his wife. "Please, what? These fuckers could help, but they won't. They've just killed my daughter."

The slap sounded like a thunderclap. Emily had struck her husband as he'd loomed over her. It was hard, fast, and clinical in its power and efficiency. It resulted in the desired effect, shutting Pagett up.

"First, Grace is not *your* daughter. She is *our* daughter." Emily vibrated when she spoke. For all her cool and calm delivery, a thin layer of restraint kept her rage contained. "Second, you are not helping the situation with your bellyaching. Finally, if you ever say our daughter is dead again, I will pack up the kids, and you'll never see us again. Do I make myself clear?"

The effect was immediate. Scott watched Brian Pagett break in that moment. All his fears overwhelmed him. He dropped to his knees and held out his arms to his wife like an injured child to his mother. His body convulsed as he sobbed. Emily stepped into his arms and embraced him.

"I'm so fucking scared, Emily. I'm scared we've lost her."

"I know, I know, baby. We all are," she cooed. Her tears streamed down her face onto his shaved head. "We just have to have faith."

"Is there anything I can get you, Mr. and Mrs. Pagett?" Sheils asked.

"We just need a minute to ourselves," Emily said.

Sheils nodded, and everyone followed him out of the conference room, including Scott. The FBI agent told his people to grab some coffee and regroup in fifteen minutes.

Scott remained at Sheils's side as the Pagetts regained their composure. Emily closed the conference-room blinds, blocking everyone from their moment of misery.

"You okay?" Scott asked Sheils.

"Yeah. It's not the first time I've seen this."

"Doesn't make it any easier."

"No."

Thorpe walked up. His expression echoed how Scott felt. It was nice to see his cocky manner contained for once. Scott guessed for all of the consultant's bravado, this was probably the first time he'd seen the ugly side of a story.

"It looked as if it got a little intense in there. Everybody okay?"

"Yeah," Sheils said. "They're just coping with the harsh realities of the Shepherd's demands."

"How much did he ask for?"

"Two hundred grand," Scott said. "He wants it by this time tomorrow."

"Shit. And I'm guessing they don't have that kind of money, and the FBI isn't fronting it."

"Correct," Sheils said.

"Thought that might be the case. I have something in mind, but I need to make a few calls to get this in motion. Excuse me, gentlemen."

Watching Thorpe go, Sheils said, "I need to make some calls, too."

Suddenly alone, Scott checked in with George to fill him in on the Shepherd's demands. Despite having the story of the year in his lap, he looked worn down by the news. That didn't prevent him from asking for Scott's piece for the paper ASAP and reminding him not to leave the building before giving a video interview for the online edition and social media.

Scott returned to the conference room. The blinds were still down, but he didn't hear any raised voices. He knocked on the door.

"Come in," Emily said.

He opened the door. The couple had a pair of chairs pulled together into a makeshift loveseat. Pagett held his wife's hand and leaned his head against her shoulder.

"Just wanted to see how you're doing."

"We're okay," Emily said.

He smiled. "Sure?"

Pagett managed a small smile. "Pretty shitty, really."

"I think that's pretty good, all things considered. Okay if I come in?"

Emily nodded.

He let himself in and closed the door. He grabbed a spare chair and wheeled it over to them.

"Look, I just want to apologize for my behavior," Pagett said. "I let it get to me, and I'm really sorry."

"Forget about it. We get it. This should never happen to anyone. Of course you're going a little crazy. If you didn't lose your shit at least once, you wouldn't be human."

"That's kind of you to say, but I really embarrassed myself. Where's everyone else? I need to apologize to them."

"They're working on what to do next."

"Can they not lend us the money? We'd pay them back," Emily said.

"No, not usually. It's just not what the government does. But believe me, they're going to try and make something happen by tomorrow."

"How did you cope with this?" Emily asked.

"By any means possible. I won't lie to you—this is the ninth circle of hell. You do what you can to survive. If that means going to church, seeing a shrink, do whatever it takes. The best advice I can give you is lean on each other. Whatever you two and your kids need, get it. Let the team know so they can support you."

"You make it sound easy," Pagett said.

"It's the gift of hindsight. I was losing my shit back then."

"God, I don't know what we're going to do," Emily said.

"How about a barbecue at my home tonight? My wife and I talked about it, and we'd love it if you'd bring your family over."

Pagett frowned and looked his wife. "We're not in much of a socializing mood."

"I know. This isn't about socializing. You need an escape. If you don't have one, this shit is going to crush you. Use it as an opportunity to draw a breath, ask us questions, talk to our kids, or whatever else you need to do. Your family should lean on each other, but you can lean on us, too."

Emily took Scott's hands in hers. "Thank you. That's very kind."

There was another knock at the door, and Thorpe let himself in. "Sorry to interrupt, but I know how we can raise the ransom."

That would be one hell of a magic trick if he could pull it off. "You do?" Scott asked.

Thorpe grinned. "We're going to crowdfund it."

• • •

As barbecues went, this one proved an unconventional get-together. The family of a kidnapped child was at the home of a family who'd had their children kidnapped. The unusual demographics were topped off by the presence of the FBI. Scott wanted this event to be momentary relief from the black cloud hanging over them, and it seemed to be working. People were talking. Kids were running around. It was proving to be a success. All in all, the mood was good.

Sheils kept the FBI presence low-key, restricting it to the two agents watching the Pagetts, Guerra, and himself. To blunt the law-enforcement edge, he'd let everyone bring spouses and partners.

Scott kept the affair simple, just burgers and hot dogs with some salad on the side. Sheils turned the cookout into a potluck by having his people bring sides and desserts.

Scott forewent his manly duties working the grill by letting everyone take a turn. He wanted to make himself available to the Pagetts and give them an opportunity to quiz him and the boys about the situation, or even escape it if they chose. It was something he'd never had available to him and wished he'd had. Being stuck in the Piper's gravity pull with no relief was crushing, and he wouldn't wish that on anyone.

Jane whispered to him that the ice chest was running low on beers. Scott went into the kitchen and grabbed a case he had in the refrigerator. When he closed the fridge door, he found Pagett standing in the doorway from the kitchen to the backyard.

"Got a minute?" he asked.

Scott put the beers on the kitchen counter. "Always."

Pagett sidled over, dropped a heavy hand on Scott's shoulder, and guided him into the living room. "I just want to ask you something."

Awkward conversation time, Scott thought.

"I looked you up on the Internet."

Scott expected this after Sheils's remark the other day. It was only natural. Pagett would want to know to whom he was entrusting his daughter's life. He wasn't afraid of what Pagett had found, but it wasn't going to be a fun conversation. Scott pointed to the sofa, but Pagett remained standing.

"You got yourself into some real trouble with this Piper and Charles Rooker."

Scott didn't know how to take that statement. Was Pagett looking for confirmation or contrition? "I did."

"Not just six months ago but eight years ago."

"A lot of things conspired to make a bad situation worse."

Scott wasn't sure where Pagett was going with all this. He wasn't about to bring it to a head. The purpose of this get-together was to give everyone a chance to get things off their chests as well as a respite from the ordeal. He'd let Pagett get to the point in his own time.

"It looks like it," Pagett said. "Is it true you're writing a book about it all?"

"Yes, it's a way of putting it behind me."

Pagett nodded. "I can see that. Are you planning to write a book about this?"

Finally, Pagett had gotten to the point. "No, I have no intention of doing that. It's not my story to tell."

"I'm officially telling you that you don't have my family's permission. I won't have our lives played out in some book for you to profit from. Am I clear?"

Scott raised his hands in surrender. "I won't be writing a book about this. The book I'm writing is a chance to get it out of my system and explain what happened. In some ways, it's my penance."

"A child died last time. What happens if Grace dies?"

It was a low blow but understandable. Pagett was a man in pain. A man left impotent by the situation, unable to protect his own daughter. Still, the insinuation burned.

"Grace isn't going to die. I will do everything to make sure that doesn't happen."

"Sounds like a good line for the book." Pagett didn't load his statement. It was simply a keen observation.

Scott put a hand on Pagett's shoulder. The Englishman glanced at it before looking Scott in the eye.

"There'll be no book, even if you ask me to write one. You have my word on it. I want one thing—to get your daughter back. Is that clear?"

Pagett peeled Scott's hand from his shoulder and shook it. "I had to be sure."

Scott nodded.

In the kitchen, he handed the beers to Pagett to replenish the ice chest. From over the hood of the grill, Jane smiled at him. He went over to her and slipped an arm around her waist.

"Okay?" she asked.

"Yeah."

"You were in there awhile."

"Brian just wanted to get something off his chest."

"But everything's cool, right?"

He nodded.

"Good," she said, handing him the tongs. "You can take over for a while. The boys need a little calming down."

She kissed him on the cheek and left him to it. He glanced at his boys, who were amped up at having so many people in the house. They charged around the cramped backyard with its high fences, which served only to whip up the younger Pagett kids into a fervor. He let Jane sort it out while he focused on the grill.

Sheils walked up with an empty plate. "Any burgers ready?"

"In about thirty seconds."

The FBI agent remained at Scott's side while he prepped a bun with veggies and condiments. "This was a good idea. I think everyone needed some relief."

Scott lifted a burger off the grill and put it on Sheils's waiting bun.

"Thanks." Sheils placed the other half of the bun on top of his burger. "Can I ask a personal question?"

What is this—The Quiz Scott Hour? he thought. Although he'd asked for this by arranging the barbecue, he hadn't thought he'd be questioned all evening.

"I'm an open book—shoot."

"How are you doing?"

It was nice to be asked. "Okay, I guess."

"I hope you don't mind my saying this, but you aren't the man from six months ago. You look tired and defeated."

It was a harsh assessment but hardly incorrect.

"I didn't know you cared." He tried to inject some levity into the answer, but it fell flat.

"Of course I care. There's a girl's life on the line, and I need to be sure that you can handle it."

So Sheils cared about him with a small *c*. While disheartening to hear, it was the right priority under the circumstances.

"If you remember, you came to me. I didn't want to be part of this."

Scott's tone had risen. Keith Draper had been on his way over to them but took a detour to the ice chest.

Scott took a breath and let it out. "To be honest, I'm struggling. Jane, the kids, they're struggling. We aren't over the Piper yet, and we've been dragged into this shit."

"Scott, if you need people to talk to, I can help with that. I can't have you crack on me."

With all that he and Sheils had been through over the years, it was easy to be cynical. The truth was, Sheils cared, or he wouldn't be asking. The old Sheils would have slammed him against a wall with his forearm against his throat.

"Thanks. If I need it, I'll ask. I just need to know you're behind me. I can't have you second-guessing me."

"Okay, you've got it."

The doorbell rang. Jane left to answer it and returned with Richard Thorpe. He stood in the doorway to the backyard, holding up two mammoth bottles of champagne.

"Everyone, I've got awesome news," he said. "We've got the ransom money."

Emily Pagett ran over to Thorpe and engulfed him in a hug. Pagett took the bottles from him before he dropped them and shook his hand. The consultant was soon surrounded by everyone congratulating him with a mix of smiles and tears. The man sucked up all the adulation offered and seemed to have room for more.

"Kickstarter paid off?" Sheils asked.

"Yeah. Two hundred and sixty-eight grand and counting. Isn't it amazing?"

CHAPTER ELEVEN

Sitting in the conference room again at the *Independent*, Scott checked his watch. There was a little more than an hour to go. Time had slowed to a crawl now. He'd been at the paper's offices since 8:00 a.m., as Sheils and his people had pulled everything together for the ransom drop. That felt like an age ago. Now he just wanted to get this done.

Having Brian and Emily Pagett there didn't help, either. Their presence just ramped up the pressure. What if he screwed it up? He could barely meet the Pagetts' gaze. Thankfully, Thorpe was there to keep them occupied while Sheils focused on prepping him.

Guerra knocked on the glass door and let herself in. She was carrying a money bag, the kind armored-car guards used for collections. She put it on the table, and Sheils removed the $200,000. As the Shepherd had requested, it had been divided into four bundles and wrapped in plastic. The wrapping was so thick, it obscured the bills, and Scott could barely tell whether they were singles or hundreds. He hoped that wouldn't be a problem.

The money didn't look like much sitting there on the table. He'd had to come up with millions for his boys. Looking at the four bundles, it hardly seemed like enough in exchange for a child's life.

"Are these your recorded bills?" Scott asked.

"Yes," Sheils answered.

"Recorded bills?" Thorpe asked.

Sheils unzipped the backpack and placed the four bundles inside. "People like the Shepherd think if they issue a tight timeline to come up with the ransom money, we won't have time to mark the bills. Marked money is a thing of the past. A while ago, we came up with a work-around—prerecorded bills. The bureau has made arrangements with the banks and the Treasury. We have a network of banks around the country that are holding large amounts of cash, all nonsequential, but all the serial numbers are prerecorded. We put all those numbers into the banking systems, and we wait. Once that money starts being spent, the banks will be looking for those serial numbers, and they'll ping us. We will literally follow the money back to who spent it. One way or another, it will take us back to the Shepherd."

"Very slick," Thorpe said.

An agent entered the room carrying a pair of suitcases. "Time to get you miked up, Mr. Fleetwood."

"You sure about this?" Scott asked. "I don't want to spook this guy."

Pagett stood. "I don't want any risks taken."

"We're not," one of the agents said, delving through his case.

"I just want eyes and ears, so we can monitor what's going on," Sheils said. "At any time, if you feel it could compromise the drop, dump them—okay?"

Scott didn't need Sheils's permission. He'd already decided he would, and screw the backlash. Grace came first.

"This is what we're talking about," the tech said and held up something no bigger than a shirt button. "This is the camera."

Scott took it from him.

"It's wireless. As is this."

The tech handed him the mike, which was no wider than a Q-tip.

"These will disappear on you. Should you want to dump them in case of a search, just pluck them off and drop them. Ready to get your James Bond on?" the tech asked with a smile.

Unlike the suave secret agent, Scott wasn't wearing a signature tuxedo. He'd gone for ransom-drop casual, sporting sweatpants, a T-shirt, and a black Giants hooded sweatshirt. More than likely, the Shepherd would have him running from pillar to post.

The tech inserted the mike into the collar of his T-shirt while the camera went into the shoulder seam of the sweatshirt. Unless someone was looking, they wouldn't be spotted. The tech spent the next couple of minutes carrying out sound and visual checks. When everything was to his liking, he wished Scott good luck and left.

Sheils checked his watch. "We've got about forty minutes before the call."

Scott's stomach churned.

"One last run-through."

"I know the procedure."

"Then you won't mind going through it again."

Sheils pulled out a chair and patted it for him to sit. Sheils took a seat opposite.

"Take the Shepherd's call. Leave here. Follow his instructions. Don't improvise. Hand him the money. Take Grace. Get out of there," Scott said.

"Good," Sheils said. "Remember, your cell phone will give us your location. We have eyes and ears on you, even though you won't be able to talk to us. That's okay. I want you to focus on delivering the ransom. We'll take care of the rest. There'll be a surveillance team following you at all times. You'll never be alone."

"But I should be. He's expecting me to do this without FBI tails. If he sees one, I don't know what will happen."

"I'm with Scott on this one," Emily said. "I don't care if you catch him as long as I get Gracie back."

"We're very good at this. We have far more experience than the Shepherd. I am guessing he will have a number of countermeasures to sniff out any tails on Scott. We have our countermeasures, too. The Shepherd won't spot a tail. We have a distinct advantage over him—sheer manpower. We'll always outnumber him. It's the power of law enforcement over any criminal."

Scott couldn't make out if Sheils believed that or was just saying it to placate them. He hoped it was the former.

• • •

Scott's cell rang at 1:03 on the dot.

"Everybody out of the room, please. Just Scott and me."

Guerra opened the door, and Thorpe ushered the Pagetts toward it.

Emily took his hand. "Do whatever he says."

"Bring our girl back," Pagett said.

"I will."

The second Guerra drew the door shut, Sheils said, "Take the call."

"Hello?"

"Do you have my money?" the Shepherd's alternating voices asked.

"Yes. I have the money and a car. I'm ready to meet you wherever you are."

"I'm assuming the FBI is with you."

Here it is—the first test. Did he lie or tell the truth? Either answer had the potential to be wrong.

He eyed Sheils. "Yes, the FBI is here."

"If they follow you, I'll know. If they interfere, I'll know. They do anything to get in the way of our business, I will kill Grace. Do I make myself clear?"

"Very. The FBI won't get in the way."

Scott said this more to Sheils than the Shepherd. The FBI agent showed no sign of giving anything away.

"Then get in your car. I'll stay on the line."

Sheils opened the door. Everyone was on their feet in the newsroom bullpen. Sheils went ahead. He signaled to everyone to stay silent with a wave of his arms.

They jogged down the stairs and out to the lobby with Sheils ahead, clearing a path for Scott. The entire time, Scott held the phone to his ear.

When they reached the lobby, Sheils shook Scott's hand and said, "Good luck."

"That was touching," the Shepherd said. "Agent Sheils, I presume?"

"Yes," Scott said, pushing the door open to the street.

"That better be the last of his involvement."

"It is."

He ran to his car, which was illegally parked on the street. San Francisco police had been told not to ticket or tow the car. Cones in front of and behind his car highlighted the fact. He shrugged off the backpack and got behind the wheel. He started it, and the car's Bluetooth synced up with the phone, linking the Shepherd to the speaker system.

So it began. He was on another ransom run. He was an old hand at these, this being his third, but it was the first time he was doing one on behalf of someone else's family.

"Okay, I'm in the car. Where to?"

"The Sir Francis Drake Hotel."

The hotel famous for its British beefeater porters standing guard outside was on the other side of Market Street, practically spitting distance. Was the exchange really going to be that close?

"On my way."

Scott lurched into traffic, driving over one of the traffic cones set out for him. All haste ended by the time he reached the first traffic light. The Shepherd couldn't have picked a worse location. The landmark hotel was less than a dozen blocks away, but it was at the heart of the city and one block up from Union Square. The streets were choked with people and vehicles, and traffic lights brought everything to a standstill every couple of blocks. It would have been faster for him to jog over there, but if Grace was in a hotel room, he wanted to grab her and get her as far away as possible as quickly as possible.

"Traffic's thick. It's going to take me some time to get there."

"That's fine. Just call off the streets as you get to them."

It took ten minutes to navigate through the series of one-way streets before he got onto Powell, giving him a straight shot up to the hotel.

"On Powell," he said.

"Call off the cross streets."

Scott did, calling off the sequence of streets.

Just as he called out crossing Geary at the corner of Union Square, the Shepherd said, "Turn right at Post."

"What?"

"Turn right at Post."

"That's before I get to the hotel."

"Just do it."

The rule of ransom drops: do as the kidnapper says. Scott turned onto Post.

"On Post. Now what?"

"Turn right on Stockton."

What are you playing at? Scott thought. It all became clear when the Shepherd asked him to turn back onto Geary.

"Do I make another turn onto Powell?"

"Yes."

He was now making a circuit of Union Square. The kidnapper wanted to see if anyone was tailing him. First blood to the Shepherd.

When he was back on Powell, he expected to resume his drive to the Sir Francis, but the Shepherd surprised him again and had him make another slow grind around Union Square.

This time when he got onto Geary, the kidnapper said, "Keep going."

"Where am I going?"

His phone beeped from an incoming text. He opened it. It read: **North Baker Beach.** He wondered if the Shepherd knew he had been miked up.

At least he was finally on the move after the Sir Francis detour. The beach was out of the way and he was looking at a good half-hour drive. That would give Sheils plenty of time to regroup his people. Scott guessed he was in for the long haul.

"Seeing as we've got some time on our hands, why don't you tell me what's going on? Why did you take this child? She can't be anything to you."

"Hoping to get a story out of me?"

The problem with the Shepherd's unsettling digitized series of voices was there was no way of getting any kind of emotional read on the man. Scott had to probe but also had to play it careful. He didn't want to set him off.

"Isn't that why you dragged me into all this? You want to make a point, and you're using me to do it, right?"

"You must think a lot of yourself."

"No, not at all. I just figure if this was just about money, you could have done it with a lot less fanfare. The way you've gone about it has sucked in the press, the FBI, and the public."

A response was slow in coming. Scott guessed he'd struck a nerve.

"The money means little to me."

"Then let's forget this. Release Grace. Let her off at a McDonald's or something. You've made your point. The Pagetts will never forget this."

"They will if they aren't forced to pay. I thought you'd be a little more understanding under the circumstances."

"What makes you say that?"

"The Piper put you through hell, but you seem to have learned nothing."

"What haven't I learned?"

"The value of a child's life. It's an awesome responsibility. People need to be reminded of that. It works best through loss. Then they understand the true value."

Scott's stomach tightened. *What does the Shepherd mean by loss? Does he have no intention of returning Grace? Is she dead?* Scott wanted to ask, needed to ask, but couldn't. One wrong word from him could get her killed. And if she was dead already, any confirmation would surely kill the ransom drop. Then it would be game over. The FBI would never find the Shepherd or Grace.

"I think when this is all over, people will learn a lesson," Scott said.

"I think so, too. Turn left, please."

"That's the wrong way for the beach."

"Just do it, please."

Scott had hoped this conversation was a distraction that was taking the Shepherd's eye off Sheils's surveillance team. It didn't look like it. The Shepherd had him make a bunch of pointless turns that had him doubling back again before putting him back on the right track for the beach.

Scott couldn't tell if he'd lost Sheils's pursuit team in this latest set of maneuvers. He didn't see any particular cars peel off. That could be because Sheils's guys were that great, or they'd been lost a long time ago. Either way, he had to assume he was completely alone playing on the Shepherd's field.

The Shepherd clammed up on him after that, leaving Scott to drive in silence. It wasn't long before he saw the sign for Baker Beach.

He followed the long, winding road to the beach's parking lot. There were no open spots. He wasn't about to wait or trawl for an open one and parked in a handicapped stall.

Grabbing his phone and backpack, he said, "Okay, I'm here."

"Go onto the beach, and head in the direction of the Golden Gate."

North Baker Beach was situated on the shoreline where the ocean met the bay. The Golden Gate Bridge loomed large in the middle distance.

As he reached the **HAZARDOUS SURF, UNDERTOW, SWIM AT YOUR OWN RISK** sign, Scott was reminded why Baker Beach was a local landmark. The north end was a nudist beach. Being a weekday, the naturists were sparse in number. He picked up a number of sideways looks, like he was the freak for being dressed. He never knew whether the nudist beaches in San Francisco were officially sanctioned by the city or not.

"I think I'm where you want me to be. Where are you?"

"Look out at the ocean. You'll see a wooden post sticking out of the water."

Scott did. It sat a couple of hundred feet out from the beach. The sea-ravaged stump only broke the surface by a foot or so depending on the waves washing by. A seagull sat atop it.

"Yeah, I see it."

"Swim out to it; follow it down to the bottom. You'll find something waiting for you."

Scott pulled the down the zip on his hoodie.

"No, you go in dressed exactly as you are."

He'd seen him pull his zip down. The son of a bitch was here. He spun around. He went from face to face, looking for a man he didn't know looking back.

"Yes, I'm watching, Scott."

A nudist with a paunch was eyeballing him. "This ain't a freak show. Either strip off or fuck off," the guy said.

"Take everything with you," the Shepherd said in his ear. "That includes the phone and the backpack, too."

"What?"

"Why did you think I asked for the money to be wrapped in plastic?"

"What about the phone? It'll be ruined."

"Don't worry about that."

Scott pocketed the phone and waded into the water. *So much for all your electronics, Tom*, he thought.

"You asshole!" the nudist yelled out.

Scott knew he was something. He wasn't sure it was an asshole.

The water was frigid. The chill took his breath away as he strode out. When it reached his waist, he threw himself forward and began swimming. It was hard going. His clothes and the backpack worked against him. Each wave shoved him back. The two hundred feet felt more like four hundred by the time he'd reached the post.

Now he was presented with a new problem—visibility. The water was deep and far from being crystal clear. It provided the cover the Shepherd needed for his planted package, but it didn't do Scott any favors.

He dove down. He couldn't make out a damn thing in the murk, so he reached out for the post and used it as a guide. Kicking hard, he reached the seabed. He fumbled around in the gloom until his hand touched a dry bag weighed down by rocks. He snatched it up and let his natural buoyancy carry him back to the surface. With the tide on his side, it didn't take long to paddle back to the beach.

As soon he was clear of the water, he dropped to his knees. He pulled the cell phone from his pocket to let the Shepherd know he had the dry bag, but the phone was fried. The FBI were now unable to track him or listen to him anymore. He hoped Sheils's surveillance team was still on him, but he had the sinking feeling he was now on his own. He opened the dry bag, hoping the Shepherd had left him a replacement. He had, along with a set of overalls.

Scott powered up the phone and went to Contacts. There was only one number stored. He dialed it. The call was picked up immediately.

"So you survived the swim," the Shepherd said.

For once, the kidnapper didn't disguise his voice. Scott detected an East Coast accent, but it was light. He didn't get New York but something close.

"Yeah. It nearly killed me. You should have picked a better swimmer."

The Shepherd laughed.

"You decided to stop disguising your voice."

"It's not needed right now."

Not when all the FBI monitoring equipment was toast. "Now what?"

"Strip. Whatever you have on you, leave it. And I mean everything—clothes, shoes, underwear, wallet, watch. Put the money into the dry bag. Change into the overalls, and get back into your car. Remember, I'm watching."

Scott had just been sanitized. Sheils couldn't track him now. The Shepherd was peeling the layers away until he was alone and naked. That had meant figuratively. Now it was about to be literally.

He peeled off his wet clothes, leaving them where they fell. He slipped into the overalls, which were a size too big for him. He dumped the cash out of the backpack into the dry bag and jogged back to the parking lot.

"You're crazy," the unimpressed nudist yelled after him.

No, Scott thought, *just desperate.*

As he reached the parking lot, the Shepherd said, "Leave your car."

"You want me to walk?"

"No, I've got a replacement for you. There's a green Ford Focus on the beach side of the parking lot. You'll find the keys in the front driver's side wheel well. Let me know when you're moving."

Changing cars really sealed the deal. If the Shepherd suspected any electronic tags were on Scott or his car, he'd successfully dealt with them now.

There was only one green Focus parked in the lot. He ran over to it and found the key in a magnetic box stuck to the wheel arch. He got behind the wheel and gunned the engine, then set the phone to loudspeaker and put it in a cup holder.

"Okay, I'm in the car. Where now?"

"Get on Twenty-Fifth Avenue and drive for a while. I'll tell you when to turn."

Baker Beach essentially exited onto Twenty-Fifth Avenue, and there was only one direction to go—south. Scott thought the guy might be quite talkative now that no one was listening in, but the Shepherd went silent once he was on the road. Golden Gate Park provided Scott with an opening.

"I'm going through Golden Gate Park. That takes me off Twenty-Fifth. You want me to dogleg over to it when I'm out of the park?"

"No. You'll come out on Nineteenth. Stay on that."

"Okay. Can I ask you a question?"

"Sure." The reply came with a sigh.

"You know what you were saying about teaching parents and the world a lesson?"

"Yeah."

"If you don't mind my saying, you seem pretty skilled at this. Have you done this before?"

"Intelligence gathering for the FBI?"

"Just thinking out loud."

"Don't bullshit me, Scott."

"Yes, the FBI is going to grill me. Thanks for that, by the way. Yes, the *Independent* will want two thousand words out of me. What did you expect? If you wanted anonymity, you shouldn't have gone public. Look, I'm trying to understand. You dragged me into this, not the other way around."

"So you're telling me you're not excited to be back in the limelight?"

"Not at all."

"Bullshit."

"Not bullshit. I learned my lesson the worst way—through my family. My kids still have night terrors. They are afraid of the dark. They're bullied. The worst part of all this is they lost their innocence. My kids fear the world now. Everyone is a potential monster looking to spirit them away. I caused that, and it'll haunt me to the day I die. So fuck you for the damage you're inflicting on Grace and all the other children you've kidnapped."

"Strong words, Scott. Be careful how you talk to me."

Scott wasn't about to apologize or placate the son of a bitch, but he had to walk a fine line with the kidnapper since Grace's life was on the line.

"I think it's time we meet," the Shepherd said. "Take a left on Judah."

After a couple more turns, it became obvious where the Shepherd was taking Scott—the Sutro Tower. The route took him into the Clarendon Heights neighborhood that stood in the shadow of the massive TV-and-radio tower. He kept following the streets until they stopped at the entrance to the tower. Without someone to let him through the gates, he wasn't getting any farther.

"Okay, I'm here. You want to let me in?"

"Just park. Bring the money, and I'll be right down. Stay on the line. I don't want you calling anyone."

Scott got out of the compact Ford, leaving the engine running. He didn't see any movement in the secure area surrounding the tower. He looked back down the street in case the kidnapper had been waiting in the wings.

A guy leaned out of the security booth next to the gate. "You can't park there. This is private property."

Scott ignored the guard. He was really getting tired of this dog-and-pony show. "Where are you?" he said into the phone.

"Patience, Scott."

"It's getting late. Let's do this thing. I just want to take this girl home."

"Look to your left. There's a covered reservoir. See it?"

The reservoir was small, no bigger than a football field. It no doubt served the surrounding area. It certainly wasn't big enough to serve the city. The concrete structure protruded three feet above the ground. Getting to it meant scaling a six-foot chain-link fence.

"Yeah, I see it."

"Wait there."

Scott jogged across the road to the reservoir. "Hey, where are you going?" the guard said. "I'll have you towed."

Scott pocketed the phone and stuck his hands into the chain-link fence. The links were close-knit and plastic coated, making it easier to climb. He clambered up the fence to the soundtrack of the security guard threatening to call the cops. He made it to the top without too much trouble, but his dismount ended with a clumsy landing on his butt.

Striding toward the middle of the concrete cover, he pulled the cell from his pocket. "Okay, I'm here. Now what?"

A high-pitched whine came from behind the trees. Scott turned toward the noise. A drone appeared.

Inventive, Scott thought. Sheils had told him once that a kidnapper lost the upper hand when it came to the money exchange. Wire transfers left a trail. Cash and diamonds required a face-to-face. A drone changed that.

The machine dropped to the ground in front of him. This was no toy from RadioShack. The aircraft with its four rotors was close to three feet across. A camera hung from the underside. No wonder the Shepherd had been able to monitor Scott's every move.

"There's a storage compartment. Insert the money inside."

"Where's Grace?"

"Insert the money."

"I need to see the girl."

"Scott, you aren't calling the shots."

He knew the man was right, and he hated that. "Please."

"Money."

Scott dropped to his knees. The camera was attached to a storage box no bigger than a shoe box. He opened it and placed the four bundles of cash inside. They fit perfectly.

"Okay, I deposited the money."

"Thank you."

The drone fired back to life and lifted effortlessly into the air.

"Now where's the girl?"

"I'll be in touch."

Panic knifed through Scott as he watched the drone climb far out of his reach. "No, you've got the money. You've got what you want. Release Grace."

"The FBI was following. I saw them. There's a penalty for that."

"But they didn't catch you. Give me the girl."

"I'll be in touch."

"No. Please. Listen."

It was too late. The Shepherd had already hung up.

"Give her back!" Scott yelled at the disappearing drone.

CHAPTER TWELVE

Sheils had carried out Scott's debriefing in an interview room at the FBI office. As debriefings went, it was a demoralizing one for the FBI agent to endure. Scott outlined how the Shepherd had dismantled his surveillance playbook. By the time Scott had handed off the ransom, only one of the pursuit cars had remained in play. For a second, Sheils thought he'd had the Shepherd when the kidnapper lured Scott to Sutro Tower. It was a dead-end road with no escape. He hadn't banked on a drone.

Losing the kidnapper and ransom didn't bother him as much as not getting Grace Pagett back. The bastard didn't have to be caught today. He'd screw up. They always did. Scooping him up in three months was fine by him. What was going to keep Sheils awake tonight was not having the girl. Percentages said the chances of getting her back alive at this point were low. The Shepherd not giving any hint to her location drove the probability down to single figures. The fact that he still hadn't called only underlined Sheils's fear that Grace was dead.

Hope was a fragile concept at the moment. Sheils had done his best to give some to the Pagett family when he'd broken the news to them that they hadn't recovered their daughter. He deserved the tears and accusations they'd thrown at him. He promised it wasn't over and asked them not to lose hope.

As pessimistic as the situation felt, he didn't think it was over. The Shepherd craved the limelight. He still had something to say. What Sheils was supposed to do in the meantime was the question. He had nothing to go on. The Ford Focus that the Shepherd had Scott drive was stolen, and the plates had been switched from another car. It was a forensic nightmare. The crime techs were combing the Ford, but with Scott's and the owner's prints and DNA all over it, the chance of finding any trace from the Shepherd was nonexistent. His electronic footprint was just as untraceable. Sheils's next lead would come when the Shepherd called again.

"Anything else to add, Scott?" Sheils asked.

"No."

"Go home. We'll regroup in the morning."

Scott nodded. He pushed his chair away from the table and stood. He looked like he'd gone twelve rounds with one of the Klitschko brothers. Sheils and Guerra watched him go.

A minute later, Assistant Special Agent in Charge Bill Travillian walked in. He slipped into Scott's seat. He'd no doubt been watching the debriefing from the monitoring suite.

"Impressions?" he said.

"It's as bad as it gets," Sheils replied.

Travillian had been Sheils's boss for many years. Sheils liked the man. He never rushed to judgment or balled him out. When investigations went sideways, he took the heat from DC. It made for honest dialogue. Sheils never felt the need to shade the truth. At moments like these, it was a blessing.

"And Fleetwood—your thoughts on him? Is he playing it square this time around?"

"You don't trust him?" Sheils asked.

"Just playing devil's advocate," Travillian said.

"Nothing makes me think otherwise."

"Those two were dark for almost half an hour. Did anything happen in that time period? Fleetwood is writing a book about the Piper. Why not strike a deal with the Shepherd for another book?"

"It's possible, but I don't think so. Scott Fleetwood isn't the guy we knew before. The Piper incident took its toll, and his priorities are different. That said, I'm still going to keep him on a short leash. I want to get his phone records."

"You think he's been in contact with the Shepherd before the other day?"

"Don't know. Maybe not wittingly. The Shepherd has a thing for Scott. He likely would have done his own reconnaissance on him. I wouldn't put it past the Shepherd to have called Scott posing as someone else."

"What's the Shepherd's next move? He has to make contact again."

"He's lost his communication channels now. The cell phone we gave Scott is toast after he went swimming with it, and we have the substitute phone the Shepherd gave Scott, which he must realize. He has to do something else to contact Scott now."

"There's still the newspaper," Travillian said.

"It's the most likely way, but I think we should also put a tap on Scott's phones. I'm not saying Scott is an accomplice, but the Shepherd might try to get in touch with him directly."

"See if he'll give you permission," Travillian said. "It would go a long way to confirm whether he's involved with the Shepherd."

"I'll do it," Guerra said. "He might be more amenable if I ask."

This informal meeting did nothing for Sheils's spirits. The shadow of the ransom-drop aftermath ate away at him—and not just because of the loss of the ransom and not recovering Grace. The Shepherd was proving to be far more insidious than he'd first thought.

"Earth to Tom," Travillian said.

"Sorry," he said.

"You dropped out of the conversation. What's on your mind?"

"This. The whole thing. The kidnapping. The Shepherd. None of it smells right. His coming up with his own boogeyman moniker is too contrived, and intentionally drawing Scott into this turns it into a circus. He indicates he's on some crusade about personal responsibility and alludes that he's done this before, but there are no other kidnappings of this nature. He's way too public about this, to the point he's practically inviting capture."

"The circus could be what he wants. It stretches our resources thin," Travillian said. "Maybe he did this before and kept it low-key."

Sheils didn't buy that. "It doesn't tie into his crusade. That needs an audience for it to mean anything. He can't go about teaching people a lesson bit by bit. And look at the way he operates. He's using sophisticated tech, from the way he's covering his digital footprints to the drone he used. That doesn't come cheap, which means he needs to go after premium victims to cover the costs. Instead, what does he do? He snatches at random the kid of some tourists who don't have a pot to piss in. That ransom is a lowball figure."

"Two hundred grand isn't cheap," Travillian said. "I couldn't cover it."

"This operation is costing him money. He needs to be asking for more. This guy is operating on a similar level to the Piper, and he asked for millions."

"But if he's truly on a crusade, then he wouldn't be asking for big money. He would be asking for what he needs to cover costs," Travillian said. "And big money is relative. To the Pagetts, he's asking for impossible sums."

It was a fair point. Sheils had already considered the issue and rejected it for one very good reason. "The reason he asked for the amount he did has more to do with weight than a crusade."

"Weight?" Guerra said.

"Drones are very impressive and make for great media coverage, but they can't carry anything particularly heavy. That cash weighed about six pounds. I doubt that drone could carry much more."

"Maybe that's why he didn't release Grace. It's only the first installment."

"Which drags this thing out, and that doesn't make sense. He had the drop on us. He got his money, and his escape was assured. He just had to let Grace go, and he would have gotten away scot-free. Then he'd be able to continue his crusade in another city with another kid. This guy is smart. Giving us a second shot at capturing him isn't."

"So what are you saying?" Travillian said.

"This is all theater, and we're being scammed."

"For what purpose?"

Sheils didn't have an answer for that.

• • •

Grace was crying again. Her muffled sobs leaked from her sound-proofed box. He glanced at the monitor. She was balled up in the corner of the makeshift cell next to the cot. He'd promised her she was going home today. He'd planned on letting her go, but then he got the text from Elvis: Don't release her.

Fleetwood had been minutes away from arriving at Sutro Tower to deliver the ransom when the text came in. A flash of fear had surged through Connors when he'd read the message. He'd thought he was blown. Maybe he'd screwed up, and the FBI was onto him. He'd taken the added precaution of waiting to collect the drone with the money from its landing site in case the ransom had a tracer. It became obvious after an hour that nothing had gone wrong with the drop. So what had changed? He'd worked with Elvis too many times for him to send that message. He'd called for an explanation and gotten voice mail every time.

Examining the bills for the third time, Connors wasn't sure what to do next. He and Elvis hadn't planned a fallback position if compromised. He didn't have a second safe house set up, but he would take steps now. He didn't know the Bay Area well, but it wouldn't be hard to come up with something on the fly. Or he could simply release the girl. He did have the money, after all. He could disappear and regroup with Elvis later. He'd give him twenty-four hours to get in contact. After that, he'd ditch the kid and bug out with the cash.

Grace's crying showed no sign of abating. He let himself into the cell. The girl's sobs seized up as she squeezed herself hard into the box's corner. He raised his hands and lowered into a crouch.

"It's okay, Grace. There's no need for all these tears."

"You said I was going home," she said, sniveling. "You lie. You break your promises. You're not a very nice man."

No, I'm not, he thought. "I try to be."

Grace palmed away a tear. "You don't try very hard."

He inched closer to her, and her sniveling grew worse. He dropped into a seated position to show he wasn't coming any closer. He didn't have any problems letting her see his face. She was six. Her ability to accurately describe him to a sketch artist was unlikely. He didn't like the idea of a mask, either. A child's imagination would create monsters far worse than they were. He didn't want to leave this child scarred.

"It wasn't safe. Like I told you at the beginning, I don't mean you any harm, and I won't let anyone harm you. I won't put you in danger."

It was a lie, but it was also the truth. The lie was he didn't know if danger would strike if he released her. The truth was he was this girl's guardian for the duration. He would die before letting anyone harm this child. It had been his job in the army, and it was his job now.

"You need to know something about me. I am a man of honor. Do you know what *honor* means?"

Grace shook her head.

"It means I live by rules and promises. It means when I say I will protect you, I mean it. Understand?"

She nodded.

"You said you'd let me go today. You broke your promise."

"I did, and someone broke their promise to me. That's why I can't let you go home."

"I don't like honor. It's weird."

"You'll get to like it when you get older. Look, I was told something about you."

She gave him a sideways look and pursed her lips.

"I heard that you like Jaffa Cakes."

Her face lit up, and she shot forward onto her hands and knees. "Yes, I do. I can eat a whole box, but I can only have two at any time. Do you like them?"

It stunned him how easily a kid could bounce from one emotional extreme to another at the simplest thing. When did adults lose this ability?

"I've never had one. What are they?"

She made a circle about two inches in diameter. "They are sponge with orange covered in chocolate."

He liked her exuberance as she mimed how this cookie went together. He used it to inch closer to her. This time she didn't flinch, or at least didn't notice.

"Sponge—as in cake?"

"Yes, I think."

"I thought it was a cookie."

"Cookie. It's a biscuit. Sort of. It's very, very nice."

He was very confused as to what this thing was.

"Do you have some?" she asked.

"No," he said. "We don't really eat them here in America, but I bet they sell them somewhere nearby. I thought I might get a box. What do you think?"

"That would be brilliant."

She jumped to her feet and charged at him. For a second, he thought she'd played him in order to escape. Instead, she smashed into him to give him a hug. He reveled in her tiny embrace. It reminded him of Aamir's generosity of spirit. He scooped her up in his arms and placed her on the cot.

"Let me see what I can do."

"Can I come with you? I know what I'm looking for."

Getting her out of this box wasn't such a bad idea, but it was a massive risk to go anywhere in public with Grace. Her face was on every TV screen and newspaper. He could disguise them. People's visual recall was terrible. It didn't take much to make yourself unrecognizable. He could turn this errand into an adventure. It would just take a little priming. It was doable.

"I don't know."

Her elation turned into a pout.

"Let me think about it. I'd need you on your best behavior."

"I'll be good."

One of his cell phones rang on his desk. It was Elvis's phone.

"I've got to take this call. I have to close the door so no one can get in, okay?" It was a subtle deception to omit any mention of locking her inside.

"All right," she said, "but you will take me shopping?"

He smiled, backed out of the cell, and closed the door, then snatched up the phone.

"Yes?"

"Took your time," Elvis's electronically distorted voice said.

He crossed the room to put distance between him and Grace. He looked out at the bay. "Talking to Grace—who should be back with her parents. What was that text about?"

"Just that the game has changed."

He hated riddles. "What does that mean?"

"An opportunity has presented itself. It's beneficial to me that I keep this soap opera going."

He didn't like this. Stick to the plan was his rule. Once greed entered the equation, everything always went sideways.

"And beneficial to me?"

"Of course. That goes without saying."

No, it did have to be said. He didn't like this.

"How much longer do I have the kid for?"

"Three, four days. Maybe a week."

He shook his head. Elvis really was screwing this up. He decided in that moment. After this job was over, he was pulling the pin. He'd close down all his communication channels and move on. He didn't need this cowboy shit.

"Here's what I need done. You reach out to Fleetwood and the *Independent*. Chew them out for bringing in the FBI. They were following you, y'know."

"I know."

"Tell them there's a two-hundred-thousand-dollar penalty for their betrayal."

"That's not going to take a week."

"I know, but I want you to stretch it out. Have fun with this. Be inventive. Really ham it up. I want this city to see the boogeyman on every street corner."

Fun didn't venture into a mission. You stuck to the mission, executed it, then got the hell out.

"This is how fuckups happen."

"They won't. You're too good at this."

The flattery wouldn't work on him. When it came to a mission, you stayed on point. You did the job and got out once it was done. Elvis's desire to string this out was putting both of them at unnecessary risk.

"The money is marked," Elvis said. "Kind of."

Why am I not surprised? "Kind of?"

"The Feds are monitoring the banks for the serial numbers. I would spend those bills abroad, or get them washed here."

He eyed the cash sitting on his table. It wasn't surprising. He could get it washed easily enough, but it did mean the $200,000 was now more like $150,000.

"You'd better not be setting me up," Connors said. "You'd be sorry."

Elvis laughed. "You're too suspicious. I'd never do that. Not to you."

I don't believe you.

"The girl's crying. I need to quiet her down," he lied.

Connors hung up on Elvis. He went over to Grace's cell and reopened the door.

"You wanna get some Jaffa Cakes?"

CHAPTER THIRTEEN

Sheils sat at his desk, his head swimming. He leaned back in his chair and closed his eyes. It was time to call it a day, check in at home, get some dinner before coming back to somehow find a way of kick-starting this investigation. When he opened his eyes, Travillian was standing there.

"What?"

"A man has just walked into the Seattle field office. He says he may know the Shepherd because he's a shepherd, too."

"What does that mean?"

"You want to ask him? Because I've got him on Skype."

Travillian had the Skype call set up in a meeting room. On the way, Travillian filled him in on what he had. The self-proclaimed shepherd was US Army Sergeant Stephen Deese, retired. He'd served in both Iraq and Afghanistan. Other than parking tickets, the guy had a spotless record.

In the meeting room, Travillian fiddled with his laptop to bring up the Skype call. Sheils hoped this was worth it. The wacko level for the investigation had been relatively low. While there'd been a few people claiming to know the Shepherd or to have seen him, numbers were running below the usual baseline. Sheils wondered if it had something to do with the nature of the abduction. The kidnapping of a foreign child made this an international incident. The thing that set Deese apart from the other witnesses was that his story tied into a growing profile that suggested the Shepherd had military training.

The familiar Skype singsongy tune burst from Sheils's laptop. He answered the call and transferred the image to the sixty-inch screen on the wall. A light-skinned black man in his late thirties sat at a conference table with the Seattle skyline behind him. The tailored suit Deese wore failed to hide an athletic build that made Sheils feel unhealthy just looking at him.

"Sergeant Deese, can you hear and see us okay?" Travillian said.

"Yes, I can, sir. Please call me Stephen. Sergeant Deese was a long time ago."

You could have fooled me, Sheils thought. Deese might be retired army, but the army hadn't left him. The man didn't sit. He sat to attention. Not that Sheils could criticize too much. His cop bearing and sensibilities weren't going to leave him anytime soon.

Sheils introduced himself and Travillian.

"You claim you know the Shepherd because you are one. Am I getting that right?" Sheils asked.

It was an attention-grabbing claim that warranted this meeting. It had originally put Deese in the crazy category, but a quick background check into the retired soldier said he was anything but crazy. He'd been honorably discharged after more than a decade in the army.

Deese raised two calloused hands. "I don't know if I do or not, but the kidnapper calling himself a Shepherd means something to me because I was one . . . for the army, I mean."

Sheils found it interesting Deese referred to *a* Shepherd and not *the* Shepherd.

"As soon as I heard that, I knew I had to come in and tell you what I know."

"Why don't you tell us everything, Stephen?" Travillian said.

"I did tours in both Afghanistan and Iraq. My last tours in both countries were protection details. My unit was charged with protecting dignitaries: local government and military officials and their families. Our unit was known as the Shepherds. Hearing it used in connection to the kidnapping, it struck a chord."

Sheils exchanged a look with Travillian before saying, "Are you saying the Shepherd is a member of your unit?"

"I don't know. I'd hate to think that, but it's a possibility."

Sheils was looking for more than conjecture.

"It's something this guy said to the newspaper that convinced me to reach out. He said something about protecting kids and people not knowing the value of their children. That stuck with me. We didn't just protect the important players in those regions. We protected their wives and kids. We'd get them to safe houses so they couldn't be used as leverage against anyone helping us. It sounds like a cushy gig. It wasn't. It got messy at times. If you want to deter someone from working for the enemy, go after their family. We had an easier time protecting those officials than we did their families."

Sheils understood. It was the art of war, from street gangs to global conflicts. You robbed people of what was most dear to them. His mind flicked back to Scott Fleetwood. It had been the technique used on him when it came to the Piper.

"Did you lose people, Stephen?" Travillian asked.

Deese's broad shoulders dropped. "More than I care to admit. People sold out our locations time and time again. Trust was a rare commodity. We lost two of our own. Losing a kid was the worst. Half the time, they didn't even comprehend how much danger they were in."

"Sounds like a tough job," Sheils said.

"It was. It got to me. It was why I left."

"What do you do now?"

"Private security."

"Essentially in the same business," Travillian said.

A sad smile spread across Deese's face. "Except I protect people who rarely have anything to fear."

"Why didn't you come forward earlier?" Sheils asked.

"I was in Abu Dhabi on a job, and I got back only yesterday."

"I know you said you hate to think anyone from your unit could be responsible for the Grace Pagett kidnapping, but does anyone come to mind?"

Deese shook his head. "I really don't know."

"You came here thinking there was a connection, so you must have someone in mind."

"Look, I may have made a mistake in thinking that."

Sheils was losing him. He couldn't afford to have him walk out the door without giving up anything.

"Stephen, I get it. No one wants to put the finger on a friend, especially a brother in arms. There's a bond that's stronger than country, commanding officer, and even family. But we all know the shit experienced in the field of battle gets to some people. You said it yourself; it got to you. Some people keep their balance. Others fall off life's tightrope. I know guys like that from this job, and you know them from yours."

Deese continued to shake his head. "Yeah, I don't know."

"You keep in touch with any of the guys?"

"I'm embarrassed to say I haven't kept in touch with them lately."

"Anyone struggle with regular life?" Travillian asked, pushing the point.

"I don't know."

Deese wasn't going to tell. He wasn't going to rat anyone out. Sheils knew it.

"Can you give me the names of the guys in your unit?"

"Yeah, I can do that."

Sheils decided this was the best he could hope for. Deese was never going to rat out a single person, but it wasn't snitching if he gave up a whole mess of names for someone else to sort through.

"There was Thomas Fortenberry, Otis Parker, Martin Grayson, Gavin Connors, Harrison Ayers, Alan Mack, and Chris Laughlin. Avery Smith and Robert Lisle were killed in action."

Sheils noted down all the names.

"So you think the Shepherd is former military?" Deese asked.

Sheils thought that was an interesting question. Was he asking for himself or a friend? "At this point, we're looking at a number of possibilities. Thanks for coming in."

"Thank you, sir. I hope you get that girl back safe and sound."

"Me, too," Travillian said. "If anything else comes to mind, don't hesitate to contact us."

"I will."

Sheils killed the connection.

Travillian leaned back in his seat. "What do you think?"

"It's an interesting tip. The way the Shepherd has gone about business makes me think he could be military or law enforcement. His use of tech from the drone to the voice modulator is very specialized. He isn't getting his kit from RadioShack."

"I didn't like that he asked if we suspected a soldier," Travillian said.

"Me, neither. He could be on a fishing expedition on behalf of the Shepherd, or he might know who the Shepherd is and wants to know if we have him pegged as a suspect."

"Do you think he has a name in his head?"

"Don't know."

Travillian looked at the names on the list. "And what about these?"

"We run a full background check on everyone—financials, phone records, criminal, the whole nine—and get statements from them

111

all." Sheils added Deese to the list. "I want to make sure he is who he says he is. Just because he came in off the street doesn't mean he isn't part of this."

Travillian laughed. "You're an untrusting son of a bitch."

"Guilty as charged. Deese did give me one thing."

"What's that?"

Sheils held up his phone. "His voice. Scott heard the Shepherd's voice in the raw. He can tell us whether this is the voice he heard."

CHAPTER FOURTEEN

Special Agent Shawn Brannon yanked the door open, and Scott ran into the *Independent*'s lobby. Lehny on reception hit the buzzer and waved them through into the offices. Sheils, Thorpe, and George were waiting for them in the conference room. The Shepherd had called again.

"What did he say?" Scott asked.

"He'd be in contact in an hour," George said.

"That was half an hour ago," Thorpe said.

It was somewhat of a relief that the Shepherd had called the *Independent*. With no prearranged communication channel, Scott hadn't slept, fearing the kidnapper would turn up on his doorstep. The greatest relief was that the Shepherd was in contact again, but the fear that had gnawed away at everyone was the possibility he was done. Maybe he was calling to say he'd gotten his money and he was in the wind, leaving Sheils and his team to find Grace.

"When he calls, I want you to push for proof of life, regardless of anything he wants," Sheils said.

Scott nodded. "Where are the Pagetts? They should be here for this. I'll need their help with details."

"On the way," Sheils said.

Brian and Emily arrived minutes later. The couple looked spent. All vibrancy had been siphoned from them. They seemed smaller, as if the planet's gravity had intensified just around them, pushing and squeezing them into the ground. The world was happening around them, and they had no influence upon it.

Scott had tried visiting them last night after he'd been picked up from the Sutro Tower, but they hadn't wanted to see him. He didn't blame them. He'd failed them. Everyone had.

He pulled Emily into a hug and made eye contact with Pagett when he said, "She's okay. I know it. You just have to believe."

Sheils asked everyone to sit, then briefed them on how the call would be handled. The FBI and the phone company were ready and waiting to record and trace the call. His people were watching the streets outside. He reminded everyone that Scott would do all the talking, but passing of notes was okay. He told Scott to keep his emotions in check and do everything he could to make the Shepherd reveal information and provide proof of life. It was all boilerplate to Scott. He'd been here too many times before.

The call came in at 11:00 a.m. on the dot.

When Sheils, cell pressed to his ear, got the green light from his people, he picked up the call and switched it to speaker.

"Hello."

"Hello again, Scott," the Shepherd said, his voice disguised once more.

"Gone back to hiding your voice, I see."

"We aren't alone."

"You have your money. I want to speak to Grace now."

"I want you to do something first."

"Screw you. I speak to Grace first."

Sheils made a calming gesture.

Yes, Sheils had told Scott to keep his cool, but he couldn't help it. He was in no mood to be jerked around by this bastard.

114

"Scott, if you want this to go smoothly, you'll do as I say."

"Do as he says," Emily blurted before breaking into sobs.

Scott took a breath. "What is it?"

"You're going to leave the building and go to the mailbox across the street. You'll find a package taped to the underside with something for you. Do it now. Go alone. I'll know if anyone goes with you."

The line went dead.

Scott didn't wait. He was out of his seat and pounding down the stairs. Fear ignited inside him as he charged across the lobby, the faces watching him a blur. *What's in the package? A lock of Grace's hair? One of her fingers? Or worse?*

Scott crashed through the doors onto the street. The Shepherd said he'd know if Sheils or anyone came with him. He looked skyward for the drone but didn't see anything. The kidnapper wouldn't be on the streets, either. He knew Sheils's people were camped outside. Then again, paranoia was the Shepherd's greatest tool. They had to assume the kidnapper was on every street corner and in every car. More than likely, the son of a bitch was holed up somewhere without a clue as to what was going on. It was the power of the boogeyman.

Scott didn't bother with the crosswalk and charged through four lanes of traffic, dodging vehicles and insults. He startled a woman mailing a couple of letters when he slammed into the mailbox. He didn't explain. He just dropped to his knees and reached underneath. His hand found a padded envelope taped to the underside, and he tore the package free.

He knew Sheils would want to have his forensics people examine the packaging. Screw that. When had the cops actually caught anyone based on the saliva left behind when they'd licked the stamp? Tiny details like this only confirmed what law enforcement already knew. He just had to know what the envelope contained, so he tore it open.

A cell phone slipped out, and Scott sighed in relief. It was different from the one that the Shepherd had left for him on Baker Beach.

The phone came without a note or instructions, so he just powered it up.

He recrossed the street, this time giving the traffic a little more respect. The cell was up and running by the time he made it back to the *Independent*'s lobby. He went to Contacts, but this time there was no number to call. Just as he thought this might be a wait-and-see tactic, a call came in.

"So you have the phone?" the Shepherd said, his voice still a digitized lie.

"Obviously. Let me get to the Pagetts."

"And the FBI."

Scott ignored the remark and climbed the stairs to the editorial offices. Everyone in the bullpen watched him run back into the conference room.

Sheils shook his head in disgust at the sight of the cell phone pressed to Scott's ear. Scott understood the agent's frustration. The cell phone was another smart move on the Shepherd's part. It changed the tempo of negotiations. With an ever-changing landscape, the FBI was forced to play catch-up. Scott knew the Feds had some gadget for capturing cell phone traffic, but the Shepherd wasn't giving them any time to deploy it.

"Okay, I'm with everybody." Scott set the phone on the table and switched it over to speaker. "We need to hear from Grace now."

"All in good time. First things first. My apology, please."

"What?"

"I told you—no law enforcement. And what did I see buzzing around you all the time you were on the road? The FBI."

Scott wished Sheils had let him go alone. It was obvious the Shepherd knew his shit. Of course he was going to spot the surveillance. At the same time, the kidnapper had to know there was no way the FBI was going to let him go stag on a ransom drop. There was nothing to apologize for, and he had no intention of doing it.

"Does it matter? You've got your money. No one knows where you are. You've got this in the bag. Just release Grace. That's all we want."

"Is it? Are Grace's parents going to let bygones be bygones?"

Scott looked over at the Pagetts. Emily was clinging to her husband for more than just comfort. Pagett's face was flushed puce. The man looked an inch away from snatching up the phone and shoving his hand down it to tear the Shepherd's heart out.

"I just want my Gracie back. You mean nothing." Pagett's words exploded between gritted teeth.

"And the FBI?"

Scott decided the Shepherd was having too much fun at everyone's expense.

"My priority is the girl," Sheils said.

"Too nonspecific. I need an assurance your investigation closes with Grace's return."

Sheils couldn't give that kind of guarantee. He didn't have the authority, even if he wasn't about to retire. Someone with a bigger title would unleash the FBI wolves to hunt the kidnapper down. The Shepherd had to know this. Scott saw through these pinkie-swear promises. The Shepherd was simply torturing everyone because he had the upper hand. So much for his noble crusade.

"Okay, you've got your assurances," Scott said. "Now Grace."

"We are the munchkins, and we're mad on Jaffa Cakes."

The nonsensical sentence sounded even more surreal spoken word by word by a host of different voices. The sentence went over Scott's head but not Pagett's.

"Jesus Christ," he said.

"What is it?" Scott asked.

"It's what the munchkins said on the telly ad for Jaffa Cakes when I was a kid. I sing it to Gracie."

Emily wept and laughed at the same time. "She's okay. Thank God."

Scott wished he could agree with her. All that meant was Grace had been alive the day of the first call, when he'd told the Shepherd she liked Jaffa Cakes. Nothing guaranteed she was alive now.

"Why don't you have Gracie sing it for us?" Scott said.

"You have to pay a penalty for not obeying my rules."

"Happy to. Let's hear from Grace."

"You'd better not have harmed her, you bastard," Pagett bellowed at the phone.

Sheils reached across the table and dropped a hand on Pagett's thick forearm. The anguished father swung his murderous gaze on the FBI agent.

"Keep it together, Brian," Sheils whispered.

"You welched on a deal," the Shepherd's disguised voices said. "You don't get to hear from Grace."

"I need to know she's okay," said Scott.

"All in good time. What I need you to do right this second is get up and leave the building."

"And go where?"

"Just do as you're told—and be sure not to have the FBI or anyone else along for the ride."

Scott looked to Sheils. He saw the frustration on the agent's face. After a moment, Sheils pointed to the door. What else could he do?

Scott picked up the cell and left the conference room, leaving Sheils and Guerra to deal with the recriminations.

"Okay, I'm on the street and alone."

Scott wasn't sure how true that statement was. Sheils had his people out on the street. As with the ransom drop, Scott had no idea how many agents were covering the *Independent* this morning. Sheils wasn't in a sharing mood when it came to his operation. Scott couldn't tell if that was because he'd act more natural if he didn't know where his guardian angels were or if Sheils still didn't trust him. He hoped, for Grace's sake, that Sheils would keep his agents in check. The Shepherd had given them a second chance. There wouldn't be a third.

"So where am I going?"

"Dealer's choice. San Francisco is a big city. You pick."

"Why the private chat?" Scott prayed it wasn't because Grace was dead.

"Too many spectators."

Scott felt exposed on the street. It had all the hallmarks of an abduction—after thinning him from the protective herd, he was now ripe for a street grab.

He crossed Mission and headed toward Market. There were plenty of people there with lunch looming. More important, it was hard to follow someone on Market with its various vehicle restrictions and congestion. If the Shepherd was following by car, he'd have to switch to foot. It wouldn't level the playing field entirely, but it would make it difficult for the asshole.

"Seeing as it's just us now, how about dropping the auto tuner? You have no idea how disorienting it is to listen to that thing."

Something clicked on the line. Then the Shepherd said in his normal voice, "How's that?"

"A lot better. How about I hear from Grace now?"

The Shepherd laughed. "You're like a dog with a bone. You won't let go."

"Maybe you should call me the Terrier. Grace?"

"The wheels are already in motion. You should have your proof of life within a couple of hours."

Why the delay? Scott thought. *Why can't he put her on the phone right now?* The only thing that came to mind was she wasn't close. He had to have her confined somewhere other than where he was calling from. That created a nasty complication. If Sheils traced the call and stormed the location, they still wouldn't have Grace. If they killed the Shepherd in the process, they'd never find her. The whole situation was built on a foundation of glass.

He reached Market and turned right, taking him toward the Embarcadero and the Ferry Building. Again, it kept him surrounded by plenty of people.

"I wish I could trust you," he said.

"It's me who should be saying that about you. I asked you to follow the rules, and you didn't. Now we are where we are. I am a man of honor. My word is true. Can you say that about yourself?"

Wow, Scott hadn't expected that. He'd struck a nerve there. What did that say about the Shepherd? *The man abducts a child and still thinks he's a man of honor?* Kidnappers with a code were dangerous. *How do I deal with someone with a deluded worldview?* How he wished this was a straightforward for-profit kidnapper who cared only about money. At least he'd know what to expect.

"Yes, I can. You want to make some quick money—that's fine with me. I don't care. I just want to get this kid back to her family so that I can go back to mine. Nothing else matters. I'm not the cops."

"I hope you mean it."

"I do."

"I brought you in because I want to deal with you . . . not the FBI . . . not the *Independent*. If you want to see Grace's safe return, everything is between just you and me from now on."

Scott's heart sank. First, he was just supposed to take the Shepherd's call and be the middleman. Then he'd been asked to deliver the ransom. Now, the Shepherd had dropped him slap-bang in the middle of Piper territory. It was a nasty spit of no man's land that in the past had gotten a boy killed, destroyed Scott's reputation, and put his family in danger.

"Okay. You said there was a penalty. Let's get this shit finished. What do you want?"

"Another two hundred thousand."

"That's going to take time."

"Nothing that another Kickstarter campaign can't fix. Have some faith, Scott. You've got two days."

"I can't promise that."

"What you can promise is to follow my rules because I won't give you another chance. Fail—and Grace dies."

CHAPTER FIFTEEN

Jane took a moment to sit down on a bench between the rhino and the big-cat enclosures. Sammy and Peter darted back and forth between the two with Matthew Pagett close behind. Phil and Karen Pagett were deep in conversation with their niece, Tabitha, by the hippos.

Their girls, Susan and Emma, were quizzing Agent Guerra. Jane knew the topic of conversation without eavesdropping. It was either what it was like to be an FBI agent, or how they could blow out their hair like hers. If the girls weren't peppering her with questions, the boys were mooning over her. Only yesterday, Sammy had proclaimed he would be joining the FBI. It was the downside of being a good-looking woman with an exciting career. Jane felt bad for Guerra, being stuck babysitting her and the boys. It made sense, though. She easily pulled off the role of friend or family member, whereas the guys Sheils had watching over the Pagetts might as well have had *FBI* stenciled across their chests.

Keith Draper walked over to her, carrying two ice-cream cones. He offered her one as he sat down next to her.

"Consider this a thank-you," he said.

"For what?"

"This. The zoo was a good idea."

The San Francisco Zoo had been Jane's idea. Anything to keep everyone preoccupied while Scott and Sheils tried to get Grace back. It was a good distraction for her, too.

She took a lick of the ice cream. "I thought it would be good to get everyone out of the hotel. I know how the waiting drives you crazy."

"Well, it's very kind of you. You don't have to put your life on hold to keep us entertained."

She frowned. "Thanks to the Shepherd, all our lives are on hold. The kids can't go to school, and I can't go to work while all this is going on. I'm just making lemonade from lemons."

"From the sourest of lemons," he said. "I'm so sorry. This can't be any fun for you and your family."

The tough thing was, she didn't know the damage this kidnapping would have on her family. At the moment, it was a distraction from their current problems. That was okay as long as it didn't spill over into their existing ones.

"It is what it is. We're all riding on the Shepherd's roller coaster," she said. "How's everyone holding up?"

"How you would expect. Not great. There's lot of guilt and self-blame. I'm sure you know the drill."

She did. Even after Scott had come home with the boys, the kidnapping's effects lingered. At one point, she'd been on the cusp of leaving him, just scooping up her sons and walking out the door. The whole ordeal had just been too much to handle. She'd held him responsible for bringing this monster into their lives. It had taken her a while before she'd come to terms with the situation and Scott's ultimate crime—answering a phone at the wrong time in the wrong place.

"And how about the kids?"

"It's a mixed bag. They're scared and confused. It doesn't help that this is a different country, and America isn't quite like it is on

TV. Your boys have been brilliant, though. We'd all be in a bubble without you guys."

Jane had to agree. She liked how her boys had opened themselves up to the Pagett family, especially the kids. They usually shut down around strangers. She wasn't sure if it was because they were going through a shared experience or because the Pagetts were exotic due to being English. Either way, she saw it as healthy. It was moving her boys on to the next phase of their recovery.

"I think Peter has a crush on Susan."

He did, although he hadn't said as much. He seemed to have a thing for long hair, and Susan had lovely, near-waist-length brown hair.

"How are you doing?" she asked.

"Okay. A little ragged. Ever seen those old variety acts where the guy has all these plates spinning on top of bamboo poles?"

She nodded.

"Well, that's me. I'm trying to keep spirits high, stop arguments, and wipe away tears. I have to be the objective one. It's the only way to keep everybody from tearing themselves apart."

She could have done with that kind of help when her world was coming apart. She and Scott had kept it within the walls of their relationship. Why hadn't they reached out to someone? Shame? Now when she looked back on it, it seemed that way.

"Where were you six months ago? I could have used you."

"Maybe I should have a side business as a family companion during kidnappings." He laughed, but it soon ran dry. "That wasn't in very good taste."

"Don't beat yourself up. Considering what you're going through, a little dark humor is allowed."

He raised his ice-cream cone, and they clinked them together.

"Can I ask a serious question?" he said.

Jane nodded.

"How did you, Scott, and the kids get through this?"

She wasn't sure they had yet. The boys were far from a full recovery, and flashes of arguments between Scott and her filled her head. But while she had her doubts now, she was sure they would mend in time. "The key is knowing recovery doesn't happen in a day and to avoid pointing fingers."

"Good to know."

"How do you know Brian?"

"We grew up together. We're practically brothers. We went to school together and were always in and out of each other's houses. Oddly, we lost touch when we left school. Our paths crossed again about five years ago or so. I own an engraving company. I do everything from trophies to industrial labels. He placed an order with the shop. Despite the twenty-year gap, we fell into being mates like it was only yesterday."

"That's cool. Where's your family?"

His gaze fell to the ground. She'd asked the wrong question and stepped on an emotional land mine.

"I'm sorry. I shouldn't have asked."

"No, it's okay. It's just one of life's regrets, if I'm being honest. Marriage, kids, family never happened for me. It wasn't for the want of trying. It's okay, though. I have friends and a nice business. I have a good life."

"It could still happen. You're young."

"No, I'm content being everyone's favorite uncle."

Tabitha broke the moment when she ran over and asked Draper to show her the penguins, or as she put it, "the *Happy Feet* birds." Watching him go, she felt bad for the guy. He seemed nice, and he deserved more happiness than he was getting. It was probably a good idea to check in with her own children, who seemed to be bugging Guerra with their questions.

The inevitable burnout came an hour later. The enthusiasm kids had for the animals petered out. No one was interested in snacks or anything the gift shop had to offer. The great barometer of this excursion now pointed to the fact that it had run its course.

She tracked Guerra down. "I think it's time to go."

She agreed and rounded everybody up. Jane and the boys said their goodbyes to Draper and the Pagetts, and everybody went their own way. Guerra drove her and the boys home in Jane's minivan.

As Guerra drove, Jane called Scott on his cell. He didn't answer. It wasn't a surprise. He'd be tied up all day with Sheils. She just wished he'd check in from time to time. She knew he wouldn't—couldn't. The Shepherd had him now. The kidnapper was now an obsession.

"Have you heard from Agent Sheils about how things are going?"

"No, I'll check in when we get back to the house."

Jane wasn't sure if the agent was giving her the mushroom treatment. She decided not to push it.

It didn't take long for Guerra to cut across the city back to Jane's house. The agent stopped Jane's minivan in the driveway. She opened the garage door but didn't pull inside.

"I'll just clear the house before we go in."

This had been the procedure since Guerra had been given protection duty. It was supposed to instill peace of mind. It did the opposite. The thought that Jane couldn't return to her home without an FBI agent going through it first turned her stomach. She handed over her door keys.

Guerra disappeared into the house, and Jane slipped into the driver's seat. This was also part of the procedure. If Guerra ran into trouble, Jane had a simple instruction—drive away and call 911.

"Can't we go in yet?" Peter whined. "I need to pee."

"You'll have to hold it for a minute while Agent Lucy does her job."

Usually, Guerra took only about a minute to carry out her sweep, but she was running longer. Peter kept whining about his need to pee, which migrated over to Sammy. Jane tuned them out. She couldn't tear her gaze away from the open front door to her home.

The clock on the dash said three minutes had passed. Three minutes wasn't enough to run. Guerra could be struggling with something. Still, the delay scared her, and she dug into her purse for her phone.

Just as she had rifled through her contacts for the number at the FBI that Sheils had given her, Guerra came running out of the house. The sight of the FBI agent's panicked face sent Jane's heart rate rocketing.

"Can I pee now?" Peter said.

She didn't answer. Couldn't answer.

Guerra ran around to the passenger door and jumped in. "We have to go. Now!"

"What is it?" Jane asked, her voice cracking on the words.

"Just go. I'll explain later."

"But we have to pee," Sammy said.

As Guerra turned to tell the boys they couldn't, Jane leaped from the car. She couldn't be run out of her home again. She had to see what had happened in there. Who had gotten to it?

"No, Jane. No," Guerra yelled.

But Jane kept going. She bolted up the steps before the FBI agent had a chance to catch up with her.

She blew through the doorway and into the living room. Visions of carnage failed to materialize. She whipped her head from left to right. Everything was in its place. She didn't understand Guerra's panic. Then she saw it—the gift the Shepherd had left on the kitchen table.

• • •

After the Shepherd hung up, Scott kept walking down Market toward the Ferry Building. He needed time to think before he called in. He faced a dilemma—tell Sheils the truth, or lie and work with the Shepherd. He'd been here before. To save his children, he'd done whatever the Piper said. It had served only to drive a wedge between Sheils and him. It wasn't until he'd brought Sheils in that he'd gotten his kids back. The likes of the Shepherd and the Piper thrived on isolating their victims. Alone, people like Scott were outplayed and vulnerable. Scott wasn't about to go down that road again, but playing by the FBI's rules wasn't going to get Grace back, either. The Shepherd had put him in a corner. Scott had only one option—put Sheils in the corner with him.

He called Sheils. The FBI agent answered on the first ring.

"It's me. I'm okay. I'm outside the Ferry Building. Come pick me up. Come alone."

"Everything's okay?"

"Yes. Tell Brian and Emily that Grace is fine. He says we'll have proof of life in a couple of hours, but you and I need to talk. Just between us, okay? What you do after we talk is up to you, but I need to talk to you off the record. Do I have your word?"

"You have it."

It was a long five minutes before Sheils pulled up in front of him. The wait had been excruciating. It was at times like these he wished he smoked. He jumped into Sheils's car.

Sheils lurched back into traffic. "What's happened?"

"He wants another two hundred grand."

"I'm getting you back to my office. I want that phone picked apart."

"Can we not do that? Not just yet."

"Why?" Suspicion filled the word.

"He doesn't just want the money. I have to pay a penalty for involving you in the ransom drop. He's going to have me do something. I don't know what."

Sheils turned onto Broadway. "What else did he say?"

Time to hit him with the big one, Scott thought. "He wants no FBI involvement."

"Well, that's never going to happen."

"It is."

Sheils stamped on the brakes and brought the car to a sliding stop at the side of the road. Scott had expected this reaction and was ready for it. He wasn't about to be bullied.

"This guy is on top of his game. He saw through your tactics during the ransom drop and sidelined you. This latest call cut you out of the loop. It was done with simplicity and skill. He's one step ahead of you because he's as good as you are, and that's all the edge he needs. So, if you want to bring Grace home safe and sound, the FBI can't be involved."

"Christ. You really want to be the hero, don't you? You want to be a superstar. Bet you've already sewn up the book rights for this one."

Scott thought they were past this, but any trust Sheils had in him was a thin veneer. He couldn't imagine Sheils talking to a civilian like this, but they had a *special* relationship. One built on a lack of trust. Scott had deserved Sheils's scorn—once. Not now.

"Will you shut up and listen to me for just one second?"

"Go ahead, superstar. I'm all ears."

"Superstar, really? If you distrust me so much, why in the hell did you bring me in? I know I sure don't need this. If you want to deck me, have at it. Get it out of your system so we can move on, because I can assure you that if Grace dies because of your obstructionism, I will make sure the world knows about it."

Sheils was silent for a long moment. "Say what you've got to say."

Scott guessed that was as close to an apology as he was about to get.

"We have to do this off the books."

"We?"

"Yes. You, me, and anybody else you want to bring in, but the FBI machine can't be part of it, because if the Shepherd sees it, then it's game over for Grace."

"The FBI isn't going to just stand down."

"That's your problem. Not mine."

"As lovely as this idea seems, the Shepherd is going to smell a rat if my people pull back."

"Of course. The FBI has to be buzzing around, but the Shepherd is expecting me to ditch you all and do his bidding. I'm proposing I do that with you backing me up. If the Shepherd believes I'm working alone, he's going to let his guard down. He's already proven that by talking to me with his voice undisguised. It's the only way we can bring him down."

Sheils spent a long moment mulling over Scott's proposal. "This is a career-ending decision. It's lucky my career is at an end. I don't know how I can make this work, but I have people who I can trust."

Sheils's cell rang. "Yeah, Lucy."

Panic swept across the agent's face. His panic became Scott's fear. Lucy Guerra was protecting his family. The Shepherd had gotten to his family. One thought kept repeating itself in his head: *Please don't hurt my wife and boys . . . please don't hurt my wife and boys.*

Sheils jammed the car into drive and slewed into traffic. "Get forensics and anybody you think we need. We'll be right there."

"What's happened? Is Jane okay? My boys?"

Sheils tossed Scott his phone. "Everyone's okay. The Shepherd left proof of life at your house while they were out."

Sheils scythed through traffic without much thought to the other drivers he cut off. There wasn't any rush to get to Scott's house. Guerra would have the place on lockdown, and it wasn't like the Shepherd was sitting on the doorstep. The kidnapper was one step ahead again, and everyone else was in catch-up mode. All the same, Scott wanted Sheils to cut every corner and run every light.

Several of Sheils's people beat him to Scott's house, judging by the number of vehicles parked in the street. Jane and the boys were on the sidewalk, leaning against Jane's minivan. Sheils double-parked, and Scott jumped from the car the second he stopped. He rushed over to them and dropped to his knees to give his boys a hug.

"Everybody okay?" he asked Jane.

She nodded.

"We had to pee in the yard because Agent Lucy said we couldn't go into the house," Peter said.

"And don't tell me you didn't get a kick out of that. Just remember that's the first and last time."

The boys giggled. Laughs were good. They hid the fear spreading through him like a cancer.

Rising to his feet, he asked, "What happened?"

"We'd been at the zoo. We came back, and Lucy found that the Shepherd had broken in."

"I'm so sorry. This is why I didn't want to get involved. I didn't want to put us at risk again. Does anyone need anything?"

No one did.

"I'll be back in a minute."

Scott got as far as the door before an agent stopped him. He called out Sheils's name, and Sheils waved him in.

"It's in the kitchen," he said. "Come see."

Half a dozen people were milling around the small kitchen. Sheils cleared them out so Scott could get a clear view. On the kitchen table sat the proof of life Scott had wanted—a simple Polaroid picture. The photo wasn't proof of life by itself. The picture could have been taken at any time during her abduction. But the Shepherd had solved that in the most provocative way. The photo showed Grace sitting in Scott's kitchen holding her bunny, Derek.

The violation terrified Scott. The Shepherd had found out where he lived and broken into his home. Had this been the first time? The kidnapper had slipped in without breaking a window or busting in a lock. Who was to say he hadn't invaded their home before? He could have slipped in anytime they were out or, even worse, while they slept. A shiver worked its way through him as he imagined the Shepherd entering the house in the middle of the night, going from room to room, watching them sleep.

"Quite ingenious, really," Guerra said. "Bringing Grace here was a massive risk, but it also means we don't have any potential leads on where he's keeping her."

Scott didn't care about any of that. "I want my family in a safe house. I don't want to know where. I won't have them put at risk. Not for anything."

Sheils grabbed Scott's bicep and spun him around. The surprise move sent Scott crashing into the doorway. Sheils pinned him there with a forceful palm to the chest.

"You want to tell me about this?"

Scott was completely bewildered. "What?"

"This." Sheils indicated the house with his free hand. "This little charade you cooked up with the Shepherd."

The agents started filtering from the room and out of the house.

"Do you think I gave him the keys?"

"Yeah, I damn well do."

"You're crazy."

"Tom, tone it down," Guerra said.

Sheils shook off the hand that she'd placed on his shoulder.

"You want to tell me how this asshole got into your home without leaving a mark?"

"I don't know."

"Don't know is pretty convenient, considering he brought the girl here while we were all across town waiting on a damn phone call." Sheils's free hand balled into a fist. "And that private call you had with the son of a bitch—did you have a good laugh about the FBI running around like assholes while you constructed this pantomime?"

Scott tried knocking Sheils's arm away, but he just intensified the pressure. "You've lost it. Do you know that? You've lost it."

"Are you helping him?" Sheils bellowed in Scott's face.

"No," he shouted back.

"I swear to God, if I find out you're lying, there won't be anything left of you to find." Sheils turned to Guerra. "Everybody out."

Scott shot Guerra a pleading look, but she ushered out the remaining agent. When the house was clear of everyone, Sheils released his hold on Scott.

"What the hell, man?"

Sheils grinned. "Don't be a baby. I just gave you what you wanted."

"Which is what?"

"Your cover story. You have to sell the Shepherd the idea that you're working alone. What better way than having word get out that the FBI no longer trusts you?"

CHAPTER SIXTEEN

Scott and Jane sat in the backyard, watching the activity inside their home. The FBI buzzed around inside in search of that vital piece of evidence that would lead them to the Shepherd. It was wasted effort, but there was always a minute chance they'd find something. Small odds had to be pursued. It was what law enforcement was all about.

"I don't want to go," Jane said.

He didn't want her to go, either, but he'd gotten the ball rolling when he'd said to Sheils, "I want protection . . . now." To Sheils's credit, he'd jumped straight on it without complaint. Scott regretted the suggestion now. The demand had been reflexive. The Shepherd had violated his home, his safe place. Protecting his family was a primary need, but having his family at his side was also a primary need. In an hour, he'd be alone.

"It was just a photo," she said.

"A photo this time. God knows what he could do next time, especially if he gets desperate. He could come back for you or the—"

"Don't say it."

The wound was still raw from the night the Piper had come for Peter. Scott guessed it was the reason Sheils hadn't balked at sending them away to a safe house. He wasn't about to have anyone snatched out from under his protection.

"Then you know this is the right thing to do."

"Goddamn him," she said.

Guilt wormed its way into Scott. It was cold and sour, leaving him sick to his stomach. He'd done it to them again. He'd invited another terrorist into their lives.

"I can walk away from this. I can refuse to be involved. It's not like the Shepherd needs me anymore. He got the notoriety he wanted by bringing up my name."

Jane put a hand on his. "You can't. The Pagetts need you. Grace needs you. Even the Shepherd needs you. You refuse him, and he will take it out on us some way. You're in this to the end."

"Goddamn him," he said.

She smiled and rested her head on his shoulder.

Sheils opened the door from the kitchen and crossed the backyard. He dragged a patio chair over to them and sat opposite.

"Okay, we're almost set. Agent Guerra is back. She has a rental car and a credit card that won't track back to the FBI. You will be totally safe in her hands."

"Thank you," Jane said.

"Agent Brannon is going to be with you 24-7 from now on, Scott. You don't go anywhere without him. Understood?"

It was. It was understood that Sheils was not only protecting him from the Shepherd but ensuring he couldn't make any side deals with the kidnapper. "How long do you envision this lasting?"

"Two to three days. A week at the very most. You know this can't go on for very much longer."

Scott did. This was going to end one of two ways—either with the Shepherd's capture or Grace's death. The longer this debacle went on, the higher the chances of the latter.

"We're ready to go whenever you are."

Jane nodded.

"Are the boys ready?"

"Probably not."

Scott and Jane checked in with the boys. In an hour, they'd managed not to pack a single thing. Instead, just about every item of clothing they owned was strewn across the room. Scott found it a comforting sight. He hoped it was a sign that they hadn't comprehended the notion of the Shepherd breaking into their home.

Scott said he had this covered, so Jane could pack her own bag. He gathered up a week's worth of clothes and put them into a couple of bags. Knowing his boys, they'd burn through everything he packed in half the time, but he couldn't come to terms with his family in hiding for longer. If they had enough clothes for only a few days, then they'd be back in a few days.

"Socks," Scott said. "You need socks."

He got socks, a random assortment dumped on Sammy's bed next to his bag.

"Can't either of you bunny ear any of these together?"

Both boys shrugged a response. It was a life lesson that would have to wait for another time.

Peter handed him a pair of his sneakers. A frown replaced the excitement that had been on his face moments earlier.

"What's up, buddy?"

"Why can't you come?"

The question brought Sammy over.

Should he paint a picture of false reality, or tell them the truth? Lying to them wasn't the answer. The truth would be frightening, but it was better than a lie. He sat on Sammy's bed and told his boys to sit on Peter's.

"You understand what happened here today?"

"The Shepherd left you a picture," Peter said.

"Yes. It also means he broke in. Luckily, everyone was out, but I can't promise that if he does that again."

Both boys tensed up. Memories of their individual abductions had to be flashing back into their minds. He had to head them off before one or both of them had a panic attack.

"That's why you two and Mom are going somewhere safe with Agent Lucy. So nothing can happen."

"But what about you? You won't be safe if you stay," Sammy said, a nervous edge to his voice.

Scott smiled. "You're joking, right? I've got Agent Tom and all his people watching out for me. I'm the safest guy in town."

"He can't leave," Peter said. "Not until he's found Grace."

"Got it in one," Scott said. "All you two need to know is you've just gotten an unexpected vacation."

From the expressions on his boys' faces, he'd stemmed their anxiety but hadn't banished it. It would be on Jane to finish the job once they hit the road.

Jane let herself into the room. "C'mon. I thought you'd be packed by now. We need to get going."

"My fault," Scott said. "I was talking."

Jane telegraphed her fears and worries with a single look. He answered her with a nod that all was well. He underlined it with a smile.

Ten minutes later, the boys were packed and buckled into the back of an SUV with Guerra at the wheel. She kept them busy while Sheils spoke to Scott and Jane on the street.

"Everything is arranged. I've got a nice place set up for you. Agent Guerra will be working alone on this one, but we have local law enforcement dialed in, so there is backup."

"What if he comes after us?" Jane asked.

The question made Scott nauseated.

"He won't," Sheils said with authority. "He's a lone wolf. He needs to be here to close this thing out. With you out of the way, he can't use you and the kids as leverage or a distraction."

"That's a frightening concept," Jane said.

"You'll be safe. Only Scott and I will be aware of your location."

"No," Scott said. "I can't know."

The implication of what he'd just said was clear to all. If the Shepherd came for him, he couldn't be squeezed. His family would be safe. That was the level that this mess had reached.

"I think it's time you got going," Sheils said. "You've got a lot of miles ahead of you."

Jane hugged Scott. Her small arms cut into him. "Be safe," she whispered.

"I will," he answered, because he knew she would be.

CHAPTER SEVENTEEN

George Moran was sitting at his desk, staring at two amazing things on his computer. First was Scott's beautifully written piece at being drawn into the Shepherd's kidnapping. It eloquently identified the Pagetts' plight, as well as his own as someone still recovering from the kidnapping of his own children. It captured his anger at being used by the Shepherd that was tempered only by the need to save Grace. It was the finest piece of writing he'd received from Scott. It gave George great pride to have one of his reporters, one he'd hired, produce work this good. It also pained him to see someone he considered a friend press-ganged into this situation. The second item to take his breath away was the circulation and advertising report. There'd been a 25 percent spike in newspaper sales—on a par with sales from a decade ago. Website traffic had quadrupled. Advertisers were clamoring to be part of the action at premium rates. All this because a man had kidnapped a child, and the *Independent* had a ringside seat to it all. It was disheartening that events like these drove the news business and kept the *Independent* solvent.

Regina Holland knocked on the open door of his office. She was a young, African American woman who'd been with the paper a couple of years. She was still a little green, but she had the makings of a good journalist. "Got a minute, George?"

He nodded. Anything for a distraction. "What is it?"

Holland took a seat. "You know I've been working on those profile pieces about the Pagetts."

These were puff pieces Thorpe had wanted. He believed having profiles about the people affected by Grace's kidnapping made them more than just names in a story and would ramp up the interest. George saw only partial value in this. It was a little too *People* magazine for his liking. Normally, he would have spiked this kind of story, but what Richard Thorpe wanted, he got, as far as management was concerned.

"Yes, I remember."

"Richard wanted me to cover everybody in the Pagetts' contingent, not just the parents and Grace. Well, something cropped up on Keith Draper. He was tried for sex offenses against kids. He wasn't found guilty, but he does have a conviction for indecent exposure."

George felt sick. He'd spoken to this guy and seen him around the Pagett kids. "You got anything to back it up?"

"Yeah, I just e-mailed it over."

George opened the e-mail from Holland. The attachment was a screen grab from a provincial British newspaper. The case was from a decade ago. The story detailed that several kids from a youth soccer team had accused Draper of inappropriate language and behavior. One child alleged molestation. The case fell apart during the trial. Conflicting accounts from the children gave room for reasonable doubt. After he'd been exonerated, fresh allegations followed but were never pursued.

Thorpe knocked on the doorframe and walked in. Holding up his phone, he said, "Just got your e-mail, Regina. Shocking stuff. What do you want to do about it, George?"

George didn't like how Thorpe inserted himself into every aspect of his job. Unfortunately, that was the authority management had given him, and George had to suck it up for the duration.

"So what's the assertion here?"

George put the question to Holland. She had brought the story in. It was on her to answer it.

"Keith Draper is a possible sex offender. The story mentions he has a previous conviction for indecent exposure."

"And?" George wasn't being obtuse. He could see where this was going. It was down to Holland to lay it out.

"He's a single man who's latched on to these two families with young kids. He's come on vacation with them. Maybe he's taking the opportunity to interfere with their kids."

"There are also family men who have committed sex crimes. Being single isn't a crime," George said.

"You're right. It isn't," Thorpe said, "but doesn't any of this unnerve you?"

It did. Any thought that a sexual predator had stalked a family's children made his skin crawl.

"Can I just say this?" Holland said. "We've got a possible sex offender and now a missing child."

"What are you suggesting? That Keith Draper is the Shepherd?"

"Possibly. He could be working with someone as part of some sex ring. I don't know."

"I don't know." The worst three words to come from a journalist's mouth. George understood the hurry. It was a massive opportunity for the paper to capitalize on all the developments that had presented themselves, but it wouldn't last long. Neither Thorpe nor Holland had the luxury of being at the *Independent* eight years ago, when he'd given Scott free reign with the Piper. George had never run fast and loose with conjecture after that.

"George, we may have the beginning of something or the beginning of nothing, but this is worth investigating," Thorpe said.

"I totally agree. I live by a single rule—citation, citation, citation. At the moment, I'm not seeing enough to support the story. Regina, keep digging until you know Keith Draper better than he knows himself. In the meantime, I'll turn this over to Sheils and the FBI. They should know about this."

"No," Thorpe said.

The dick-measuring contest has just begun, George thought. "Could you give us a minute, Regina?"

She nodded and left his office, closing the door on the way out.

"What do you mean, *no*?"

"We're sitting on a golden opportunity here. We're running this story now."

"Really?"

"Yes, really. If we run this, Draper will do one of two things—cry foul or run, and innocent men don't run. He runs, and we've given the FBI a big break."

"And if he does cry foul, what then?"

"We print a retraction, but my gut says he won't. There's too much smoke."

George shook his head. "No, I want to see more work on this before I sign off on it."

Thorpe cocked his head. "I'm not asking your permission, George."

"I'm the editor in chief. I have final say," he said, keeping his contempt in check.

"In this case, you don't. I have carte blanche to run any story I wish, with or without your sign-off."

The *Independent* needed Thorpe's talents. George didn't deny that. It was why he got to dictate his terms. In spite of all that, this was wrong. He was trading sensationalism for good journalism. George picked up his desk phone.

"If you're calling Cardone, I wouldn't bother. I got his sign-off before I came in here. I'm working with legal to ensure we don't cross any lines."

But you'll run right up to them, George thought and put the phone down.

"Now if you'll excuse me, I have to go work with Regina."

George watched Thorpe leave. He'd been outplayed. It meant his days were numbered at the *Independent*. If this was what passed for journalism, then it might be time for him to go.

CHAPTER EIGHTEEN

The sound of banging woke Keith Draper. Sunlight blazed through the hotel window. He winced against its intense brightness. He couldn't decide if his dulled senses were the fault of the jet lag or all the drinking he'd been doing.

"Keith, get up, you bastard."

It was Brian Pagett. Draper rolled out of bed and traipsed over to the door. "Coming."

He unlocked the door. Before he could pull it back, it smashed into him, sending him staggering across the room. He tripped over his own feet and went crashing to the floor.

Pagett shouldered his way into the room. He loomed over Draper, red-faced and breathing hard, dressed only in a T-shirt and boxer shorts.

"Jesus, Brian. What the hell?"

Draper knew to keep his outrage bottled up for the moment. Pagett had a hair-trigger temper. He'd punch first and think later.

"Is this true?" Pagett threw a newspaper in Draper's face. "Is this fucking true?"

Draper opened it. He scanned the page, but he was too bleary-eyed to make out anything beyond a headline. He wiped a hand over his face to focus his vision.

His insides clenched when he saw a picture of himself with the simple two-word headline—

SEX OFFENDER?

"Oh, Christ," he murmured.

"So it's true, you tosser."

"It's not what you think."

Pagett dropped on top of Draper, straddling him. He clamped his hand on Draper's throat and drew back his fist. Pagett's vise grip on his throat and the body weight he put behind it stopped Draper's airflow. He wrenched at his friend's wrist, but it didn't move.

"Not what I think? Don't tell me what I think. Are you a convicted sex offender—yes or no?"

Draper tried to answer but couldn't. He managed a single shake of his head. It felt more like a spasm.

Pinpricks of white light exploded in his vision. He caught a glimpse of himself in the wall mirror. His face had turned plum purple, a stark and frightening contrast against his pale body. The air trapped in his lungs stagnated. He slapped at Pagett's arm to tell him he was killing him. It stunned him, what little strength he could muster.

"I fucking trusted you," Pagett snarled.

The room door flew open. Phil charged into the room with Emily behind him.

"Brian, no!" she screamed.

Phil enveloped his older brother. The combined weight of both brothers on top of Draper intensified the pressure on his neck. Bile climbed up his throat with nowhere to go. He tore at Pagett's arm.

"For Christ's sake, let go. You're killing him," Phil said.

Phil slid an arm across Pagett's throat, clamping a hand onto his shoulder, and heaved back. Pagett's neck arched. His brother kept the pressure on, peeling him back.

"Think about what you're doing, Brian," Phil urged.

The moment Pagett's grip on Draper's throat ebbed, Draper knocked Pagett's hand away and scrabbled to his feet. A breath had never tasted as sweet.

Phil dragged his brother to his feet. The second he released his hold, Pagett charged. He slammed into Draper, sending him barreling across the room. His head connected with the bed frame, sending a lightning bolt through his skull. He ignored the pain and jumped to his feet, ready to fight it out or run for his life.

Phil grabbed Pagett and drove him into the wall before he could attack again. Emily embraced her husband, yelling at him again and again to stop.

Draper backed up in the room until he bumped into the window. There was no escape. The Pagetts filled the narrow hallway out of the room. The window wasn't an option. Even if it opened, it was too high up.

"I made you part of this family, and this is my reward."

Pagett was on the verge of tears, with Emily clinging to him and his brother propping him up. Their family was in pain. Draper wanted to reach out and give his love and support, but he couldn't—and he wasn't sure if he would ever be able to again. Their friendship had just shattered. How did anyone fix that?

"It's not what you think," he said again.

"Fucking liar. Why didn't you tell me?"

"There was nothing to tell. I was on the lash. I took a piss against a wall. The cops did me for indecent exposure. That's it."

"I left you with my kids."

"Brian, stop," Emily said. "Please."

He wasn't listening. The truth existed in the black and white of newsprint. Nothing else could change that. Not even reality. *How had it come to this?* Draper thought.

"What are you saying, Brian? You think I've hurt your kids?" He couldn't bring himself to say *touched*. Taking advantage of a child was so beyond his comprehension that to even acknowledge the notion was beyond him. "You have to know that I would never do that."

He looked to Emily and Phil for support, but they couldn't even make eye contact with him. He didn't know how to sway them. How could he prove the unprovable?

"Did you touch them? Any of them?" Pagett kept his voice quiet and restrained.

Draper wished he could do the same. He'd done his best to be calm. He understood Pagett was going through a nightmare he could never know. He didn't want to show his indignation, but he couldn't contain it any longer.

"I never touched your kids. Anyone's kids," he barked. "For God's sake, you know me, Brian. I'm not what some damn headline says. I pissed against a wall. That's it."

He hoped his contempt, frustration, and rage were penetrating Pagett's brain. He rubbed at his chest at a pain that radiated from within.

"Did you take her?"

The world had just come off its rails.

"You really think I could do that? Seriously? Besides, how could I? I was with you. You're not thinking, Brian. I get it. You want to find this bastard, but it's not me. It would never be me."

"If you know where she is, just tell us," Emily said.

It wasn't just his friend who didn't believe him. It was all of them. These people were family, and they believed the worst of him. A sob escaped from Draper. Just one. He hadn't meant for it to. It just slipped out on the back of his frustration. He went to answer, but there was nothing to say.

"Tell me."

The rage had returned. Emily and Phil fought to hold Pagett back, but it wasn't working. Phil usually had more than enough strength to hold back his older brother, but he was losing the battle.

"I can't."

The simple, defeated answer only served to take Pagett's rage to another level. "I'll kill you. That's not a threat. It's a fucking promise."

"Clear out, Keith," Phil said.

He reached for his suitcase at the bottom of the bed.

"Leave that. Just go."

He snatched up the clothes from the night before that were hanging off the back of the desk chair. Grabbing his shoes, he squeezed by the trio.

"I'm so sorry you're in pain," he said on his way out in the hope it healed something in his friend.

"If she dies, I will kill you," Pagett bellowed as the door shut.

Draper stood in the hallway in his underwear. He pulled on his clothes to the sound of Pagett's shouts. It was only when he'd finished tying his shoes that he saw all the Pagett children standing in the hallway, watching him. A family he loved was staring at him like he was a monster.

• • •

Sheils stared at the Pagett family. He'd gathered them all in one of the meeting rooms. This hadn't been how he'd expected to start his day. He should be focusing his attention on the Shepherd, not dealing with this bullshit. He'd gotten the call over breakfast from his protection detail that Brian Pagett had half killed Keith Draper after the *Independent* ran its sex-offender story. What the hell had they been thinking, running a story like that? He'd thought George Moran was smarter than that.

"Anybody see where Keith went?"

He looked to the kids as well as the adults. Draper had been an integral part of the Pagett family. They'd all seemed to love him.

He got a conclusive round of head shakes.

He cast a look over at his two agents. They looked suitably sheepish. He didn't expect them to have stopped the fight, but they shouldn't have let Draper run out on them.

"Anyone know where he'd go now? Does he know anyone in the city or close by?"

More head shakes.

"If he gets in touch with any of you, please tell me right away. Or tell him to call me. You all have my card."

"He won't be in touch if he knows what's good for him," Brian Pagett said.

That wasn't helpful or useful. No doubt Draper wouldn't contact Pagett, despite their long friendship. Again, he pinned his hopes on the kids or one of the others.

"I have a few more questions, but I don't need the kids for them. Is it okay if my guys look after them for a bit?"

He didn't get any objections, so the agents escorted the kids out.

"Right, what can you tell me about Keith?"

"He's a sodding pedophile," Pagett snapped. "Don't you read the papers?"

Pagett was going to be worse than useless, but Sheils needed him around. The man was closer to Draper than anyone in the room.

"Any truth to the rumor?"

"Rumor? He's a convicted sex offender. He admitted it. I let that scum around my family."

"Brian, please," Emily said.

"As far as I'm aware, the conviction was for indecent exposure and public urination," Sheils said.

"Yeah, that was what he was convicted for. You should be looking into what he didn't get caught for."

Sheils already was. The initial background check that he'd run on the Pagett contingent revealed nothing out of the ordinary. Now he'd be digging deeper.

"You've all known Keith a long time, right?"

"Since we were kids," Phil said.

"And this conviction is news to you all."

"We'd lost touch. We met up again only a few years ago," Pagett said.

"He's been a good friend to us and the kids," Emily said.

"And to ours," Phil's wife, Karen, said.

"Have you spoken to the kids about any impropriety?"

The mothers shifted awkwardly in their seats.

"Yes," Emily said. "They said Keith never did or said anything that made them feel uncomfortable."

"Mine said the same," Karen said.

"Any doubts? I can have a child psychologist speak to them if you feel any of them are holding back."

Emily shook her head. "No. They love Keith. He's been so good to them."

"That's how the bastards work," Pagett added.

"For God's sake, Brian," Emily said. "Keith is your friend. How can you believe he'd do anything to our kids?"

"Because anyone is capable of anything. If they weren't, Grace would be here now. I don't trust anyone outside my flesh and blood from now on." Pagett jumped up, sending his chair flying back into the wall, then onto its side. "I don't have time for this bollocks. I'm done."

Sheils let Pagett storm out of the room. He was being more of a hindrance than a help.

Emily got up to follow her husband. "Brian, wait."

"No, you stay," Phil said. "I'll see if I can't knock some bloody sense into him. My apologies, Mr. Sheils."

Phil saw himself out.

Emily was now in tears. Karen moved into the chair next to her sister-in-law and slipped an arm around her. Sheils offered a Kleenex, which she declined.

"Will Brian get into trouble for what he did to Keith?" she asked.

"I understand tensions are high, and things happen. As long as Keith doesn't press charges, it'll be down to you to sort out the apologies."

"Do you think you'll find him?"

"I have his passport and credit-card numbers. One of those should ping back to us. I imagine we'll pick him up later today if he doesn't return to his room. I will be questioning Mr. Draper as soon as we find him. My request to you is to keep a level head, and remember you're all after the same thing—Grace's safe return. Easier said than done, but please do your best."

"Will you find out what the *Independent* knows?" Emily said. "I called them, but I haven't had a call back."

Bet you haven't, he thought. "They're my next port of call."

He walked the half a dozen blocks from the hotel to the *Independent*'s offices and strode into the lobby. He made no attempt to check in with reception. Lehny Corbin, the receptionist he'd interviewed, must have read his expression. She stood up and said, "I'll let Mr. Moran know you're on your way up."

"You do that."

George sighed when Sheils stormed into his office and tossed a copy of the paper with the sex-offender headline on his desk. He made no attempt to touch his own product.

"What the hell were you thinking, George? I thought you were smarter than this. This is nothing more than half-assed speculation."

"I agree. I didn't want to run the damn thing, but I was overruled. Trust me, I'm not happy about this."

"You're going to be even less happy about it seeing as Brian Pagett almost strangled Keith Draper this morning. Now Draper is in the wind."

"Shit."

"I want everything you have on this story."

"Hold on one second. I need to make a call."

A minute later, Thorpe came in with a reporter named Regina Holland. Both had to know why Sheils was there, but Thorpe looked like everything in the world was just peachy. Holland looked like she had been summoned to the principal's office.

Sheils pointed to the paper on George's desk. "Anyone want to explain this?"

"I'm not sure we have to explain anything," Thorpe said.

"Yes, you do, if you want further access to this case."

Thorpe smirked. The man might think he had an edge because the Shepherd was contacting the *Independent* and they had Scott on the payroll, but Sheils could freeze him and his damn smirk out in all other areas.

"I've been writing profile pieces on the Pagett party," Holland said. "In my research, I came across Draper's conviction."

"His conviction was for public urination, but you made the man out to be a sexual predator."

"There was an accusation of inappropriate behavior. It made the papers in the UK."

"Paper," Sheils corrected. "You cited one account."

Holland struggled to maintain eye contact. Sheils hoped this would be a powerful lesson for the young reporter.

"Why didn't you come to me with this before you ran it?"

"It was an executive decision," Thorpe said.

More like your decision, Sheils thought. There was only reason for running a hatchet job like this—to sell newspapers. He expected more from the *Independent*.

"It was a reckless and sensationalistic one. You basically intimated that Keith Draper is a sex offender who might be in the pocket of the Shepherd, if he's not the Shepherd himself—which is impossible, by the way. This isn't journalism. This is guessing."

"We reviewed the story, and we knew it was inflammatory in tone, but we wanted to beat the bushes to see what came flying out."

"Well, you did that. Brian Pagett attacked Keith Draper, and now he's missing. That means I have to divert resources away from Grace's recovery in order to find him."

"Oh, Jesus," Holland said.

"Now I want everything you dug up on Draper, so my people can check it out properly."

"You've got it," George said.

Holland took that as her cue to get the information and scurried out of the office.

"You two should think hard about writing a retraction. Hopefully, it'll bring Draper back in."

CHAPTER NINETEEN

Sheils arrived back at the field office in time for his meeting with Stephen Deese. He had a text saying the retired army sergeant was waiting in an interview room. He left his office with the file he'd built up on Deese. In the corridor, Bill Travillian approached him from the opposite direction.

"Deese is here," Sheils said.

"I know."

"You want to join me?"

Travillian shook his head. "I'll observe. I'll tap in if you need to come at this guy from a different angle."

Sheils knocked on the interview door and let himself in. Deese stood upon Sheils's arrival. The soldier had looked to be a big guy from the Skype interview, but in real life, he was far more imposing. He stood close to six-three, and he was all muscle. The man had lost none of his army conditioning since mustering out. Sheils guessed maintaining his physique worked as good advertising for his new career in private security. He shook the former soldier's hand. His grip was strong, but his hand was smoother than Sheils had expected.

"Thanks for flying down, Sergeant Deese. I really appreciate it."

"The least I could do."

Both men sat with just a plain table between them. Sheils opened his file and slid over a sheet of paper with the faces of the men Deese had served with. The array included Deese's own military ID photo.

"This is your unit, correct?"

Deese nodded and slid the paper back. Sheils left the paper where it lay. He wanted Deese to keep the image in his field of vision.

"Kept in touch with any of the guys?"

"Not as much as I would have liked. I've seen Otis Parker and Martin Grayson a couple of times. I'm social-media buddies with Harrison Ayers and Alan Mack."

"But not Thomas Fortenberry, Gavin Connors, and Chris Laughlin?"

"No."

"Any reason for that?"

"You get on better with some guys than others. Some aren't that social, and eventually, everyone moves on, y'know?"

Sheils nodded. "So no specific reason."

"No."

"I'm going to be candid with you, Stephen. I checked out all the members of your unit. You included."

If this revelation surprised Deese, he didn't show it.

"The good news is everyone checked out, including you. I had agents from six different field offices carry out interviews and check out unit members' movements over the last few weeks. I reviewed all your military records and spoke to your CO's. Nothing but commendations, by the way."

Deese cocked his head. "Why am I here, then?"

Sheils pulled out a single headshot. He put it between them and tapped the face of Gavin Connors with his index finger. "Because of this guy."

Deese picked up the picture and examined it.

"As far as I can tell, this man is nothing more than a PO box. There are no property records, tax returns, or job history going back several years. His army pension payments have gone untouched. Have you had any contact with him?"

Deese shook his head. "It doesn't surprise me, though."

"What makes you say that?"

Deese stood. He retreated to the corner of the room and leaned against the wall with his arms crossed.

Trying to escape your past? Sheils wondered.

"The guy was wound tight to begin with, and tour after tour only tightened his spring."

"Was he unstable?"

"No, he was worse—he took his role personally, especially as a Shepherd. That wears on you when you lose people."

"You mean fellow soldiers?"

"Yeah, but also the people we were assigned to protect. We did our best to keep those people safe, and we failed more than once."

Deese's gaze fell to the floor, and Sheils lost the former soldier to his memories. Whatever he was reliving, it wasn't good. The confidence Deese had exhibited during their first interview and moments earlier had ebbed away. His body sagged under a revisited sorrow.

"What was the mission that went sideways on you?" Sheils asked.

The question snapped Deese back into the present. "Huh?"

"In my kind of work and yours, a case or an assignment gets away from you. You follow the standard operating procedure as your training dictates, but the cosmos doesn't want to play ball, and it blows up in your face. You know you did nothing wrong, but the self-doubt never goes away. You can do a thousand missions right, but it'll never make up for the one that you didn't. You bury it deep, but it'll eat away at you."

Deese flashed Sheils a wry smile. "Sounds like you're talking from experience."

Nicholas Rooker's corpse lying in Golden Gate Park flashed through Sheils's mind. "I am. Now what was Connors's?"

"Aamir Shah. He was the son of Bahram Shah, schoolteacher turned politician. He was shaking things up, which put him on Al-Qaeda's shit list. Our military cocooned the man. We'd been charged with the task of getting Shah's family to a safe house. Someone talked or they got lucky, but they found us. A sniper took Aamir's head off. Connors liked the Shahs, especially the kid. He blamed himself for not protecting him."

Sheils knew that feeling.

"The kid's death was a game changer. Shah went on a rampage. He gave us everything he knew about Al-Qaeda, the Taliban, and just about anyone he suspected. His intel took down a lot of assholes until they took him out with an RPG, and our unit was recalled. Our combat days ended with that kid's death."

"That had to suck."

"Sure did."

The army had done the Shepherds a disservice by recalling them and essentially giving them the military equivalent of desk duty. They'd never been given the chance to reclaim their reputations. Their military jackets said they finished out their combat career as guys who'd failed. Shit like that ate away at people. A second chance could have changed that for them. It was the one thing he'd always thank Travillian for doing for him. After Nicholas Rooker's death, Travillian had let him stay in the line of fire. He continued to work cases. There was no such thing as closure. Scars never healed. Nicholas's death would always be with him, but he'd had a significant body of work after that boy's death. He'd made a difference.

"When was the last time you talked to Connors?"

"Years ago."

"Any ideas where we could find him?"

Deese shook his head. "If he doesn't want to be found, you never will."

That wasn't the kind of answer he was looking for. "Know anyone who would know where to find him?"

Deese pushed himself off the wall and retook his seat. "Karima Shah. Aamir's mother. If Connors is talking to anyone, it's her. The only problem is, I doubt you could find her."

"Why?"

"She's in witness protection."

CHAPTER TWENTY

In the remnants of the TNT factory, Connors sat at his desk with the ransom cash in front of him. He slipped the bundles of bills into a prepaid FedEx box along with Karima's address.

He popped another Jaffa Cake into his mouth. *How come these haven't been introduced to the United States?* he thought.

He'd developed quite a liking for them. He couldn't put his finger on exactly what he liked about them—the orange jelly or the sponge-cake layer. Either way, they were addictive. Whereas it took Grace two or three bites to polish one off, he could put one in his mouth whole. He'd bought four boxes at Grace's urging, thinking they'd last a week. They were down to their last box in less than two days. He should have bought more.

Grace ran around the factory, lost in play with Derek, the stuffed bunny. The Jaffa Cakes had been the breakthrough in their relationship. She now saw him as her protector. With the fear element gone, he could trust her. He let her have free run of the place while he worked. In their downtime, he took her hiking through Nitro Park. At night, he locked her in her room. He didn't fear her escaping, but he knew he had little control over a curious child.

He put the last of the Jaffa Cakes from that box into his mouth and picked up one of his cell phones. Grace ran by him. He put out a hand to halt her. She stopped in front of him.

"I've got to make a call, so I need you to be on silent running for a few minutes."

She nodded. "I'm hungry. Can I have dinner soon?"

"Right after this call."

She smiled and disappeared into her room. She got into some whispered conversation with Derek, and he smiled.

He dialed Jason Powers's number from memory. He never programmed any numbers into his phones in case of capture. His database was in his head. The brain remained the securest of computer servers.

"Clean Right Laundromat."

It was a cute joke for the service Powers provided.

"It's Jeff Mann." It was another of the aliases he used and one he used with only three contacts, Powers being one.

"Long time no hear, *amigo. ¿Qué pasa?*"

Despite the informality, they'd never met, which was how Connors liked it. Anonymity provided the best security. That wasn't to say Connors didn't know everything about Powers. He had a good rep in money-laundering circles, and Connors had checked the man out before he'd gone to him for the first time. He'd performed his own background check. Beyond the usual financials and property checks, he knew Powers's virtues and vices, his liabilities and responsibilities, and anything else that had made him the man he was. Every facet was a weapon he could use against Powers should the man screw him over.

"Got space for me?"

"Always. How much needs cleaning?"

"Two hundred."

"Nice. I can do some good work with that. Any particular stains I should worry about?"

"Federal."

Powers sucked air through his teeth. "That'll have to be carefully handled. I'll have to charge forty because I'll have to call in my cousins to help me."

The 40 percent cut instead of Powers's usual 30 percent would take a big bite out of Karima's money, but it had to be done. Nothing could come back to her.

"That's fine. I've included an address where I want it sent."

"Is this a gift like that other time?"

"Yes."

"Man, you're a generous guy. You should spread that generosity in my direction."

"You're getting forty. I'm being plenty generous."

Powers barked a laugh. "So you are. I should be able to turn this around in three to four weeks—that cool?"

"That's fine," he answered and hung up. "I'm off the phone, Grace. You want to help me make dinner?"

Dinner was an exaggeration. All meals had to be prepared on his camping stove, which meant whatever he could put in a skillet or in boiling water. Oatmeal for breakfast. Pork and beans for dinner. Grace didn't mind. The whole thing was an adventure now. He told her she'd make one heck of a cowgirl.

He pulled out the stove while Grace cleared the card table he used for cooking. She handed him things he needed to make the simple meal. Her gaze never left his hands. She gave a running commentary to Derek, informing him of all the necessary steps. It made him smile.

Six was a fun age to be around kids. Everything was new and amazing. There was an eagerness to learn and unquenchable curiosity. The best part—no cynicism. It was a joy to be around that purity of spirit.

He would have liked kids of his own, but the military and mercenary life had made that an impossibility. It provided no foundation for marriage, let alone children. There was time to escape this life, but not enough to switch to another. He was too hardwired. It was this or a bullet to the head.

They ate and cleaned up. Later, in the quiet of the night, she asked for a story. In the comfort of a folding camping chair, she lay stretched out on his lap. He told her a story of a boy prince who embarked on a treacherous quest. The story was an amalgam of two or three fairy tales with a few of his missions mixed in for authenticity. The boy prince had Aamir's face and spirit, although Grace couldn't have known that. It was a fairy tale for his benefit. An alternative narrative where a good kid got a shot at living a full life instead of having half his head blown away by a sniper's bullet.

A noise shook him from his reverie. He caught the sound of someone moving through the undergrowth, then a cough. Here on the deserted headland, sound traveled. He guessed it was one person a hundred yards upwind of him.

He sat up in his chair. Grace stirred. She'd dozed off during the telling of the story.

"I have to put you in your room. Someone's here," he whispered.

"Is it a bad person?" she whispered back.

"I think so. Silent running, okay?"

She nodded and disappeared into her room. He closed the cell door and locked it.

He killed the lights. The lights had drawn his unwanted visitor. He'd kept them low so as not to draw attention. Once Grace fell asleep, he always switched to a headlamp. He hadn't wanted to use blackout drapes. He wanted the connection to the outside world that the missing windows in the derelict building afforded him. He knew it was a risk, but he thought the desolate location played in his favor. He'd been wrong.

He grabbed his gun from his pack. He'd kept it out of Grace's sight so as not to scare her. He thumbed off the safety.

He pressed himself against a wall next to a busted-out window. It would be several minutes before his eyes adjusted to the dark. They were a distraction until then. He closed them and listened.

The footfalls continued. Branches cracked, and dirt slipped underfoot. Clothing snagged on thorns. Labored breaths continued to close in on him.

Definitely one person, he thought. Which person was the question. It couldn't be Scott. The reporter couldn't have found him. It wasn't the FBI. They would have sent a full tactical team, and they would have been a damn sight quieter than this lumbering jackass. It could be his client, but he didn't know his location, either. It had to be the one person who could screw up his plans—a stranger. Some blundering asshat put there by happenstance.

He opened his eyes. His natural night vision was in full effect. He peered out the window in the direction of the movement. He failed to make visual contact among the eucalyptus trees. From the rising noise, he estimated his gate-crasher was forty yards away. It was time to draw his quarry out. He slipped out through the doorway.

Instead of coming at his target head-on, he first wanted to draw him away from Grace to another of the derelict structures, in case it got messy. She didn't need to see his true nature.

He moved with precision to the blown-out building two over from his makeshift camp. He crossed behind the buildings, using the thick concrete walls to muffle the sounds of his movements from his target.

He slipped inside his decoy structure. There wasn't much of it— just two and a half walls and no roof. On one of the two remaining voids the windows once occupied, he placed his headlamp. He switched it on and ducked out.

He rounded the building and moved into a flanking position with a clear view of the building and his unwanted visitor. The visitor's next move would help identity his intentions. Should the stranger approach the light surreptitiously and without announcing himself, he was dealing with a predatory agent. If the visitor just lumbered up to the light, he was dealing with an unwanted pest. Either outcome would be dealt with effectively.

The target emerged from the eucalyptuses and into the open space between the trees and the building. It appeared to be a man in his thirties, although it was hard to tell for sure in the dark. He was dressed in hiking gear with a pack on his back.

The sight failed to alleviate Connors's fear. This wasn't an official campsite, and the trails were way off the beaten path. In fact, there was no beaten path. The park service had abandoned the trails long ago. So what was he doing out here?

"Hey, there, fellow camper. How goes it?" the guy called out to the light.

An unwanted pest, it is. He couldn't know for sure. The dumb-hiker bit could be for show, but his instinct said his assumption was right.

The pest continued to walk up to the light. He raised his hand to the glare.

"I thought I was the only one to find this modern oasis."

Connors was in the pest's blind spot now. He pulled on his ski mask and moved out, falling in behind him. He kept his distance. Jumping the guy with the pack on would be awkward.

"Hey, is there anybody there?"

Connors aimed the gun at the back of the pest's head. "Yeah, right behind you."

Before the pest could turn his head, he added, "Don't turn around. I have a gun pointed at you."

The hiker shot his hands up. "Look, I don't want any trouble. I didn't mean to crowd you. I'll go."

"Too late for that."

"Jesus Christ." The pest turned his head.

"I said, don't turn around."

He jerked his head back toward the headlamp's glare.

"What are you doing on private property?"

"Private property? I didn't know."

"Does this look like a goddamn campsite?" He was laying it on thick on purpose. It helped him dominate the situation.

"No, sir. I'm sorry. I'm just backpacking my way up the coast. I'm trying to do it by hitchhiking and not staying at campsites."

"Why, for God's sake?"

"Just a challenge, y'know?"

The pest was just that—a pest. Still, he presented a problem. He now knew someone was staying at Nitro Park. Even though he hadn't seen Grace and more than likely was unaware of her kidnapping, he knew someone was holed up here.

"Anyone know you're here?"

The pest didn't answer. He was no doubt debating his next words. Everybody had seen *Deliverance*. He'd be guessing a no answer got him a bullet to the head. The key was to not give him time to formulate a plan.

"I said, anyone know you're here?"

"No," the pest blurted. "Nobody knows."

So this was a predicament, but at least it wasn't a total disaster.

"Drop your pack, and get on your knees."

"Sir, I'm sorry. I'll leave."

"Do as you're damn well told."

"Why?"

Connors gave the pest full marks for moxie, even if his voice lacked the conviction to follow it through.

"Just do it."

The pest shrugged the pack off, letting it fall to the ground. Illuminated by the headlamp, he stood there looking like a kid who'd pissed his pants. He wasn't making any attempt to kneel.

"Knees."

He dropped to his knees.

Connors moved in, pressing the gun to the back of the pest's head.

"Oh, God."

Connors felt for the guy. He wasn't trying to intimidate him. It was just his bad luck that he'd blundered into something much bigger than him.

"Please don't kill me."

This mess was Elvis's fault. If he hadn't insisted on dragging this kidnapping out, Grace would be back with her family by now, and he'd have been out of here before this guy had stumbled over them.

The big issue now was what to do with him. A bullet to the head was the smart move. It solved his immediate problems. By the time anyone found the pest's corpse, he'd be long gone. But killing this putz was hardly fair. He killed only out of necessity, not out of expediency. Holding on to this guy wasn't an option, either.

"I'm not going to kill you."

Just as the pest's shoulders sagged from releasing a pent-up breath, Connors tossed his gun aside. The sound of the gun bouncing off the ground gave him the perfect distraction. He slipped an arm around the pest's neck and applied more pressure with his other arm before wrapping his hand around the back of the pest's head for extra leverage. The pest bucked and twisted. Connors took care of that by lifting the backpacker off his knees, robbing him of his stability. He made sure not to let the pest slip into the crook of his arm. A sleeper hold was all about pressure on the carotid artery on both sides of the neck, not on the throat. It wasn't long before the pest went slack in his grasp, and he lowered him to the ground.

He grabbed his headlamp off the ledge and put it on, then searched the pest's pockets and jerked out his wallet. He pulled out the ID and shone his light on it—Erich Covey.

"No, I'm not going to kill you, Erich, but I'm not sure what I'm going to do with you."

CHAPTER TWENTY-ONE

It had been a pig of a day. It had left Draper dazed and heartbroken. He'd stumbled through it bouncing from one thing to another. Anything to kill time. He wanted to leave. He'd get out of this damn country and soak his head in England. Anything to put distance between him and this debacle. Except he couldn't.

After the fight with Pagett, he'd taken the BART train out to the airport in the hope of rebooking his flight for the first available, but his ticket was nonrefundable and essentially worthless against a new one. He'd have to pay a small fortune to catch the next flight home. It was money he didn't have. That left him with the prospect of having to endure another week in California before sharing the same flight home as the Pagetts. He had to just hope Grace's safe recovery would mean they'd leave the country early or that they stayed beyond their scheduled flight. He could only imagine how ugly it would get if he had to share a twelve-hour flight with Brian. He'd taken the precaution of moving his seat away from them.

He returned to the hotel to shower and get a change of clothes. With no desire for a second bout with Brian, he made sure none of them was around before taking the stairs to his room.

If he'd been harboring any hope his friend had come to his senses, he lost it when he let himself into his room. Pagett had trashed the place. The bed had been overturned and the drawers yanked out onto the floor. Every stitch of clothing had been pulled from closets and his suitcase, then shredded. He couldn't tell if the carnage had been part of some attempt to look for proof of his involvement in Grace's kidnapping or just willful vandalism. He gathered up what was salvageable into his case and left the hotel, not bothering to check out.

He found a crappy hotel a few streets over from Fisherman's Wharf. In spite of its condition, it wasn't cheap. Damn, this city was expensive.

He asked around about where he could buy some clothes and toiletries. He burned a couple of hours getting enough things to last a long and undoubtedly lonely week.

Then he drank. He went anywhere that had a beer logo hanging from the place. By midafternoon, his head was swimming. He slept it off at a cinema. He bought a ticket for whatever was playing and crashed before the opening credits. He awoke to night and a thick head.

He couldn't do this to himself for another week. Tomorrow it would be museums and a sight-seeing bus. Maybe a walk across the Golden Gate Bridge. Anything to eat up time.

Tonight was different. He'd indulge in some well-earned self-pity. He'd eat food that would scare a cardiologist and get well and truly shit-faced. *That's the thing to do when everyone thinks you're a pedophile.*

He was off one of the city's main drags. The city was too alien to him to know which one. All he knew was the street was narrow and ill lit, with the exception of the backlit signage for the various businesses.

The street might have been off the beaten track, but it was still lively. He passed a nightclub that seemed busy; a number of people waited outside. He considered going in. It was somewhere dark where he could hide for a bit, but the thumping baseline bleeding from the walls and into the night air did nothing for his head. His brain would be reduced to pulp after ten minutes.

He kept going until he reached a place with an Irish name punctuated with a shamrock. The burble of voices and the low lighting looked so inviting. Just what the doctor ordered. He thought the place was a restaurant, but it was more of a pub, judging from the hardwood floors and long bar running the length of it. A pub was fine. He could drink his dinner.

Booths lined the walls not taken up by the bar, and tables filled the open space. He pinballed his way to the bar and dropped onto the first empty bar stool. He gave the clientele the once-over. None of them was giving him the time of day. Just the way he wanted it.

"What can I get ya?" the barman asked.

He never rated America when it came to pubs. They never got the vibe right, but this barman was on the money. He might have had one of those hipster beards and haircuts that came from the 1920s, but he had the hard stare and broad shoulders of a publican who can handle any drunk. The tattoo sleeve just underlined the fact.

"Can I get a pint of lager?"

"A beer?"

"Yeah."

The barman indicated a row of taps. None of the names meant anything except for one.

"Actually, I'll take a Guinness. And a double whiskey."

"What brand?"

"As long as it's made from fermented grain, I don't care."

"Dealer's choice?"

"Sounds good."

The barman returned two minutes later with the whiskey and a perfectly poured pint of Guinness. The guy knew his stuff.

"Do you do food?"

"Yeah, I'll get you a menu."

"Just tell me you do a steak."

The barman grinned. "We do. How'd you like it?"

"Medium rare."

"Sure thing."

He sipped the Guinness. Its bitterness raised his spirits. Yes, his best friend hated him. Yes, a newspaper had branded him a sex offender. Yes, he was thousands of miles away from home and confined to a country he didn't know. Yet a Guinness was always a lonely man's best friend.

The barman worked his way back down to him by the time his pint was down to the dregs. "Another?"

"Sure. You've talked me into it."

The barman put a fresh glass under the tap and pulled the stick back. "English, right?"

"Yeah."

"Thought so. Get a lot of tourists in the city. You get an ear for accents after a while. Here on vacation?"

It had been. Now it felt like purgatory. He nodded.

A cute waitress with thick black hair delivered his steak. It came with a jacket potato the size of a rugby ball. He would have preferred chips, but a big spud would do. All the cheese and sour cream it came covered in would soak up the booze he'd put away today and planned to tonight.

The steak was good and bloody. Eating it made him feel human again. He hadn't realized how empty his stomach was until that first bite of meat hit it.

"How's the vacay going?"

"Don't ask."

"That good, huh? I thought you'd had a rough one." The barman ran a finger back and forth across his own throat.

Draper pressed the sides of his neck lightly. His throat hurt from the inside out. He hadn't thought there were any external marks. He checked his neck in the bar mirror. An ugly red band ringed his neck. *Polo shirts for the rest of this train wreck*, he thought.

"I got into a fight with a buddy of mine."

"Over something trivial, I bet."

No, but he said that it was.

The barman put the third Guinness in front of him. "That's on me, then."

It was the first nice thing to happen in what seemed like forever. "Thanks, mate. You don't know what this means. I'm Keith, by the way."

"Craig," the barman said.

Craig kept checking in on him during the night and introduced him to a group of friends that came in. Conversation flowed with the drinks. He slowed his pace, switching to spirits only. The people were young, which made him feel a little older than he was, but their unfamiliarity with each other and their respective countries made for easy banter. They chatted about sports, England, America, and cultural differences. He easily forgot himself and his troubles. He liked being the center of attention and having this little crowd hanging on his every word.

Eventually, the booze caught up with him. He was having to work hard at standing up without wavering. When a couple of Craig's guys said they were going out for a smoke break, he followed them out to the street to get some oxygen to his brain.

He hadn't smoked in years, but he took a cigarette, hoping the nicotine would sharpen him up. He was aware he didn't have a clue how to get back to his hotel.

"I'm guessing you've never been to a baseball game," Luke, one of Craig's friends, said.

"Never even seen one on telly," he said.

"Dude, you have to see one while you're here," said Brett, another of Craig's buddies. "There's a night game on Friday. We can get tickets. You'll like it. You won't understand it, but you'll like it."

Two guys walked out of the restaurant. They were closer to Draper's age than Craig's friends. The taller of the two brought out a pack of cigarettes and asked if anyone had a light. Luke brought out his Zippo lighter. The man used it to light a cigarette.

"We're all smoking, but what are we talking about?" he asked.

"Giants," Brett said.

"This year is going to be a wash. No World Series this season."

"They'll make the playoffs."

The conversation stayed on baseball. All of it went over Draper's head, leaving him feeling excluded.

The only one not talking was the cigarette man's mate. He just kept eyeballing Draper. It was getting a little disconcerting. He finally broke the silence saying, "I know you, don't I?"

The question was asked with such vehemence, it cut the baseball conversation stone dead.

"I doubt it," Brett said. "He's from England."

"Your name is Keith, right?"

Draper examined the guy but didn't recognize him. Was he from the hotel or the FBI?

"Keith, I thought we were your only friends in town. You been holding out on us, buddy," Luke said.

"Your name is Keith Draper."

Shit. Draper had been slow on the uptake. This guy knew him from the newspaper. What the hell were they thinking, publishing a story like that?

"Look, I need to be getting back," he said. "It's been great meeting you."

"Hey, what about the Giants game?" Brett said.

"Sounds good."

"Want to give me your number?"

He took a step back. "Let Craig know, and I'll check in with him. Good meeting you, lads."

"Yeah, Keith Draper. You're with that family who had their kid snatched."

This time it was the cigarette guy jumping in with a thinly veiled attempt at recognition. These guys knew exactly who Draper was. Why hadn't he seen it earlier? He blamed it on the alcohol making him dumber than usual. He shot a look down the street for a passing cab. Nothing. Just his sodding luck.

"You with the Pagett people? You know that missing girl?" Luke asked with genuine curiosity.

"He knows that girl much more than any grown man should know her," the intense guy said.

Draper kept backing away from the group. They matched him step for step.

"What's that mean?" Luke said.

"This asshole is a pedophile. He's the Shepherd's sidekick."

"What?"

"You're hanging out with a pedo," the cigarette guy barked at Luke and Brett.

Draper raised his hands in surrender, but before he could say anything, the cigarette guy kicked him in the balls. The pain was instantaneous and crippling. He collapsed to his knees to protests from Luke and Brett.

He looked up in time to see the intense guy whip a beer bottle from his jacket pocket and smash it over his head. The bottle didn't break, but the brain-jarring impact felled him, sending him sprawling to the sidewalk.

The kicks came fast after that. To the stomach. To the back. To the head.

The shouts came just as fast. Over the blood pumping through his ears, he heard a muffled mix of hate-filled accusations and the continued protests from Luke and Brett. The voices blurred after a time, and the voices defending him faded—or was that just his fatalistic voice conceding defeat? It certainly felt like more than two people were attacking him now. He looked up for a second and caught a kick to the mouth.

Did I feel a tooth break? he thought. He lay down after that and took the beating he started to believe he deserved.

CHAPTER TWENTY-TWO

The doctors had briefed Sheils on Keith Draper's condition before he'd entered his hospital room. Draper's catalogue of injuries included a concussion, broken ribs, a broken arm, contusions, a bruised lung, four broken fingers, three broken teeth, and some internal bleeding. That information still failed to prepare Sheils for the horror show lying in the hospital bed. Draper's left arm was in a full cast from hand to elbow and rested on his chest. All but his thumbs were splinted together. The Englishman's face was a parody of its former self. Swelling distorted it, pulling it different directions, depending on which injury screamed the loudest. The flesh around his right eye had ballooned, forcing it shut. Black, purple, and red bruising shaded his whole face to the point where Sheils would have sworn it wasn't the man he'd spoken to just days earlier. The sheet covering Draper's body spared Sheils from seeing the rest of the injuries inflicted upon the tourist.

Sheils stopped at the end of Draper's bed. "Mr. Draper, could I have a few minutes of your time?"

"Sure, why not," he lisped through his broken teeth. "I'm not busy."

Too much bitterness tinged the remark for it to be construed as levity. Sheils thanked him and sat in the chair next to the bed.

"I'm so sorry this happened to you. I just wanted to let you know the police are investigating the attack. The FBI is providing any and all assistance."

"Sounds fantastic." Draper smiled, showing his broken and missing teeth. Then he cursed. "I'm sorry. I'm being a dick."

"Totally understandable under the circumstances."

"What can I do for you, Agent Sheils?"

The lisp reduced Sheils's name to a whistle.

"Why don't you call me Tom? It's easier to say."

Draper smiled again. It was so abhorrent this time around. "Call me Keith. I hate formalities. Could you get me some water?"

Sheils picked up a cup with a straw in it and held it out for Draper to drink. When he was finished, Sheils put the cup on the overbed table so it was in reach.

"What are the chances you people will catch these guys? Be honest."

"Pretty good. These guys acted in the spur of the moment. They won't have covered their tracks too well. We'd already have them in custody if they'd used credit cards at the bar instead of cash. Thanks to the barman you spoke to, we do have the suspects' first names. We have the barman's friends assisting SFPD. Security cameras from inside the bar snagged a pretty decent image of them. It's only of a matter of time before we have these jerks."

Draper swiped his food tray off the overbed table. It clattered to the ground. Sheils made no attempt to retrieve it.

"That sodding story. Why did the newspaper publish it?"

"I don't know. Any truth to it?"

"Of course not."

"So there was no court case?"

"No, I've never coached a kids' team."

"Where'd this story come from?"

"I don't know. It's probably some other Keith Draper, because I can sure as shit tell you it wasn't me."

"The story says you have a conviction for indecent exposure. Is that true?"

"Really?" Draper closed his one good eye and shook his head. "I should have known this was no social visit."

He was right. It wasn't. Sheils was probably going to piss him off even more with the questions he had lined up.

"I have to ask, Keith. There's a question mark surrounding you. I have to clear you as a suspect. It's my job."

"Yeah, yeah, yeah."

"You haven't answered my question—the indecent exposure."

"I was caught pissing in the street after I got wrecked one night. I got done for indecent exposure. Everything else in that story is bullshit. Talk to the police back home. They'll tell you."

"We are talking to police back in the UK."

Sheils looked for a flinch from Draper at that small bombshell but didn't see one. Although it was hard to tell with his face being in the condition it was.

"I've gone over your statement for the day of Grace's abduction, and I have questions."

"Now you think I had something to do with Grace's kidnapping? Do I need a lawyer?"

"If you think you need one."

"I thought you were on my side. What I wouldn't give for a friend right now. This holiday was such a big mistake."

Sheils felt for the guy. He could only imagine how alienating this moment must be. Having your best friend try to kill you, then getting the shit kicked out of you by a mob must suck, but having it happen in a foreign country must really amp up the disorientation factor.

"Would you like a lawyer?"

"No, just ask your damn questions."

"You weren't with the Pagetts the night before Grace's abduction. Where were you?"

"Seeing the sights."

"Alone?"

"Yes."

"Which ones?"

"Is that important?"

"Yes."

"A strip club."

"Which one?"

Draper named three.

"Why strip clubs?"

Draper shifted in his bed. "I'm a lonely guy, okay? Satisfied?"

Sheils said nothing, letting the silence leech the truth out of Draper.

"I don't have family. It's why I hang around Brian. I haven't had a girlfriend in years. I'm not the sort of bloke a woman swoons over. I still have needs, though, so I go to strip clubs. It's not something I can do with Brian with his family around."

In the end, Draper was just a lonely guy looking for some human interaction. Sheils pitied the man for it.

"Would anyone remember you at any of these places?"

"Probably. I spent a bit of money there. The accent sticks out, so I'm sure someone will remember me. That work for you?"

"For now," Sheils said and stood. "Anything I can do for you?"

"You want to do me favors now? Thanks."

"Look, Keith—"

"Yes, I get it. You're only doing your job."

Sheils thanked Draper for his time and crossed the room. Before he got to the door, Draper stopped him.

"Has Brian asked about me, do you know?"

"I don't believe so."

"Shit."

"I'll talk to him and get him to reach out."

"Thanks."

"Anything else?"

"Yes, get me out of here. I just want to go home and put this behind me."

"Let me see what I can do," Sheils said and left Draper to his misery.

In the hospital hallway, one of his agents jogged toward him.

"I've got news."

"Good, I hope."

"Depends on your point of view. First, the cops in England confirm Draper isn't a sex offender. He was picked up for public urination, and that was it. He's never been a person of interest in any sex crime of any kind. Second, the story in the local UK newspaper about him was totally bogus."

"What?"

"The newspaper confirmed that it's posted on their website and the reporter on the byline is real, but the story is fake. They never published a story of any kind relating to Draper. It looks as if someone uploaded the story to their server."

The Shepherd had to have done it, but why? What was the purpose of putting a story like that out there? Sheils struggled to see what it gained the kidnapper. It provided a distraction. It wasted FBI resources. If that was the aim, mission accomplished. The action told Sheils a couple of things. The Shepherd worked fast and could improvise. He'd chosen the Pagetts at random, but he'd put time in to research the Pagett camp, find an angle, and exploit it by manufacturing a story.

"Okay, ask that newspaper if they'll let our people go over their server to see if we can trace an IP address or something back to whoever uploaded the story. I'll check in with you later."

"Where are you going?"

"To inform George Moran that his newspaper needs to do a better job."

The *Independent* wasn't far from the hospital. Sheils knew it was after hours, but he figured George could still be there, seeing as the Shepherd dominated the paper's livelihood. He didn't announce his visit because he didn't want to give George advance warning he was coming.

The *Independent*'s doors were locked. He rapped on the glass and held up his credentials. The guy on security came over and let him in.

"Is George Moran in?"

"He's gone."

The ass chewing could wait. "What time will he be in tomorrow?"

"No, he's gone. Resigned."

Sheils had always thought the only way George would ever leave the *Independent* was feetfirst. "Do you know where I can find him? It's important."

The guard gave him an address in the Outer Sunset district. George lived on Lower Great Highway facing Ocean Beach and the Pacific. It was a modest house squeezed by its equally modest neighbors, although there was no such thing as a modest house in San Francisco anymore. Despite the house's average size, the place had to appraise in the seven figures. He rang the doorbell and was surprised to see Scott open the door.

"What are you doing here?"

"Consoling a friend," Scott said. "Come on in."

Brannon emerged from the kitchen with a coffeepot. "Want some?"

Sheils shook his head.

181

He followed Scott into the living room, where an aged chocolate lab greeted him. He petted the dog, and it wandered back to George. The newspaper editor sat in a recliner with a generously filled whiskey glass resting on his potbelly. The bottle on the side table was only half-filled. Sheils hoped that hadn't all been drained tonight.

"I know about Draper. Come to gloat?"

Sheils's intentions had changed now. "I just found out you resigned."

"I have. I did." George shot back half the contents of his glass.

Sheils glanced over at Scott. He shrugged in a "what are you going to do" gesture.

"You want to put that glass down, and tell me about it?"

George popped his seat into the upright position, slopping some of the whiskey onto his lap. "I'll talk, Copper, but I ain't gonna put my drink down. Sit. Sit. Why is everyone standing?"

Sheils and Scott sat next to each other on the sofa.

"You were right to tear me a new one over that Draper piece. I didn't want to run it, but Thorpe overruled me."

"I thought he was just a consultant."

"A consultant who is spinning gold for the *Independent*'s much-needed coffers, so management has given him veto power. I should've walked when he pulled that shit on me, but I stayed. I still saw merit in what I was doing, but when I got reports of Draper's assault, I knew I couldn't be a part of it anymore. Journalism comes with a responsibility to tell the truth. For me, that died when we ran that story."

Sheils didn't blame the man for walking. "Who's in charge now?"

"Thorpe," Scott said.

"The golden boy can finally call the shots."

Great, Sheils thought. "I hate to be the bearer of bad news, but it gets worse. The sex-offender news story you used as a source is fake."

"Jesus Christ," Scott said.

George killed off the remaining contents of his whiskey.

"My people ran background on the Pagett group and found nothing. Someone inserted the fake story on that British newspaper's website in the last couple of days."

"Who? The Shepherd?" Scott asked.

"Yes, more than likely, or someone he employed. I have computer forensics looking into it."

"Hopefully, that'll take the shine off Thorpe's golden reputation. Please let me be the one to tell him. Please." George stretched out the second *please*.

"Have at it," Sheils said.

His cell rang. Travillian's name and number appeared on the screen. "Yes, Bill."

"We just caught a break. Do you know the old TNT factory on the Marin Headlands?"

"Nitro Park, yes."

"It looks as if the Shepherd was camped out there. There's been a fire. Get over there."

Sheils's stomach turned. "Grace?"

"With the Shepherd. A witness stumbled upon the camp. The Shepherd trussed the guy up, torched the place, and bolted."

"On it," he said and hung up.

"What's happened?" Scott asked.

Brannon came in with a couple of cups of coffee. He set one down next to George, whether he wanted it or not.

"The Shepherd's been sighted in the Marin Headlands with Grace. He torched his camp after it was discovered."

"Can I come?" Scott asked.

Sheils nodded at George, who was refilling his glass.

"I'll stay with him," Brannon said. "I'll make him something to eat. Anything to soak up the booze."

"Okay, let's go," Sheils said to Scott.

CHAPTER TWENTY-THREE

In jeans and sneakers, Scott was better prepared for the hike across the Marin Headlands than Sheils in his FBI-issue suit and wing-tips, especially in the dark. Negotiating the terrain wasn't too bad over the official trails, but once they ended, it was a slog. The park ranger walking with them had given them massive flashlights. They lit up the landscape for more than a hundred feet. The waning full moon provided additional illumination. The world had been reduced to gray scale.

"Why's there no trail in this part of the park?" Sheils asked the ranger.

"The terrain. It's not impassable, but it's not practical for park needs. The average hiker would have a hard time."

Scott could see how navigating the headlands proved difficult. There was a perfect line of demarcation. The headlands rose to a steep ridgeline. The westerly side was flatter and somewhat treeless compared with the side facing San Francisco Bay. The drop-off on the eastern side was far steeper and unpredictable. Trying to put in a service road to support this side of the park would have required significant engineering and tree removal. Sometimes nature didn't always give the human race an access pass.

"There's nothing stopping anyone from getting to this side of the park," he said.

"No," the ranger said. "It would be impractical to fence off this amount of land. There's plenty of signage stating the risks. As a deterrent, the park service let nature put up as many obstacles as she decides."

As if to prove the point, Sheils lost his footing and kept himself from falling by grabbing a tree for support.

"We come out here only to carry out maintenance work."

Making it the perfect kidnapper's hideout, Scott thought.

"I can't see how this guy got across here with a six-year-old," Sheils said.

"I doubt he did," the ranger said.

"What makes you say that?" Sheils asked.

"It's easier to come in by boat. It was how they did it when this was home to the TNT factory. The only reason they'd gotten permission to operate was because it was well away from homes. The fact the terrain was so difficult—remember, it wasn't parkland back in the thirties and forties—provided added security."

"And that's how this place came to be known as Nitro Park," Scott said.

He'd come here as a kid. The thought of an abandoned gunpowder factory filled his prepubescent mind with visions of sticks of dynamite left around for anyone to pick up. Naturally, he'd never found any. He'd never even reached the remnants of the old factory.

"So our man has a boat," Sheils said more to himself than to either Scott or the ranger.

Scott saw the gears turning in the FBI agent's head. If the Shepherd had a boat, the odds of catching him increased by the simple virtue that there were a limited number of boats in the Bay Area. Now that someone had stumbled upon the Shepherd's hideout, there was also the prospect that he was homeless and scrabbling for a backup location, which made him vulnerable and more likely to make a mistake. For the first time, the scale was swinging back in their favor.

The stink of smoke permeating the night air told them they were close. The glow of lighting and the burble of voices came next. It wasn't long before they entered the crime scene.

A dozen or more FBI agents and crime techs swarmed over the smoldering ruins of one of the factory buildings. It was hard to say how much damage the Shepherd's fire had done, seeing as all the buildings were little more than ruins. Every window had long since been kicked out. Very few of the structures had a roof or four walls, for that matter. One structure was nothing more than a concrete slab. Everything else had been lost to sixty years of decay and neglect. It might have been a good hideout, but it was far from a luxurious one.

Their work for the night complete, park rangers and firefighters were off to one side, packing up.

Agent Dunham jogged over to Scott and Sheils.

"What have you got for me, Terry?" Sheils said.

"Too early to tell on the fire, but I don't think it's going to give us much. I do have a witness—Erich Covey. I've got a statement from him."

"I want to talk to him." Sheils turned to Scott. "You can observe, but no questions."

Scott nodded.

Dunham walked them over to a man who sat leaning against a tree with an oxygen mask over his face. A firefighter attended to superficial wounds on the man's face. He looked pale under the glare of a battery-powered, portable light unit. It was one of many dotted around the scene.

"Mr. Covey, this is Tom Sheils. He's the agent in charge of the investigation."

Sheils raised a hand in hello. "I know you've been through the wringer, but could I talk to you for a minute?"

Covey nodded.

Scott put Covey in his late twenties. He had a mess of dirty-blond curls hanging down over his face. The quilted North Face jacket made him look pudgy, as did the unkempt beard, but his narrow face said otherwise.

"Could you tell me what happened?" Sheils asked.

Covey pulled the mask from his face. "I'm on a kind of personal *Rumspringa*."

"Are you Amish?"

"No, it's just what I call it. I'm seeing America while I can, so I've been hitching down the coast from Seattle and camping along the way."

It sounded like the reverse of a *Rumspringa* to Scott, but he didn't bother pointing that out. He was just observing.

"I was looking for somewhere to bed down for the night, and I saw lights, so I went down to check it out. I've spent most of my time on my own, and it's nice to have some company from time to time, so I thought I'd introduce myself. Make a friend for the day, y'know?"

Sheils nodded. "This spot isn't exactly an obvious place to happen upon. I just about broke my neck getting here. There are a dozen spots where you could have bedded down for the night without having to risk breaking an ankle—so why go the extra mile? It's not like the lights would have been visible from the park entrance."

Covey put the oxygen back over his nose and mouth. Sheils pulled it away.

"I'll make it easy for you. I'm not interested in you illegally camping or looking for a spot where you can smoke some weed. I have bigger things to worry about—namely, a kidnapped child. Just tell me what you were doing here."

Covey swallowed before answering. "I don't believe in government ownership, okay?"

Sheils shook his head. "I don't get what you mean."

"This is public land. It belongs to the people."

"Correct."

"But this is one of many national, state, and regional parks that restrict access. I refuse to be denied access. I will not have my rights infringed upon."

Sheils held up his hand, ending Covey's soapbox speech. "You saw a light, and you thought you'd encountered a kindred spirit— then what?"

"I called out. I made it obvious I wasn't a threat or barging in. Some of these people are a little odd."

"I can imagine," Sheils said.

Scott used the cover of night to disguise a smile.

"No one said anything. I kept walking toward the light. Then he came up on me from behind with a gun. He told me I was on private property, and I knew that was bullshit, but I wasn't telling him that, not with the gun and all."

"I don't blame you," Sheils said. "What else did he say?"

"He asked me why I was there. I told him. Then he jumped me. He had his arm around my neck. I'll tell ya, I thought he was going to kill me, but he choked me out or something because I lost consciousness. When I came to, he'd bound my hands and ankles up."

"He trussed him up with flex cuffs," Dunham added.

"Where did he attack you?" Sheils indicated the smoking ruins.

Covey shook his head and pointed to another of the dilapidated buildings. "The light was coming from over there. I walked toward it, but when I got close, I could see it was just a flashlight sitting on a ledge. That was when he jumped me and knocked me out. When the fire woke me, I was all the way over there. He must have dragged me."

Covey pointed to a clearing a good distance from where the Shepherd had jumped him.

"Did you ever see his face?" Sheils asked.

"No. I never saw him when he jumped me, and when I came to, he had a ski mask on. When he started that fire, I thought I would die tonight."

"I can imagine," Sheils said. "What else happened?"

"Nothing. He lit that building up and bounced."

"Which way?"

"Down to the water."

That confirmed the boat theory.

"What did he take with him?"

"Just a pack as far as I could tell, but he could have taken more while I was out."

"You said you saw him with a girl," Dunham prompted.

"Yeah, he was disappearing into the shadows. I thought he was alone, but then I heard this girl. Young."

"Did you see her?" Sheils asked.

"Just a glimpse. The flames lit her up. I heard him call her Gracie."

Sheils dropped to his knees and moved in, invading Covey's personal space. The backpacker pressed himself into the tree supporting him. It was the first time Scott had witnessed Sheils putting the squeeze on anyone other than him. It was no less intimidating.

"It's vitally important that I believe you, Erich. Are you telling me the truth?"

"I've got no reason to lie." Covey opened his mouth to say something else, then closed it. His expression changed. "What did I walk into? You said this involves a kidnapping?"

"The Shepherd."

Covey gave Sheils a blank look. "Is that supposed to mean something? I've been off the grid for weeks. I don't know what's happening in the world."

Sheils fixed Covey with a stare that didn't quit. It was a long moment before he rose to his feet. "Thank you for your time, Mr. Covey. Can we get you anything?"

"I'd like to sleep in a bed tonight."

"We'll get you into a motel."

Sheils told Dunham to organize a motel stay for Covey, then thanked the backpacker for his time. He headed over to the scorched building. Scott fell in at his side.

"So you believe him."

"I do."

Sheils asked one of the crime techs combing the burned-out building if it was safe to enter.

"This place was built to be blast-proof. This fire didn't scratch the surface."

The tech handed them two pairs of booties to put on. Sheils told Scott not to touch anything.

The crime tech wasn't wrong. The building was all concrete. The walls were a foot thick. The fire had failed to make a dent, but it had done its job on everything the Shepherd had left behind. A couple of tables, camp chairs, a cooler, and a camp stove were reduced to skeletal forms. The most interesting casualty was a six-foot wooden cube. It contained what looked to be a camp bed.

"Was this where he kept her?" Scott said.

"Looks that way," Sheils said with a sigh.

Poor kid, he thought.

"He's panicking," Sheils added.

Scott wasn't so sure about that. Yes, the Shepherd had been forced to ditch his safe house, but he'd made off with a decent head start, thanks to Nitro Park. It took time before anyone had seen and reported the fire. The shitty terrain slowed down the official response. It all played to the kidnapper's advantage.

Then a couple of tumblers fell into line in Scott's head. "We just learned something about the Shepherd."

"What's that?"

"He's no killer."

"Where'd you come up with that?"

"Look at this place. It's a pretty sweet setup. He didn't have to burn it down. He could have simply put a bullet in the back of Covey's head and buried him. Chances are, it would have been years before someone would have found a body. In the meantime, the Shepherd would be long gone."

"Leaving Covey trussed up did the guy no favors. If the fire didn't kill him, the wildlife would have."

Scott shook his head. "I don't think so. Look at this fire. If he was looking to burn down the headland, he did a shitty job. It didn't spread beyond this room."

Sheils ran his gaze over the extent of the fire.

"This fire served two purposes," Scott went on.

"Two?"

"Yeah. First, it destroyed anything to identify him."

"And second?"

"It told us where we could find Covey. Pretty slick if you ask me."

"You really believe that?"

"Yeah, I really do."

Sheils sighed. "So do I."

CHAPTER TWENTY-FOUR

Yes, that was exciting," Connors said over his shoulder. Grace was chatting away at a mile a minute in the back of his minivan about the "bad man," the fire, and their daring escape by boat across the bay. Now they were heading across the Bay Bridge in search of Jaffa Cakes before moving on to his backup location—an Airbnb rental. The accidental discovery of his setup at Nitro Park was a setback but not a devastating one. He always had a fallback position. Not that he should have needed one. But his training taught him you had one, anyway. Nothing was guaranteed. For a first-timer, he was getting good at the kidnapping game. For years, he'd been on the other side of the equation. He'd extracted captives. Now he'd flipped the script on those experiences to identify the weaknesses to any extraction. It seemed the key to pulling off a gig like a kidnapping was timing and speed. Law enforcement was an effective machine, but it needed time to warm up its engine. This job should have been wrapped up in twenty-four hours. Stretching it out, as Elvis wanted, had lost him the element of surprise. He could still pull this job off clean, but every hour he prolonged it increased the chances of capture.

At the moment, he was irritated by the situation, not concerned. The boat was moored up in Berkeley. Erich Covey, the backpacker, couldn't identify him. The fire was diverting FBI resources away from him as they sifted through the ashes for a scrap of meaningful evidence, which they wouldn't find. Despite their skills, Agent Sheils and his FBI task force didn't have a handle on his identity. They also had no clue about the vehicles he was using or inroads on his digital footprint. All in all, he was still good.

"Are we getting more Jaffa Cakes?" Grace asked.

"Yes, we are."

His charge squealed with delight.

Over the Bay Bridge, he stayed on 101 heading south for Belmont, home to the Full English. It surprised him that an English specialty store could survive in the Bay Area. He guessed there were a lot of Brits and anglophiles to keep it ticking along.

It was slow going in evening traffic, made slower by his decision to ditch the interstate at Daly City in favor of Highway 82. He'd hoped the long drive and night would catch up with Grace, and she'd fall asleep. No such luck. She continued to bombard him with kid questions that took more out of him than her. A kid's adrenaline. You could power the city's lights with it.

The Full English was located in a strip mall on the corner of Ralston and Alameda de las Pulgas. He had about twenty minutes before they closed. More than enough time to stock up on Jaffa Cakes.

He guided the minivan through the parking lot and parked in a "safe" spot. Every store sported some sort of surveillance camera. He made sure he wasn't in range of their gaze by parking away from the building and using other vehicles as shields.

He pulled on a baseball cap and thick-rimmed reading glasses. Those were a couple of simple tricks to change his features in case anyone tried to identify him.

"I'll be right back," he said.

"Can I come?"

"No. I'll only be a minute."

Just as he reached for the door handle, he paused. The car—correction, *cars*—caught his attention. Three sedans surrounded the Full English. The other cars around them failed to disguise the fact. One was parked in front of the store. One was in the central bank of stalls close to the south exit. The final car was parked in a similar location, covering the northern exit. The two vehicles had been reversed into their stalls, which placed them counter to the traffic flow. However, that made complete sense if the occupants wanted to make a quick exit to grab someone leaving the store. All three vehicles had two-man teams inside them. It could be his paranoia kicking in, but he didn't think so.

He opened the minivan's door. "What's the golden rule, Gracie?"

"Silence is golden."

"That's my girl," he said.

He avoided the Full English and went into the Starbucks. He ordered a cappuccino for himself and a chocolate milk for Grace. While the barista made his drink, he surveyed the scene and smiled.

Definitely Feds, he thought. What sealed it for him was the pile of tossed food items sitting next to the vehicles. Those guys had been parked there for a long time.

"Cappuccino for John."

He grabbed his drink and left. Crossing the parking lot back to the minivan, he watched the enemy from the corner of his eye. None of them were watching him. Their focus was on the Full English.

Sheils had just gone up in his estimation. He'd almost fallen for the agent's little trap. Despite using cash, the FBI had traced him to this store. How? They'd influenced him into buying a traceable item in the name of keeping Grace happy, and it had almost worked. He got back into the minivan.

"Jaffa Cakes," Grace shrieked.

"Sorry, they've run out. I got you chocolate milk instead."

He held the milk out to her.

"I wanted Jaffa Cakes."

"Me, too. You'll have to have the chocolate milk instead."

Grace didn't take the milk.

"I know you're bummed out, but there's nothing I can do about it. But if you drink your milk, I promise we'll go looking in another store. Deal?"

"Deal," she said and took the milk.

"You're a good kid, Gracie," he said, and started the engine.

Reversing out of the stall, all his admiration for Sheils turned into contempt for his client. This stakeout showed exactly why you didn't drag out a job. *You're going to get me caught, Elvis*, he thought and disappeared into the night.

CHAPTER TWENTY-FIVE

Sheils sat at his desk in his office and smelled smoke. It was coming from him—or more accurately, coming from his hair. The fire at Nitro Park had clung to his clothes. The suit he'd worn to the scene stank and was currently hanging in his garage before it took a trip to the cleaners. He should have washed his hair this morning.

Luckily, hardly anyone was around to complain about his wood-fire-barbecue aroma. He'd come in early for a Skype call with the US Marshals. A video conference was the only way he was able to speak to one of their protected witnesses. Face-to-face meetings weren't an option. Travillian had jumped through a bunch of hoops to get this meeting for him. He understood the precautions, but it was a drag. They were on the same team, after all.

The incoming Skype call lit up his screen. He hit the video-link icon, and a pair of women filled the screen. It wasn't hard to determine who was Karima Shah and who was her handler. The Nordic-looking woman in the pantsuit left nothing to debate.

Karima was a strikingly attractive woman in her forties. Her black hair was pulled back to reveal a narrow face with delicate features. Her skin was flawless, but it was her slate-gray eyes that really caught his attention. Every other feature came in second to those eyes. For all their beauty, Sheils saw sadness in them. There was no wonder to it. She'd lost her husband and her child and was left to live in a country that wasn't her own.

A crude yet effective attempt had been made to disguise her location. A white drop cloth filled the camera's field of vision. The women could be in an office anywhere in the country, but more than likely, they were in Karima's actual home.

"Hello, I'm Special Agent Tom Sheils. Thanks for agreeing to meet with me."

"I'm US Marshal Jane Burfield."

Burfield managed to say her name without exhibiting any warmth or congeniality. Sheils got on pretty well with all the various branches of law enforcement except for the Marshals Service, especially when it came to protected witnesses. He'd entered three witnesses into WITSEC, and the marshals had been a pain in the ass to deal with every time. They always took the agency and themselves way too seriously. There was no interagency cooperation because they treated everyone as a potential leak. He understood the seriousness and importance of their work, but they could be professional without being douchebags. Burfield was following the marshals' standard operating procedure.

"Mrs. Shah—is it okay if I call you Mrs. Shah? I'm not sure if you'd like to be addressed by your WITSEC name."

"It's not necessary that you know Mrs. Shah's assigned name," Burfield chimed in.

"Karima will be fine, Agent Sheils."

Her English was accented but clear and precise.

"Seeing as we're on a first-name basis, call me Tom."

Karima smiled. Burfield scowled.

"I wanted to ask you about Gavin Connors. He was part of a unit assigned to protect you and your children in Afghanistan. Do you remember him?"

Karima's smile faded. There'd been a glimmer of what she must have been like in her youth in that smile. She must have been the center of attention in those days.

"Yes, I remember the men who tried to protect my family."

Sheils found the use of *tried* particularly sad. The Shepherds bookmarked what had to be the saddest moments of her life.

He held up a picture of Connors close to the screen. "Hopefully, you can see this okay. This man. Do you recognize him?"

"Yes, I remember him. He was very good to me and my children. All the men your military provided were."

"That's good to hear. By any chance, have you had any contact with him since you relocated to the United States?"

"Agent Sheils, Mrs. Shah hasn't had contact with anyone from her former life. For reasons of security, no one is even aware of her location. She stopped existing the moment she entered our program. I am sure that's something you are aware of."

He was. He also knew that drawing a line under your life wasn't that easy. Witness protection might be a fresh start, but it was also a lonely one. It was freedom with a small *f* and with a large slice of solitary confinement thrown in. He'd set people up in WITSEC. Some couldn't handle it and ditched the program. Some could handle it as long as they got to reach out to an old friend from time to time.

"The question was for Karima."

"Do I have to remind you that this agency goes to a lot of trouble to ensure Mrs. Shah's anonymity?" Burfield barked.

Sheils knew one thing. No system was perfect. Not when a human element was involved.

"Then it should be a simple question for Karima to answer."

"No, Tom," Karima said. "I've not had any contact with anyone from my former life."

"See?"

Sheils ignored Burfield and focused on Karima. He watched for any tics or tells to indicate she was lying. It was hard when his view was reduced to just her head and shoulders. That was why he liked to interview subjects in person. He could watch their body language. It was surprising what people gave away about themselves with just their hands and feet. Unfortunately, Karima was giving him nothing. This woman wouldn't be an easy read. She'd lived in a country where one wrong word meant death. In that environment, people honed their deceptive skills to a keen edge. For all that, he had no reason to doubt her, and despite Burfield's protestations, she was right. Connors would have one hell of a job tracking Karima down. Still, it didn't mean he hadn't.

"So you haven't received a call or letter or e-mail or anything?"

"Agent Sheils."

"No," Karima said.

"You may not have realized it was him at first. Are you sure? It's vitally important."

"I'm sure."

"Satisfied, Agent Sheils?"

Not really, he thought, but it was all he was going to get. "I believe so."

"Good. That means we can draw a close to this highly irregular meeting."

"Why are you asking, Tom? What has Mr. Connors done?"

Sheils saw an opportunity and pounced. "He's a person of interest in a crime involving a child's abduction."

He hoped the child-in-peril aspect appealed to her maternal instinct. It was a base move, but he didn't care. Grace mattered more than this woman.

"That's none of our concern," said Burfield.

"Should he reach out to you, please contact me. Anytime."

"That concludes this interview."

Sheils thanked them for their time, never once taking his gaze off Karima. *Am I imagining it, or did I see a flicker of something in your expression, Karima?*

CHAPTER TWENTY-SIX

Burfield closed the laptop. "That was a waste of everyone's time."
Karima said nothing. All she could think about was Connors.
What have you done, Gavin?

"The FBI should never have been allowed to interrogate you."

Interrogation? You don't know the meaning of the word, Karima
thought. "They are just doing their job."

She helped Burfield remove the bedsheet they'd hung on the wall
to disguise her bedroom. She balled it up and tossed it on her bed.

"They can do it elsewhere."

Burfield was her second handler since relocating to the United
States. She actually liked her. Maybe that wasn't the right word. She
respected her. She was conscientious and diligent. She just scored low
on people skills.

"I'll be going," Burfield said. "Anything you need before I go?
Everything good? No issues that need resolving?"

"No, I'm fine."

"Good."

Karima saw Burfield to the door. Burfield opened the door for
herself instead of letting Karima do it for her as the host.

The marshal lingered on the threshold. The New Mexico heat poured into the condo's air-conditioned cool.

"You haven't been in contact with anyone from your past, have you, Karima?"

There was no one left to be in contact with. Everyone she cared about was dead. She hadn't even been allowed to bury her dead. Going forward was hard. She was confined to a country she didn't understand. It was a country that had sworn to protect Bahram while trying to save his homeland and failed. Yet there was nothing to go back to.

"No, I haven't. There's no one to stay in contact with."

"I understand the need to want to speak to someone from your home. Someone who speaks your language. Someone who understands your world. You've been here for some time, but it doesn't get easier. Homesickness strikes at any time."

"I know. I know these things."

"I know you do. I'm just saying it gets hard from time to time, so I get it if you do reach out to someone. If you do, that's fine. You just need to let me know—okay? So that we can ensure your safety."

She knew what that meant. If she broke the rule, they wouldn't kick her out of the program. They'd relocate her. The thought of starting over depressed her.

"If anyone reaches out to you, let me know."

"I will."

"And if by some miracle, this Connors character does contact you, call me. Not Agent Sheils. Understood?"

"Yes. Thank you, Jane."

Karima slumped against the door the moment Burfield left. She couldn't tell if Burfield suspected she had talked to Connors. The woman was so straitlaced she was hard to decipher. She felt the marshal was more concerned with the marshals' reputation than whether she had talked to anyone.

Confident Burfield wasn't about to return on some pretense to quiz her again, or worse, search her home, she went to the trash can and pulled out the bag. She removed the cell phone taped to the side of the can. The phone, like many things over the years, had come from Connors.

She called his number.

• • •

Grace giggled as Connors ran the towel over her hair. "You ready for your big reveal?"

She grabbed the edge of the towel to jerk it off her head. He placed his hand over hers to stop her from spoiling the surprise.

"I said are you ready?"

She giggled again. "Yes."

He jerked the towel off her head with a magician's flourish and topped it off with a "Ta-da!" for good measure. At first sight of herself in a condensation-streaked mirror, she shrieked and covered her face with her hands.

"Don't you like it?"

She peeled her hands away. "I don't look like me."

That was the point. The Nitro Park hideout gave him an element of seclusion that meant he didn't have to resort to any countermeasure when it came to appearance. Now that he'd had to ditch Nitro Park for the Airbnb house, he had to switch up their looks for their neighbors. That meant Grace's long blonde hair had to go. He'd cut it short, halfway up the nape of her neck. His hairdressing skills left a lot to be desired, but the end result wasn't too bad. He'd given her this slightly punkish asymmetrical pixie cut. He'd dyed her hair black, too. The little girl certainly looked different. Not enough to fool her family, but that wasn't the point. She just had to look different enough to fool the general public. It was a strange quirk of human nature that it didn't take much to throw a person off a face once they had a preexisting impression.

"But you look good, though."

Grace ran her hands over her damp and irregular hair. "It looks weird. I don't think Mummy will like it."

"I think your mom will love you as a brunette."

"Brunette," she said, trying the word out for the first time. "What's a brunette?"

He toweled off her hair. "Someone with dark hair."

"Oh." She shook her head. "She won't like me as a brunette."

"But what do you think?"

She looked up at him and away from her reflection. "It looks weird."

"I think you look cool. Like a mini Joan Jett."

"Who?"

"You know how to make a guy feel old."

She laughed. "You sound like my dad."

"Anyway, what do you think about me?"

She wasn't the only one to have gotten a makeover. He'd bleached his hair and given himself a buzz cut. He was also using colored contacts to throw people off.

"You look silly."

"Just the look I was going for."

A phone rang in another room. He left Grace in the bathroom, telling her to dry off and get into fresh clothes. He went into the spare room, which was his revised command center. On the table was a bank of cell phones. He thought it was his client calling, but to his surprise, it was Karima.

She'd never once called him in all these years. The fact she was calling now made him both happy and apprehensive. A call from her had the potential for comfort and fear. He answered the phone.

"Gavin, are you in trouble?"

It was a curious way for her to start a conversation. "No. What makes you say that?"

"The FBI interviewed me about you."

Shit. "When?"

"Just now."

"Tell me everything."

"I received a call last night from my US Marshal handler that the FBI wanted to interview me. Today, an agent spoke to me via a video link. He asked me if I had any contact with you."

"They mentioned me by name?"

"Yes."

That ruled out the client. He didn't know his name.

"Who was the agent?"

"Tom Sheils."

How the hell had Sheils learned his identity? It didn't mean game over, but it did make things more difficult. The Feds would put his face out there. It was a good thing he'd changed his appearance.

"What did you tell him?"

"Nothing. I said I had no contact with anyone. How could I? I'm in witness protection."

He smiled at the sarcasm, but it was short-lived. A fresh prickle of fear ran down his back. Karima had rebuffed his every call, even one just a few nights earlier. Yes, he understood her reticence. He'd been with her at the worst moment of her life. He probably came on too strong, but he owed this woman. He just wanted the chance to make amends, but she'd kept her distance. So why the change now? It could be that she liked him, understood him, cared about him. It could also be that she was an FBI honey trap.

"Tom said you'd abducted a child."

Tom, is it? he thought. *First-name basis after just one call. Quite astounding.*

"Is it this English girl that's on the news? Do you have Grace?"

How long had he been on the phone? He checked his watch. Two or three minutes, he guessed. More than enough time for a trap and trace. He might have just fucked himself.

"If you've got her, release her. Think of her mother. You of all people have seen what a lost child does to a parent."

Grace bounded into the room with her newly dyed hair towel-dried and shabbily combed. "How does my hair look now?"

"Is that her?" Fire lit up Karima's voice. "Let her go, Gavin. Do it now."

"I have to go," he said and hung up. "What have I said about talking when I'm on the phone?"

"Sorry," she said.

"That's okay. Just don't do it again. Okay, I have a job for you. I need you to pull a bunch of supplies together—snacks, drinks, books, and Derek—because I have to go out. Can you do that for me?"

She snapped her head up and down.

"Good girl."

She scampered out of the room.

"Your hair looks great, by the way," he called after her.

He pulled the battery and the SIM card from the phone, then broke the SIM card. He couldn't take any chances with Karima. She wasn't an enemy, but she couldn't be trusted from now on.

He helped Grace gather up her things and took her down to the basement. He'd been particular when it came to the house he rented. It had to have a basement. He hadn't asked for it by request, but real-estate databases told you if a home had one or not, and this place did.

It was a finished basement with a half bath, guest bed, and TV hookup. This was the family den and the perfect romper room for Grace.

He made sure she had everything before he said, "I have to go out, which means what?"

"I have to be quiet," she said in a hushed tone.

"Got it in one. I'll be a while, so don't get worried, but when I get back, I think I'll be able to take you home."

Hope and apprehension played themselves out across her face. "Promise?"

He crossed his heart. "I promise."

CHAPTER TWENTY-SEVEN

Scott was making breakfast for Brannon and himself when the doorbell rang. He cursed under his breath. This debacle didn't give him a break. It would be Sheils or Thorpe, setting him up with his day's events. It wouldn't be any of his media colleagues, as they wouldn't have rung the bell. They would be banging on the door, demanding to be let in, or phoning him nonstop.

"I'll get that," Brannon said.

"Yes, dear," Scott said. He and Brannon had become quite the couple.

Over the sound of brewing coffee, Scott listened to the person at the door ask for him. The man's voice wasn't familiar.

"You can give that to me," Brannon said.

"No, I have to hand it to Scott Fleetwood only."

"I'm with the FBI. You can give it to me."

"I don't give a shit."

Scott took the eggs off the heat and went to the door. Brannon was reaching for a package, but the man on the stoop was holding it high above his head. The situation bordered on the tipping point between farcical and violent.

"Hi, I'm Scott Fleetwood."

The schoolyard antics stopped. Brannon stood back to give Scott room.

Scott didn't recognize the man holding a bulging UPS envelope. He was in his fifties with thinning, straw-colored hair. He wore a pale-blue polo shirt over khakis.

"Sorry, do I know you?" Scott said, shaking the man's hand.

"No. I'm Richard Sprague, a neighbor. I live the next street over, and I found this leaning against my door when I was leaving."

Sprague held out the UPS envelope to Scott. The package bore no UPS-processing markings. Instead, across the envelope had been written in thick black ink: *Hand-Deliver to Scott Fleetwood*, followed by his address and signed *The Shepherd*.

Brannon handed Scott a cotton handkerchief. "Don't touch it with your hands."

Scott understood the caution, but it was a waste of time. The Shepherd wasn't dumb enough to leave his prints behind. Still, the FBI would have to jump through the hoops as part of the police protocol. He took the package from Sprague using Brannon's handkerchief.

"I know you're trying to get that kid back from that Piper wannabe. I didn't want to screw anything up for her. You get that, right?"

Scott shook the man's hand again. "I do. Thank you."

"Do you have a minute to answer some questions?" Brannon asked.

Sprague said that he did, and Scott retreated into the kitchen to let Brannon do his job. Looking over the envelope, he was forced to admire the Shepherd. Knowing the Feds were surveilling his home, he'd circumvented the whole problem by leaving the package on a stranger's doorstep. The Shepherd had enough notoriety that he could use any person in the city to be his courier. There was no way law enforcement could counter that. If they tried, it just stretched their resources thinner than they already were. He yanked back on the pull tab, and a cell phone fell out onto the kitchen table.

"I hope you've got stock in the phone makers of the world at the rate you go through these things," he said.

A Post-it Note with the simple message *Call Me* was stuck to the phone.

"It's another phone," he called out to Brannon.

The agent ran into the kitchen. "You opened it?"

"I was careful."

He picked up the phone with the handkerchief and powered it up.

"Don't call until we're all set up for it."

That wasn't in the cards. The Shepherd had said no Feds, no cops. He was going to stick by that. He went to the phone's Contacts and selected the only number stored in its memory.

"Damn it, Scott."

"I'm not going to wait around for you guys to get your act together. He left that phone with someone, knowing they'd see it on their way to work. He's expecting this call now."

Brannon had his phone out, and he was scrolling frantically through it. "You're an asshole. Do you know that?"

"Don't be like that. You know you're not going to get anything off this phone."

"Tom, it's Shawn. The Shepherd just had a cell delivered to Scott. He's calling him now."

Scott left Brannon to explain the situation to Sheils and went into the backyard. It was a gorgeous morning—sunny tempered by a cool breeze. He sat on the bench to let nature work its rejuvenating magic on him.

"Got your gift," he said when the Shepherd picked up.

"Are you alone?" the Shepherd said in his variety of manufactured voices.

He looked back into the kitchen at Brannon talking to Sheils with one hand to his forehead. *Poor guy*, Scott thought. "Yeah, I'm with one agent, but no one is listening in. How about talking to me in your own voice?"

"You'd better not be lying. I warned you."

"I know. I didn't give them the chance to set up. It's just you and me. We only have long enough for you to say your piece, so can we get this moving along?"

Clicking sounds followed.

"You're being pushy," the Shepherd said in his own voice. "Not a morning guy?"

"No, just fed up. My wife and kids are in hiding, and I have an FBI agent as a permanent shadow. I just want this to end."

Brannon walked into the backyard with his phone pressed to his ear and headed toward him. Scott held up a steadying finger to him. The FBI agent stopped.

"He's got him on the line," Brannon whispered into his phone.

"I didn't expect to hear from you today," Scott said. "Not after you torched your camp last night."

"A minor setback."

"Looked like a big one to me."

"Looks can be deceiving, you know."

Scott wanted to irritate the Shepherd a little. Not so much to piss the guy off but enough to get him to realize his tenuous predicament. The Shepherd's empire had almost been felled by a passing backpacker. It had to be a wake-up call to the fact that he was not invincible, and every minute he stretched this debacle out increased his chances of a messy showdown.

"I do. What do you want?"

"My two hundred thousand. I saw the Kickstarter has raised the new amount."

Scott hadn't checked the page on the *Independent*'s website, but it didn't surprise him. "Okay, how do I get it to you?"

"Parceled up as before."

For another drone delivery? he wondered. "Okay, when?"

"Now."

"You've got to be joking. I don't have the money. It'll take time to get it from Kickstarter."

"I thought you wanted to move this along."

He deserved that. "I do, but I can't get the money just like that."

"You've got four hours to pull the money together. I'll call," he said and hung up.

CHAPTER TWENTY-EIGHT

Brannon pushed his way into Scott's kitchen, which had become the center of operations. Despite the supposedly low-key approach Sheils had promised Scott, an army of FBI agents filled the place. Thorpe's presence compounded the population swell. He'd brought a photographer as well as Emily and Brian Pagett. Scott had hoped the Shepherd's hurry-up play would have prevented this kind of circus.

Brannon put a bank bag on the kitchen table. "Two hundred thousand, as requested."

Scott checked his watch. "With fifteen minutes to spare."

Sheils removed the bundled packs of cash from the bag and placed them in a backpack. More than likely, this second payoff was going to be another complicated and drawn-out affair.

"Can we talk?" Scott said to Sheils.

"I was just about to suggest the same thing."

Sheils pointed to the backyard, and Scott nodded. Thorpe took a step to follow, but Sheils put out a hand, halting the consultant.

"Your story isn't here."

Thorpe looked to Scott for backup. Scott gave him nothing.

Scott followed Sheils into the backyard, closing the door after him. "Is this your hands-off approach?"

Sheils raised his hands. "There's only so much I can do. Any less, and it would be dereliction of duty."

Sheils worried him. He wanted to trust the FBI agent but felt Sheils viewed him as expendable if it meant capturing the Shepherd.

"All those guys in there—none of them will be following me, right? Because the Shepherd's got your number. He'll know if you're following me."

"You won't have a tail."

Scott detected a lie. Sheils was hiding something. "But you've done something."

"We'll be tracking your phone. That's the only surveillance we'll have on you."

Scott hoped so. Trust was on thin ground for both of them. "Look, I just want to get Grace, get my family back, and get my life back. That's all that matters. Please don't jeopardize that."

"That is understood."

"Thank you."

"You can help me in one way, though. The phone he gave you? We've loaded a simple GPS-tracking app on it. Slip that phone to him."

Scott looked at the cell. The simple device that everyone took for granted these days took on so many guises. It was a lifeline to Grace. It was a connection that kept him and the Shepherd united. It was a GPS locator. Ultimately, it was a bomb, capable of destroying so many lives if the wrong word was uttered or action carried out.

"Only if I've got Grace back first."

Sheils frowned, then nodded.

"Any last instructions?" he asked.

"Everything is on you now. I really am pulling back. Other than that phone app, you're on your own. That means I'm relying on you to give me all you can on this guy, so we can bust him."

Somehow Scott knew the Shepherd had made it a condition he'd deal only with him so everything would rest on him. He was again responsible for a child's life.

"Christ, this never gets any easier."

Sheils rested a hand on the back of Scott's neck. "I know. I'll tell you what, though: there's no guy more experienced than you at handling this."

That's some accolade, he thought.

The cell rang. He answered it.

"You have my money?" a choir of alternating voices asked on behalf of the Shepherd.

"Got it right here."

"The FBI with you?"

"Yeah, but they've learned their lesson. They've assured me they won't interfere."

Scott looked straight at Sheils when he said this. He wanted the FBI agent to remember this moment if he was lying. He wouldn't take the blame for another child's death if anything went wrong from this moment onward. He'd see to it that everyone knew Sheils was responsible this time around.

"You don't sound convinced."

"Hey, I can't be sure of anything. You two are dictating terms. I'm just the grunt following orders."

"You're playing yourself short, Scott. You're just as big a part of this as I am."

Only if this goes wrong, Scott thought. "Shall we do this, then?"

"Yes, I know Grace is eager to go home. Get in your car. I'll tell you where to go."

Sheils put a hand on his shoulder and guided him back into the house with the phone still pressed to his ear. Scott felt like a presidential candidate after an attempted assassination. He grabbed the ransom-laden backpack off the kitchen table. Emily Pagett hugged him. Brian Pagett shook his hand, and the agents wished him luck as he and Sheils snaked through the house. From the corner of Scott's eye, he spotted Thorpe directing his photographer to capture the moment.

"Sounds like you've got yourself quite a crowd there," the Shepherd said.

"Don't worry. They won't get in the way."

"They'd better not."

Sheils opened Scott's car door, and Scott slid behind the wheel.

"Good luck, Scott."

Scott thanked him, and Sheils closed the door. It was all down to him now.

"That was touching," the Shepherd said.

Jerk, Scott thought. "You want to tell me where I'm going?"

"Get on Market and drive toward the Ferry Building."

Scott noted an issue with what the kidnapper said. Drive *toward* the Ferry Building, not drive *to* the Ferry Building. He wouldn't reach the Ferry Building. What would happen to him in between was in the Shepherd's hands.

He put the cell phone in the holder stuck to his windshield and set the phone to speaker. He reversed onto the street without making eye contact with Sheils. He didn't need the weight of his expectation draped onto his back. He'd heaped enough of his own onto his shoulders already.

He picked up Market and drove on the laser-straight road that cut a diagonal line across half the city. He scanned every vehicle on the road. Who was in front of him? Who was behind? Who turned onto Market? The Shepherd could be any of them.

His breath bound up in his chest. He felt like he was breathing through a straw. *Shake it off*, he told himself. *Don't let this get to you.* He powered down the window a couple of inches and took in a long breath.

"You okay there?" the Shepherd asked. The alternating voices served to give the question a mocking tone.

"Yeah, I'm fine. Seeing as it's just us, why don't you turn off that box of tricks and talk to me in your normal voice."

"Is it just us?"

"Yes."

"Sure the FBI aren't listening in?"

"It's just us."

"That's what they told you."

Scott didn't think Sheils would lie to him. It would be a dumb move to try anything, but the FBI had rules to abide by. Sheils had only so much leeway. *Break a few rules, Tom*, he thought, *for Grace's sake*.

He slowed to an annoying pace to weed out anyone following him. Anyone who stuck with him was one of two kinds—the FBI or the Shepherd. Vehicles piled up behind him but pulled out to pass him. He picked up a couple of honks for his trouble.

"What was that?" the Shepherd asked.

"Somebody doesn't like my driving." He sped up. "You want to tell me where I'm going?"

"Just keep going. You've got a ways to go."

How did the Shepherd know his location? The drone again? He stared at the phone. No drone required. The phone was sending his location. It was everyone's little spy.

"Why don't you give me the address, so we can dispense with the cloak-and-dagger bullshit?"

"Getting impatient?"

"I just want this over and done with."

"Well, follow my instructions, and this will be all over before you know it."

The response didn't surprise him. He had no bargaining chips. He didn't have any goodwill or trust. He served at the Shepherd's pleasure.

He kept driving. The Ferry Building grew bigger in his view as he entered the heart of the city. He tried second-guessing the Shepherd's next move as Market Street ran out of road. For a moment, it looked as if he was going to the Ferry Building, then the Shepherd spoke.

"Take a left on Drumm."

Scott drove past the last couple of intersections before turning left, passing the Hyatt Regency. He wouldn't be on this street long. The turn put him in the heart of the Financial District, which was a patchwork of short streets that dead-ended.

"Turn left on Washington."

That was only a couple of blocks ahead. He sped up and made the turn.

"Now slow down."

Was he stopping? Was this it? Where was the Shepherd having him go? The Financial District was an odd location for the drop. It was just office buildings and a few stores.

"Go straight at Davis. Then look to your right."

He did as he was told.

Crossing Davis, he found himself in a concrete canyon. To his left were nothing but entrances to the parking structure to One Maritime Plaza. To his right was just the private parking garage for a town-house complex and a row of angled public parking bays. A couple of people walked along the sidewalk, and a car jerked out from behind him to pass.

"What am I looking for?"

"A silver Chevy Malibu. Recent model. The blocky-looking one."

Scott scanned the parked cars and found the Malibu midblock, parked in a stall. He stopped behind the car. No one was behind the wheel.

"Found it. Now what?"

"Get in the car. Take nothing but the money and get in the car. The keys are on top of the front driver's side wheel."

So this was the start of a second song-and-dance act. "What about this phone?"

"Leave it. There's another in the Chevy's door pocket."

Once he ditched this phone, Scott was alone again. He wished he'd brought his own phone so that Sheils's people could track him. There wouldn't have been much point in it, though. The Shepherd would no doubt do some kind of electronic sanitization before he made the drop.

The Shepherd had hung up on him. Scott backed his car up to give himself room to get the Malibu out. He found the keys where the Shepherd had said and reversed the car onto the street. He pulled forward and jumped out. He parked his car in the Chevy's spot, much to the chagrin of a woman in an Audi who thought parking karma was on her side. By the time he got behind the Malibu's wheel, the cell phone in the door pocket was ringing.

"Yes," he panted down the line.

"Took your time. Where were you?" the Shepherd said in his voice.

"Getting my car off the street."

"Did I tell you to do that?"

"Can we just get on with this, please?"

"Get on 101. Head south."

Scott took a left on Battery and drove across the city to Harrison for the long drag for the on-ramp onto 101. City driving during the day made the simple act of getting on the freeway a chore, giving him plenty of time to talk.

"Am I coming to you now?"

"If your FBI friends are smart."

"They are."

"We'll see."

Scott stamped on the gas, running the light for the southbound 101 on-ramp. He merged with freeway traffic.

"I'm on 101. Now what?"

"I'll tell you when to get off."

"We're all alone now. No one knows this phone. No one knows this car. Why don't you just tell me where to go?"

"We're on my schedule. Not yours, Scott."

Scott was glad the Shepherd had dispensed with the digital-voice disguise. Now he had a read on the Shepherd's mood, and he detected a little irritation.

"Now that you're sure there's no one listening in and it's just us, do you mind if I ask a few questions?"

"Hoping to get something out of me for your FBI pals?" Bemusement replaced the irritation.

"More out of curiosity."

"You won't catch me out, so ask away."

The Shepherd really was paranoid. Scott guessed he had to be. He had to fear the FBI nipping at his heels. It was the only way to survive.

"How are you set since you left Nitro Park?"

"Just fine."

"Good. Can I ask you something about that?"

"I don't think I can stop you. You seem quite chatty today."

Scott smiled. "I'm a little excited that Grace gets to go home today."

That wasn't the reason for his chattiness. The Shepherd was revealing elements of himself. He might not think it, but he was. He'd done a good job keeping everything to the point. He hadn't made much in the way of statements, verbal or otherwise. Still, the longer he dragged out this kidnapping, the more he gave little pieces of himself away. Nitro Park was one of those giveaways.

"Why'd you burn down your camp?"

"Why do you think? I wasn't going to leave your FBI friends any physical evidence, now was I?"

"Oh, I get that. What I don't get is, why do it at all?"

Silence.

"I mean, you didn't have to do it at all."

"What are you getting at?" The Shepherd's jocular tone was now gone.

"Erich Covey, the backpacker who found you, he's on some vision quest or something. He'd dropped out of society. He didn't know anything about you or Grace."

"So?"

"You could have killed him, and it would have been months before anyone would have thought to look on that side of Nitro Park, if at all. You could have buried him and kept your camp with no one being any wiser."

"It wasn't worth it. If Covey could find me, then others could. Bugging out was the smarter option."

"But starting a fire at night wasn't. I get junking your camp after being found, but you could have easily covered your tracks without setting the fire. You know what that fire did more than anything?"

"No, what?"

"It directed authorities straight to Covey. That fire ensured he was found. That was thoughtful."

An exhale came down the phone line. "What's your point?"

"That you're no killer."

The Shepherd laughed. "And you know killers. Is that it?"

"I've met a few. Some killed by accident. Some killed because they wanted revenge. Some felt they had no choice. And you're none of those."

"Really? Think you know me?"

"I'm starting to."

"What's your game here, Scott? You're different. You've got your big-boy pants on today."

"In your position, killing Erich Covey was the smart play. Doing what you did tells me you're not a killer and that you won't harm Grace."

"You underestimate me. I can kill. I have killed."

"Who have you killed?"

A belly laugh exploded from the phone. "Scott, I'll give you points for trying. I don't know if you're trying to goad me or data mine, but rest assured, you'd be wrong to underestimate me. I'm no schmuck. Just know this: screw me over, and you will have two dead kids on your conscience. You're coming up on the 280 exit. Take it."

Scott let the Nicholas Rooker crack bounce off him. It was just the Shepherd hitting back. He'd gotten what he'd wanted from the kidnapper. The simple fact that he wasn't a killer. He guided the Chevy Malibu over to the I-280 exit lane.

"I'm on 280. What now?"

"Radio silence for a while. You've talked too much. Don't hang up, though. I don't want you talking to anyone."

Scott rewarded himself with a smile. He shouldn't be provoking the Shepherd, but the son of a bitch deserved it. He'd upturned a bunch of lives. He deserved some pushback.

His smiled faded. It was unlikely the kidnapper was a sensitive snowflake. It dawned on him that the ransom drop was moving into its final phase. He needed to have his shit together and not distract himself with verbal potshots.

How would this go down? He could see the drone being used again. It had been the perfect getaway vehicle last time. Why change the system if it ain't broke? But somehow he didn't think so. The Shepherd would want to put on another show for the headlines.

Sheils had wanted him to plant the phone on the Shepherd. That option had gotten the kibosh when he'd had to ditch his car for the Chevy. But he could install a tracker app on the phone in the Malibu. It was doable. The Shepherd wouldn't know. Slipping it to the kidnapper was the tricky part, but he could do it. Then again, the Shepherd was smart. He'd no doubt strip him of everything electronic before he even got the chance. That was, if he even showed. Scott could see this being a cold drop. Leave the cash at one locale and pick up Grace at another. He could second-guess every scenario. All he could do was be ready for all of them.

He minimized the call screen and scrolled to the app shop on the phone. It beeped when he selected the app. He cursed under his breath. He switched on the radio to mask any further noisy keystrokes.

"What are you doing?" The Shepherd put a hard edge on the question.

"You don't want to talk, so I'm just putting on the radio."

"Well, don't."

"Look, man, I'm trying to keep my shit together. Music keeps me grounded."

"If you're getting cute, don't. Remember what's at stake."

"I think everyone's well aware of that. That's why there are no Feds or backup. Just me."

"Just drive, Scott. You don't have far to go."

Scott hit a couple of the radio's presets and stopped on KFOG. It was a station he listened to, and he could rely on them to have music loud enough to cover what he was doing. He typed *spy* into the phone's shop app and hit the search. A bunch of apps filled the screen with the word *spy* in them. The majority of them were tracker apps, and half of them were free. He hit "Download" on something called iSpy.

While the software downloaded, he went to the settings function and looked up the phone's number. It was a 415 number, a San

Francisco number. He focused on the seven digits. He murmured the number to himself again and again to get it to stick in his brain. The number was going in, but it wasn't sticking. He looked at the number again for patterns. Memorable numbers tied to dates and events in his life. He didn't see any, but he noticed the number possessed a useful quirk. All the numbers were a function of three. He made an equation of them. To his surprise, the number finally stuck.

Sheils, he thought, *I might not be able to slip a phone to the kidnapper, but I've got you a number to trace.*

He flipped back to the iSpy app. It had finished downloading, so he quickly set up the tracking app.

"Get off at Serramonte Boulevard and turn left."

This was it. "Where am I going?"

"The City of the Dead."

CHAPTER TWENTY-NINE

Brannon shook his head. Sheils peered at Brannon's laptop over his agent's shoulder. According to the tracking software on Scott's phone, he hadn't moved from his position on Washington Street in ten minutes. Stationary for a minute or two wasn't a concern. The Shepherd could easily have Scott jumping through some hoop. Even after five minutes, it was still a possibility. But ten minutes meant something had gone wrong. The Shepherd could have forced Scott to ditch the phone, or worse, Scott had been mugged for the ransom and left by the kidnapper. Sheils cursed.

"Is something wrong?" Brian Pagett said, his wife at his side.

With everything happening so fast, Sheils and his team had remained at Scott's house. That included Brian and Emily Pagett. He'd tried sending them back to the hotel, but they weren't having it. He felt for them. He'd want to be ringside if he were in their shoes. Their presence did cause one problem. He couldn't protect them from witnessing a tragedy. If Grace was found dead, they'd see it raw and unfiltered. He didn't wish that on anyone.

"Scott's phone locator says he hasn't moved in ten minutes."

"What's that mean?" Emily said, panic rising in her voice.

"More than likely Scott's been forced to switch phones."

"So you have no idea where he is," Pagett said.

"Not right this second, but I trust Scott. He's doing everything to gather information and get it back to us."

He did trust Scott. Truly, he did. It hadn't always been that way. Whatever he'd thought of him before, the journalist was willing to walk through fire to recover a child that wasn't his. Involving himself had brought him nothing but problems. Chiefly, he was separated from his family and was bearing the emotional weight of what would happen to him if another child died during a kidnapping.

"Get a couple of units over to this location," Sheils told Brannon. "Just a drive-by to see if they get eyes on Scott."

Brannon nodded and called it in.

He'd promised Scott he would keep his distance during the ransom drop, but he wasn't letting him go completely unsupported. He'd ordered half a dozen unmarked cars to remain in Scott's vicinity. No one was to get within a mile of him. That should be more than a big enough margin to stay off the Shepherd's radar if he was patrolling from the skies with his drone.

A few minutes later, Sheils's cell rang. He hoped it was a call from Scott, but it was from one of his people.

"We have Fleetwood's car on Washington. It's parked, unlocked with the phone on the passenger seat."

"Shit. The son of a bitch has benched us. The Shepherd had Scott ditch the car and phone. Now he's either on foot or in a new car with a different phone. Hit all the surrounding stores and buildings for their surveillance video. I want to know which way he went, and if he's driving now, I want the plates. I'll be with you in fifteen."

Nothing more could be learned by staying at Scott's home, so he broke up the team at the house. He sent the Pagetts back to the hotel with their babysitter and left one person at the house in case Scott or the Shepherd showed up. Everyone else he took down to Scott's car on Washington.

With sirens blaring and lights flashing, it took less than fifteen minutes to get to the scene. He parked on the sidewalk across from Scott's car. It had been cordoned off. He and Brannon climbed from his car.

He ran his gaze up and down the block from Davis to Battery. It was a smart location for the Shepherd to pick. This stretch of Washington was a no-nothing block. No stores or businesses to speak of. More important, it was a street with no security cameras on it, which meant no one to see the Shepherd arrive with a switch vehicle or see Scott leave in it. But it wasn't all gloom and doom. One thing did play in their favor. They were slap-bang in the middle of the Financial District's network of one-way streets. That meant Scott could only go in one of two directions—stay straight on Washington, or turn left on Battery. That simple restriction cut down his workload when it came to checking out security-camera feeds.

He had his people coordinate with the agents already on the ground and canvass an initial four-block grid spreading out from the corner of Washington and Battery. It took less than twenty minutes before he got two hits on the CCTV footage belonging to Wells Fargo and Citibank. Trust the banks to have great security footage.

Walking into the Wells Fargo lobby, he introduced himself and was whisked over to the security office. He found Brannon hunched over a video screen with a Wells Fargo guard.

"Here he is," Brannon said, standing back for Sheils to see.

The video footage gave a clear shot of Scott at the wheel of a silver Chevy Malibu. The time stamp put it less than five minutes after the phone-tracking app said Scott had stopped moving. In that short a time frame, there was just enough time for him to switch cars, and that was about it. No time to make Scott jump through any hoops.

"Any shots of the plates?"

The guard ran the video back and forth and switched between the various cameras the bank had dotted around the perimeter of their building, but none of them had captured the Chevy's license plate.

Sheils hoped for better luck at Citibank and got it. Their video feed picked up Scott driving on Battery, and they had the perfect angle for reading the front plate, but fate had stepped in to ruin everything. Just as the camera was about to catch the plate, another vehicle pulled ahead to block the shot. By the time it had passed, Scott's Malibu was out of range.

"Son of a bitch."

If he could just get the plate number, he could feed it into the automatic license-plate-reader system, and he'd have Scott's location and direction in minutes. Every city and freeway in the Bay Area had smart cameras reading every license plate. It would be just a matter of time before he pinged one somewhere. But without a plate number, he was screwed.

"I thought we had him this time," Brannon said.

You and me both, Sheils thought. "We know the direction Scott was heading. Keep the canvass moving down Battery. We can still get lucky."

"With the head start he's got, I'm not sure we'll find him in time."

Sheils didn't think so, either. Well, Scott had wanted it this way. It was all on him now.

CHAPTER THIRTY

"City of the Dead" was one of many nicknames for Colma. Cemeteries covered the majority of the land. The city had more residents below the ground than it did above it.

"Which graveyard am I going to?" Scott asked.

"Holy Cross."

The Shepherd fed Scott the directions, but he didn't need them. He knew the cemetery's location well. Holy Cross was the largest of Colma's cemeteries and belonged to the Catholic Church. It had a number of notable Bay Area figures interred in its grounds, including baseball legend Joe DiMaggio. But for Scott, Holy Cross was most notable for one family—the Rookers. Young Nicholas Rooker had been buried here after his kidnapping had gone wrong. Scott slowed for the turn into the cemetery's main entrance.

"I'm here. Where am I going?"

"Do I have to say?"

"No." Scott did little to hide his contempt.

He turned left at the second traffic circle. The Rookers' plot lay at the end of this road. He realized he was driving slower and slower the closer he got to his shame. He was barely driving above walking pace when he stopped the Chevy. He cast a look across the rows of varying grave markers until his gaze found Nicholas Rooker's.

"I'm here." His voice registered barely above a whisper.

"Put the money on his grave, Scott."

He snatched the backpack off the seat next to him along with the cell phone and climbed from the Malibu. His legs buckled under his weight. He grabbed the sedan's door to stop himself from falling.

He trudged over the lawn between the grave markers until he reached the Rooker family plot. Despite Charles Rooker's millions, there was no elaborate gravestone marking his son's final resting place. Just a simple black-marble plaque set into an angled, concrete marker that stood only a few inches above the ground. The inscription was simple: *Our Loving Son, Nicholas*, followed by his birth and death dates. It was a tragically short period of time. Charles Rooker lay on one side of his son, while his wife was buried on the other. A family reunited in death.

What a fucking mess it had all been. He'd inadvertently contributed to Nicholas's murder. To avenge his son, Charles Rooker had been behind Sammy's and Peter's abductions, and he'd died hating Scott. Cancer had claimed Rooker's wife, Alice, and she'd died never knowing the identity of her son's murderer. Rooker got his justice but at a horrible cost to himself and everyone else.

"I'm so sorry," he said.

A sob slipped out of Scott, taking him by surprise. It was the wake-up call he needed. He'd failed this family, but he wouldn't fail Grace's. He backhanded the tears running down his face.

He dropped the backpack with the $200,000 in it on Nicholas's grave. "I've delivered the money," he said into the phone.

"Sounds like you choked up there."

"Fuck you."

He looked around for the Shepherd. He had the place pretty much to himself. He'd passed only a couple of cars and seen only a smattering of people paying their respects to loved ones. No one seemed out of place or watching him.

"You've got your money. Where's Grace?"

"Behind the mausoleum."

The admission stunned Scott. He expected another trip down misery lane. He didn't expect her to be here.

"Get back in your car. Do a one-eighty, drive all the way to the end, and take a left. There's an open grave. She's in there. Hurry, though. They're filling it in later today."

"You son of a bitch."

He raced back to the Chevy, throwing himself into the driver's seat. He stamped on the gas and wrenched hard on the wheel. The sedan went into a tire-squealing turn. The road was too narrow to keep the U-turn on the asphalt. The Malibu bumped over the curb and tore up the manicured lawn. Luckily, he managed the one-eighty without clipping a gravestone.

He raced the Chevy across the cemetery, blowing through every intersection. A crew of three landscapers yelled something at him as he raced by them. Something smacked off the rear windshield. He cast a look in his interior mirror. Whatever the object was, it had taken a chunk out of the glass, sending out a spiderweb of cracks in all directions.

He threw the car into a left turn. He whipped his head left and right, searching for an open grave. Then he saw a heap of dirt between the graves to his right.

He stamped on the brakes, and the Chevy came to a juddering and untidy halt. He leaped from the sedan, calling Grace's name. He lost his footing and crashed to all fours, then gathered himself up in the same instant. He yelled Grace's name again but didn't get a reply.

He reached the pile of dirt. A tarp covered the grave next to it. He tore the green plastic sheeting back, but only a gaping hole stared back at him. No Grace.

Confusion filled his mind.

Then the sound of squealing tires disturbed the cemetery's respectful quiet. He whipped his head around to see a minivan racing back to the street. It was the Shepherd. The son of a bitch had screwed him. He sent him here so he could grab the cash and bolt.

He cut across the graves back to the Chevy and snatched up the cell phone sitting in the foot well.

"Where is she?" he screamed into the phone, but the line was dead. "Son of a bitch."

He threw the sedan into another ugly one-eighty, again riding the curb and churning up grass and dirt. As he raced back to the street after the Shepherd, everyone in the cemetery, both visitors and workers, ran toward him to hurl abuse at him. He ignored it all. Catching the Shepherd was all that mattered.

Scott reached the cemetery entrance in time to see the Shepherd's minivan heading southbound. He threw the Malibu into traffic, sending one car into a skid.

The minivan was small in the distance and getting smaller as it stretched its lead. Scott had his foot planted on the gas pedal. The Chevy's engine screamed in pain as it carried him faster and faster.

Wherever the Shepherd was going, he was following. It didn't matter if the bastard kept to the surface roads or got on the freeway. He would catch him. He'd slam him off the road if need be, but he wasn't letting him get away again.

He glanced over at the cell on the seat next to him. It was useless. The Shepherd wouldn't be answering now. He could call Sheils—should call him—but there was no way while he had this car up to this ludicrous speed.

In the distance, the Shepherd's minivan turned left. Scott swore again. He could easily lose the kidnapper with the lead he had. A few quick turns, and the chase would be over.

"C'mon," he yelled, urging the Chevy to go faster.

He slammed on the brakes. The deceleration threw him against the steering wheel. There hadn't been time to bother with a seat belt. He overshot the turn but managed to make the corner by skidding into oncoming traffic.

The minivan was ahead. So was traffic. Not a lot, but enough to cause problems. It could slow the Shepherd down, which would be good for Scott, or it could slow Scott down, which would be good for the Shepherd. He activated his hazard lights and leaned on the horn to tell everyone to get the hell out of his way.

The Shepherd made another left, blowing through the light. Scott did the same with his hand still on the horn.

Now Scott was on a wide, four-lane residential street with bike lanes. He followed the Shepherd, weaving from one lane to another, crossing into oncoming traffic when there was no other option. The insane driving was worth it. He was reeling the minivan in. Not by much, but he was making inroads on the son of a bitch.

A compact van was dead ahead. Scott hit his horn and jerked the Chevy right to go around him. Just as he was about to pass, the van moved into his lane. Scott's speed almost beat the narrowing gap, but then the van clipped the driver's rear door and fender with a squeal of grinding metal.

Scott glanced in his mirror. The driver was screaming at him as he put increasing distance between him and the injured van. No time to stop and exchange details. The van driver would have to take this one on the chin.

"Sorry, pal," he said and kept going.

The road dead-ended at a T-junction. The Shepherd hung a right at the lights, causing a two-car crash when one rear-ended the other stopping for the kidnapper. Scott rode up and over the curb to get around the wreckage.

That fender bender gave the Shepherd an edge. Scott had been forced to slow more than he wanted, and he saw his advantage evaporate. He didn't lose hope. The road they were on now was a main artery leading into the heart of suburbia. Scott liked his chances. The Shepherd wouldn't risk getting stuck on some cul-de-sac. He'd blow through the housing development to get to a place with more options. Regardless of the distance between them, all Scott had to do was to stay in visual contact and whittle down the gap if he could.

The sound of distant sirens overwhelmed the scream of the Chevy's engine. It looked as if their car chase had attracted attention. That was just what Scott wanted. He had little game against the likes of the Shepherd, but the Shepherd had even less against a bunch of cops.

The road curved lazily to the right. Scott exited the bend to see the kidnapper's minivan only a hundred yards ahead with a seemingly never-ending straight road ahead. The siren wail behind him intensified. He glanced in his mirror to see five cop cars closing in on him.

"You're done, asshole. And you brought it on yourself."

Scott couldn't believe the Shepherd had been so dumb after being so smart. He didn't have to collect the ransom in person. He had other options, but the idiot had to be the showman. He had to rub Scott's nose in it by bringing him out to Nicholas Rooker's grave and watching his anguish. Of all things, bravado would bring the Shepherd down. What a moron.

Scott kept the pace up. On this long, straight road, the Chevy had the speed advantage over the Shepherd's minivan. He reeled the kidnapper in a yard at a time. Ninety yards. Eighty yards.

And he wasn't alone. The cops were reeling the Shepherd in, too. Scott had the Chevy up to 110 miles per hour, and the cops were now twenty yards off his bumper and closing.

One of the cop cars pulled alongside Scott. Scott waved a hand at the Shepherd's minivan in the distance.

"Driver, pull over," the cop's voice boomed over the car's bullhorn.

It was time to let the professionals take over. Scott took his foot of the gas. The Chevy dropped below the hundred-miles-an-hour mark within seconds.

The police cars didn't blow by him. No one was taking off after the Shepherd. Instead, they crowded around the rear of the Malibu as the lead car maintained its speed to stay ahead of him.

"No, no, no, what are you doing?"

Scott sped up so he was back alongside the lead car.

"Driver, pull over now. I won't ask again."

Scott powered down his window. Again, he pointed at the Shepherd's minivan. "That's the Shepherd. Get him."

To his credit, the cop in the lead car lowered his window.

"I'm Scott Fleetwood. That's the Shepherd kidnapper," he yelled, pointing again. "You need to stop him."

The cop shouted something back, but Scott couldn't hear a damn word he was saying over the roar of wind noise. He shook his head, guessing the cop could hear his voice about as well as he could the cop's.

The rear impact was short but effective. It shunted Scott forward in his seat, but the effect on the Chevy was far more profound. It lifted the sedan seemingly by a fraction of an inch, but that fraction was all that was required. The rear wheels took on a floaty sensation as they lost grip with the road surface. The rear end stepped out slowly to the right. Scott held the skid until the Malibu banged into the lead cop car. The impact bumped the sedan back around in the opposite direction. The spin wasn't so gentle. It gathered momentum and went into three-sixty after three-sixty. He worked feverishly at the wheel, trying to catch a spin that couldn't be caught.

Just as he thought the roller-coaster ride was coming to an end, the rear wheels hit the curb, sending the rear of the car into the air. When the wheels hit asphalt again, the car lurched across all four lanes of the road. It looked as if he'd end up flying off the road into a drainage ditch until one of the cops slammed into him broadside. Windows exploded, spitting safety glass all over him. He cracked his head off something hard. His vision disintegrated into white light for a moment. The Chevy Malibu came to an ugly stop at a cockeyed angle on the wrong side of the road.

Seconds later, cops surrounded him, guns drawn.

"You okay?" a cop at his driver's door barked.

"Yeah," Scott croaked.

"Then get out of the damn car. You're under arrest."

"The Shepherd. He's getting away."

The cop wrenched Scott's door open and dragged him out on the road. He hit the ground before two cops landed on him. His arms were whipped behind his back before he was cuffed. Someone was reading him his rights. He couldn't tell who under the wail of sirens.

"Do you understand your rights as I've read them to you?" a cop said.

"Yeah, just get the Shepherd. He's getting away."

"I suggest you exercise your right to remain silent and shut the hell up."

What's the point? Scott let his head drop to the warm asphalt. No one was going after the Shepherd. He'd gotten away again.

CHAPTER THIRTY-ONE

The text said: Change of plans. Call me.

It came in twenty minutes after Connors had collected the second ransom from Scott Fleetwood and lost him in the car chase. The thought of another script change unnerved him.

He wouldn't call until he got back to Grace. Elvis might like chopping and changing the rules; he didn't. He had a procedure to follow. He couldn't just pull over and make a call. He was in the middle of an exit strategy. He had to give Scott and the Feds the slip and get back to the Airbnb first before even considering making any calls. There was no celebrating until his position was locked down.

It was an hour before he was back with Grace. She was still asleep, tucked up with Derek the bunny. The sedative he'd put in her lunch ensured that she'd slept while he'd given Scott the runaround during the ransom drop. He stroked her hair. She stirred but didn't wake.

"Not long now, sweetie. You'll be home soon," he whispered.

Her release would be easy. He'd drop her somewhere safe, then call it in when he had a head start. He'd be on a train out of San Jose taking him south, then he'd catch a plane out of L.A. He'd take a number of flights using different IDs that would have him home the day after tomorrow.

To the sound of Grace's small breaths breaking the silence, he called Elvis. The phone rang and rang. For a moment, he thought the call was going to switch over to voice mail, but Elvis finally picked up.

"Got the money?" he asked.

"Yes. It all went very smoothly."

Both of them used voice changers. Connors saw that as a reflection of their working relationship. Neither of them trusted each other.

"Good. Did you get my text?"

"I did."

"I was a little worried there was a problem when you didn't call me back after I sent the text." Elvis backed up his fear with a nervous-sounding laugh.

"It wasn't convenient. What's the change? I'm prepping to release Gracie."

"That's the change."

"You want me to hold on to her and go for a third ransom? No way. The odds of pulling that off diminish every time I go to the well. The Feds aren't stupid."

"I don't want you to push for another ransom."

"I can't hold on to her any longer."

"I want you to kill her."

There needed to be a damn good reason for justifying a child's execution, and Connors didn't think there ever could be one. "Why?"

"You're right. We've pushed our luck. That backpacker exposed your hideout. Has the girl seen your face?"

"Yes," he admitted.

"You're blown, John. If you're compromised, the FBI has a direct road to me. I can't have that. The girl has to die."

Connors looked across at Grace, who was still sleeping. "I don't see what killing her achieves."

"It eliminates a vital witness."

"We've been paid. Twice."

"Money isn't worth anything if you can't spend it. Just kill her."

It was oh so simple to his client. It always was to someone a million miles away from the problems at hand. Everything was in the abstract. When a problem presented itself, the solution was simple—either navigate it or eliminate it. And decisions were always easy to make when you didn't have to carry them out yourself. Connors pictured Elvis in a room someplace with an image of Grace from the newspaper in front of him, drawing a big *X* across her face. He could pretty much guarantee Elvis had never killed, never had to take a life with his bare hands, never watched the life go out of a person up close. If he had, he wouldn't be asking what he was asking. He'd be seeking out any and all alternatives to cold-blooded murder. No, he was a button man, used to pressing a button to make problems go away.

"There are alternatives to this," he said.

"There aren't."

Are you that insistent on taking a life? Connors thought. "What if I say no?"

"Then you leave me no option."

Elvis didn't elaborate. It was obvious that he wanted to play games and have him ask.

"No option other than what?"

"Let me be clear. If you don't kill Grace, I will burn you. I know who you are—despite your alias game—and I know where you live. I will turn it all over to the Feds. You'll either be in custody or dead before the end of the business day."

Connors wondered how much of that was bullshit. Yeah, the FBI had unearthed his identity, but did they know where he lived or where he was now? He doubted it. He'd installed many firewalls—electronic and otherwise—between him and everyone he did business with to prevent anyone from tracking him down. He was confident no one had. Not that it was impossible for his anonymity to be breached.

Someone with the right skills could do it. Had Elvis hired someone with those skills?

"Have I made myself clear?"

"Yes."

"So you'll do it?"

"I'll call you when it's done," he said and hung up.

He wouldn't be calling because he had no intention of killing Grace. His association with his client was over. He went into Grace's room and gave her a gentle shake.

"Hey, Gracie, you up for an adventure?"

CHAPTER THIRTY-TWO

Sheils stood in the doorway to the holding cell with a Colma cop at his shoulder. "You look like shit."

Scott felt like it, too. He had a ringing headache to accompany the smack to the back of the head. His knees, chest, and back were bruised from the bouncing around he'd taken in the crash. A dozen or so nicks covered his face from where the safety glass had peppered him. A paramedic had checked him out at the scene and said he was well enough to go to jail. He thought about making some crack about police brutality, but judging from the scowl on the Colma cop's face, it wasn't the time.

"Has he released her?"

Sheils shook his head.

"Shit."

He didn't much care about what he'd endured over the last few hours as long as the Shepherd had released Grace.

"Have you heard from him?"

"No, but we'll talk outside."

"Am I free to go?"

The Colma PD might not have been all that enamored with Scott, but the feeling was mutual. They'd kept him for hours. He'd tried explaining the situation, but they were more interested in laying out the litany of charges he'd racked up, including grand theft auto. He regretted some of the things he'd said to the detectives during the heated interrogation. When it became obvious that trying to reason out what had happened and explain that the Shepherd was getting farther and farther away wasn't working, he invoked his constitutional right to say nothing and demand his phone call. He used it to call Sheils, and Sheils asked for the detective in charge. He didn't know what Sheils had said, as he had been put back in his holding cell until now.

"You're in my custody now," Sheils answered.

Custody didn't sound good. That meant charges were still pending.

Scott groaned when he stood. The headache and the bruising worked their magic against him in perfect harmony.

Sheils guided him through holding and back out to reception, all under the watchful eye of the scowling cop. He wasn't alone in his disapproval. Every officer eyed him with contempt. He got his possessions back after signing for them. Sheils threw a general thanks over his shoulder at whoever wanted to take it, and he held the door open for Scott.

Crossing the parking lot to his car, Sheils said, "You're persona non grata with these guys. I'd stay out of Colma for the time being."

That wasn't a problem for Scott. "You said I'm in your custody. Are charges still pending?"

"Yeah, but they'll be dropped. Bill Travillian is working on it. We aren't their flavor of the month, either. They're pissed that we didn't loop them in on the ransom drop."

"It wasn't like I knew I'd end up here."

"Forget them. The damage is done. Tell me what happened."

They got into Sheils's Crown Victoria, and he pointed the car north back to San Francisco. Sheils set up his phone to record the debriefing and told Scott to go. He laid out the events of the ransom drop, from driving through the city to the switched car to the drop at Nicholas Rooker's grave. He left nothing out. He shared his thoughts on the Shepherd's inability to kill after the conversation. They were down a lot of points against the kidnapper, and that felt the closest to a point in their favor.

"What I don't get is why he came to the ransom drop," Scott said.

"Because he had it covered. I have to give it to this prick. He's good. The switched car wasn't his. He stole it and set you up. After he picked up the money, he called 911, telling them his car had been stolen from the Holy Cross Cemetery. It was one of the few details we managed to get out of the Colma chief."

"Son of a bitch. Why bring me to the Rooker family plot?"

"Simple. To fuck with your head. Tell me it didn't throw you for a minute."

It had. He couldn't lie.

"It makes great theater, too. What other location could he have picked to beef up his image as the great kidnapper?"

It was true. Spectacle was becoming the Shepherd's thing. This moral crusade was sure as shit fading into the background. The true motivation of this mess had yet to be revealed.

Screw this guy, he thought. *Screw him and his bullshit games.* He thumped the dash. This whole thing was getting to him. He wanted Grace home and this bastard in jail.

"Take it easy," Sheils said.

"He's got his money. Twice now. Why hasn't he let Grace go?"

"I don't know. I don't understand why he's stringing this thing out. He could be going for a third ransom."

"A third? You've got to be shitting me."

"It's a possibility. I'm not counting anything out. My hope is that he's been waiting for your release. He wants to talk only to you, and he can't do that when you're behind bars."

"Great."

"You'll like this even less. We need the Shepherd to know you're out of jail. That's why I'm driving you to the *Independent* for a press conference."

He wanted to say, "Can't it wait?" But he knew it couldn't. It was for Grace's good and her family's sanity, if nothing else.

"How much do people know about today?"

"Not long after your apprehension, the incident made the news from a crime-and-traffic perspective. Then the news outlets got wind that you'd been arrested, and it forced us to make a statement that connected it with Grace's kidnapping."

That was another reason the Colma Police Department wasn't too happy with Scott. They were the cops who'd arrested the man who'd been trying to seek Grace Pagett's release while letting her kidnapper escape scot-free. Not a banner day for law enforcement. It wasn't a banner day for anyone. The FBI, in spite of all their resources, had failed again. And so had he. He was supposed to be the guy to get Grace back, and he'd blown it twice now.

His thoughts went to one person. "Does Jane know?"

"Yeah, she called when the news broke."

He sighed. She should have heard it from him first. He'd wanted to use his one call from jail to let her know he was okay. He'd also wanted to call her for more selfish reasons. He'd needed propping up, and she was the one person in the world who could do that. But that hadn't been an option. His needs had to wait. As did Jane's. As did his kids'. As did life itself. Finding Grace came first. Jane understood that, but he still felt he was failing her.

"I want to call her. Can I use your phone?"

"Sure. You'll find her number in my phone log."

He scrolled through the dozens of calls Sheils had taken over the last few hours until he found Jane's. He hit "Call," and she picked up after the first ring.

"It's me," he said.

"I wondered when I'd hear from my jailbird," she said with a smile in her voice.

It was just the response he needed. Only Jane could fix his broken day and dented spirit. It was like a piece of him was missing when she was away. A tear leaked out when he smiled. The salt in the tear singed the grazes on his face, but he didn't care.

"Yeah, Tom broke me out. He didn't even have to put a file in a cake to do it."

"Tell her I said you're welcome," Sheils said.

Scott relayed the message.

"How was jail?"

"Can't say I recommend it," he said, remembering the officer who had pushed him to the ground when they'd arrested him.

"At least you didn't spend the night there. I definitely don't recommend that."

A knowing tone had entered his wife's voice. "Is that the voice of experience talking?"

"Afraid so."

This was news to him. "You're telling me you spent a night in jail? How come I didn't know about this?"

"I don't tell you everything."

"Maybe you should."

"Another time."

She was right. He shouldn't be bantering with his wife at a moment like this.

"Sorry. I would have called earlier if I could."

"I know," she said, the levity gone from her voice. "You're okay, though? They said you were in a car wreck."

"I was. I'm a little banged up but okay."

"Any word on Grace?"

"No."

She exhaled down the line. It said everything that needed to be said.

"How are you and the boys?"

"Worried but fine. Let me put them on the phone."

They had questions about everything. He gave them answers as best he could. He'd hoped speaking to them would lift his spirits. Instead, it lowered them. It brought home the simple fact that he couldn't protect them. They were there, and he was here. He'd failed to do anything to bring Grace home. He was failing them. Jane took the phone back from them.

"I wish you could all come home," he said to her.

"Me, too. It won't be long."

He wished he had her confidence. "I'm going to the *Independent* for a press conference. Call you later?"

"Sure. And hang in there."

"Trying to."

He gave the phone back to Sheils.

"Your wife spent a night in the drunk tank after being brought in on a drunk and disorderly when she was eighteen," he said.

Scott looked at the FBI agent in surprise. "How do you know?"

"During the Piper investigation, we were just shooting the breeze. I was talking to her to keep her mind off the situation. It came up in conversation. You two need to talk more."

There was more humor in that last remark than anything else. It was nice that Sheils was warming up to him. It was amazing what humiliation and a high-speed wreck could do.

On the drive into the city, Sheils got a call from Thorpe, telling him to bring Scott through the back. As they approached the *Independent*'s building, it was easy to see why. Arc lights lit up the front of the building. News trucks occupied the street as they had on previous occasions, but this time around, a significant number of people also packed the sidewalk. SFPD officers did their best to keep everyone contained. Thorpe was at the rear entrance, ready to welcome them inside.

"We'll start the press conference whenever you're ready. I've not promised anyone a specific time, so we're not on the clock."

Aren't we? Scott thought. He'd told Thorpe he wanted to go on as soon as possible.

"You need a new shirt. That one's torn to shit."

Thorpe was right. Scott hadn't noticed himself, but his shirt was ripped in the front and across his back, not to mention the tiny pulls and tears peppering it. He guessed he'd picked up most of them during his apprehension rather than the crash.

Thorpe took Sheils and Scott up to the conference room. Brian and Emily Pagett were there. Emily put a hand to her mouth when she saw him.

"I'm so sorry," he said. "I did everything he asked."

"We know, mate," Pagett said. "You don't have to explain."

His words lost their strength as he said them. The man was breaking before them.

"This isn't over yet," Sheils said. "The Shepherd isn't done yet."

Thorpe left and returned with a fresh polo shirt still in its packaging.

Scott pulled off his shirt and Emily gasped. His bruises had moved into the glory stage, a mix of reds and purples.

"It's not as bad as it looks," he lied. Now that the adrenaline had burned off, his body was stiffening up, his bruises throbbed, and someone was ringing an alarm bell in his head.

He pulled on the shirt. The feel of a clean, new shirt felt good against his skin.

"Your face, Scott," Emily said. "I can apply some makeup to cover things up."

"No, people should see him raw," Thorpe said. "It'll play better with the audience."

As much as Scott wanted to, he couldn't fault Thorpe's logic. They needed sympathy on the Pagetts' side. How many times had public opinion swung in cases like this? At the beginning, the public was on the side of the parents, but when things dragged out, it changed. Doubts crept into people's minds. Blame got apportioned. Or even worse, interest turned into apathy. Once people lost interest, then it was over. Cases died, taking the victims down with them.

"You ready, Scott?" Thorpe asked.

He nodded.

On the way down to the lobby—which was fast becoming the *Independent*'s de facto TV studio these days—Thorpe coached the Pagetts, Sheils, and Scott on how the press conference would play out. Scott didn't need coaching. He knew exactly what he was going to say.

In the lobby, a flurry of voices greeted them as they took their seats on the dais. Thorpe calmed everyone down and started the press conference. He introduced himself, then everyone else, before explaining that a second ransom payment had been made to the Shepherd, but Grace remained in his custody. The reporters hit him with a barrage of questions. He swatted them down with a single sentence.

"I'd like to turn the proceedings over to Scott Fleetwood, who will comment on today's events."

This was the reason everyone was here. They wanted all the juicy details of his encounter with the Shepherd. But this was also what the Shepherd wanted. Scott wasn't about to give it to him.

"I'd like to address my comments to the Shepherd directly, because I know he's watching." Scott stared down the barrel of the TV camera in front of him. "You've been paid your second ransom, and I followed your rules. Law enforcement kept their distance. You received your payment unmolested. Now let Grace go. You've got no reason to keep her from her family any longer. Drop her off at any fire department, school, restaurant, store, or wherever. It doesn't matter. Just do it. It's time to end this. That's all I've got to say. Thank you."

Scott got to his feet and walked behind everyone to get off the dais. A fresh barrage of questions chased after him.

On the way by, Thorpe caught his arm. "Well done. That was journalism gold."

CHAPTER THIRTY-THREE

Brannon parked his FBI-issued car in Scott's driveway. It wasn't even 8:00 p.m. Scott couldn't believe it had only been five hours since he'd left the house with the ransom. It seemed like days ago. Scott handed his house keys over to Brannon. The FBI agent let himself into Scott's home for the obligatory sweep while he waited on the stoop. It would be nice to come home and not have law enforcement check for boogeymen hiding under the bed. After a couple of minutes, Brannon appeared back on the threshold with the all clear.

It would also be nice to come home to his wife and kids. The house felt a couple of degrees cooler without their presence. It didn't smell the same, either. The air went stale without their chatter to keep it circulating. Scott didn't know if he was imagining it or not, but he was no less depressed.

"I want to call Jane and the kids."

"No problem," Brannon said. "You're off the clock."

I'm not, or my family would be here, he thought. "Make yourself at home."

He went upstairs to his bedroom and called Jane's number on the cell. He fell back on the bed, and the phone rang. Jane answered before the fatigue could hit him.

"How'd it go?" she asked.

"Okay, I guess."

"You don't sound sure."

"I'm not. I paid him again, but still no Grace. Not yet, anyway."

"He's gotten everything he asked for. What more does he want?"

That was a good question. "I'm convinced he's working alone. He can't give me the runaround and handle her at the same time, so he needs time to get back to where he's holding her to release her."

"That sounds like a fairy tale you're telling yourself to stay sane."

It was. He was the plaything in this pantomime. "Can we talk about something else?"

Jane's tone softened. "Sure."

"How are the boys?"

"Good. We went out to—"

"Don't say where. I can't know."

"This has gotten old fast."

"I know. I'm sorry."

"I want to come home."

"I want you to. The boys are good, though?"

"Yeah. They're getting to miss school, so it's a win in their eyes. They're having fun, but they're worried. They want to know you're okay."

He palmed away a tear. "They around?"

"Outside. Playing. Want me to put them on?"

"Yeah."

Jane put the boys on. It was funny listening to their rapid-fire chatter as they talked over each other. Despite being twins and essentially looking the same, he could tell them apart by their voices. They had their own particular vocal tells. His boys were growing up. More tears slipped out.

Jane finally wrestled the phone away from them and came back on the line. "Are you sure you want that noise back in your life?"

He laughed. "Always."

251

"I need these two to clean themselves up, so I can get them some dinner."

"Okay. Love you."

"Love you, too. Call me later."

"I will."

She hung up on him, and he tossed the phone aside. He jumped in the shower to wash the stink of fear off himself. He toweled off and trotted down the stairs back to Brannon. The FBI agent had ESPN blaring by the sound of it.

He cut through the hallway into the kitchen and tugged open the refrigerator door.

"Shawn, I was thinking of pulling dinner together. I can go the full caveman and throw some steaks on the grill, or do a stir-fry with vegetables and tofu if you're feeling adventurous. Gotta cut down our dependency on red meat."

Brannon didn't answer.

Scott put his head through the doorway to the living room. "I said . . ."

His words shriveled up in his throat. An unconscious Brannon lay in the middle of the floor with his hands cuffed behind him and his ankles bound together with a thick plastic tie. Standing over him stood a black-clad figure in a ski mask with a gun in his hand.

Scott lunged for the kitchen stool. The figure raised the pistol. Scott froze.

"I'm not here to hurt you, Scott."

The voice was unmistakable. It was the Shepherd's.

"Then you don't need the gun."

The Shepherd looked down at it. "I do for the moment. Is there somewhere we can stash this guy? We need to talk."

Scott considered the situation. He had little in the weapons department close at hand. Going for the Shepherd and the gun wasn't an option, either. He'd be dead before he made it across the room. A

911 call wasn't going to help. He could bolt, but he wouldn't get far. Only one option presented itself to him.

"We can put him in the garage."

"Don't like that. He could raise the alarm. Pick again."

That hadn't even occurred to him. "My office upstairs. It has a window, but nothing else."

"Grab his feet, and lead the way."

Scott did as he was told. His gaze went to the Shepherd's gun as he jammed it into his waistband at the small of his back.

"Don't get any ideas, Scott. I don't need a firearm to kill you."

They lifted Brannon off the floor. Scott had it easy with the FBI agent's feet. The Shepherd shouldered most of the man's weight by lifting him under his arms. But dragging Brannon up the stairs was harder for Scott, while the Shepherd seemed to deal with his burden with ease. That was all the indication he needed that the Shepherd would have the upper hand in any fight.

They deposited Brannon in Scott's office. Scott stood there while the Shepherd hog-tied the FBI agent's feet and hands together. He looped a length of cord between the cuffs and plastic tie and cinched it tight, drawing Brannon into a back-breaking pose and tying an elaborate knot to hold him in place.

The Shepherd pulled out a small hypodermic and jammed it into Brannon's neck. "That'll ensure he doesn't give us any trouble while we talk in private."

Retrieving his gun from his waistband, the Shepherd ushered Scott out of the room and closed the door. Scott led the way down the stairs into the living room.

"Sit there," the Shepherd said and pointed at the armchair with its back to the window.

Scott sat, and the Shepherd sat in the armchair opposite with just the coffee table between them. Scott noticed the Shepherd had chosen to face the street. The man didn't want anyone creeping up on him.

The Shepherd settled back in the chair, letting the cushions take the strain. He rested his gun hand on the chair's arm. The weapon was lazily trained on Scott.

"What do you want?" Scott asked.

"To explain."

Something was wrong. The Shepherd was all about the big production. His coming out of the shadows to talk to him didn't make sense.

"I need your help," the Shepherd said.

"Haven't I helped you enough?"

"I'm not who you think I am."

"You're the Shepherd. You're a household name. Am I wrong?"

"It's all a fiction."

"It is?"

The Shepherd reached behind his head and pulled the ski mask off. The kidnapper was a few years younger than himself, late thirties. He was good-looking with a strong jawline, although the buzz cut hardened his features. He looked tired. It was good to see he was being run ragged, just like the rest of them.

The Shepherd rubbed a hand over his cropped hair. "I'm a hired gun. I was paid to kidnap a child, any child, then phone the *Independent* and ask for you."

Scott seized on the revelation. *Is the Shepherd bullshitting me? Is this just another wrench dropped in the machinery to throw everyone off?* He wanted to believe the answers were yes to those questions. Those were more palatable truths to believe. Grace's kidnapping being part of someone's game other than the Shepherd's was far harder to stomach. Why draw him into this? For what purpose? The Piper sprang to mind, but it couldn't be anything to do with him or anyone else involved with him. Everyone was dead.

"Who hired you?"

"I don't know."

"What do you mean you don't know? How can you not know?"

"I don't know his name—he calls himself Elvis. He doesn't know my name, either. He knows me as John. It's that kind of business."

"What business—the abduction business?"

The Shepherd's hand tightened on the pistol. "I'm not a bad man. I don't hurt people. I protect them."

This man had kidnapped a child and God knew what else. It was clearly a delusion he told himself to soothe his conscience. "What is it you do?"

"Troubleshooting."

That was a nice meaningless term. "For corporations?"

"Sometimes. Sometimes not."

More meaningless answers. "How do people find you?"

"These days, the dark net."

Scott could only imagine the kind of clientele the Shepherd found there. "Is this the first time you've worked for Elvis?"

"No, I've done a few jobs for him over the last couple of years."

"Have they involved abductions before?"

"No." The Shepherd spat the word as if it had been poisoned. "It's been straightforward stuff in the past. Steal files. Get information out of someone. Pay someone off. Basic shit like that. Never kidnap a child. I said no at first. I didn't want anything to do with it, and he said he'd get someone else to do it. I know the other people out there. They would not have looked after Gracie as well as I have."

Scott thought about the charred wooden box he'd seen at Nitro Park. It had hardly been the Ritz.

"So Grace is safe?"

"Yeah, I'd do nothing to hurt her."

"Is somebody with her now?"

The Shepherd was slow to answer. "She's an independent girl. She's fine."

So she was alone. It confirmed everyone's suspicion that the Shepherd was working solo. There might be someone else calling the shots, but he wasn't playing an active role. It was all good intel for Sheils.

One question remained now. It was the one that came to mind the moment he'd seen the Shepherd in his living room. "Why are you here?"

The Shepherd shifted in his seat. He looked down at the weapon in his hand. He pocketed it. If that was supposed to be a sign of good faith, Scott took it at face value. The man had skills. If Scott tried anything, the kidnapper would break his neck without losing breath.

"The assignment has changed again."

"Again?"

"My assignment was just to pull you into a simple kidnap and ransom. Then Elvis told me to hold on to Gracie and draw it out. Now he wants me to kill her."

"Christ. Why?"

"I think he knows he's overplayed his hand, and it's time to destroy anything that could come back to incriminate him."

"You know that means you have a target on your back, too."

"I realize that. That's why I'm here."

"Who's Elvis trying to hurt? Does he know the Pagetts? Is it me? Is he trying to punish me?"

His own questions took him by surprise. They had come from his subconscious, slipping out without thought. Had he been drawn into this so he could be punished for Nicholas Rooker's death? It hadn't been his fault. It was just a mistake. A mistake he had to live with every day of his life. Killing Grace did what—acted as a reminder? Who the hell was behind this?

"I don't know."

The Shepherd barked the answer at Scott. It shook him from his thoughts.

"You don't have to do it. You're running this show. You've got your money. You can drop Grace at any street corner and disappear into the night. The Feds would never catch up to you."

The Shepherd was already shaking his head. "That's not good enough. I'm done with this asshole. I want to serve him up to the FBI. I want to make a deal with Sheils. I'll deliver my client as long as I'm allowed to slip away in the exchange."

Scott couldn't see Sheils going for it, but for Grace's sake, he couldn't say that. He had to make the Shepherd believe anything was possible.

"I'll get him on the phone." Scott reached for his cell. "I can get him here in minutes, and we can thrash this thing out."

"No. We do this on my terms. You tell him my offer. If he's interested, you call me." The Shepherd pulled a cell phone from his pocket and tossed it to Scott. "Now it's time I go. Stand up."

"What?"

"Stand up, and turn around. You know what I have to do."

Scott didn't, but he turned around all the same.

"I need a head start. I apologize. This won't be pleasant."

Scott whipped around, but it was too late. The Shepherd was on him. The kidnapper's arm snaked around his neck. He tried to shake the man off, but the Shepherd was far too proficient. Within seconds, he was immobile in the stronger man's grasp. The pressure on the sides of his neck was incredible. The sound of his heart pounding in his ears roared. Dizziness swept over him from his scalp on down.

"Just let it happen, Scott. Just play your role. Make this happen."

CHAPTER THIRTY-FOUR

S cott came to and checked his watch. He'd been out a couple of minutes. Three at most. He jumped up and regretted it instantly. A wave of dizziness washed over him, and he slumped against the sofa for support while it passed.

He peered out the window. However the Shepherd had arrived, there was no sign of him now.

He called Sheils, then checked on Brannon. The FBI agent was still out. Scott cut the plastic ties off Brannon and uncuffed him using keys he found in the agent's pocket.

Brannon was coming around as Sheils arrived. To his credit, he'd kept the response low-key, just a couple of agents and himself. The agents bundled Brannon into their car and drove him off to an ER. Scott found himself sitting in the same chair but this time opposite Sheils.

"What happened?"

"We came home. Shawn cleared the house, but the Shepherd had hidden himself in the yard next door. He moved in and he jumped Shawn."

"Did you catch him in the act? Was he trying to leave another proof of life?"

Scott shook his head. "He had a far more important message. He showed me his face. He wants to make a deal."

"A deal? What kind of deal?"

"He says he was hired to kidnap a kid and pull me into it. Now his client wants him to kill Grace. He'll serve up his client as long as you let him slip away."

"He's got some stones on him. I'll give him that. Did he say who his client is?"

"He doesn't know. He deals anonymously with him."

Sheils jumped to his feet. He paced between the kitchen and the living room, shaking his head. "There's no way I can let him walk. He kidnapped a kid. He has to be out of his head to think I can get a sign-off like that."

Scott understood that. Sheils had the law and his oath to uphold, but a little girl was still out there. He believed the Shepherd when he'd said he wouldn't harm Grace, but if it turned into some firefight to take him down, she could be collateral damage. Grace had to come first, and Scott couldn't let Sheils forget that.

"He just has to believe you'll let him walk."

"He'll want paperwork to back it up if he's smart. Answer me this. Do you believe this line about an evil client telling him to kill, or do you think it's a line of bullshit that's the next phase of his game?"

That was a good question. Scott had believed the Shepherd. He couldn't see what was in it for him by doing what he'd just done. He held all the cards. He had the ransoms. He had Grace. Sheils was no closer to capturing him. He could ditch or kill Grace and disappear without any fear of capture, unless there was more to it all than just the kidnapping. He believed the Shepherd, but the fear he was preparing to drop a bombshell ate away at that belief. Scott hoped to God he was reading the Shepherd right.

"I believe him."

"You believed Redfern."

Bringing up the superfan who pretended to be the Piper all those years ago was a low blow, but not unfair. He had believed Redfern, and it had gotten Nicholas Rooker killed.

"The circumstances are different. I'm a little less inclined to believe."

"Willing to bet Grace Pagett's life on it?"

"I am. Not that we have much of a choice either way."

"What makes you believe him?"

"He let me see his face."

That stopped Sheils. After a moment, the FBI agent pulled out his cell phone. He tapped away at it for a second, then slid it across the coffee table to Scott. "Is this the guy?"

Scott took the phone and looked at the photo. "The hair is different—cropped and bleached—but it's him. Who is he?"

"Gavin Connors. He's former military. He was part of a unit known as the Shepherds because they protected dignitaries. We narrowed it down to Connors as the man who had ceased to exist since leaving the army."

"You could have told me."

"I am."

Now, Scott thought. What else had Sheils kept from him? He had to concede their partnership would always be a limited one. Sheils's allegiance would always be to the FBI. With that thought, Scott's irritation subsided.

So Sheils had been keeping him in the dark about developments. Not surprising. He should have known Sheils wouldn't clue him in on every facet of the investigation. Scott slid Sheils's cell back to him along with the one the Shepherd had given to him.

"What's that?"

"The phone he gave me to discuss the deal."

Sheils picked it up.

"Do you want to call him, or should I?"

• • •

Scott dialed the single number stored in the cell's Contacts directory. The Shepherd answered. Scott switched the phone over to speaker and placed it on the coffee table between Sheils and himself.

"I have Agent Sheils with me."

"Hello, Mr. Connors. How would you like me to address you?"

The kidnapper didn't respond. Scott bet he wouldn't have been expecting that. He thought Sheils was taking a big risk to come out swinging by revealing he knew the Shepherd's identity. It had the potential to scare him off, but he saw the value of Sheils's move. It underlined the fact that the FBI was onto him, and he was on rocky ground.

"Gavin is fine. So you worked out who I am," the kidnapper said with a note of admiration in his voice.

"The Shepherd thing worked against you. It led us back to your unit."

"It looks as if I revealed a little too much of myself. Are you okay with my terms?"

"I think we've got a lot to discuss before I can agree to anything."

A girl giggled in the background. Scott and Sheils looked at each other.

"Is that Grace?" Scott asked.

"Yes."

"Could I speak to her? It would mean a lot to her family."

"Sure," Connors said. "Hon, I've got a couple of friends of your mom and dad with me. Come and say hi."

A moment later, a girl said hello in a funny little English accent. It was the most wonderful sound Scott had ever heard. Finally, he could tell the Pagetts their little girl was safe.

"Hi, Grace. I'm Scott. I'm a friend of your mom and dad's."

"Are they with you?"

They weren't. Scott and Sheils were operating off book at the moment. No one knew about this call. No one was monitoring it. Not that there was much point. Connors had proved time and time again he could disguise his digital footprint. Sheils had gotten Scott to record the call on a digital recorder. Scott saw that it doubled as their protection. If anything went sideways, they had something showing they weren't being entirely reckless with the law and Grace's life.

"No, sweetie. They're not here at the moment, but I'll tell them we talked."

"Oh," Grace said, sounding disappointed.

"Grace, this is Tom. I'm a buddy of your mom and dad's, too. They wanted to know how you're doing. You're not hurt or anything?"

"We're out of Jaffa Cakes. Can you get some?"

That told Scott the girl was more than fine. "I'll find you some."

"Brilliant."

"Okay, hon, go play. I need to talk to my friends," Connors said.

"Bye!" she yelled.

"You've got your proof of life. She's doing well," Connors said. "Now let's finish this thing."

"Totally," Sheils said. "I need you to come in so we can square this away."

"Don't game me, Sheils. I thought you were better than that. You aren't calling the shots on this. I am."

Scott's stomach tightened. They were close to pulling this off as long as Sheils didn't spook this guy. "Okay, how are we supposed to do this thing?"

"You meet me."

"When?"

"Now."

"Where?" Sheils asked.

"The end of the Aquatic Park Pier. Next to Fort Mason. It should make for a cozy chat. You're close to bringing this home, so don't do anything stupid to fuck it up," he said and hung up.

The hurry-up play was smart. Sheils couldn't muster much of an FBI response in the half hour it would take them to meet Connors at the Aquatic Park Pier. But the pier was a poor choice of meeting places. It was a dead end. Connors had pinned himself in.

"Let's go," Sheils said.

Scott grabbed Connors's cell and followed Sheils out the door. They jumped into Sheils's bureau Crown Victoria.

"You calling this in?" Scott asked.

"I want to, but I'm not. I want to pitch him first."

"Pitch him what?"

"The idea of surrendering himself as part of the deal."

Scott doubted Connors would go for it and kept the thought to himself. Letting the kidnapper think he dictated the terms was their best chance of getting Grace back. If Sheils played by FBI rules, that chance was gone.

Sheils cut across the city. The nighttime traffic was thick but moved swiftly.

Along the way, the FBI agent issued instructions. Don't improvise. Don't antagonize. Don't promise anything. And stay down if a firefight breaks out. The last instruction was a queasy reminder that they were going into a gunfight with the power of tact and little else behind them.

Van Ness dead-ended into the pier. Sheils didn't bother to find parking. He just parked in front of the bollards lining the front of the pier.

Climbing from the car, Sheils said, "Don't run. There are people here. I don't want anyone spooked."

It was late enough that most tourists had dispersed for the night, but many still took in the sight of the Golden Gate Bridge. Scott estimated more than a dozen people dotted the length of the curving pier. As they walked to the end of it, no one took much notice of them.

"I don't see him," Scott said.

"He'll be waiting for us to arrive before showing himself, to make sure I haven't brought anyone."

Scott glanced skyward for Connors's drone but didn't see or hear it.

He pulled out the cell and texted: We're here. Where are you?

A moment later, the phone rang.

"Are you at the end of the pier?" Connors asked.

"Just walking up on it."

"I see you. Just keep walking. Stay on the line. Tell Sheils to keep away from his service weapon. He's got nothing to fear from me."

Scott glanced down at Sheils's right hand. He kept it close to his pistol on his hip. It made for an awkward gait.

"What's he say?"

"He says keep your hand away from your gun."

"He's got eyes on us?"

"Apparently."

Sheils dropped his hand. "Goddamn it."

Scott felt for Sheils. It couldn't be easy for the FBI agent to play by someone else's rules. *Welcome to my world*, he thought.

They reached the end of the pier. Scott turned around and leaned against the concrete barrier.

"Okay, we're here. Come join us," he said into the phone.

"Turn around."

As he did, a spotlight hit them in the face from a cabin boat around fifty yards from the pier's end. The boat was small, twenty-five feet or so, and nothing fancy. It blended in with the boats you'd commonly see out in the bay. He made out a figure waving, standing off the stern.

Scott had to admire Connors. He really knew how to color outside the lines. If Sheils had called in the cavalry, the water was the best place for a getaway.

"Now you see me," Connors said. "Tell Sheils to toss his weapon in the water."

"He wants you to ditch the weapon."

"No way. I'm not risking a government-issued firearm falling into someone else's hands."

"You know he can't do that."

Connors was silent for a second. "Okay, he keeps the gun, but he gives you all the rounds. Remember, I'm watching."

"He says—"

"I heard."

Sheils ejected the magazine from the automatic and handed it over to Scott with the two spares he carried. Scott had never handled weapons, and just stuffing the magazines into his pockets felt alien to him.

"Okay, done. Now what?"

"You come to me."

"You're going to have to come a little closer."

"I think you can swim it."

"Goddamn it. See you in a minute." Scott pocketed the phone. "Time to ruin that suit of yours. We're swimming for it."

Scott thought he caught a smile from Sheils as they clambered over the barrier and jumped. If Connors had wanted to keep everything on the down low, he'd blown it when he and Sheils hit the water. The sound drew everyone on the pier to marvel at their stupidity.

They swam toward the boat to cheers and insults from the small crowd.

The impromptu swim wasn't for effect but for purpose. The water would take care of any nonwaterproof tracking devices. At least Connors hadn't had them strip like he had with Scott on Baker Beach.

Trust was still an issue, and that worried Scott. He and Sheils were making all the concessions. Connors had to do some quid pro quo at some point.

They finally reached the boat. The swim had winded Scott. Fifty yards in open water was about his limit, although it didn't seem to bother Sheils much.

"One person aboard at a time, please," Connors said. "Scott first."

Yep, no trust, Scott thought.

He helped pull Scott aboard. The second he was on the boat, he retreated into the cabin and retrieved a gun. He pointed it at Scott.

"Now you, Sheils, and don't be dumb."

Scott helped Sheils aboard to a cheer from their fans on the pier. He acknowledged with a wave. Anything for appearances.

"Gun, please. You'll get it back when we've concluded our business."

Sheils didn't argue, instead removing the weapon from the holster and placing it in the dry bag Connors held out. Scott dropped the magazines into it, glad to be free of them. The kidnapper sealed the bag, which was tied to a line on the side of the boat, and tossed it overboard.

Next, Connors subjected them to a pat down. Sheils, staying true to his "don't antagonize" instruction, didn't object. The kidnapper tossed them a blanket each and told them to sit on the bench seat by the outboard motor. They did as they were told, and Connors hit the throttle and pointed the boat out into the bay. He positioned himself sideways to the controls so he could steer the boat and keep the gun trained on them.

"As a sign of good faith, any chance you can put the gun away?" Sheils said. "We've done everything you've asked, and none of my people know I'm here."

"Okay."

As Connors ejected the magazine from the pistol and placed both pieces in a storage cubby, Scott stared at the entrance leading to a small berth. Connors caught him looking.

"She's not in there," he said.

"Where is she?"

"Safe."

"You're working alone," Sheils said. "How sure of that are you?"

"Very. She's secure." Connors cut the engine and let the boat drift. "You ready to deal?"

CHAPTER THIRTY-FIVE

Sheils quizzed Connors on his client, Elvis. He had the kidnapper lay out his contact with his boss from the first time to when he'd told him to kill Grace.

"Did he give a reason why Grace has to die?" Sheils asked.

"He said Grace was a liability."

"You've never met your client?"

Connors shook his head. It was a shining example of technology's capabilities. Crimes could be assigned, executed, and paid for without any physical contact.

"But your guy says he'll expose you if you don't kill Grace," Scott said. "How's that possible if you've hidden your digital tracks?"

Connors looked grave. "I don't know. It could be bullshit. Something to scare me into doing this."

Scott felt Connors was holding something back. It was there in the man's expression. He was working the permutations.

"What else?"

"He could have hired someone to dig into you to unearth your identity," Sheils said.

Connors nodded. "I can cover my tracks, but I'm no genius at it. No digital footprint is completely invisible. Someone could track me down."

Scott guessed some paranoia was talking, but no wonder. Everything Connors did was potentially life ending.

"How long before he expects you to follow through on his instruction?" Sheils asked.

"He didn't say, but twenty-four hours. Thirty-six at the most."

"Tell him you did it," Scott said. "It'll get him off your back. It'll reset the clock and give us more time."

Connors nodded. "He'll want proof, though."

"And that's how we'll take him down," Sheils said. "You tell him you've killed Grace. He'll do one of two things—pat you on the head and disappear into the shadows, or he'll burn you and disappear into the shadows. He wants proof of death? Let's have you give it to him in person."

"I think we've got our plan," Scott said. "When do we call?"

"Now," Sheils said.

• • •

Scott felt a million miles from the world on the boat. The San Francisco cityscape glowed in the night, but it was silent. For all its energy, it couldn't reach across the water to connect them to its presence. It seemed fitting, considering the stunt they were about to pull.

Sheils gave Connors the go-ahead, and he punched in the number.

Scott hoped to God this worked.

All three of them huddled around the phone as it rang.

"It's done," Connors said when his client answered.

Elvis was silent for a few seconds. "You surprised me. I didn't think you'd do it so quickly."

Like Connors, Elvis used a voice changer that made him sound like a digitized Barry White.

"You made it pretty damn obvious I didn't have much of a choice in the matter."

"I did at that."

This was all dynamite stuff, but there was no record of it. It was the problem with this whole meeting. Connors had ruined everything electronic Scott and Sheils had with them. It was what had to be done to win the kidnapper over, but it left them ill equipped. It had to be killing Sheils.

"How did you do it?"

"Oversedated her."

"Must have been peaceful."

"There's nothing peaceful about someone dying. You'd know that if you'd ever seen it happen," Connors barked.

That wasn't acting. Something had happened to this guy. It probably explained why he did what he did for a living. Scott glanced over at Sheils. The FBI agent made eye contact for a second before focusing on Connors.

"Can I see her?"

Scott shifted in his seat. This was it. It was all on Connors to sell the plan. Sheils had coached the kidnapper, then hammered him with mock calls for more than an hour before giving him the green light to call. Everything hinged on Connors to sucker his client in.

"Sure. I'll give you a location."

"A picture will do."

"No, it doesn't work that way. Not for this."

"It doesn't?"

The voice changer did little to hide Elvis's smugness. Scott wanted to reach down the phone and throttle the asshole.

"No. This was supposed to be a simple kidnapping and ransom. Your words. I should have been in and out in forty-eight hours.

Instead, you've strung it out, exposing me to unnecessary risk. I don't kill people. Especially not kids."

"But you did."

"Yeah, and it's going haunt me for the rest of my life. That's why if you want to see your prize, you can do it in person. I'll even toss in a bonus. You can help bury her."

"I don't want her buried. I want her delivered."

"What?"

"I want her body left at the doors of the *Independent*."

Grace was alive. They were talking in hypotheticals, but it sickened Scott. One question continued to be at the forefront of his mind ever since Sheils had come to his door, requesting his help. *Why? Why is Elvis doing this? Why did he draw me into this? Why murder an innocent child? Why this unnecessary act of cruelty? What is the point of any of this?*

Sheils urged Connors to keep going with a hand gesture.

"That's pretty cold," Connors said.

Elvis laughed. "I'll take that as a compliment."

"I'm not doing that. If you want her body dumped at the doors of the *Independent*, you do it. It's about time you did your own dirty work."

"Remember who is calling the shots. I tell you—"

"You don't tell me anything. We're done. You can make all the threats you want. I'm out. Trust me, after this call, I'm gone. Now, do you want her body or not?"

Scott decided Connors was a cool customer. He was forcing Elvis to a make-or-break decision, and there wasn't a bead of sweat on the man's forehead.

"When and where?"

Sheils made a stretching gesture with his hands and mouthed the words, "Tomorrow."

"I'll call an hour before the meet with a location. So be ready to leave at any time. And bring a hundred grand goodbye money. You owe me."

Sheils gave Connors the thumbs-up.

"I look forward to meeting you, John," Elvis said and hung up.

Scott's shoulders sagged. "Christ, that was intense."

Sheils shook Connors's hand. "Good work. I think you've got him on the hook."

"I do, too," Connors said.

Connors went to take his hand away, but Sheils maintained his grip. Scott didn't like where this was going.

"Everybody getting what they want is dependent on you," Sheils said. "It all comes down to whether I can trust you. Can I trust you, Gavin?"

Connors's expression remained stoic. There wasn't a hint of shame or embarrassment. He met Sheils's gaze pound for pound. Scott felt he was ringside at a heavyweight boxing match.

"You can trust me."

"I'm taking you at your word. I know you're a military man. Can I rely on your honor as a soldier that we are a team?"

"Yes."

Sheils released Connors's hand.

Scott exhaled. "Now that's out of the way, where do we want this thing to happen?"

Connors retreated to the boat's wheel and rested a hand on it. "Somewhere public. I don't want him trying anything."

Sheils dropped into the seat next to Scott. "No way. I'm not getting into a potential gun battle with the public around. It has to be isolated. Somewhere I can control the environment."

As Sheils and Connors bickered over the terms, Scott mentally combed the Bay Area for a safe meeting place. He smiled when the perfect spot came to him.

"I got it. Candlestick Park. The place is a construction site now. It's a massive open space, close to the water. There are what—three, four roads that feed into it? Tomorrow being Sunday, nobody's going to be on site. It's perfect."

Sheils looked at Connors. The kidnapper nodded.

"Okay, tell Elvis to meet you at Candlestick at ten a.m.," Sheils said. "Now, communications. How do we stay in contact with each other?"

"Give me a number where I can reach you," Connors said. "I'll call you."

Scott thought that was a smart play on Connors's part. Not giving his number out meant Sheils had nothing for a trace until the very last minute. Sheils didn't balk at the request. It was a small concession to make.

Connors fired up the outboard. "I'll take you guys back."

Sheils joined him at the wheel. "Come in with me. I can protect you. Grace can go back to her family. My people can button up the situation and take this prick down without any fuss."

The kidnapper was already shaking his head. "That's not the agreement."

"Think about it, man. There are too many moving parts for you to do this alone."

"I've got you two."

"Still too many parts."

Connors jammed a forearm under Sheils's jaw and slammed him into the side of the boat, pinning him. The FBI agent fought against the kidnapper's hold.

"I thought I could trust you. If I can't, once you go over the side, you'll never see me again."

Scott lunged across the deck and grabbed Connors's shoulder to pry him off Sheils. The kidnapper fixed him with an angry stare.

"Be cool. He's doing his job. You and I don't have to play by the rules. He does. Cut him some slack. We all want the same thing."

Scott's words got through, and Connors dropped his arm. Sheils shoved the kidnapper away and slumped into a seat.

"I'm not going down for this."

"Do it my way, and you won't," Sheils said. "You know it makes sense."

Connors retook the wheel and jammed the throttle forward.

Scott fell in at the kidnapper's side. He grabbed the rail for support as the small boat bounced over the water.

Connors looked at him with disdain. "Don't you start."

Sheils's approach had been far too pragmatic. Connors needed romancing. Scott needed to appeal to the man's soul.

"I wasn't going to. You know he's right, though. We're going to get one shot at this. We'd be better off with backup than without it."

"No." The answer was as unforgiving as a gunshot.

"What if Tom got you your immunity paperwork first? Then everyone works together, and you walk away the second this jerk's in custody."

"Sit down before you fall down."

Scott guessed they were doing this the hard way and fell into a seat next to Sheils. He gave the agent an "I tried my best" shrug.

It wasn't long before the boat was barreling toward Aquatic Park Pier. Connors eased back on the power. This time Scott and Sheils didn't have to swim for it. Connors eased the boat alongside the pier as best he could.

True to his word, Connors returned Sheils's service weapon back to him and helped give them a boost onto the pier. Both men scaled the concrete barrier. Relief at being back on dry land and alive swept over Scott.

"Think about what I said. You know I'm right," Sheils said. "Call me anytime."

"I won't," Connors said.

"You've got the money. I don't care about getting it back. Do me this favor. Please."

"Sure, I have the money. Are the serial numbers logged like last time?"

"Yeah," Sheils said, stretching the word out.

"I should have known," Connors said and pulled away from the pier.

"What's wrong?" Scott asked.

"He knew we were tracking all the ransom money's serial numbers. How?"

CHAPTER THIRTY-SIX

Scott and Sheils trudged back to the FBI agent's car, still sodden from their impromptu swim in the bay. Their bedraggled appearance attracted looks, but no comments.

"I didn't think you were capable of so much male bonding. You were pretty friendly toward Connors, considering all he's done," Scott said.

"Jealous?" Sheils asked with a snort.

In a way, Scott was. He couldn't help but be slightly resentful toward the kidnapper after all the shit the FBI agent had given him over most of their association. "Just surprised you'd give him so much latitude."

"The key to working with an informant is making them feel loved."

Scott laughed.

"I'm serious. An informant needs to believe he has a friend. Someone who understands his situation. Compassion goes a long way. Right now, Connors has dug himself a deep hole, and he needs to believe I'm the only guy in the world who has rope to pull him out."

"And are you? Or are you the guy with a shovel ready to bury him?"

"It'll depend on him. If he does what we agreed, I'll make sure he's treated fairly. If he screws me over, I'll bury him in a New York second."

When they reached Sheils's Ford, Sheils drove Scott back to his home. A briny stench overwhelmed the car's interior. Scott made no move to crack a window. His thoughts were still focused on what Connors had just said. He knew the ransom cash was tainted. That led Scott to a frightening conclusion.

Sheils handed Scott his phone. "See if you can get that working."

Water beaded the smartphone's surface. Scott wiped the phone off with a couple of paper napkins he found in his door pocket, then he powered the phone up. To his surprise, it went through its boot-up cycle.

"I think you got lucky."

Sheils grinned. "Hallelujah for modern technology. They claimed it was waterproof."

Scott handed the phone back to Sheils. The FBI agent hit a speed-dial number, then set the phone in its holder on the dash as the Bluetooth synced up with the phone.

"Travillian."

"Bill, it's Tom. I just met with the Shepherd. It is Connors."

"Fantastic."

"I've got more, but it'll have to wait. He's in the bay, piloting a cabin cruiser called *The Other Woman*."

Scott couldn't believe Sheils was selling out Connors. They'd just made a deal with the kidnapper, and now Sheils was reneging? "What the hell are you doing?"

Sheils held up a hand to silence Scott.

"He has to moor it somewhere. We need to check out every marina between here and Suisun," Sheils said.

"I'll check out that boat name. It has to be registered to someone."

"Good. No one is to approach Connors or even get close. This guy will spot a tail from a hundred miles away, so we need to stay one hundred and one miles away."

"Got it. Let me get this in motion, and I'll call you back."

"One second, Bill. We've got a problem. We have a possible leak. I think Connors has been getting privileged information from someone within the Pagett camp, the *Independent*, or us."

"Shit. Who are you sure about?"

Sheils glanced over at Scott. "Scott and myself."

Travillian was silent for a long moment. "And me?"

"I haven't vetted you, and I don't have the time, but you're the only one I've shared this information with, so if anything goes wrong, I'll know you're the leak."

Travillian laughed. "Fair enough. I'll use outsiders for everything from now on. I'll be in touch."

Travillian ended the call.

Scott was seething. "What the hell happened to keeping this investigation off the books?"

"Scott, I just let a confessed kidnapper go. I am hanging my ass out here, but there's only so much I can do. I'm an FBI agent. I have to do my job, and that means covering the bases. I believe Connors is on the up-and-up, but he could be bullshitting me. Elvis could be an invention, and this payoff could be nothing more than a diversion to effect an escape."

Scott shook his head. "Grace's life is on the line."

"I know that. That's why I am giving him leeway but not free reign."

Scott noticed a change in Sheils. The FBI agent was keeping his tone level. A year ago, the man would have been railing on Scott.

"What about the ransom money? How did Connors know the cash was traceable?" It sounded alien to him to speak the Shepherd's real name. "Someone must be talking to him. He's got an inside man."

"Not necessarily. Connors isn't some thoughtless punk. He's skilled. He'd know there was a good chance any money he received from us was tainted in some fashion. The smart play would be to assume it is and launder the cash. But slinging that remark at us, especially as a parting shot, might have been a bluff. If he didn't know if the ransom was being tracked, he does now. Basically, we confirmed his suspicion."

"You believe that's the only option?"

"No. I consider everything. There's a possibility that Connors just screwed up and gave me a massive break by giving away the fact he has an insider feeding him information. That could be someone at the *Independent*."

The thought of George or anyone at the *Independent* being the inside man was beyond Scott's comprehension, but it wasn't without precedent. Hadn't he been the one suckered by a voice on a phone? If the leak came from the newspaper, he hoped it was due to foolhardy ambition and not someone taking a bribe.

"There's also the possibility that someone from the Pagett contingent is involved. Even Brian and Emily Pagett are suspects to me now."

Scott shook his head. "I've seen these people. You've seen these people. You can't believe that."

"Statistics say different. Crimes of this nature are rarely random. The victim usually knows the perpetrator."

"Yeah, but you can't believe that in this case."

"I count nothing out. Not even you. You could be one of the Shepherd's flock. You've been out of the game for a while, so you cook up a scam, a kidnap-and-ransom deal to get you back on the front pages. There's no chance of a rematch with the Piper, so you conjure up Piper 2.0 in the guise of the Shepherd."

If Sheils had hoped to knock Scott off balance, he had, but he wouldn't get a rise out of him. Scott had played these games with

Sheils before, and that was what they were—games. He was looking for a reaction. Provocation revealed truths suspects didn't intend on showing. His truth was solid. He didn't have anything to reveal. And the real truth of this moment was that he and Sheils had been through too much with each other to be keeping secrets. If Sheils suspected Scott for a second, he'd be in jail by now.

"Bullshit. You know I'm not the inside man."

Sheils gave Scott a sideways look and smiled. "No, but I have to consider it."

"Jerk."

"It's a job requirement."

"You forgot someone among your list of suspects. What about your people? The leak could be coming from the FBI. If you're considering everybody, you have to consider that, too."

Scott expected fireworks from Sheils and received a simple admission instead.

"I have," Sheils said with a sigh. "You wanted trust. You got it. Right now, I trust you. The jury is out on everyone else for the minute. That's why this one piece of information doesn't leave this vehicle. You don't breathe a word of it to any of your pals at the *Independent*. Got it?"

He did and nodded. Their relationship had come a long way.

Sheils's cell rang, and he answered it.

"Tom, I'm back," Travillian said. "I have the boat search under way. What else have you got?"

"Connors wants to surrender the girl in exchange for a deal," Sheils said and outlined their meeting with Connors.

"There's no way I can let him walk," Travillian said. "No one is going to sign off on that."

"I know," Sheils said.

Red flags were going up in front of Scott. "This guy is expecting you to stick to your word. You can't screw him over. There's no knowing how he's going to react. You know he's ex-military. He's not going down without a fight. Do you want to take that risk with Grace in the crossfire?"

"He's got nothing in writing."

Scott looked at Sheils. "You gave him your word."

Sheils was quiet for a moment. "I think we'll have to play it by ear. If we can take Elvis and the girl without incident, we'll let Connors go. I know this guy is a ghost, but we have his face and prints. He won't be able to hide from us long-term. We'll pick him up after the fact."

It was a good tactic, and Scott breathed easier.

"How do you want to play this?" Travillian asked.

"I want full tactical in place to take down this Elvis character. The priority is Grace's recovery, then Elvis, then Connors."

"Where's the location?"

"Candlestick Park at ten a.m. tomorrow. I want control of the location."

"I'll get on it."

"Scott, it looks like your part in this is done," Travillian said. "You have my personal thank you."

That caught Scott unaware. He thought he'd be there for the take-down, but he realized he wasn't needed. His job was finished. He'd brought them the Shepherd. It wasn't his job to land the fish, only hook it. It was a relief, but it felt like unfinished business.

"Thanks," Scott said. He heard the fragility in his answer.

"Thanks, gentlemen. If all goes well, the drinks will be on me this time tomorrow."

Sheils said he'd be in touch soon and hung up on his boss.

A few minutes later, they arrived back at the house. With Brannon in the hospital, Sheils cleared the house before letting Scott go inside. Once inside, Scott changed into dry clothes. He gave Sheils a pair of sweats and a T-shirt. Unfortunately, they weren't the same shoe size, which forced the FBI agent to pad around Scott's house barefoot.

Scott went to the fridge and pulled out a couple of beers. He offered one to Sheils, but he turned it down.

"You've got to celebrate the little victories," Scott said.

Sheils caved and took the beer with a smile. They clinked bottles and retired to the living room.

"I think it's okay for Jane and the boys to come home," Sheils said.

"Let's wait until this is over." Scott didn't want to take any chances, especially if Connors felt aggrieved. He didn't want the kidnapper coming for his family.

"Have it your way."

The doorbell rang.

Sheils went for his weapon, sitting in its holster on the coffee table.

"It's okay. It won't be Connors," Scott said. "He wouldn't ring the bell."

Sheils ignored him and went to the window. He peered out and cursed. "It's Thorpe. Remember the situation. We have a leak. Nothing about Connors."

Scott nodded and answered the door.

"There you are," Thorpe said. "I've been trying you for hours."

"Yeah, sorry. The battery died on my cell."

Thorpe didn't wait for an invitation and let himself in, bumping Scott to one side. He stopped short when he found Sheils in the living room. The consultant took in the FBI agent's casual attire and beer and smiled.

"Everything looks pretty cozy."

"It's been a long day. I thought it was better to finish the debriefing here."

"Looks like it. Can I get one of those beers? It's been a shit of a day."

"Sure," Scott said and went to the fridge.

Scott returned to the living room to find both men sitting. He handed Thorpe the bottle and sat in the remaining armchair.

The consultant took a long pull on the beer. "God, that tastes good. I've been babysitting the Pagetts all evening. Needless to say, they're frantic after this second botched ransom payoff."

Scott winced at the word *botched*. Connors had outplayed them. He hadn't botched it.

"I'll give them a call."

"That would be good. Look, I hate to be that guy. I know you've been through the wringer today, but I need something from you tonight."

"Can't it wait?" Sheils said. Scott could feel the FBI agent willing Thorpe out of the house.

"I want to get Scott's insight on the ransom drop—what happened, the implications, et cetera. Everyone knows the second ransom was lost, and there's still no sign of Grace. Speculation is rife. I don't want fiction getting in the way of fact."

"Yeah, you don't want another Keith Draper situation."

Thorpe frowned. "I've admitted my mistake there. Can't we move on?"

"As long as you remember that my investigation comes before your headlines."

"We have a deal, Agent Sheils."

"I can do it," Scott said, "but I want it done quick."

"How about this?" Thorpe said. "I'll send someone over to get your statement. That way it'll be low stress."

Scott stifled a laugh. There was nothing low stress about any of this.

CHAPTER THIRTY-SEVEN

As the former home to the San Francisco 49ers and Giants, Candlestick Park checked all Sheils's boxes when it came to a location for the payoff between Connors and his client. Seated right on the bay, it was big and isolated. In effect, it was its own peninsula. The old stadium was gone, demolished. The planned development hadn't progressed to construction phase yet. The mammoth parking lot that had once encircled the stadium remained. Line of sight was open for hundreds of yards in every direction. If Connors approached from the water or by road, Sheils and his team would see it. There was no place to hide. If anyone bolted, options were limited to the couple of roads in and out of the park. This place was a steel trap. Whoever went in wasn't getting out.

Candlestick wasn't without its drawbacks. Its tactical strengths gave Sheils his fair share of headaches. While the flat and open landscape provided no hiding spots for either Connors or his client, it meant Sheils didn't have any, either. Snipers were forced to take position beyond the boundaries of the park with one team on a boat in the bay. Should anything go sideways, his tactical team lost valuable response time from having to breach the massive development from the streets. There wasn't much in the way of high ground to give him a tactical advantage. He had lookouts on the hillside, and he'd taken up a position closer in the neighboring RV park across from Candlestick. He didn't have the best view, but he was as close to the action as he could get. Despite the location's shortcomings, he liked his chances of a successful takedown.

Travillian sat alongside Sheils in the RV with all that they needed stretched out in front of them—cell phone, walkie-talkie, binoculars, and coffee. Unlike the tactical team, they had the luxury of a bathroom in the RV. Their colleagues were reduced to pissing in the bushes or into water bottles.

The RV came with a further advantage. Inside, he and Travillian were out of Candlestick's infamous wind. Despite the bright sunshine, the tactical teams were freezing their butts off, buffeted by a frigid bay wind. Sheils had come out for 49ers and Giants games throughout his life, and this was the only place where he could catch a sunburn and frostbite at the same time. It would be some fool who bought into the waterfront lifestyle the new development advertised. The twenty-mile-an-hour winds that smashed this place daily weren't going anywhere.

Sheils stood and stretched. He and the tactical team had set up camp long before the agreed meeting time in case Connors tried anything.

Sheils's cell burst into song. No name came up on the screen, just a number.

"This is him," he said to Travillian and answered the phone.

"It's me," Connors said. "You ready?"

"Yeah. On your way?"

"Yeah."

Sheils gave Travillian the thumbs-up.

Travillian picked up the walkie-talkie. "Stand by all teams. Subject inbound."

"Have you notified your client?"

"He'll be here within the hour."

"And you?"

"In the next five to ten."

He sounded relaxed. There wasn't a single note of tension in his voice, which was somewhat surprising, considering Connors was essentially walking into a potential ambush. His stress levels should be off the charts. Sheils knew his blood pressure was up a few points, and he wasn't in any danger. Sure, Connors had been in plenty of dangerous situations during his military days, but no one went around with a resting heart rate during those moments. It was a concern. Either this guy was beyond caring, or he had something up his sleeve.

"Which road you coming in from?"

"I'm not. I'm coming in from the water."

The water was a good move. Traffic cams and license plates made a getaway difficult. The water was far less congested or patrolled. It was also far more difficult for Sheils to intercept.

You really think you're walking away from this, Sheils thought. He didn't know whether Connors was that naive or just that determined.

"You have Grace with you?"

"No."

"C'mon, man. The deal was your boss and Grace for your freedom."

"Don't fret. You'll get Grace. As soon as you have my client and I'm back on the water, I'll tell you where you can find Grace."

"That's not how this works."

"I say how this works."

The son of a bitch was leveraging him. The chances of Connors getting his free pass just got an uptick. Fine. The man would never be free and clear. Sheils would track him down eventually. Just one factor concerned him. What if Connors wouldn't give up Grace's location?

"You'd better give her up, because if you don't, I'll hunt you to the ends of the earth."

286

"You'll get her back, but on my terms. Is Scott with you?"

"No."

"Get him on the road. As soon as I'm back on the water, I'll text him Grace's address. Signing off now. I'll call back when I'm in position."

The line went dead, and Sheils tossed the phone. It bounced across the table and off the window before skidding back across the table toward him.

"The son of a bitch doesn't have Grace with him. He won't give up her location until he's back on his way. He'd better not be screwing with us."

"We roll with it," Travillian said. "Give him all the slack he needs, and jerk it back in at the end. He's not getting out of this."

Sheils hoped Travillian's optimism played out, and he picked up the walkie-talkie. "All teams, the Shepherd is coming in from the water. Report in when someone has eyes on him."

Sheils called Scott and told him to get on the road and expect a text from Connors.

"Echo Team, potential eyes on the Shepherd. Boat inbound from the south. High speed." Echo Team was stationed on the unmarked boat in the bay.

Unfortunately, Sheils's position in the RV park gave him a first-class view of Candlestick but nothing on the water. It was galling not to see Connors's approach.

"Charlie Team, boat homing in on our location. He looks to be hitting the shoreline on the south side. I'd estimate he's going to enter the park via the Gate One entrance."

"Do not engage," Sheils said. "No one is to engage the Shepherd without my authorization. A girl's life is in the balance."

"Understood, Charlie Team."

"Charlie Team, radio in developments."

"Understood, Charlie Team."

Travillian patted Sheils on the back. "He's here. That's a step in the right direction."

Travillian was right. The guy could have simply sold him out, arranged the meet somewhere else, and left everyone holding their dicks. It scared Sheils how much of the success or failure of this mission rested with Connors sticking to his word.

"Charlie Team, the subject has beached on the shoreline. Subject is emerging. I can confirm it is the Shepherd."

"Yes," Sheils said between gritted teeth.

"Damn it. The Shepherd is armed. Repeat, the Shepherd is armed."

"Do not intercept," Sheils said into the radio. "How armed?"

"He has a pistol on his hip—can't identify caliber. And an AR-15."

"Shit," Sheils said to himself.

"The Shepherd has jumped the barrier, crossed the Hunters Point Expressway, and scaled the fence at Gate One. He's in the park. Do you want us to disable the boat?"

"No, Charlie Team," Sheils said.

"Alpha Team, we have eyes."

"Bravo Team, we have eyes also. Subject is jogging northbound through the parking lot."

Connors was coming straight toward Sheils. Sheils grabbed his binoculars and stared through them. He picked up Connors on his binoculars, jogging across the lot. Just as Charlie Team had reported, he had a pistol in a thigh holster and an AR-15 slung across his back. Connors stopped and turned around, the semiautomatic rifle in full view.

Sheils put down his binoculars. Connors was eight to nine hundred feet from his position and easily the same distance if not more from any of the team's positions.

He dialed Connors and put the binoculars back up to his eyes. He watched the kidnapper answer the phone.

"You shouldn't be calling me, Agent Sheils. You're distracting me from my mission."

Connors turned a full 360 degrees. He was no doubt scanning for Sheils and the tactical teams' positions. Sheils didn't think he'd spot any of them, but with Connors's military training, he wouldn't show any sign if he did.

"I'm just a little worried by the hardware you brought with you."

"Did you think I'd come here unarmed?"

"No, but that AR-15 raises the stakes unnecessarily. Stash it somewhere. You've got time."

"Relax, Sheils. I won't do anything stupid, but I need my backup," he said, tapping the rifle with his free hand.

"We're your backup."

Connors chuckled. "I'll stick with something I know, if you don't mind."

"Goddamn it," Sheils said when Connors hung up on him.

"Take it easy, Tom," Travillian said, peering through binoculars. "One half of the equation is here. Just waiting on the other."

Connors got on the phone again. Sheils's phone didn't ring, but Connors got into a conversation with someone.

"I wish we could have wired this guy up," Travillian said.

It would have been good, but there was no chance of that happening. Connors would never have agreed to it. While a recorded confession would have been handy, Sheils didn't need it. As long as Elvis turned up with the payoff, it was game over.

A directional mike wasn't an option. At close to a thousand feet, a mike picked up wind noise and nothing else.

Sheils's cell rang again. "Sheils."

"Just spoke to Elvis. Says he's en route. Should be here in thirty."

"Good to hear."

"I expect this to be the last time we'll ever speak."

It won't be, Sheils thought. "I'll need you to testify."

"Nice try, but you won't."

"I had to try."

"All the best with your future endeavors, Agent Sheils," Connors said and hung up.

"He expects Elvis in thirty minutes," Sheils said to Travillian.

It would happen very quickly once Connors's client arrived.

Sheils keyed his radio mike. "All teams, second subject expected in thirty minutes. Report all sightings. No action without my authorization. All teams confirm."

Each of the teams radioed in the confirmation of the order.

"Now we hurry up and wait," Travillian said.

Sheils tried eating away at the time just watching Connors through his binoculars. The kidnapper stood, occasionally walking tight circles. The wind pulled at his pants and T-shirt. How the man survived the driving wind was beyond Sheils. The guy was made of sterner stuff. He put it down to Connors's relative youth. Connors was fifteen years younger than himself.

The man was right there. He wished he could send a tactical team in, but so many things prevented him. Grace wasn't safe. Elvis had yet to arrive. Worst of all, Connors was a trained professional. If he sent anyone in to grab the kidnapper, someone would get hurt. It was bizarre to think Connors was merely the bait and not the big fish.

"Bravo Team, we've got visitors." Bravo Team was bedded in on the hillside overlooking the park.

Travillian checked his watch. "He's early."

"Where?" Sheils said into his radio.

"A single vehicle on Jamestown Avenue. Two occupants. One male, Caucasian. One female, African American. They've left the vehicle, and they're looking down on the subject's position."

"Lookouts?" Travillian said into his radio.

"Possibly. Could be tourists."

That was the problem with Candlestick. People wanted to see what had happened to the Bay Area landmark.

"Permission to approach?"

"Denied," Sheils said. "Run the vehicle's plate. Let's see who we're dealing with."

"Will do."

"All teams watch for lookouts coming into the area via Gilman and Harney." These were the only two other streets that fed into the Candlestick Park area.

"I wasn't expecting this Elvis guy to have watchers, were you?" Travillian asked.

"No," Sheils said, but he wasn't too surprised. Elvis had enlisted Connors to do his dirty work, so it was likely he'd draft others to watch his back for the payoff.

"Bravo Team, subjects have returned to vehicle and are following the road down to Candlestick."

"To all teams, no action without my say-so."

"Bravo Team, vehicle is registered to Daniel Hutton. San Francisco address. No priors."

"Military?" Sheils asked.

"Negative."

"Charlie Team, subjects have passed our position and stopped at the Gate 2 entrance. They're getting out."

Sheils swung his binoculars away from Connors to where Charlie Team indicated. He picked up movement, but at over half a mile, his binoculars weren't strong enough to bring the figures into sharp focus.

"Charlie Team, subjects have hopped the fence and entered the parking lot."

"Shit! This is Alpha Team. The Shepherd has seen them. He's shouldered the AR-15 and called out to them."

Sheils swung his binoculars to Connors. He had the rifle raised. Sheils hit redial on his phone.

"Pick up. Pick up. Pick up."

Connors did not.

"Charlie Team, both subjects have raised their hands."

Fuck, fuck, fuck. It was all going wrong. He should send in the tactical team, but Connors was a professional. If these people were connected to Connors's client, he had to let this play out. If this pair were dumb tourists getting in the way, Connors would call him to mop up this mess.

"All teams, hold fast," Sheils said into his radio.

"Christ. Charlie Team, the Shepherd has told the female subject to freeze, but she's not complying. She's backing up to the fence."

Impotently, Sheils watched Connors swing the rifle toward the woman and saw his grip on the situation hang in the balance.

"Alpha Team, the male subject is now walking toward the Shepherd and talking. The Shepherd is yelling at both subjects, but they aren't listening. Shit. The male subject is reaching for something in his back pocket. The son of a bitch is reaching."

A gunshot split the air.

"He opened fire. He opened fire. Male subject down."

"Move in! Move in!" Sheils screamed into the radio as he burst from the RV.

With Travillian right behind, Sheils sprinted toward Connors as best he could as a middle-aged man. Sheils watched the train wreck play out before him. Being closest, Charlie Team closed in on Connors first. As they yelled instructions to the kidnapper, he swung his aim away from the prone figure on the ground to Charlie Team.

"No," Sheils bellowed.

Connors either didn't hear over the cacophony of voices scream-ing at him, or he didn't want to hear. He did the one thing you never did when surrounded by law enforcement. He didn't lay down his weapon. He fired once. His shot took down one of Charlie Team.

"Don't shoot," Sheils screamed into the radio, but it was too late.

An Alpha Team sniper fired once. The bullet smashed into Connors's back, and he went down.

"All teams stand down. Call medical!" Sheils yelled into the radio.

Like vultures, Charlie Team descended upon Connors, yanking the rifle and pistol away. When Sheils reached them, he shoved the men aside. He dropped to his knees over Connors. One side of his chest was a mess of torn flesh. Blood poured from the ragged wound. The bullet had decimated the man's lung. All color had drained from his face. He was gray, and his eyes were glazed.

Sheils glanced over at the Charlie Team member Connors had taken down. He was being helped to his feet by a colleague. His Kevlar vest had saved him.

Why didn't you wear one? Sheils thought as he applied pressure to the devastating injury. "Gavin, Gavin, it's Tom Sheils. Can you hear me?"

Connors's lips opened and closed, but his words failed to make it beyond his lips. Sheils put his ear to the dying man's mouth. He couldn't make out a word. It was just breath escaping the kidnapper's mouth.

"Where is she, Gavin? Nothing else matters. You know you want to tell me."

Connors continued to talk, but all Sheils heard was blood filling the man's throat.

"He's going for something," someone yelled.

Connors was reaching inside his pocket. Sheils pulled the kidnapper's hand free and grabbed the cell phone.

"Is it here—the address?"

Connors took the phone from Sheils. He tapped at the screen.

"Just tell me, Gavin," he said and put his ear to Connors's mouth again.

"G-g-good g-g-girl," Connors managed between ragged breaths.

"And where is she?"

His words trailed off, never to be finished because Gavin Connors, aka the Shepherd, was dead.

CHAPTER THIRTY-EIGHT

It had already been a rough morning when Scott walked into the *Independent*. First, he'd met with the Pagetts at their hotel. They looked to him for answers on the failed second ransom drop. He had the answers, but he couldn't share them, because one of them could be the person employing Connors. He didn't really believe any of them were behind it. The truth of it was in the pain in their eyes. Still, for Grace's safety, he couldn't give them the information they craved.

After that, he did two local morning shows, where he lied through his teeth. The lying didn't bother him. As he gave his superficial answers to the hosts' questions, his mind was on Sheils's sting operation. He wasn't really needed there—he was needed on these shows. If he maintained the line that the FBI was at a loss after this second failed ransom, Connors's client would continue to believe he was on top. Sheils was relying on a false sense of security to bring this guy down. As Scott talked, he kept hoping for an interruption to say Elvis had been caught and Grace recovered. It didn't come.

He left the second of the TV studios with Brannon at his side.

"Where to now?" the agent asked.

"The *Independent*."

Brannon dropped Scott off while he parked. As Scott walked through the lobby, Lehny on reception waved and told him she'd call Thorpe to let him know he'd arrived. She smiled at him, but he could barely muster one in reply.

The *Independent* had been responsible for so many highs and lows throughout his life, but he'd never regarded the place and its people with suspicion until now.

The realization that someone close to the investigation might be working with Connors's client had kept him up all night. He recounted every person who'd had contact with the investigation. He discounted the FBI and the Pagetts. The leak could only have come from the newspaper. From his people. Maybe that was just the guilt talking. For all he knew, Sheils could be convinced it was someone at the FBI. Scott didn't think he was deluding himself. The *Independent* was the weakest link in the chain. The Pagetts were too closely knit to do this to their own flesh and blood. The FBI was too reputable. No, it was at the newspaper, where the personal stakes were lowest and it was the easiest for someone to exploit.

During the night, he'd made a list of possible names. George and Thorpe were on it, along with the *Independent*'s board, as they were fully aware of the investigation, but it soon occurred to him that anyone at the newspaper could be the client's ally. There was a collegial atmosphere at the place. People talked. It wouldn't be impossible for someone to talk to George or Thorpe about the Shepherd story. Thorpe had brought in several reporters to write pieces on various aspects of the story. Any one of them could be the leak. Eventually, he'd tossed the list because it couldn't be narrowed down.

Thorpe came out of his office. He took Scott's hand and pumped it two-handed. "How are you doing? You look fried. You okay?"

"Just a little burned out."

"And a little banged up." Thorpe pointed to the abrasions he'd picked up from the car crash and his arrest.

Scott ran a hand over his bruised right eyebrow. "Yeah, well . . ."

"How'd the interviews go?"

"Fine."

"Good. Good. Come in the office. Tell me all about them. Jenna, could you rustle up a couple of coffees? Thanks."

Scott followed Thorpe into his office. Thorpe fell into his seat behind his desk. He listened as Scott went through his TV interviews.

"Sounds like they went well," Thorpe said. "Naturally, with the aftermath of this second ransom drop, I want to get some video of you going into yesterday's events. Also I'd like a written piece from you on where we go from here. Feel free to speculate. Readers are hanging on your every word right now."

Scott marveled at Thorpe. As far as the world was concerned, it had woken up to a second devastating blow that Grace was still captive after two ransom payments. Yet to Thorpe, it was business as usual. The man put the business in the phrase *news business*.

"Have you heard from the Shepherd since the drop?"

"No," Scott said.

"Well, that's too bad. Regardless, I'd like to record an appeal from you to the Shepherd. This guy has gotten his money—twice—so what more does he want? We need to get him talking. I think time is of the essence now. He's held on to Grace too long. I'd like you to call him out on his bullshit to get him to surface and start communicating with us again."

"You really want me to provoke him while he's still got Grace?"

"Of course, I don't expect you to go Royal Rumble with the guy, but we haven't heard from him. We need him to come out of the shadows and explain himself. At the very least, he needs to state his new demands."

Thorpe made a decent point.

"Is Tom Sheils with you?"

"No."

"Where is he? I expected him to be all over you today. You're the Shepherd's button man, and you've got to be on the button today."

"I think he's tied up reviewing yesterday's events."

"He should have dealt with yesterday's events yesterday. Instead, he was kicking back with you at your place in his sweats with a beer in his hands. Today's today. He needs to stay ahead of the curve here."

"I don't know what to tell you."

Jenna came into the office with a couple of coffees. She'd made them both with cream, the way Thorpe liked it. Scott said that was fine.

Scott spotted Brannon crossing the bullpen. He waved, and the agent waved back. Brannon put his head through the door.

"Do you mind giving us ten minutes, Agent . . . ?" Thorpe said.

"Brannon."

"Thank you, Agent Brannon. Much appreciated."

Brannon closed the door and took a seat at an open desk.

"Look, Scott," Thorpe said. "Can I be honest with you? Something else happened yesterday, didn't it? Sheils is holding out on me. And so are you."

You're an insightful prick, Scott thought. "I'm not holding anything back."

"Do I have to remind you that you signed a contract?"

"Don't make threats."

"Then don't force me to make them."

This was getting dumb in a hurry. "I can't speak for Tom Sheils, but I'll tell you this. He isn't my pal. We have a relationship built on miserable occasions. I have no sway over him. He's an FBI agent. He's not required to involve us. With yesterday's fiasco, I think he's of a mind that this real-time reality show he's been forced to play to keep the Shepherd happy has gone far enough. And I'm reading between the lines here, but I think he's taking heat from his people for not reeling this one in. Now, where do you want me to do this video recording? I'm ready to tell the Shepherd what I think of him."

Thorpe grinned. "That was good. You hit just the right tone of indignation."

"I'll write that piece up for you."

Leaving Thorpe's office, Scott spotted Brannon getting a soda from the vending machine and jogged over to him.

"Okay, what's the plan?" Brannon asked.

"I'm going to be holed up for a few hours working on a story for Thorpe."

The FBI agent mulled the information over. "Do you need me?"

"Not really. I'm going to be desk bound."

"Can I trust you not to be a jerk and to stay here?"

Scott smiled. "Yeah. Scout's honor."

"Okay, I'm going to check in with my family. They haven't seen much of me lately."

Scott went in search of a desk to work at, namely, one with a desktop, as he hadn't brought his laptop. Regina Holland had one, and she wasn't there. Perfect. He sat down and switched her machine on. As he watched it boot up, he looked at the Post-it Notes fringing the outside of her screen like petals of a rectangular sunflower.

He smiled. It was nice to see somebody liked to make physical reminders like he did. Then his smile dropped.

He pulled a Post-it off the screen and read it. *Candlestick Park 10:00.*

"Anyone know where Regina is?" he asked everyone in earshot. "I need to ask her a question."

"Don't know. She and Danny Hutton went off to work on something. You want her cell?" asked a reporter Scott didn't know.

"Yes."

He called the number he was given. The call went to voice mail. He hung up.

"Who sent Regina off?"

"Thorpe, I think."

A draining sensation overwhelmed Scott, as if all the blood in his body was pouring out from his feet. He stuck the Post-it back on the monitor and went back to Thorpe's office. An explanation built itself in his head with every step. It made sense. It made horrible sense. He pushed open Thorpe's door.

Thorpe flashed a smile. "Help you with something?"

"Yeah, I asked Regina to look something up for me, and I need it. Do you know where she is?"

"Yeah, I sent her off to Candlestick . . ." The smile fell away.

The man had just fucked up.

"You're right," Scott said. "I have kept something from you. And I think you've kept something from me."

Scott entered the office and closed the door.

CHAPTER THIRTY-NINE

Connors lay with his eyes and mouth open, his chest still. Sheils couldn't believe it. Their only tether to Grace was gone. The girl was out there somewhere, but where? A building? A truck? A boat? A hole in the ground? Wherever she was, Connors had just taken that location to the grave.

What were you thinking? Sheils thought. Connors had called himself a shepherd, a guardian. He'd fallen down on the job.

"I'm sorry, sir," a Charlie Team member said. "We had no choice. He opened fire."

"What did he say?" Travillian asked.

"Not enough."

Sheils picked up Connors's cell. The kidnapper had tried typing a text, but it was nothing but gibberish.

"Get over to that boat. Look for anything to show where he's been. That girl is somewhere."

The members of Charlie Team broke into a run. They were no doubt looking for an excuse not to be part of their handiwork anymore.

He looked over at the prone figure of the man Connors had shot. Tactical officers crowded around him.

"How is he?" he yelled over at them.

One of the black-clad figures shook his head.

A woman burst into sobs. Sheils turned to see Bravo Team marching the African American woman in cuffs toward them. She walked with her head down, tears and snot running down her face.

Were this woman and man Connors's clients? If they were, they hadn't been what he was expecting.

She looked up, and her face knotted in misery. "Why'd he shoot him?"

Sheils recognized the distraught woman's voice. He rose to his feet. "Regina Holland?"

She nodded.

"Who is this?" Travillian said.

"She's a reporter for the *Independent*." Sheils grabbed the reporter by the arm. "Who sent you?"

"Mr. Thorpe."

That son of a bitch. He should have known. "Why did he send you?"

"Is Danny dead?"

"Yes. How'd he know to send you here?"

"He said he followed you here. He said something was happening, so he sent us to cover it. God, I can't believe Danny's dead."

"He's fucked everything for a headline."

Travillian checked his watch. "We've still got time. The client isn't scheduled to arrive for another ten minutes."

That was if he hadn't arrived early. Even if he hadn't, the meeting place was now a crime scene. Bodies couldn't be moved.

"Get her out of here." Sheils pointed at Regina Holland. "I want every vehicle stopped coming this way on Jamestown, Gilman, and Harney. Anyone who doesn't have a good reason to be here, hold them."

Thorpe would have to wait for the moment. The situation was pulling him in two directions—find Connors's client, or find Grace. Someone needed to pay for this mess, and the client was all that remained, but that child was alone now. She needed to be found.

As two officers marched Regina Holland away, Sheils dropped to his knees. He went through Connors's pockets. Travillian helped. They found a car key, a door key, cash totaling over $500, two credit cards, and an Ohio driver's license with Connors's face on it but under the name of Andrew Walker.

Travillian took the ID and looked it over. "It's fake, but I'll get it checked out. We'll see what he's been doing with it."

The boat came up clean. The only thing Sheils had left was Connors's cell phone. He hadn't programmed any numbers into it. The phone log revealed only three numbers—Sheils's, Scott's, and one other. That had to be Elvis's. He had the son of a bitch.

He called the telecommunications unit at the FBI field office. "Larry, it's Tom Sheils. I have a cell phone here, and I'm going to call a number. I want you to do whatever you do to locate this phone."

"What's the number?"

Sheils gave Larry the number of both cell phones and told him to stand by.

"All teams, are you holding anyone?" Sheils said into the walkie-talkie.

The tactical team was holding three people.

"I'm going to call the client's number. If anyone's phone rings, hold the bastard."

Sheils hit "Dial."

• • •

Thorpe's cell phone rang. It took Scott a moment to realize the ringing phone wasn't the cell on his desk.

"You have two phones?" Scott said.

Thorpe removed the phone from his suit jacket and tossed it on the desk.

"Aren't you going to take it, *Elvis*?"

Thorpe smirked. "I think what we have to discuss is a bit more important, don't you think?"

Scott did. "You hired Connors to be the Shepherd."

"Who?"

It wasn't a joke. It wasn't Thorpe playing dumb. He genuinely didn't know Connors's identity.

"The man who's been holding Grace. His name is Gavin Connors. He's former military."

"We dealt in aliases. I didn't give him my name, and he didn't give me his. It's safer that way."

The phone stopped ringing. Either the caller hung up, or it switched to voice mail.

Scott pulled out his cell to call Sheils.

"I wouldn't do that."

"I bet you wouldn't. It's over. You're done."

"This is far from over."

Scott paused.

"I have Grace."

"Bullshit. Connors does."

"Not as of this morning. I have her now. I'll make a deal with you. I'll take you to her in exchange for your silence."

"Why would I do that? Sheils has Connors. You've got nothing."

"I've got Grace. Sheils has got nothing. Connors can say what he likes. None of it comes back on me. Only you and I know the truth. Say nothing, and I release Grace to you unharmed. Sell me out, and I will never reveal her location. Do you really want to have Grace's slow, lingering death on your conscience? I don't think you've got room there for another dead kid."

Rage lit Scott up. "You're a piece of shit."

"So I take it that we have a deal."

• • •

The call went to voice mail. Sheils hung up and pocketed Connors's phone. He said into his own phone, "You get anything, Larry?"

"Yes, I did. It's in the vicinity of Mission and Third. I've got an IP. I can backtrack to the carrier and get you a more accurate location."

Sheils didn't need it. He knew exactly where the client's phone was—the *Independent*. He thanked Larry and hung up.

"My call went to the *Independent*," Sheils said.

"Son of a bitch," Travillian said.

"I want that building locked down. No one enters or leaves."

"I'll take care of it," Travillian said. "You get over there."

Sheils grabbed one of the tactical officers, and they jumped into a team SUV. The tactical officer drove. He sliced through traffic with lights flashing and sirens blaring. The need for stealth was no longer required. Vehicles got out of their way. The twenty-minute journey would take half that at this rate.

He called Scott's cell. The reporter was scheduled to be at the newspaper today. It would be good to have someone on the inside. He could ring the client's phone number again, and Scott could see who had it.

"Pick up, Scott. Pick up." The call went through to voice mail. "Call me back. I need your help."

He hung up and called Brannon. His agent answered.

"Shawn, I need you to lock down the *Independent*. The person behind it is there. I need you and Scott to do something. I'm going to give you a number. Call it. Whoever answers is the Shepherd's employer."

"I'm not at the paper. I'm at my desk."

"What?"

"Scott was going to be there for the day, so I left him there."

"Dammit. Get back over there with whoever you can. No one leaves. I should be there in ten."

He tried Scott's number again and got voice mail again. The reason Scott wasn't answering could be innocent enough, but ugly alternatives kept filling Sheils's head.

"Don't be a part of this, Scott," he murmured.

Sheils arrived at the *Independent* to see agents staked out in front of the building. The lobby teemed with visitors and staff arguing with his agents. He went directly to reception.

The receptionist smiled at him. She was about the only one pleased to see him. "Agent Sheils, I believe we have you to thank for this situation."

"You do," he answered. "It's Lehny, isn't it?"

"Yes."

"You have a PA system or something?"

"Yes."

"I'd like to broadcast a message."

She hit a couple of buttons on her switchboard and gave him the handset. "You're good to go."

"Attention, please." His voice echoed throughout the building. "I'm Special Agent Tom Sheils, and I require everyone's assistance. This is in connection with the Grace Pagett kidnapping."

The mention of Grace's name quelled the tension in the lobby.

"I require everyone to present their cell phones to an agent. Agents don't require access to your phones. We have one small test to perform. I'd like to meet the *Independent*'s board, Richard Thorpe, and Scott Fleetwood in the conference room, please. Thank you for everyone's assistance and patience."

He gave the handset back to Lehny, then jogged across the lobby and up the stairs to the office level. Everyone was on their feet. No one looked happy to see him. Brannon came running toward him.

"We've got a problem," Brannon said. "Scott and Thorpe aren't here. They left twenty minutes ago."

"Shit. Anyone know where they were going?"

"No."

The *Independent*'s board emerged from the conference room. At this point, they were no good to him. He ignored their demands for an explanation.

"I require a minute of everyone's cooperation. I'm going to call a number. I need absolute silence. If you hear a phone ring, please point it out."

Sheils called the number Connors had called this morning. He heard a faint ringing.

"Where's that coming from?"

"Mr. Thorpe's office," a woman said, pointing at a corner office.

Sheils ran toward Thorpe's office with Brannon behind him. "Thank you for your assistance. Everyone is free to go about their business."

He reached Thorpe's office as the call went to voice mail. He hung up and called the number again. The ringing came from Thorpe's desk. Sheils yanked open a drawer. Three phones sat inside. The custom case with a picture of Jane with her arms around the twins on it said one of the phones belonged to Scott.

Sheils nudged Scott's phone to one side and picked up the ringing phone with a handkerchief. "I want this phone printed, then handed over to the techs for analysis."

"Sure thing," Brannon said, taking the phone from him.

Sheils's phone rang now. It was Travillian.

"What is it, Bill?"

"Good news, Tom. Connors's alias, Andrew Walker, booked an Airbnb rental in Berkeley. I think we've found her, pal. I think we've found her."

"But we've lost Scott and Thorpe."

• • •

Scott was at the wheel of Thorpe's BMW on 101, going south out of the city. A black SUV with lights flashing and siren wailing tore past in the opposite direction. Was it too much to believe that was Sheils? Probably. It didn't matter if it was Sheils coming for him or some cop responding to another call. Whoever it was wasn't coming to save him.

Thorpe was wedged against the passenger door with a gun trained on Scott's stomach. He'd pulled it when they'd gotten on the road. Scott hadn't expected that—Thorpe didn't seem like a gun guy. That was what he had Connors for, right? The gun itself wasn't much, just a little automatic. Scott imagined it wasn't too accurate, but at close quarters, it didn't have to be.

Scott was unarmed. His one weapon, his cell phone, sat in Thorpe's drawer. With it, Sheils could have tracked him. Without it, he was on his own.

Losing the phone wasn't such a bad thing at the moment. If the FBI scooped them up now, Grace was screwed. Thorpe wasn't talking, but Scott got the feeling he'd reveal Grace's location only as part of a plea deal. His only course of action was simple—get Grace, then sabotage Thorpe's escape.

"You're quiet," Thorpe said. "I expected questions."

"All I care about is getting Grace back. How much farther?"

"Just drive. I'll tell you when we're close." Thorpe switched on the radio. "We'll keep an ear out to see if anyone is missing us."

Scott got the feeling that Thorpe hadn't planned his exit strategy. He'd been relying on Connors to take the fall. Where would Thorpe go after he released Grace? Every law-enforcement agency in the country would be looking for him. He'd never outrun a manhunt. Connors lived off the grid. Thorpe didn't. He wouldn't last the day. Maybe it was worth sharing these facts of life with him.

Scott eyed the BMW he was driving.

"What's wrong?" Thorpe asked.

"Is this yours?" Scott asked.

"No, it's a rental."

"Rental companies have GPS trackers and immobilizers on their vehicles, especially nice ones like this. You'll have to ditch it soon."

There was a look of absolute surprise on Thorpe's face. He might be a dynamite media consultant, but he was a useless fugitive. Scott remembered Sheils telling him that the average criminal planned no more than ninety minutes ahead. Thorpe didn't look to have planned nineteen minutes ahead.

"Shut your mouth, and keep driving."

He'd drive, but he wouldn't shut up. "You manufactured this whole thing—why?"

"I took a leaf out of Churchill's book. History is written by the victors. We're in an age where news is written by the newsmakers."

"You kidnapped a child and put her and her family through hell for a headline?"

"No." Thorpe's denial was emphatic. "This newspaper was dying. I ran the numbers. It had eighteen months left at most. Now—who knows? Why? Because it is now at the center of the journalistic world."

"And all because of you."

Thorpe grinned. "All because of me. Do you know how much revenue Grace's abduction has generated?"

Scott shook his head.

"Circulation is up forty percent. Advertising revenue is up eighty percent. The *Independent* is better off to the tune of fifteen million. Not bad for a week's work."

"And what's your cut?"

"Ten percent. I'm not greedy."

The son of a bitch was actually proud of his achievement. Scott saw no point in lecturing him on the role of the fourth estate. There was no point. The importance of journalism would be lost on him.

"How did you get to Connors?" Thorpe asked.

"He came to us."

"Really?"

"He was willing to kidnap a kid for you, but he wouldn't kill one for you."

"Yeah, I didn't buy that whole 'help me bury the kid' line. Connors always kept the job anonymous. There was no way he'd agree to a face-to-face, even for what he was asking. That's why I didn't go to the meeting today. I assumed Sheils was waiting for me." He looked back at the Candlestick Park development now behind them. "Without me, Sheils will have to make do with Connors."

"How did you find Grace?"

"It wasn't hard. I have a guy who can trace any phone. I made a bogus call, got a location, waited for Connors to leave today, grabbed Grace, and hid her. Simple really."

"I'm surprised you didn't kill her, considering you want her dead."

Thorpe sneered. "Sarcasm doesn't suit you, Scott. Get on 92. Head toward Half Moon Bay."

Scott guided the BMW onto the off-ramp.

"I had no reason to kill Grace once Connors had sold me out. In fact, her value has dramatically increased. Like now. Don't look so disgusted, Scott."

"I can't believe you'd kill a girl for a story."

"You'd be surprised what you can do with the right motivation."

Scott couldn't talk to this man any longer. Everything he said made him nauseated.

He caught a glimpse of a vehicle close behind him. It was a San Mateo sheriff's cruiser. He eyed the deputy at the wheel in his rearview mirror. The deputy showed no sign of being interested in them. *More's the pity.*

Thorpe caught him looking and turned his head. "Don't do anything stupid."

"Wasn't planning on it."

The sheriff's deputy did that annoying tactic of tailgating. Scott swore it was a ploy to spook drivers into doing something dumb, so they could pull them over. He checked his speed. It was one mile an hour below the speed limit. They just had to suffer through it for the next half mile, and the deputy would get bored and blow by them.

But then the radio ruined everything.

"Breaking news," the DJ on the radio said. "Grace Pagett, the child kidnapped by the Shepherd, was rescued moments ago. She was recovered from a house in Berkeley. We're also receiving unconfirmed reports of a shootout at Candlestick Park. It's believed the FBI has killed the Shepherd and another suspect."

In that moment, Thorpe's last great deception imploded. Whatever this road trip was for, it wasn't to get Grace. Thorpe had said it himself. Only he and Scott knew he was behind the kidnapping. This wasn't a rescue mission. It was his execution.

"You lying piece of shit."

Thorpe jammed the gun in Scott's side. Before he could pull the trigger, Scott did the one thing he could do to save himself—he stamped on the brakes.

Both men lurched forward against their seat belts under the brutal deceleration. The gun went off, and a bullet punched a hole in the driver's door. This was followed by an explosive force from the rear as the sheriff's cruiser slammed into the back of the BMW. The impact snapped them back into their seats, and the rear windshield burst, spraying them with glass. The rear of the now-crumpled sedan collapsed, sending the car into a spin. For a second, Scott caught the deputy's stunned expression.

All will soon become clear, Scott thought.

The sheriff's cruiser slammed into the BMW again, this time clipping the front fender. Any hope Scott had of catching the tail slide evaporated, and the car smashed into the concrete. The impact sounded like a cannon roar as the vehicle deflated. Finally, the car jolted to a stop.

The sheriff's deputy skidded to a halt along with the rest of the traffic bearing down on them. Tires shrieked in unison. One of them ended in a boom of colliding metal.

The deputy jumped from the crippled cruiser with his weapon drawn. "Let me see your hands. Let me see your hands!"

Raising his hands, Scott turned to Thorpe. "It's over, asshole."

CHAPTER FORTY

Sheils stood in the interview-room observation suite. On the video monitors, Richard Thorpe sat in an interview room alone, with a big smile plastered over his face.

What the fuck do you have to smile about? Sheils wondered.

The door opened, and Brannon showed Scott into the room. The reporter looked drained and battered. Fresh nicks marred his face. In nearly killing himself by orchestrating a wreck with a deputy, he'd more than likely saved his life.

"You okay?"

"Yeah. Fine. A slight headache. Nothing a week of sleep can't fix."

"Remember, you're here as a courtesy. Observation only. I don't want to see anything you witness today in the *Independent*."

"There's no one to report to."

That was true. Sheils imagined the newspaper had bigger problems to worry about right this moment. The *Independent* had gone from reporting the news to being the news. The story had already dropped that the person behind Grace's abduction was the newspaper's own consultant.

"How is it out there?" Sheils asked. He'd been holed up in the protective bubble of his office.

"The circus is in full effect. My home is packed with people looking for comment. The rumor and speculation mills will be working overtime until there's a statement from you guys."

"That'll be some time."

"That's why I've gotten a hotel room until it happens." Scott peered at the monitors. "He doesn't look too concerned, does he?"

"No."

"He's probably relying on an army of lawyers to get him off."

"He hasn't asked for a lawyer."

Scott turned away from the monitors to Sheils. "What?"

Sheils had been just as surprised that Thorpe had turned down his right to legal representation. He couldn't work out what the guy would gain by not having a lawyer. He got the feeling the consultant was attempting to control the situation, as he'd done throughout this staged kidnapping. If Thorpe thought he could game him, he was sorely mistaken.

"What's he playing at?"

"I don't know, but why don't I find out?"

Sheils called in Brannon to record the interview and babysit Scott. He trusted the reporter to behave himself, but no one went unsupervised in an FBI office.

He grabbed the file on Thorpe. It was slim now, but it would be fat within days. He'd work the interview alone for now. The situation was fluid from this point, and it would change as evidence came in. He'd bring people in as he needed them and step out when he needed a rest. The only person not getting a break would be Thorpe. Sheils let himself into the interview room.

"Sorry to have kept you, Mr. Thorpe, but you've given us a lot of things to sift through."

The media consultant beamed. "Call me Richard."

"Do you require anything before we begin, Mr. Thorpe?" Sheils wasn't about to let this asshole dictate terms.

Thorpe held up a half-drunk bottle of water and shook it.

Sheils took the seat opposite his perpetrator and placed the file on the table between them. "I thought I'd share some quick news with you. We've interviewed and released Regina Holland with no charges. And we've delivered the death notification to Danny Hutton's family."

Thorpe shrugged the information away.

"That was pretty cold, sending those two reporters to Candlestick to be your sacrificial lambs."

"I don't know what you mean. I received a tip and sent them to follow it up."

Sheils had been hoping Thorpe's house of cards had finally crashed down around him and he'd come clean. He should have known the man would maintain the charade, considering the monstrous crime he'd masterminded.

"I'm not going to play games with you, Mr. Thorpe. We know the events and your part in them. I'm just going to state the facts, and I'm looking for your confirmation at this point."

That damn smile he'd been sporting since the day Sheils had met the son of a bitch broadened. "I doubt that very much, but carry on. I'll correct you where I can."

What do you have up your sleeve? Sheils pondered. Thorpe had to have something—or thought he did—to justify this level of bravado. Sheils shook the idea off. Whether Thorpe had something or not, it didn't matter. Whatever he had, Sheils would crush it the moment Thorpe presented it. He'd sat opposite plenty of people who'd thought they'd beat the system, only to see themselves end up in prison. Thorpe was no different.

"Have it your way, Mr. Thorpe. You hired Gavin Connors to kidnap Grace Pagett in order to create a media storm around the *San Francisco Independent* for the sole purpose of boosting its circulation. Isn't that correct?"

Thorpe leaned back in his chair. "I think you're giving me far too much credit."

"I don't think so. I think it succinctly describes the situation. The *Independent* was withering on the vine. It needed a miracle worker to save it. A miracle worker like you. You have a track record of turning media outlets around. This one proved a little tough for you. Print media is dying. There's only so much even a rainmaker can do. So what to do? Simple. When a rainmaker can't make it rain, you create a media storm. You hire a gun for hire like Connors, tell him to grab a kid, any kid, off the street; it doesn't matter. Then you have him call the *Independent* and ask for Scott Fleetwood. Fleetwood is news. This guy went twelve rounds with the Piper and lived to tell the tale. Now we've got intrigue. The Piper is dead. What does it mean? Do we have Piper 2.0? Could be. Read all about it exclusively in the *Independent*."

Thorpe clapped his hands together. "That's impressive. You make me sound like a genius."

"And you're not?"

Thorpe pointed to the cramped, windowless room around him. "Would a genius be here?"

Sheils had been hoping that Thorpe's plan was to angle for a plea deal. It wasn't shaping up that way. He guessed he was in for a long one.

"Okay, then, why don't you tell me your involvement in Grace Pagett's abduction?" He held up a hand. "And don't tell me you weren't involved. You wouldn't be in this room if you weren't."

Thorpe leaned forward. "You're right. I attempted to orchestrate a news story in order to boost the *Independent*'s circulation, and yes, I hired Gavin Connors to do it."

Now they were getting somewhere, but Sheils hid his pleasure. The word *orchestrate* did it. Thorpe had hustled the *Independent*'s board, and now he was going to try this on Sheils. There was a key difference between the *Independent*'s board and him. He wasn't desperate to accept everything Thorpe said.

"You told him to kidnap a child, yes?"

Finally, his smile slipped. "Yes."

"You told him to involve Scott Fleetwood and extort two hundred thousand dollars."

"Yes."

Sheils had the son of a bitch. The slam dunk came quicker than he'd expected. No matter what Thorpe said from now on, an admission of guilt had been made. He'd set this whole thing up. All he needed to do was drill down on the finer details.

"And you had Connors plant that fake story about Keith Draper being a sex offender on that British newspaper's website?"

Sheils cocked his head. "Yes and no. I had the story planted, but I had someone else do that, not Connors."

"I have to give it to you. You pulled off an amazing feat. You achieved what you set out to do. The *Independent*'s circulation has been off the charts."

"It has, but circulation is only one half of the equation. Advertising revenue is up, too."

"Really? Amazing. Is that why you decided to double down and go for a second ransom?"

The smile was back. "That wasn't my idea."

"Wasn't it?"

Sheils's celebration looked to be short-lived. Thorpe was entering the bob-and-weave phase.

"This was where I unfortunately lost control of the situation. When Scott made the ransom drop, I was like, 'Great, we've got the money; let Grace go,' but Connors saw how easy it was and wanted more. You have to understand, he operated entirely off the grid. I didn't have a clue where he was. He was just a voice on the phone. I had no control over him. That was when I knew I'd pushed it too far, and I was out of my depth."

"You'd worked with Connors before, correct?"

Thorpe cocked his head to one side. "Yes, but how did you know that?"

"Let's be honest: this isn't the first time you've done something like this. This scam was too well thought out for that. That means you'd choose to work with someone you knew and trusted."

Thorpe held up his hands. "I'd worked with him four or five times in the past, but they were small jobs. I had him plant things, steal things, or do surveillance. So yes, I trusted him, but when he saw the money he could make from this, he was a different person. My fault was trusting him, because I sure as shit didn't know him by the end."

Keep talking, Sheils thought, *because you're talking yourself into a big, dark hole.* "So you didn't tell him to hang on to Grace and demand a second ransom?"

"Like I said, no."

"So I take it that you didn't instruct Connors to kill Grace after the second ransom."

"Good God, no."

It was time to drop the hammer on Mr. Richard Thorpe. Sheils tried not to take too much pleasure in it.

"That's interesting."

"What is?"

"What you've just said. Connors reached out to Scott after the second ransom drop and asked for my help. Can you imagine that?" Sheils waited for Thorpe to chime in with something, but when he didn't after an uncomfortably long pause, he carried on. "Your hired gun turned to the FBI for help. He told us everything. That's got to piss you off."

Thorpe was immobile. Sheils enjoyed the son of a bitch's silence. It was nice to see the asshole on the back foot.

"No? Don't worry. It happened. I met with Connors, and we called you. That's how we caught you, and how I know you're full of shit. You're the mastermind behind all this, so you're going to take the fall for it. It's what you deserve. Now, what have you got to say about that?"

Thorpe said nothing. Sheils wanted to see every person who sat opposite him get treated fairly, as the law dictated. He was pleased to see that at last, Thorpe was exercising his right to silence.

Sheils stood. "I'll leave you to think about that while I check on developments, but I'll tell you another thing. Connors might not be a straight-up guy, but his moral compass pointed north. He was no child killer. I've spoken to this little girl. Connors treated her well. Right now, she's crying because she misses the man who looked after her. That has to tell you something."

He picked up the file and turned to leave. Thorpe stopped him with a word. When he turned back, the consultant was smiling again. The son of a bitch worked fast.

"What was that?" he said.

"The money," Thorpe said. "Have you found the ransom money?"

"I can't comment on that."

"I'll take that as a no, then. Let me tell you a few things, Agent Sheils. You've no doubt ransacked my hotel suite here in the city and my home back in Seattle. You won't have found any of the ransom money. I never received a cut because Connors was beyond my control by then. He was money mad. Connors told you I told him to kill Grace. Got anything to prove that—like an e-mail or a recording? I don't think you do."

Thorpe was goading him, but Sheils wasn't falling for it. He'd been around too long for that. "That's your opinion, Mr. Thorpe."

"You're oh-so-right there. That's my opinion. I admit hiring Connors to kidnap a child to drum up business for the *Independent*, and I will accept whatever punishment the court deems fit." Thorpe waved his hand in the air. "But all this stuff about my instructing him to go for a second ransom and to kill Grace . . . I'm sorry, but that just isn't true. Connors was a deranged man who went rogue on me. I'll do the time for my crimes, but I won't do them for someone else's."

"Nice try, but it won't wash."

"Won't it?"

Sheils smiled. "No."

"Then produce your witness." Thorpe snapped his fingers. "That's right; you can't. The only person who can dispute my account is dead."

There it was. The whole reason for Thorpe's smug attitude. The state didn't have a witness. It was a defense but not an impregnable one. "We'll see."

"We will, because at the end of the day, it's my word against a dead man's. My narrative versus his. In that situation, whom do you think will come out on top, Agent Sheils?"

Sheils felt that with a persuasive lawyer, Thorpe might be right, if it weren't for one thing. "Not everyone is dead. What about Scott?"

"What about him?"

"You kidnapped him. There's no arguing that."

Thorpe feigned confusion. "I didn't kidnap Scott. I asked him to accompany me, and he did—of his own free will."

"You told him you were taking him to Grace Pagett. That was a lie."

"That's not exactly a felony, now is it? Yes, I lied to Scott. I knew I was in trouble, and I panicked. I wanted to get away, and I thought Scott would be a good person to act as intermediary."

"Bullshit. You held him at gunpoint, and you fired a round at him."

"No, I had a gun, and it went off when Scott almost killed us. I hope someone is charging him with reckless driving."

"Don't play games. You were driving him somewhere to kill him. Admit it."

"I don't have to admit anything. You have to prove it. At the moment, I'm still hearing his word against mine. So, give it your best shot, and we'll see how far you get. I wish you the best."

Sheils left the room. In the corridor, Scott emerged from the observation suite. The reporter sped toward him.

"Is he right? Will he get off? The man has proved he can distort the news."

Sheils held up his hands. "He can try and no doubt will, but with the weight of evidence against him, not to mention public sentiment, he's deluding himself if he thinks he can wriggle out of this one."

"Do you honestly believe that?"

Sheils wanted to, but at the back of his mind, he wasn't so sure.

CHAPTER FORTY-ONE

The road for international departures at San Francisco International was slow going. Scott pulled in behind the Marriott courtesy van when he reached the drop-off for Virgin Atlantic.

"Okay, everyone out," he said to the family.

Jane and the boys jumped out as the Pagetts piled out of the van. The boys ran over to help the Pagetts unload their luggage.

Grace waved at them. Scott waved back. He was still taken aback by the child's black, bobbed hair. It would go back to normal in time, and he hoped Grace would, too.

He hadn't seen much of the Pagetts since Grace's rescue. They'd been on a whirlwind adventure for the last week. Disney had flown them down to Anaheim for an all-expenses-paid stay at Disneyland. Universal Studios wasn't to be outdone, so it gave them a VIP tour. Anything the family wanted, someone came forward to provide it, from car rental to hotel stay. Even their flight home had been bumped up to business class. It was quite an ending to a nightmare vacation.

It warmed him to see them all going home together, intact. Except they weren't. Keith Draper wasn't with them. Thanks to a dose of airline goodwill, he'd gotten a flight back to the UK the day the hospital had discharged him.

Pagett extracted himself from the kids buzzing around the van driver as he unloaded bags. He called over to his wife, and the two of them approached Scott and Jane.

"Good to be finally going home?" Scott asked.

Pagett ran a hand over his bald head. "Yeah, this is a holiday to remember and forget."

Scott totally understood.

"How is she?" Jane asked.

"Good," Emily said, "but with so much going on, I don't think it's really sunk in what happened to her."

Maybe that was a good thing, Scott decided. He guessed some of that was because of her age, too.

"Have you told her yet? That Connors is dead?" Scott asked.

Pagett shook his head. "As far as she knows, he's protecting someone else."

"We'll let her keep believing that for a while," Emily said.

The one good thing to come out of Grace's abduction was that Connors had treated her like she was his own child. In her mind, he'd been her protector and not her kidnapper. In a way, he had been. He was the one thing that had kept her safe from Thorpe's deadly endgame.

"Keep it moving, people," a passing sheriff's deputy said. "This is for drop-offs only."

The hurry-up ignited a round of hugs and handshakes. Everyone took a turn making farewells.

"If you ever come to Britain, you've always got a place with us," Emily said.

"Thank you," Jane said.

Pagett hugged Jane, then took Scott's hand and squeezed. His grip was intense. "I'll never be able to repay you for all you did for this family. If you find yourself in trouble and you need someone's help, never hesitate to call me, yeah?"

"I hope I never have to."

Pagett intensified his grip. Scott felt his blood pulse in his hand. "I mean it, Scott."

Scott saw the sincerity in the man's eyes. This was no idle promise. This was an oath. Pagett had been forced to stand aside and let another man take on his fatherly duty. It would be a debt that any father would want to settle up. It was a debt Scott knew all too well from when Sheils had rescued Sammy and Peter. It was a debt he doubted he could ever repay. Maybe paying someone back was the wrong way to look at it. Paying it forward might be the better solution, putting it all on the line for someone else.

"If you get the chance to do for someone what I did for you, that'll be repayment enough, Brian."

Pagett smiled. "I will."

The sheriff's deputy told them to move it along again. Scott wasn't budging until he finished his goodbyes. Kneeling before Grace, he realized this was a girl he felt he knew well despite meeting her only a couple of times.

"Have a safe trip home, Grace."

"Thank you."

"You're a very special girl, do you know that?"

"That's what everyone tells me."

Scott laughed. He didn't have to be told this girl was going to be okay. With an attitude like hers, he knew it.

Watching the Pagetts disappear into the depths of the airport, he held his own family, knowing they'd be okay, too.

• • •

The package arrived on a Tuesday. A FedEx deliveryman knocked on Karima's apartment door. Her instincts told her not to accept the package when the man asked her to sign for it. She eyed the sender's details on the box but didn't recognize them. Still, she knew the sender's true identity.

"Looks like a gift," the deliveryman said. "Birthday, maybe?"

"No," she answered without taking her eyes off the box.

"Just need a signature," the deliveryman said again.

She signed his electronic reader, and he handed her the large box. It was heavier than she expected, close to fifteen pounds. She couldn't decide if that was a good or bad thing. The FedEx man told her to have a good day, and she closed the door on him without saying a word.

Her stomach churned as she carried the package into the dining area. She sat at the table and sliced the box open using a pair of kitchen shears.

Karima didn't know what to expect, but it wasn't bundles of cash. These weren't crisp, new bills straight from the bank but crudely bundled stacks of creased and grubby twenties and fifties. Each bundle consisted of a hundred bills. She counted the amount. It came to exactly $110,000. No note was included, but she knew it was from Connors.

"Oh, Gavin," she said. "What were you thinking?"

Connors didn't get it. Aamir's death wasn't his fault. It wasn't America's fault. It wasn't even the Taliban's fault. It was no one's fault. Circumstances dictated events. Her heart ached for her dead son, and that pain would never leave her, but she accepted the situation life had handed her. Connors hadn't. He'd been trying to fix a problem that couldn't be fixed. That was the road to ruin, and it had ruined him. Connors was dead, and all that was left was a gesture that meant nothing. Money never fixed a broken heart.

She examined one of the bundles in her hands. This was ransom money. Did he really think she could accept it? Connors's blood was on this money. A child had been held captive for it. A family had gone

SIMON WOOD

through hell for it. Connors was a good man, but this was the product
of a damaged soul.

"I'm sorry, Gavin. I can't."

Karima grabbed a bunch of used paper grocery bags from the
kitchen and double-bagged them. She dumped all the cash into two
bags. She covered the tops of the bags with a bunch of old clothes.

She put on a big pair of sunglasses and a baseball cap. In her jeans
and T-shirt, she could pass for American if she didn't speak.

She took the bags out to her car, a Honda the marshals had set
her up with, and drove into town. Although a life-changing amount
of money sat in the foot well next to her, she never looked at it once.
It was dead to her, but it wasn't without value.

She pulled into a strip mall and parked. Grabbing the bags, she
cut across the parking lot and into the Goodwill store. The woman
behind the register smiled.

"Donation?" she said.

Karima nodded.

"Straight through to the back. Someone there'll help you."

Karima nodded again and walked down a long aisle to the
rear of the store. A sign above an open doorway said, STAFF AND
DONATIONS ONLY.

She went through and found herself in a poorly lit stockroom.
A man stood hunched over a pile of clothes. He snatched up various
items, tossing them into different bins. Each one was marked with
a different designation: men's shirts, women's pants, and so on. He
looked up.

"What you got there—clothes?"

"Yeah," she said, doing her best to disguise her voice.

"Just put them down there." He pointed to a stack of bags and
boxes. "You need a donation receipt for taxes?"

"No, I'm good."

He scooped up an armful of clothes. "Thank you for your donation, and have a nice day."

She walked out of the Goodwill, knowing she would. The money wouldn't help her, and it couldn't save Connors, but it would help someone.

• • •

Thorpe stood on the deck of his Bainbridge Island home. He looked across the bay at the Seattle skyline with a cell phone to his ear. His lawyer, Simon Duringer, outlined all the plays he had in mind, but the upshot was simple. He was going to prison. Thorpe smiled at the probable outcome.

Prison didn't really bother him. He knew whatever time he did would be a fraction of what he should get. The key was, he still controlled the narrative. Connors was dead. He wasn't telling his side, which meant Thorpe could tell the story for both of them. The narrative was his to dictate. Yes, he'd hired Connors to kidnap a child to drive up the *Independent*'s circulation, but that was it. He'd lost control of the deranged army vet. It had been Connors's idea to go for the second ransom and his alone. It was also Connors's idea to kill Grace Pagett. Anything Connors had told Scott and the FBI was the mad ramblings of a damaged mind. Anything that poor, broken soul had said had to be taken with a pinch of salt. Yes, he had made a terrible mistake. Yes, he'd created the monster the world knew as the Shepherd. But he'd never had any control over that monster. He'd done his best to reel Connors in, but to no avail. Yes, he, Richard Thorpe, would throw himself on the mercy of the court and pay the (small) price for the role he'd had in this misguided plan. Duringer feared he'd get ten years with a deal and twenty-five at the worst. Thorpe was more optimistic. After he'd worked his magic, he surmised he was looking at a five-year sentence, out in three with good behavior. He'd known the risks. Prison was the cost of doing business. Three years was a win in his book.

"It's okay," he said. "You're freaking out over nothing. Everyone thinks I was hand in glove with this Connors character, but I wasn't. I'm happy to sit down with the Feds and explain everything as part of a deposition or whatever."

"You did enough talking. What the hell were you thinking, talking to the FBI without legal counsel?"

Laying the groundwork, he thought. "I know. I was a fool. I've got you now, so let's talk to them properly this time. They'll see that I had only a small part in all this. Hell, the asshole kept all the money. I never saw a penny of it."

Duringer sighed. "You know you're finished in this business, don't you?"

"Yeah."

He was as a media consultant, but not as a rainmaker. Some people would see the value in what he'd done. He guessed he would be working with less savory people, but it would be far more lucrative work. He'd more than likely lose this house, but he'd have somewhere better before he knew it. It was why his arrest was far from a failure. He'd put himself on the market with the biggest media blitz in world history.

"You need me to bring anything by?"

He looked down at the ankle monitor sticking out from his pants. It was a condition of his bail arrangement.

"No, I'm good. I'll call you if I do. For some reason, people don't like delivering out here anymore, and if they do, I tend to find unwanted toppings on my pizza."

"Richard, you're far more chipper than I would be in your position."

"That's why I've got you to do my worrying for me," he said, which he punctuated with a laugh. "In all seriousness, I did what I did and got caught. I'm ready to face the music."

"Then you're a better man than me, Richard."

No, just a different man. He thanked Duringer and hung up.

He turned around to find a black man holding a gun on him. The man was his age, forties, and built like a running back. He looked like a nightclub bouncer dressed in a dark suit with a T-shirt instead of a button-down. All he was missing was an earpiece and a clipboard.

He glanced left to the stairs from the deck to the beach. If he got to the beach, he'd set off the ankle monitor, and the Feds would be here in a flash. They were aching for an excuse to throw him in jail.

"Don't even think about it," the man said. "Your head will be all over your neighbor's yard before you take a single step."

Thorpe raised his hands and hoped one of his neighbors was witnessing this.

"Come on in. We need to have a little chat."

Thorpe walked through the French doors into his living room. The gunman backed up a step for every one Thorpe took forward. He didn't understand why the gunman should be afraid of him. He was the one with the gun. Thorpe might not have a gun, but he wasn't unarmed. The ankle monitor was his weapon. If he could buy himself some time to get it off, then the cavalry would save him.

"Who are you?" Thorpe asked.

"Stephen Deese. My friends call me Stephen, but you can call me Mr. Deese."

"What do you want, Mr. Deese?"

"I want you to sit down because we need to have a little talk about a mutual friend."

For a second, Thorpe relaxed. *A new client already. How nice.* The approach was a little unorthodox, but he could get used to the new norm. But as quickly as the thought hit him, it left him. This was no new client.

"Could I go to the bathroom first? You kinda scared me, I'm embarrassed to say."

"Just sit."

Thorpe did as he was told, sitting on the sofa while the gears turned. He needed a minute alone, tops, to get the monitor off. There were two ways of doing that—either he pushed again for the bathroom, or he got this muscle-bound asshole to leave the room. As soon as he saw an opening, he was going for it.

Deese sat across from him on the other sofa, ramrod straight. The automatic stayed pointed at Thorpe's chest.

Only the coffee table separated them. The damn thing was carved from solid oak, and at six feet long, it weighed a ton. It made for a decent barrier if it came down to it.

"Who's our mutual friend?"

"Gavin Connors."

Every muscle in Thorpe's body tightened. He should have known. "If you're going to kill me, just do it."

"I'm not here to kill you. I will if you do anything stupid, but I just want to talk to you about Gavin."

Thorpe hoped to God that Deese was telling the truth. He'd always thought Connors worked alone, but Deese could be his partner. There was no way he did all the things he did without working with someone. This could be a shakedown. A shakedown was good. He could work with a shakedown.

"Did Gavin tell you much about himself?" Deese asked, his words slow and reassuring. His cadence bordered on hypnotic. Thorpe certainly found it comforting.

"No, I didn't even know his name until after he was dead."

Instantly, Thorpe regretted mentioning anything to do with death.

"That name he gave himself—the Shepherd. That name meant something to him because he was a shepherd, as was I."

"It was a military thing, right? The FBI told me."

Deese nodded. "It was my unit's nickname because we kept people safe from harm. We took being shepherds very seriously. We looked after the vulnerable. It wasn't sexy work, but it was important."

"Thank you for your service."

Deese frowned at him. "Really?"

"Sorry."

"We were shepherds for countless people over the years—good people and assholes who had some value—but Gavin's death taught me one thing."

"Which was what?"

"The shepherds need shepherding, too. I failed in that respect. The guys in my unit failed. We needed to look out for each other. Gavin fell, and we should have been there to pick him up. If we had, a piece of shit like you wouldn't have preyed upon him."

Thorpe's mouth had gone dry at some point. He noticed only when he tried to speak and his tongue seemed glued to the roof of his mouth.

"Anything happens to me, and you'll be the first person the Feds go after."

"You're right, but I'm not here. I'm in Tahoe with my army buddies. The shepherds look out for each other now."

"So what is it you want from me—money for his family?"

Deese smiled. "You guys think it's all about the green. But you would. If you don't mind my saying, you're short on honor."

The insult carried little weight compared to the potential of what Deese would ask of him.

"You're right in one respect. I do want something from you. I want you to make a sacrifice."

"Sacrifice?" The word had been so hard to say. The shape of it didn't fit in his mouth.

"Yes, it's only a small one in the scope of things, but it would change your legacy. I've got it set up in your bedroom. Let me show you."

Deese stood. Thorpe didn't. He didn't want to see it.

The former soldier came around the coffee table and grabbed him by the bicep. His long fingers bit into his flesh. The gun was right there, just inches from his face. He could knock it from Deese's hand with a simple chop. Somehow he didn't have the strength. The idea of breaking free from his ankle monitor slipped into the shadows of his mind.

Deese guided him to his feet and walked him to the master bedroom upstairs. The soldier truly was a shepherd, as Thorpe felt safe and secure in his charge. He would not have made it to his bedroom without him.

What awaited him in his bedroom was simple, but its impact was visceral. It was simply a chair and a rope with a noose at one end. He recoiled from the setup but got only as far as Deese's grasp allowed him.

"You won't get away with this."

Deese pressed his gun into Thorpe's chest. "I won't be doing anything. You will."

"No, no, I won't do it."

Deese shook him. "Time to wise up. This is happening one way or another, and you need to realize I'm giving you a way out. If I kill you, it's going to be long and dragged out, and I guarantee you'll wish you could come back to this moment. Now what's it to be—my way or your way?"

• • •

Scott stood across the street from the *Independent*'s building—its door closed forever. He'd given more than a decade of his life to this organization, and now it was over. The tidal wave of criticism from the public, politicians, and media outlets had washed the newspaper away. There was no coming back from the damage Richard Thorpe had done, or management's complicity by hiring him in the first place. There was only one option—to shut the newspaper down. Of all the things he'd thought could take down a newspaper like the *Independent*, he would have never guessed it would be a self-inflicted wound.

Although unoccupied for only two weeks, the place seemed to have withered. That may have had something to do with the graffiti and the boarded-up doors where the glass had been kicked out. He hated the vandalism, but the newspaper deserved it, in a sense. It had let down the city and its people.

Scott wasn't alone in paying a visit. Nelson Marsters paraded back and forth in front of the building in full rant. Scott had had the occasional run-in with San Francisco's resident conspiriologist over the years. Naturally, Marsters saw the *Independent*'s demise a little differently. Government interference was to blame in the ongoing war on the First Amendment.

Sheils appeared at his shoulder. "Jane said I'd find you here."

"Just saying goodbye to the place."

"What's that guy's problem?"

"A die-hard reader not ready to let go."

"What'll happen to the place now?"

"Hard to say. They may be able to sell off some of the printing equipment. The archive will be donated, I'm guessing. There's over a hundred years of recorded history inside that place. The 1906 earthquake made this place."

"And a man-made one took it down."

Scott nodded. "Standing here, I feel like Charlton Heston at the end of *Planet of the Apes*, screaming at the Statue of Liberty."

Sheils laughed. "No chance of resurrecting the paper?"

Scott shook his head. "Nope."

"What will everyone do?"

"Find other jobs. George is looking to start an online news outlet. It only took a catastrophe like this to get him to embrace new media."

"Think he can pull it off?"

"I do. He's the only one to come out of this with his reputation untarnished."

"And what about you?"

"George wants me to be part of the setup. I haven't decided yet. I've got a book to finish first. You didn't come down here to discuss my prospects. What do you need?"

"Nothing, for once. I just have some news for you. Got time for lunch? Name the place. I'm buying."

With an offer like that, Scott couldn't turn it down. He suggested MarketBar in the Ferry Building. Sheils agreed, although the menu came with prices that would make a humble FBI agent wince. As they strolled toward the Embarcadero, Scott turned his back on the *Independent* for the last time.

"How are the boys doing?" Sheils asked.

"Good. They start a new school next week. I hope it works out for them."

"Heard from the Pagetts?"

He'd spoken to them a couple of times since their return to England. He'd become their sounding board when it came to handling the media and Grace's adjustment back to normal life.

"They're going to reach out to Keith Draper in an attempt to reconcile."

Sheils sucked in a breath. "I don't envy that call."

"Neither do I. SFPD picked up the two guys who assaulted him, which is good. You heard about the ransom money?"

The ransom had become contentious. Only half the money had been recovered from the house in Berkeley. The serial numbers identified the money as coming from the second ransom drop. So what to do with it? Return it to Kickstarter to distribute back to the donors? That would be a little unfair to the people who had donated to the first ransom. An alternative was to split the money among all the people who had donated during both Kickstarter campaigns, essentially giving everyone half their money back. Another suggestion was to give it to the Pagetts. In the end, the decision had been left to Brian and Emily Pagett. Their solution had been the fairest.

"I heard the Pagetts wanted to donate it to charity. Did they decide on one?"

"They've split the money between St. Jude's and Childhelp."

"Two good choices. Makes you wonder what happened to the other half."

"In a bank vault, most likely."

They continued to talk, or more accurately, Sheils continued to ask him questions. It was all small talk. When they reached the Ferry Building, he stopped Sheils at the entrance. People walked by them in both directions, either entering or leaving the building. No one paid them any attention.

"Tom, you're stalling. You said you had news. You're playing for time, so it must be bad."

"It's bad news of a kind, but it depends on your point of view."

Sheils was pissing him off. "Just tell me."

"Thorpe is dead."

Scott was stunned. He'd expected something else—Thorpe skipping the country or having found some way to weasel out of the charges. Something of that ilk. But dead didn't even feature in Scott's thoughts.

"How? When?"

"He hanged himself. His lawyer found him this morning, when he didn't answer his phone, but it looked to have happened sometime yesterday. The postmortem is in progress as we speak."

Scott had read the man all wrong. Suicide hadn't seemed like Thorpe's thing. Then again, maybe the realization of what he was facing had sunk in.

"I would have bet a million bucks he would have wanted his day in court just to see how many retweets he could generate."

"Me, too."

"So what's this mean?"

"The case is effectively over. The bad guys are dead. Grace is safe. Everyone goes home. There's just the paperwork to complete. Thorpe did us a favor. He saved the taxpayer a very expensive trial with what would have been an even bigger media event. He would have topped O. J."

"If I'm honest, I can't help feeling cheated. I wanted him to rot in jail. Feels like he got away with it."

Sheils nodded.

"There was a task force being assembled to investigate Thorpe's other media campaigns. This wasn't his first rodeo. The audacity of this scheme had come from a history of stunts like this one."

"And now?"

"There'll still be a task force. It'll just vet his clients for any impropriety."

"I'll bet there are a lot of nervous people out there. You going to be part of the task force?"

He shook his head. "My retirement is overdue. I'm just going to cross the *t*'s and dot the *i*'s on all my open cases, then I'm done."

"That means our paths will never cross again."

Sheils smiled. "Now that's something worth celebrating."

ACKNOWLEDGMENTS

I'd like to thank my readers who answered my "casting call" and volunteered their names to be part of the book. Those people being: Jeff Mann, Regina Holland, Harrison Ayers, Dani Hutton, Alan Macdougall, Thomas Fortenberry, Simon Dusty Duringer, Martin Grayson, Andy Walker, Otis Parker, Jason Powers, Stephen Deese, Karen Richards, Jane Burfield, LaTanya Roberts-Fisher, Lehny Miller Corbin, Vivian Nichols, Tracy DeVore, John Teehan, and Erich P. Covey. I hope some of you don't mind that I played with the spelling of your names and, in one case, your gender.

ABOUT THE AUTHOR

Photo © 2003 Barry Evans Studio

*U*SA *Today* bestselling author Simon Wood is a transplant from England who now lives in California. He's a former competitive race-car driver, a licensed pilot, an endurance cyclist, an animal rescuer, and an occasional PI. He shares his world with his wife, Julie; a longhaired dachshund; and a multitude of cats and chickens. He's the Anthony Award–winning author of *Deceptive Practices*, *Working Stiffs*, *Accidents Waiting to Happen*, the Aidy Westlake series, and *The One That Got Away*, which has been optioned for film. *Saving Grace* is his second novel in the Fleetwood and Sheils series, following *Paying the Piper*. He also writes horror under the pen name Simon Janus. Curious people can learn more at www.simonwood.net.